I'LL BE SEEING YOU

Orphaned Linda Bellwood has grown up looking wistfully through the windows of Fernwood Hall on to the lives of the glamorous Hyltons, knowing theirs is a world she can never be part of. But when she is hired as companion to the old Mrs Hylton, she becomes inextricably linked with the house and its inhabitants. Linda soon finds herself drawn in as confidante to the beautiful, spoilt daughter Cordelia as her dramas are played out. It's Florian, the youngest son, whom she has the strongest connection to, however, and when their friendship blossoms into something more, she feels as if dreams really have come true.

I'LL BE SEEING YOU

I'LL BE SEEING YOU

by

Benita Brown

Magna Large Print Books
Long Preston, North Yorkshire,
BD23 4ND, England.

British Library Cataloguing in Publication Data.

Brown, Benita
    I'll be seeing you.

    A catalogue record of this book is
    available from the British Library

    ISBN   978-0-7505-3712-4

First published in Great Britain in 2012 by
Headline Publishing Group

Published in Large Print 2013 by arrangement with
Headline Publishing Group

Magna Large Print is an imprint of Library Magna Books Ltd.

Printed and bound in Great Britain by
T.J. (International) Ltd., Cornwall, PL28 8RW

Every effort has been made to fulfil requirements with regard to reproducing copyright material. The author and publisher will be glad to rectify any omissions at the earliest opportunity.

To Norman with love as ever.
And to our new granddaughter, Cara,
and her brother and sister, Gabriel and Aurelia.

Part One

The girl emerged from the wood. Ahead of her the grass stretched like a frozen lake, each blade crisp with frost. Beyond it the house loomed; its mass sharply defined against the winter sky. It was only mid-afternoon but the light was already fading. For the moment Linda kept to the shelter of the leafless trees, looking at the house impatiently. At last some of the windows blazed with light and curtains were drawn. Now it would be safe to complete her journey.

Once she stepped out onto open ground the wind met her and tried to blow her back the way she had come. Soon her cheeks were stinging. She could hear her footsteps crackling on the stiffened blades of grass. She supposed she must be leaving a trail, but surely no one would forsake the warmth of the house to examine the lawn on a day like this.

The stone steps leading up to the terrace sparkled with hoarfrost and Linda trod cautiously. She smiled with relief when she saw that, as usual, the curtains of the drawing room had not been properly closed. The heavy folds of crimson velvet drawn across the bay by a careless maidservant sagged open just enough for her to peer into the room beyond.

Linda pushed her way through the rose bushes below the window. She suppressed a cry of pain when a branch sprang back and a thorn scratched her face. Not that they would hear me, she thought, or would even dream that a trespasser has invaded their territory in order to spy on them.

They were all there tonight; the Hylton family. The

15

grandmother was sitting in the chair nearest to the fire; she did so whether it was winter or summer. As usual her large handbag was on her knee. The younger Mrs Hylton, blonde and glamorous, sat at the other side of the hearth, flicking through the pages of a magazine and looking up occasionally to smile and exchange a word or two with her mother-in-law. Mr Hylton sat a little apart near a low table on which there was a decanter and whisky tumbler. He was engrossed in a book.

The children never stayed still for long. Sometimes they would sit over a board game but of late they had had a new distraction, a gramophone – and Rupert was in charge. His twin sister Cordelia might complain but he didn't trust her with the precious records. And with good cause, for once when she had insisted she had managed to scratch the record so that the needle jerked in the groove and the first line of the song repeated itself indefinitely. If you… If you… If you … If you…

Tonight Rupert and Cordelia were dancing to some jazzy sounding music. How stylish they were and how attractive they looked as they performed the latest dance steps. They were fourteen years old, and Cordelia, already as beautiful as her mother, was beginning to take on the same air of sophistication. Rupert, tall and handsome like his father, exuded the natural confidence of the comfortably rich. Florian, the youngest of the Hylton children, was twelve years old, the same age as Linda herself. He was sitting on a pile of cushions on the floor. He held a page torn from a newspaper which must be a sheet of dance step instructions, for while he watched his brother and sister dance he consulted it occasionally and waved his other hand as he shouted out directions.

Linda wished with all her might that she could join in, be part of the happy scene. She would have Florian for her dancing partner. But that would never be. Not only because she would never be invited to enter Fernwood Hall, but because Florian would never dance; not with her, not with anyone.

Enchanted by the cheerful exuberance of the scene, she remained at the window until she heard the sound of the dinner gong resonating through the house. It was time for the meal which people like the Hyltons called 'high tea'. She ought to have gone home some time ago. Miss Agnes would have awoken from her Sunday afternoon nap and she would have seen to the fire in the parlour by herself. She would be vexed with Linda for staying out so long.

Linda turned to go but then paused and glanced over her shoulder. Inside the room the elder Mrs Hylton, clutching her handbag, was already on her way to the door. The younger Mrs Hylton was laughing as she ordered the twins to stop dancing, while Mr Hylton crossed over to Florian and offered a hand to help him rise. Florian shook his head and scrambled up himself. His father smiled approval and then the two of them followed the rest of the family, leaving the room empty.

She lingered a few moments longer. The family had gone but the room remained full of their presence. Mr Hylton's book waited on the table. His wife's magazine lay open on the chair where she had been sitting. The pile of records on the lower shelf of the gramophone stand was askew, some of the cardboard sleeves lying on the floor. The cushions where Florian had been sitting were scattered invitingly. If only she could go in and wait for them too.

*Linda made her way across the lawn reluctantly;
her physical body retracing the way she had come.
But in her imagination she remained at Fernwood
Hall; not standing at the window looking in, but
somehow, just as in her dreams, she had entered that
magical place and become part of the family who
lived there.*

Chapter One

Autumn 1937, Redesburn, Northumberland

'I'm sorry, Linda, but I cannot see how you could stay here.'

John Sinclair looked at the girl sitting opposite to him at the late Agnes Taylor's dining room table. Linda Bellwood looked younger than her twenty-two years. Today, although her dark curls were neatly combed and her black dress was clean and well pressed, her forlorn expression reminded him of the unkempt child she had been the first time he had seen her.

Linda's mother, Joan Bellwood, had been the Sinclairs' cleaning lady; she came in twice a week to do the rough work, and one morning she had not turned up on time. Instead a weeping child had appeared at the door and told Mrs Sinclair that she could not waken her mother, and she didn't know what to do. Muriel Sinclair called her husband from the breakfast table and he went with the girl to the mean little cottage where the Bellwoods lived.

Her mother was dead, as he had suspected. There was no obvious cause, but the doctor had said the poor woman must have had a weak heart and was probably worn out. So Linda found herself alone in the world. She had never known her father, and maybe he had never known that he had fathered her before going off to die in the first Battle of Ypres.

Muriel Sinclair was a good-hearted woman, and she had been sorely tempted to offer a home to the dark-eyed, elfin-faced child, but her husband had pointed out that they had four children of their own to raise and he was only a country solicitor. However, like his wife, he was reluctant to pack the child off to an orphanage.

How relieved they had both been when Agnes Taylor had suggested Linda should come to her. Miss Taylor, a recently retired school teacher, had fled the grimy streets of Newcastle where she had taught all her working life and bought a small house in the village of Redesburn. Although overly formal in the solicitor's opinion, she was intelligent and kind. He could think of no reason why the orphaned child should not go to live with her. The arrangement had been most successful. But that had been seventeen years ago, and now Linda was alone again, and he had come here this morning to tell her she would have to leave the house she had come to regard as home.

'But the house is mine, isn't it? Miss Agnes always said she would leave it to me.'

'And so she has. But that is all there is. The house. Your guardian was living on her pension, which obviously dies with her, and her savings have gone.'

'I don't mind about that!' Linda flushed. 'I wasn't expecting to inherit any money. But if the house is mine, why can't I stay here?'

'If you did, what would you live on? How would

you buy food? Clothes? Coal for the fires?'

She looked relieved. 'Oh, is that all? I'll get a job.'

'Where? There's nothing here in Redesburn.'

'I know that. I shall have to travel to Newcastle.'

'It is an hour's journey and before that a mile's walk to the railway station.'

'Only a mile?' She smiled. 'That's nothing.'

'Linda, you know times are hard. There are very few jobs to be had and you have – forgive me if this sounds blunt, you have no training of any kind. You would be lucky to be offered the lowliest of jobs and it is unlikely that you would have enough money left to live on after you had paid the train fare.'

The girl's bright smile wavered, making John Sinclair feel guilty. But he also felt responsible for Linda Bellwood. Agnes Taylor had fully intended that Linda should continue her education after she left school; that she should either go to a commercial college to learn secretarial work, or train to be a teacher. Perhaps she would even gain a place at university, although that would depend on her winning a scholarship. Agnes could not have foreseen the massive stroke that would all but paralyse her, and that Linda would insist on caring for her twenty-four hours a day.

Linda looked troubled. 'Mr Sinclair, I have to confess that I simply cannot think of any solution to my problem.'

Her expression was bleak but her voice was firm; it seemed there was no danger of her giving way to tears. John Sinclair was filled with relief and also with admiration for this most likeable girl.

'There is a solution, Linda. And – erm – it's one

that I'm sure Miss Taylor would have heartily approved of.'

Linda frowned. 'Oh dear,' she said.

'What's the matter?'

'By the way you hesitated just now I suspect that you doubt that *I* will approve of it.'

He smiled. 'How perspicacious you are.'

'And it means I shall have to leave here.' It wasn't a question, just a statement of fact. 'Well then, you had better tell me what you think I should do.'

'You should sell the house.'

'No!'

'Let me go on. I think you could get at least two hundred and fifty pounds for it. Maybe more – Redesburn is a very attractive village and a good place for comfortably off people to retire to.'

'And what would I do with the two hundred and fifty pounds?'

'You could find comfortable lodgings in town and go to the commercial college. You would have enough money to see you through until you qualified, and you would have some to spare.'

'And then what should I do?'

'I beg your pardon?'

'What should I do when I leave college?'

'You would find a job, of course. That would be much easier if you had some sort of qualification. Shorthand – typing – bookkeeping ... you know what I mean.'

'But there would be no suitable jobs in Redesburn, would there? If I sell the house and move away I don't see how I could ever return. Until I'm comfortably retired, that is.' She smiled ruefully.

John Sinclair shook his head. 'Well, I've done my best to put to you what I believe Miss Taylor would have wanted,' he said.

Linda looked at him speculatively. 'You say that as though there is another solution.'

He sighed. 'Yes, there is another solution to your problem. I feel duty bound to tell you about it, but I hope very much that you will decide to go to college.'

'Mr Sinclair, I wish you wouldn't procrastinate.'

'Very well, Linda. When Mrs Hylton–'

'Mrs Hylton?'

'Yes, Mrs Hylton. When she heard that Miss Taylor had died and that you were alone in the world she came to see me.'

John Sinclair heard Linda's sharp intake of breath and observed how still she had become. Her eyes blazed with an intensity that had not been there a moment ago.

'Mrs Hylton came to see you about me?'

'Yes. She has offered you a job.'

'A job? At Fernwood Hall?' Linda's eyes were huge and John took her intensity for puzzled apprehension.

'Don't worry, she doesn't need a new house-maid. She would like you to be a companion to the elder Mrs Hylton.'

'Companion?'

'Mrs Hylton knows how good you were with Miss Taylor.'

Linda frowned. 'But the elder Mrs Hylton isn't ill, is she? At least, I haven't heard so.'

'No, she's not ill in any physical sense. Most of the time she's perfectly all right, but every now

23

and then she needs somebody to ... to keep an eye on her.'

Linda frowned. 'Why is that?'

'She's not exactly senile, but she is becoming a little forgetful and is not always as alert as she used to be. Apart from that, she is physically more fit than many other people in their seventies. You would not have to care for her in the same way you looked after Miss Taylor.'

Even so, John Sinclair hoped that the prospect of being a companion to the elder Mrs Hylton would not appeal to her. He sensed that Linda Bellwood had a keen intelligence that would be wasted on the duties of a companion. Now that women were beginning to make their way in the world, Linda ought to take the chance to further her education. He did not understand why she couldn't see this.

Unfortunately she seemed to be interested. 'Would I live in the Hall?' she asked.

'You would. The position would be all found, as they say. You would have your board and lodging as well as a reasonable salary. But perhaps a live-in position would not suit you?'

'Oh, but it does.' Linda's eyes were shining. 'To live in Fernwood Hall would be so ... so interesting, don't you think?'

'Linda, no matter that officially you would be called a companion, it still means that you would be a servant.'

'Don't worry, Mr Sinclair. I know that. I've read enough Victorian novels to know that the life of a governess or a companion was not always easy, resented by the other servants and looked down on by the family. But this is the twentieth century and the Hylton Family are not like that. They're very up-to-date and modern, aren't they?'

John Sinclair was about to tell Linda that, no matter how modern the family might appear on the surface, old traditions die hard, when he realized that her eyes were shining and she was smiling in a way she hadn't since the day of Agnes Taylor's funeral. With a flash of insight he thought he understood why.

Linda had been lucky when Agnes Taylor decided to take her in. Life with the retired schoolmistress in a comfortable house in the village was infinitely preferable to life in an orphanage. But John sensed there had been something missing.

He thought of the games he had played with his own children; the stories Muriel had read to them when they were tucked up in bed; the picnics in the summer; the excitement of going to the pantomime in Newcastle at Christmas. Linda had been well fed and respectably clothed, but there had been no fun in her life; no excitement.

It was entirely probable that she thought life at the Hall would be not only exciting but glamorous as well. Perhaps she thought that the Hyltons were like people in a novel or in a Hollywood movie. The Hylton household was undeniably luxurious. Maybe having started life in a run-down cottage and then being brought up in a house where pennies were counted and nothing was wasted, Linda craved a bit of luxury. No matter that this was not what he wanted for her; John Sinclair could not deny her the chance to taste a different way of life. He only hoped that once she had, she would eventually decide to follow his advice. With this in mind, he told her that if she took up the position she ought not to sell the house.

'Not sell?'

'You will not be working every minute of the day, every day of the week, and you ought to have somewhere of your own to go on your days off.'

'My own house. I still can't get used to the idea that I own a house!'

'That's settled then. And now I'd better tell you what will be expected of you as the senior Mrs Hylton's companion.'

Linda smiled and rose from the table. 'First let me offer you a cup of tea and a slice of cake. I had it all ready for you, you know.'

She hurried through to the kitchen, where she could be heard filling the kettle and lighting the gas stove. John had observed the lightening of her mood and he supposed that he should be glad. Her upbringing by Agnes Taylor had been sober, not to say austere, no wonder she was elated by the thought of living in the Hall. At least she had agreed to keep the house; if she was disappointed or disillusioned by her position as companion she still had the option of selling up and going to college.

He hoped that was what she would do but wisely he didn't mention it again. Instead, as they sipped tea from Agnes Taylor's willow pattern teacups and enjoyed the Victoria sandwich cake that Linda had baked only that morning, he told her about his meeting with Mrs Hylton and what had been said. He also told Linda that she must not hesitate to come to him for advice if ever she needed to.

By the time John Sinclair put his papers back in

his briefcase he felt reassured. No matter what I believe she ought to do, he thought, I want Linda to be happy. There is no doubt that she deserves to be.

Agnes Taylor's house – now Linda's – was at one end of a terrace of six opposite the village shops. It was only a short walk to John Sinclair's detached home, set back from the road and surrounded by well-kept gardens. On the way he passed the village hall. The door was open and he paused for a moment, thinking he might venture in to see if his wife was ready to come home. He smiled and shook his head when he heard the raised voices. They belonged to the local women who were busy organizing the Autumn Fayre. It sounded as if they were disagreeing about something. Well, that was nothing new. However, he knew it would all be resolved by the time the big day came, and he looked forward to hearing the details from Muriel this evening. His wife had a gift for making the most commonplace incident sound interesting and amusing. He decided to go straight home.

The house was empty. Once the children had left home Muriel had decided that they did not need a live-in housemaid, so Mrs Coxon went home as soon as she had prepared the vegetables for the evening meal. Muriel liked to do the cooking herself. She told him that she much preferred to be in charge of her own kitchen. She was a very good cook.

John opened the door to his study where he had been visited by Mrs Hylton only the day before. He couldn't imagine that lady ever cooking anything. Indeed he would be surprised if she had ever set foot in the kitchen at Fernwood Hall. He had been intrigued when she had telephoned and asked if she could visit him. The Hylton family had been dealing with the same firm of solicitors in Newcastle for more than a hundred years, and he couldn't imagine why she should want to consult him. On most days he worked in his office at Hexham, but it was more convenient for Mrs Hylton to visit him at home.

An over-awed and intensely curious Mrs Coxon had shown Mrs Hylton into his study and left most reluctantly. When the door finally closed behind her, John had suppressed an amused smile at an image that sprang to mind; that of their stolidly sensible maid hovering at the other side of the door and even stooping to peep through the keyhole. But he assured himself that she would never do that, and he motioned Mrs Hylton to the chair placed before his desk. When she had taken it he sat down himself.

His visitor was the most beautiful woman he had ever seen. He did not feel guilty in acknowledging this. His own Muriel had been a pretty girl, and now she was comfortably womanly and attractive to him in a way this woman could never be. Emerald Hylton, who must be in her late forties, had retained her figure despite the fact that she had had three children. Her skin appeared to be flawless, although he realized that she was probably very skilfully made up. What little of her hair that could be seen was platinum blonde and he doubted very much if that was natural.

John Sinclair tried not to stare, but he knew he

28

must take in every detail of the way she was dressed because Muriel was bound to quiz him later. Well, he did not know the correct terminology, but it was safe enough to say that Mrs Hylton was wearing a black-and-white checked pencil-slim skirt, a white blouse and a bolero-type black jacket. He could hardly peer over the desk to examine her shoes, so he contented himself by briefly scrutinizing her hat.

He thought it looked like something a Cossack might wear, tilted forward at a jaunty angle. Tilted so far forward in fact that it almost covered Mrs Hylton's eyes. As a result she inclined her head sideways and back a little so that she appeared to be looking down her nose a trifle snootily. However, her smile, when it came, was charming.

'I won't waste your valuable time,' she said. 'I have come to ask you a favour.'

He was mystified. What could the immensely rich Hylton family want of him, a moderately successful country solicitor? Looking at the fashionable woman sitting before him a wicked thought crossed his mind. Had Mrs Hylton become involved in something less than respectable? An affair of the heart, perhaps, with complications that needed sorting out? Complications that could not be revealed to her husband's solicitors?

One look at her open-hearted smile dismissed these thoughts. Everyone knew how devoted a couple the Hyltons were. After more than twenty years of marriage it was said they still adored each other.

'You are intrigued?' his visitor said, and she smiled.

John Sinclair felt acutely uncomfortable. Surely she could not have read his mind? Fortunately she did not seem to expect a response.

'I've come about the Bellwood girl,' she said.

'Linda?'

'Yes. Her guardian, Miss Taylor, was buried last week and now the girl is alone.'

'That's right.'

'I was wondering if she would like to come and work for us.'

'Work at the Hall? Oh no, I don't think—'

'I don't mean as a domestic servant. Linda Bellwood is educated and well spoken; furthermore she is kind and capable. She looked after Agnes Taylor after she had her stroke, and village gossip has it that Miss Taylor was very fortunate indeed to have such a companion.'

'Village gossip?'

'Don't look so surprised. We are not the sort of family that cuts itself off from local day-to-day affairs. I have many friends here in Redesburn.'

Maybe she really believed that, John thought. There were women in the village who felt flattered whenever they were invited to one of her afternoon tea parties, but he did not think any one of them was naïve enough to think of herself as Emerald Hylton's friend.

'And you have been given good reports about Linda?'

'I have. That is why I think her the ideal person to be a companion to my husband's mother.'

'Mrs Hylton senior wants a companion?'

'We have persuaded her that she needs one.' Mrs Hylton's engaging smile had vanished. 'I

30

think I had better explain. I'm sure you will realize that this is confidential.'

John Sinclair was an honourable man. So much so that later that day he did not even tell his wife the true state of affairs. The story was to be that the elder Mrs Hylton, now that she was growing older, wanted someone to fetch and carry for her; someone on a more intimate footing than that of a maidservant. Someone who would read to her, write her letters, accompany her on little trips to town.

'You know the sort of thing,' he said. He slipped off his dressing gown and climbed into bed. His wife was busy creaming her face at the dressing table.

Muriel turned her head and gave him a knowing look. 'I do,' she said. 'And if the gossip from the Hall is to be believed, it's a very good idea. And I think Linda Bellwood would probably cope very well. I imagine she will accept the position.'

John watched fondly as his wife began to brush her hair. 'Why do you think that?' he asked.

'She's young. She has not exactly led a life of luxury. Imagine the excitement of living at the Hall. I'd be very surprised if she turned the position down.'

And his wife had been right, John thought as he put his papers away, closed the study door behind him and went upstairs to change out of his business suit before Muriel came home from the meeting. It struck him that he was dressing down, whereas up at the Hall the Hyltons would do the exact opposite and dress more formally for their evening meal. He frowned when it occurred to

31

him that Linda would not have clothes suitable for such a way of life. He could only hope that the younger Mrs Hylton would see to it that the girl had no cause to be embarrassed.

The Hyltons had been rich for several generations. The family pottery had made their fortune even before William Hylton's great-grandfather Thaddeus had built Fernwood Hall in the early part of the last century. Thaddeus, his wife and his children had left their perfectly respectable home in Newcastle and moved into the Hall on the eighteenth of June, 1815; the day when the Duke of Wellington won a decisive victory over Napoleon at the Battle of Waterloo.

Thaddeus's flighty young second wife, Caroline, had immediately started planning for a celebration ball. Extra servants were employed from the village and the Hylton family became popular with the locals at once. Since then their relationship with the village had been good.

Succeeding generations of Hyltons had continued to work hard and the firm had prospered, comparing favourably with the largest of the Staffordshire potteries. Their only sin in some people's eyes was that they became increasingly grand, behaving, it was said, more like gentry than honest tradespeople.

Even though he thought she had made the wrong decision, John Sinclair hoped that Linda would be happy at Fernwood Hall. She must learn from experience, he supposed, and after all there was no harm in that.

Just as the shadows were beginning to gather,

Linda pulled on her coat and slipped out of the house. She turned to close the door behind her and, without thinking, started to call out, 'I won't be...'

She stopped herself and smiled. There was no one there to care how long she was going to be. No one to worry and fret and tell her how unkind she was to stay out so long.

Poor Miss Taylor had never got used to being so incapacitated, to having to rely so much on another human being, even if that human being was Linda, the girl she had taken in as an orphaned child. Linda had been incredibly patient with her. She left the house only to do the shopping or, after a long day, go for a quick walk. But it had been a long time since she had been able to venture so far as the woods she loved so much. The woods that belonged to the Hylton family and where she should not have been walking at all.

Lights were going on in the houses and people were drawing their curtains. Smoke rose from the chimneys. The day had been warm, but the autumn evening brought a chill and a hint of the colder weather to come. Once Linda had left the village behind her, she pulled her collar up around her ears and wished she'd had the sense to wear gloves.

As soon as she was out of sight of the nearest house, Linda climbed the low drystone wall and hurried across a small strip of open ground to seek the shelter of the trees. She took a torch out of her pocket and switched it on, although she knew the paths so well she was sure she could have found the way to her destination blindfold.

The leaves were beginning to fall and the paths crackled underfoot. As she neared the stream, she saw mist advancing through the trees. Although she had not planned to, she turned and took the trail that led to the water's edge and the stepping stones. There was a splash. She couldn't see what had caused it – some water creature? Circles rippled towards her across the surface of the water.

She gazed at the stepping stones and remembered a hot summer's day when she was thirteen, when the boy had slipped from the stones and fallen into the water. She remembered his startled expression when he looked up and saw her sitting in the overhanging branches of the tree.

Forgetting his own predicament, he had called out furiously, 'You're trespassing!'

Even though she was worried about the consequences, she knew with a flash of insight that his rage was more to do with his feeling of humiliation at being seen like this than anger at her wrongdoing.

Linda swung down from the tree and stood on the bank. She leaned forward and stretched out her hand.

'Go away. I can manage,' the boy said.

'Maybe you can, but there's no shame in accepting help.'

He glowered at her for a moment and then sighed and reached for her hand. As soon as he had hold of it, he gave it a vicious tug, pulling her forward until she lost her balance and ended up in the water beside him.

'You beast!' she cried. 'How could you? I only

34

wanted to help you.'

'I didn't need help. I told you.' Florian Hylton struggled to his feet and made his way cautiously to the bank. He turned and looked at Linda. 'Well, are you just going to sit there?' he asked. He held out a hand. 'Go on, take it.'

'How do you know I won't pull you back in?' Linda said.

He looked startled for a moment and then burst out laughing. 'I don't know,' he said. 'But I'll risk it. You look too nice to act in such a mean way.'

'Like you did.'

'Yes, like I did. But for heaven's sake get up. You must be soaked through.'

Linda didn't need him to help her, but she sensed it was important to him, so she took his hand and clung on tightly, allowing him to pull her up. She realized at once that he was very strong, completely belying his delicate looks and the impression given by his limping gait. They stood and looked at each other.

'I say,' he said. 'You're soaked through. Will you be in trouble when you get home?'

'It would be better if I could dry off a bit. The sun's warm enough. I just need to find somewhere to sit.'

'I know a place,' he said. 'A little clearing not far from here. I should dry off too, or Mother will fuss and ask why I wandered off on my own instead of staying with my brother and sister.'

'Why did you?'

'Because they're always saying I can't do this and I can't do that. Mother's got them trained to treat me like a baby just because–' He stopped suddenly and looked down at the ground.

'Because you have a limp,' Linda said. 'It's all right; you don't have to tell me about it. Let's go and sit in the sun and get as dry as we can.'

There had been no consequences – at least not bad ones. Florian did not refer again to the fact that she undoubtedly was trespassing. They lay down in the clearing, turning over now and again to dry off their backs as well as their fronts. They laughed at their predicament, and they talked about the books they had read and the films they had seen.

They had both read *The Thirty-Nine Steps*, *The Prisoner of Zenda* and *Lorna Doone* and enjoyed them thoroughly.

'We seem to have similar tastes,' Florian said. 'But what about films?'

'Well, I've only seen cowboy films and Charlie Chaplin. There's a film show at the village hall once a month.'

'Mother takes us to the cinema in Newcastle but it's the same for me. Cowboys and Charlie Chaplin. She won't take us to see anything more grown-up.'

'Miss Taylor's the same.'

'Miss Taylor?'

'My ... guardian.'

'Are you an orphan?'

'Yes.' Linda stood up abruptly. 'I think I'm dry enough to go home now.'

She began to brush bits of grass from her clothes. She noticed with dismay that there were green stains on the skirt of her blue gingham dress.

'Do you have to go?' The boy sat up and shielded his eyes with a hand as he gazed up at her.

''Fraid so.'

'Shall I show you the way to the main gate?'

'That's not the way I came in.'

He laughed. 'I didn't think so.'

'I know the way back to the stream,' Linda said. 'And from there to – to the place I came in.'

'Will you come here again?'

'Perhaps.'

'Come back soon – before I have to go back to school. I'll look out for you.'

'Will you?'

'Yes. And I won't tell, you know.'

'Thanks. Bye.'

'Hey – wait – I don't know your name.'

'Linda.'

'And I'm–'

'Florian. I know.'

Abruptly she turned and fled. She had wanted to go from the moment she had mentioned her guardian. Until that moment she had been living in her dreams. She wasn't a trespasser; she actually belonged here in the grounds of Fernwood Hall. Then, with Florian's questions, real life had intruded. As she hurried through the woods she brushed tears from her eyes. But no matter how upset she was, she knew she would return.

That day had changed everything. After that she was no longer the complete outsider. Now she had an ally – an accomplice. Whenever they met Florian would talk about his family and what went on in the Hall, although sometimes she had to tease it out of him. For she had soon discovered that Florian seemed to want to get away from the Hall as much as she would have liked to get in.

The air had grown colder while Linda had been standing by the stream remembering the first time she had met Florian Hylton. She turned away from the water and made her way back to the wider path. She was going to her usual place. She was going to stand in the shelter of the trees and gaze across the lawn at the Hall, and watch the lights go on and the curtains being drawn. She would be doing this for the last time, because the next time she entered these grounds she would have every right to be there.

Chapter Two

'Linda! I'm so pleased you have agreed to come and help us.'

Emerald Hylton hurried across the imposing entrance hall, her high heels click-clacking on the black-and-white marble squares. She was wearing a day dress made from some silky fabric; it was white with broken black stripes. Her blonde curls looked as if they had been sculpted perfectly to frame her lovely face. She reminded Linda of one of those glamorous photographs of movie stars on display in a cinema foyer. Mrs Hylton was followed at a more leisurely pace by the middle-aged housemaid who had opened the door and greeted Linda just a few moments before.

'Wait here,' the maid had said. 'I will tell Mrs

Hylton that you have arrived.'

Her less than enthusiastic greeting had made Linda feel uneasy, and as Mrs Hylton came to a stop before her she blurted out, 'Did I come to–I mean should I have used some other door?'

Mrs Hylton looked surprised. 'The servants' entrance, you mean?'

'I suppose I do.'

'Of course not, my dear. You must use the same entrance as the family. Although if you go for a walk in the grounds you will find it more convenient to use the door at the end of the passage near the kitchen. The cloakroom and the boot room are there.'

Emerald Hylton's smile was brilliant, but over her shoulder Linda glimpsed the maidservant's impassive expression. She wondered if, just as in the novels she had read, she might be resented by those who did not use the same door as the family.

'Did you walk up from the village?' The welcoming smile faded. She looked distressed.

'Yes.'

'Carrying that case?'

Linda nodded.

'Oh, dear. I do apologize. I should have sent a car for you.'

'Please don't be concerned,' Linda said. 'It's a lovely day. I enjoyed the walk.'

'It's kind of you to say so.' Mrs Hylton's smile returned, expressing grateful relief. 'Now, I suppose you will want to see your room. Saunders will take you up and unpack your case, and then you must come to my little sitting room and we will have a chat. Saunders will show you the way.'

Emerald Hylton gave an encouraging smile, then turned and hurried away. Saunders stepped forward and picked up Linda's case.

'Come with me,' she said.

'Oh, I'll carry that – please don't bother.'

The woman identified as Saunders looked doubtful but surrendered the case readily enough. 'Goodness, lass, that's heavy. What have you got in there?'

'Just my clothes and – erm – books. I have a lot of books.'

'Like reading books, do you?'

'Yes.'

'Well, you'll find plenty more in the library here. Hundreds, there are. Now I suppose we'd better use that grand staircase over there – not the stairs the servants use.'

The words could have been interpreted as hostile, but the maidservant's smile was wryly humorous. She's making fun of me, Linda thought. But not in a spiteful way. Her seemingly cool manner when she first opened the door might have meant that she was withholding her judgement until she'd had the chance to sum me up. Hopefully, she likes what she sees.

'Are you sure this room is for me?' Linda exclaimed when, finally, Saunders opened a door and led the way into a room on the first floor of the house. She gazed around in awe.

'Why do you ask that?'

'It's very luxurious.'

'It's no different from any other room on this floor. But this room is definitely for you. Look.' She pointed to another door set in the wall to the right. 'That door opens into a bathroom, and a further door leads to the old lady's room. That's why you must sleep here. To be near to your charge.'

'I see.'

'Don't worry. I imagine you've been told what the problem is. That's only right and proper. But she's not that bad. If she likes you, and I don't see why she shouldn't, you'll find her easy to get on with. Now, shall I unpack your case?'

'That's all right. I can do it. I don't have much.'

'Apart from your books. No, we'll do this together then you can freshen up and I'll take you to Mrs Hylton's sitting room. Her little boudoir, she calls it.'

'Thank you – erm – what shall I call you?'

Saunders raised her eyebrows. 'Well, the Hyltons call me Saunders but my Christian name is Vera. When you're with the family you had better do as they do. When we're on our own you can call me Vera, if you like.'

'And I'm Linda.'

'I know that. I was at school with your mother. She could have had a position here too, but she fell in love with Josh Bellwood.'

'You knew my father?'

Vera Saunders smiled. 'He was a proper catch. Big and bonny. All the lasses in the village set their caps at him – including me. But he chose your ma, God bless them both. I wish the story could have had a happier ending.' The maid-servant sighed. 'But come along, Miss Bellwood. We mustn't keep Mrs Hylton waiting.'

'Oh, not Miss Bellwood. Call me Linda, please.'

41

'No, Miss. You are Mrs Hylton senior's companion. You are living in Fernwood Hall with the family. You'll be using the same door as they do and you'll eat at their table. You can call me Vera if you want to, but to me you will be Miss Bellwood.'

Emerald Hylton was sitting on a delicate little sofa by the fireplace. There was no fire. Instead a large wide-necked blue-and-white vase filled with flame-coloured flowers stood on the hearth. A small table bore a tray set with coffee and biscuits.

Vera Saunders had knocked before they entered, and Mrs Hylton had looked up and smiled. 'You may go now, Saunders,' she said.

The moment was so formal that Linda almost expected the maid to curtsey, but she simply said, 'Yes, Madam,' and left, closing the door behind her.

'Come and sit down, Linda.' Mrs Hylton gestured gracefully towards a chair that matched the sofa and which was set at the other side of the hearth. 'Coffee?'

'Yes, please.'

The delicate little coffee cups were cream with a pattern of gold stems and brilliant green leaves. Linda gazed at them admiringly.

As she poured the coffee Emerald Hylton looked up, saw Linda's expression and smiled. 'Pretty, isn't it?'

'Very.'

'Have you ever seen anything like it before?' Mrs Hylton's smile suggested that she already knew the answer would be no.

'I haven't.'

'It was made specially for me when William and I got married. Very apt, don't you think?'

'Apt?' Linda stared at the little cream jug that Mrs Hylton had just picked up. 'Oh, of course. The leaves. They're emerald green.'

'Clever girl. Cream and sugar?'

Linda said yes to both.

'And do help yourself to one of those cinnamon biscuits. Have as many as you like – each one is barely a mouthful!'

Linda took a biscuit, and then another, but Emerald Hylton ignored them. She put her coffee cup down on the table and gave her attention to a silver cigarette box, a small lighter and a jewelled cigarette holder. Linda watched, fascinated, as she lit the cigarette and then inserted it into the holder. Once she had inhaled deeply, she gave every indication of being more relaxed.

'That's better,' she said and then, 'Oh, but forgive me. Would you like one?' She indicated the cigarette box with one graceful hand. The beautifully manicured scarlet nails contrasted shockingly with her very pale skin.

'No, thank you. I don't smoke.'

'Not at all? I mean, not even when you're on your own? Many people consider smoking a vice to be enjoyed in secret.'

'I don't smoke at all.'

'Good girl.' Mrs Hylton smiled ruefully. 'I sometimes wish I'd never started. More coffee?' Linda nodded. 'Would you mind pouring it yourself?'

Emerald Hylton sat back and crossed her legs. Linda couldn't help contrasting her sheer silk stockings with her own serviceable lisle. Linda

43

drank her coffee and Mrs Hylton closed her eyes. She wasn't sleeping; she was simply enjoying her cigarette. Linda observed her through a haze of bluish smoke. Eventually she sighed, sat forward and knocked the remaining stub into an ashtray.

'Now to business,' she said. 'Although I'm loath to leave here, it's been so relaxing sitting here with you.'

Linda would have liked to have believed her, but she was sure it had been the cigarette that had enabled Mrs Hylton to relax, not the fact that they were sitting here together.

'Before I take you to meet my mother-in-law I'd just like to go over what your duties will be.'

The instructions that followed were exactly what Linda had been expecting. Mr Sinclair had been very thorough. When Mrs Hylton was satisfied that Linda understood everything, she rose gracefully and pulled a tasselled bell cord at one side of the fireplace. Vera Saunders appeared almost immediately.

'You can clear this away, Saunders,' Mrs Hylton said. 'And do you know if Mrs Charles is down yet?'

Linda was momentarily confused. Who was Mrs Charles?

Emerald Hylton saw her puzzled expression and said, 'There are two of us. To avoid confusion we call my mother-in-law Mrs Charles. That was my father-in-law's first name. And I, of course, am Mrs William. It's less bothersome sometimes than Mrs Hylton senior and Mrs Hylton junior, don't you think?'

Linda nodded.

By now Vera Saunders had cleared the little table and was standing patiently holding the tray. Mrs Hylton turned to her and asked again, 'Mrs Charles?'

'She's still in her room, Madam. Still in bed, actually.'

'Thank you, Saunders. Come along, Linda.'

The maidservant stood back to allow them to leave the room before her. Emerald Hylton hurried ahead in a nervous manner which Linda was to learn was characteristic of her. Then, half-way up the grand staircase, she paused for a moment and reached for the banister rail to support herself. Linda noticed that she was slightly out of breath. However, she soon hurried on again. At the top of the stairs they turned and went along the wide corridor, past Linda's own bedroom to the room next to it. Mrs Hylton's knock was peremptory. She didn't wait for a reply before hurrying in.

The curtains were closed and the room was dim. A small lamp on the bedside table revealed the elder Mrs Hylton sitting up in bed, propped up by what seemed a mountain of pillows. A pale pink chiffon scarf was tied turban-like around her head, making her strong-boned face look rather intimidating.

'There you are,' Clara Hylton said. 'Come to chivvy me, no doubt.'

Her daughter-in-law made no reply. She hurried over to open the curtains at both windows then turned and smiled. 'Really, darling,' she said. 'How can you bear to lie about in bed on such a lovely day?'

'And how am I to know it's a lovely day if I'm lying in bed? I mean, nobody came to tell me, did they?'

Emerald Hylton crossed to the bed and, sitting on it, took the older woman's large wrinkled hands in her own small white ones. 'Don't be difficult, darling,' she said. 'You could have asked the maid what kind of day it was when she brought your breakfast, couldn't you?'

'I suppose so. But what's the point?'

'The point is you should be up and about. Surely it's boring just lying here. You don't even read the newspapers or a magazine.'

'I would devour them if I could see them properly.'

'I've told you. We're going to take you to the eye infirmary in Newcastle and get that sorted out. There's a new man starting there in January. He's supposed to be the tops. Meanwhile Linda, here, will read to you. Newspapers, magazines, books, whatever you want.'

The older woman reached for a pair of gold-rimmed spectacles that were lying near the lamp on the table. She put them on and peered in Linda's direction.

'Linda, did you say? Are you sure you didn't mean Grace Poole?'

'Grace Poole? What are you talking about?'

'Standing there all in black. I wouldn't be surprised if she has a bunch of keys at her waist and intends to lock me up at night to stop me from burning the house down.'

'I haven't the faintest idea what you're talking about.' Emerald Hylton sounded worried. She ob-

46

viously thought her mother-in-law was rambling.

'No, I don't suppose you have, Emerald. But surely you didn't have to dress the girl in unrelieved black?'

'Oh ... that.'

Emerald Hylton was struggling to connect the fact that Linda was dressed in black with the completely incomprehensible – to her – remarks about someone called Grace Poole. Linda would have liked to explain things and put her mind at rest, but she was afraid she might seem to be presumptuous.

'Well?'

'Linda is in mourning, you see.'

'Who died?'

Emerald Hylton winced at the abrupt question. 'Her guardian. The woman who brought her up.'

'So she's a Jane, not a Grace.'

There was a silence, and then the younger Mrs Hylton, totally defeated, said, 'If you say so. And now I'm going to leave you to get to know each other. I'll see you at lunch.'

She leaned forward and kissed her mother-in-law's brow. The gesture was tender and suggested that she was very fond of the old lady. She rose gracefully and turned to Linda. 'Perhaps you would help my mother-in-law to get dressed? If she wants a cup of coffee or tea, just ring for Saunders.'

She stood for a moment, looking perplexed, then she blinked and smiled before hurrying from the room, leaving Linda and Clara Hylton staring at each other. Linda was trying to conceal a smile. The older woman did not bother to hide

47

her own amusement.

'My daughter-in-law's taste in reading is for society and fashion magazines. I don't know if she has ever read a book of any kind in all her life, but she has certainly never read *Jane Eyre*,' she said. 'However, I see from your expression that you have.'

'Don't you think that was rather cruel?' Linda asked.

Clara Hylton looked surprised. 'Cruel?'

'You were teasing her.'

'Teasing, was I?'

'I think so, but it was worse than that. You must have known very well that your poor daughter-in-law would take your words as a sign of – oh, dear... I mean...'

'A sign of my increasing senility?'

Linda, aghast at what she had nearly said, re-mained silent.

'Well, you may be a little slip of a thing but you certainly don't beat about the bush, do you?'

'I didn't mean to offend.'

'Don't worry, you haven't offended me. It will be good for me to have a companion who is not afraid to speak her mind. I know what they all believe of me, and in all truth they may be right. But I'm not totally gaga yet, and I have to amuse myself somehow.'

'One of my duties will be to read to you.'

Clara Hylton raised her eyebrows. 'Duties? You will look on it merely as a duty?'

'Certainly not. I love reading. It will be a plea-sure.'

'We have a good library here, you know, but we

48

shall order what we want to be sent from the Army and Navy Store. Or we will go into town and browse the shelves at Robinson's. Would you like that?'

'Very much.'

Clara Hylton frowned. 'If we are going to go out together I really cannot have you dressed in black like this. I need cheering up, not the opposite. I know you are in mourning, but you are only a young girl. No one expects you to wear black for months on end these days.' She paused. 'What's the matter? You look uncomfortable.'

'I don't mind putting aside the black, but the other clothes I have are hardly cheerful. Miss Taylor – my guardian – believed that one should dress sensibly.'

'Oh, poor you. I had a nanny like that when I was a little girl, but fortunately my mother was a frivolous woman and she sent the nanny packing, sent all my clothes to the orphanage, and we started again with a fashionable young woman from Paris. But do sit down, Linda, while we decide what to do. Bring that little chair over. That's right. Now, we'd better have a trip into town, hadn't we? Fenwick's? Bainbridge's? Fenwick's, I think, then we can have lunch in the Tivoli. Goodness, child, I'm feeling more enthusiastic about life already and you've only just arrived. But now what's troubling you?'

'Why should anything be troubling me?'

'Don't deny it. Your expressions are transparent. I have said something to upset you.'

'No, you haven't – I mean, yes ... but why are we going to Fenwick's?'

49

'To buy you some new clothes, of course.'

'No, I can't allow you to do that.'

'Why ever not?'

'Well, I mean, I am being paid generously. It won't be long before I can buy new clothes for myself. And I will be only too pleased to, I promise you.'

'And until then do you propose that I should put up with you looking like a prison warder?'

'I'm sure I don't look like a prison warder!'

Clara Hylton tilted her head to one side and observed Linda thoughtfully. 'Well, perhaps not. You are far too pretty. Those dark curls, the brown eyes and the delicate features give you an almost waiflike look. You have a good figure; perhaps a little too slender but altogether womanly. No, you don't look a bit like a prison warder.'

Linda, at first bemused by the older woman's forthright manner, recovered herself enough to say, 'First you upset your daughter-in-law and now you are amusing yourself by making me feel uncomfortable.'

'I didn't intend to. You will have to get used to my ways. But there will be no argument about the new clothes, you know. For goodness sake, allow me to enjoy a day's shopping, won't you?'

Linda smiled weakly. She knew the battle had been lost.

'Good girl. Now you'd better help me get dressed as Emerald requested and we'll go down in time for luncheon.'

There were five of them at the dining table: Emerald Hylton, Mrs Clara Hylton, Cordelia

Hylton, Florian Hylton, and Linda herself. She assumed Mr Hylton and his elder son Rupert would be at the pottery in Newcastle.

Emerald Hylton introduced Linda first to Cordelia, who smiled and said, 'I hope you will be happy here.'

Then to Florian. Florian, her childhood friend, who was now a handsome young man. Strikingly so, Linda thought, and she held her breath as they stared at each other. Florian's eyes widened momentarily. What was he seeing when he looked at her? Then almost immediately he concealed his emotion with an easy smile.

'Welcome to Fernwood Hall, Miss Bellwood,' he said, but his tone was cool.

Linda thought she knew why. She hoped it wouldn't be too long before she could explain what had happened.

As he walked away to take his place Linda looked around the formal dining room and re-membered all the times she had imagined being in here with the family. And now she was. The five of them were sitting round one end of a large table with Emerald Hylton sitting at the head. Her mother-in-law sat next to her, then Linda. Cor-delia sat next to her mother on the other side of the table and Florian was directly opposite Linda.

A different housemaid served their meal. She was younger than Vera and very pretty, with naturally fair curls restrained by her maid's cap and startlingly blue eyes. She wore the same ser-vant's garb as Vera: a neatly cut dark grey dress and a clean white pinafore. But whereas the effect on Vera was to take something of her personality away, make her blend into the background, nothing could quench the vibrant attractiveness of this young woman.

Linda soon learned that the maid's name was Hawkins and thought that name completely unsuitable for one who possessed such grace and, surprisingly, an accent-free and melodious speaking voice.

At one point she realized that she had been staring at the girl with open curiosity, and when she looked away she was embarrassed to see that Florian was looking at her with an amused smile on his lips.

'I'll tell you later,' he mouthed silently.

Florian's mood seemed to have warmed slightly and Linda smiled at him. He responded with an almost imperceptible shake of his head and turned his attention to the meal that was placed before them.

They had fish pie and peas, followed by steamed fruit pudding with custard. It was a meal of which Miss Taylor would have heartily approved, but she might have raised her eyebrows at the grand manner in which it was served. The snow-white damask cloth, the silver cutlery, the fine china plates and dishes, and crystal glasses seemed altogether too ornate for such a humble midday meal.

The conversation was cheerful but inconsequential. Cordelia and her mother were discussing hats; particularly something called the Florentine, and the surreal, zany hats shaped like lamb chops, shoes, fruit baskets and even bird's nests designed by the Italian couturier Elsa Schiaparelli. Mrs Hylton senior joined in now and then, and surprised Linda by seeming to approve of fashions that would have made Miss Taylor bridle with outrage and derision.

Florian barely spoke but was happy enough to offer his opinion if his mother or his sister asked for it.

'But what do you think, Linda?' Cordelia suddenly asked.

'Me? What about?' Linda was startled to be singled out.

'About the demise of the cloche? My mother used to love them, thinking them very stylish and flattering, but I always thought they looked like inverted pudding basins, and they completely ruined your hairstyle. Do give us your opinion, and don't worry that in doing so you will have to disagree with one of us.'

'Oh, but I don't disagree with either of you.'

Across the table Florian raised his eyebrows and waited expectantly. Next to her Clara Hylton turned towards her slightly and Linda sensed her amusement.

'Don't say you are too timid to voice your opinion,' the elder lady said. 'From our limited time together I would not have thought that likely.'

'No, I'm happy to tell you what I think. A cloche hat could be very flattering indeed worn by someone with exquisite features, but worn by lesser mortals it could certainly remind one of an upturned pudding basin.'

'Well done, Linda,' Clara Hylton said. 'And you're absolutely right. Emerald always looked marvellous wearing a cloche hat, as did Cordelia if she would but admit it. But my bone structure is far too rough-hewn for such a fashion.'

'Oh, not rough-hewn, Grandmamma,' Florian said. 'Your face is full of resolution and character.'

Clara Hylton looked at him with raised eyebrows and she sounded amused when she said, 'Kind of you to say so. But now, if we are all finished, why don't we go through to the drawing room for coffee?'

Grandmother, mother and daughter rose gracefully and, placing their napkins on the table by their plates, they left the dining room, still talking together about hats. So Linda and Florian were alone. They looked at each other across the table and she felt suddenly exposed. She glanced uncertainly at Florian, seeking reassurance, but his glance was enigmatic.

'Don't worry, I'll never give you away,' he said.

'Give me away?'

'Tell them that you are an imposter.'

'Imposter! What do you mean?'

'Well, here you are, respectably employed by my mother as a companion for my sainted grandmother, and neither of them knows that you were once a ragged village child who trespassed on our land at will.' Florian rose from his chair and smiled down at her.

'I was never ragged!' Linda stood up.

'Of course not. I exaggerate. I'm afraid it's a habit of mine, but you cannot deny that you were a trespasser. And please put that napkin down before you rip it in two.'

Linda put her napkin on the table and stared down at it, unwilling to meet his eyes.

After an uncomfortable pause he said, 'I'm

54

sorry, Linda. I've upset you and I didn't mean to, especially as, despite my less than enthusiastic welcome, I'm so very pleased to see you here.'

'Are you?' she asked doubtfully.

'Of course I am. We were friends, weren't we? You were the only person I knew who could talk about the things I liked. Books ... music ... cowboy films and Charlie Chaplin.'

'I thought you said you were sick of those – the cowboy films and Charlie Chaplin?'

'I was. And so were you. You told me they were the only films your guardian allowed you to see when the film show came to the village hall.'

'You remember that?'

'Of course. I think I can remember all our conversations. We were very earnest children, weren't we?'

'Not all the time. I think we laughed a lot, too.'

'We did. I can't tell you how much I looked forward to the school holidays and coming home to seek out my secret friend in the woods. And then, when I was at university, you stopped coming. Quite suddenly; with no warning. I was worried you must have found another boyfriend.'

'I couldn't come. You see, Miss Taylor – my guardian – she had a stroke and–'

Florian held up his hand. 'I know, and I'm sorry. Mother told us why she had chosen you to be Grandmamma's companion. I was looking forward to seeing you again, but just now when I saw that my little trespasser had become such a beautiful woman, my old world shifted on its axis. For a moment I didn't know how to behave. But it's all right now, isn't it? We can start again.'

Linda was about to ask him what he meant by start again and if he had really considered himself her boyfriend, when they were interrupted by the maid who had served the meal.

'Are you coming through to the drawing room, sir, or shall I bring your coffee here?'

'We'd better join the others, I think. Thank you for asking, Hawkins.'

Linda was surprised to see the near scowl Hawkins gave in response.

The maid hurried ahead of them as they left the room. Florian's limp was noticeable and Linda adapted her usual brisk gait so that she could walk beside him.

'You were going to tell me about her,' she said softly as they crossed the hall.

'About who?'

'The maid – Hawkins. You saw me looking puzzled and I'm sure you mouthed, "Tell you later," or something like that.'

'I did. She surprises everyone.'

'Well?'

'What do you make of her?'

'What do you mean?'

'Why were you surprised? Not by her beauty, surely. Beauty is quite indiscriminate. It is not unusual for the maid to be more beautiful than the mistress. Even a mistress as lovely as my mother.'

'No, not her beauty.' Linda was embarrassed. 'Does it sound snobbish of me to say that it was her voice... I mean, the way she speaks?'

'Not like the sort of person who becomes a servant, you mean?'

'Mmm.'

56

As they entered the drawing room they saw Hawkins standing by a trolley, waiting to pour their coffee. Linda knew it was silly of her, but for a moment she imagined that the maidservant knew they had been talking about her. Florian's mother, sister and grandmother were sitting near the fireplace at either side of a low coffee table. Just as in days of old, the elder Mrs Hylton had her chair pulled close to the fire. They were still talking animatedly about hats. Linda wondered when, if ever, they would exhaust the subject.

The room was just as large as Linda remembered, and Florian indicated a sofa some distance from the cosy group and nearer to the window. As he and Linda took their seats, Hawkins pushed the trolley towards them and poured their coffee.

'Will that be all ... sir?' she asked.

'Thank you, Hawkins. You may go. If we want more coffee I'll ring for it.'

His tone was curt and Linda was surprised. She waited until the girl had left the room before she asked, 'Why did you sound so cross? Hawkins was being perfectly polite.'

'No, she wasn't,' Florian said. '"Will, that be all, *sir?*"' he mimicked, but made the innocent question sound sarcastic. 'She was playing games again. She doesn't dare behave like that towards my parents or my grandmother, and Cordelia isn't bright enough to notice, but I am and as I have no power in this household she takes it out on me.'

'How do you mean?'

'Poor girl. It's perfectly natural that she should be resentful, but there is something about her that makes it impossible for me to feel sympathetic.'

'You have made it sound so mysterious. I wish you would explain. And please begin by telling me if her name really is Hawkins.'

Florian laughed. 'Of course it isn't. My mother chose the name because she thought it suitable for a servant. Pamela Hawkins is better than Pamela Delafontaine.'

'So she was allowed to keep her first name?'

'Don't look like that. It's not a matter of my mother allowing anything. There is a perfectly good reason why Pamela herself wanted to change her surname.'

'And that is?'

'Notoriety.'

Linda was surprised. 'She had become famous for some unsavoury reason?'

'Not Pamela. Her father. Does the name Jack Delafontaine mean anything to you?'

'The disgraced financier! It was in all the newspapers, and the case was reported in the news on the wireless. Is he Pamela's father?'

'Yes, poor girl. And not only did he steal large amounts of money from his trusting clients, but when he was found out and brought to justice, his wife, Pamela's mother, committed suicide.'

'That's dreadful. Poor Pamela.'

'And that's when my mother stepped in. She had known Pamela's mother at school. They weren't exactly friends, but Mrs Delafontaine wrote to my mother and told her what she was going to do, and asked her to care for Pamela. I suppose she realized that Mother has a soft heart and would be the most likely one to help her.'

'Could your mother not have stopped her killing herself?'

'She tried. She hurried to London but found she was too late. There were policemen all over the house in Belgravia, and Pamela was sitting sobbing at the bottom of the stairs. The worst thing was, there were already reporters hanging around outside. Godness knows how they find out about these things so quickly.'

'So your mother brought Pamela here. To be a maidservant.'

'She could hardly be part of the family. Mother thought it best if the girl became totally anonymous, and what is more anonymous than a house servant? None of the other servants know who she is; they think Mother got her on a whim from a London employment agency. Only the family know the truth, and that is because Mother thought it her duty to tell us that she was bringing the daughter of a convicted criminal into the house. And please don't judge my mother by today's more egalitarian standards. The Hyltons have the reputation of being very good to their servants.'

'So the problem, in your opinion, is that Pamela does not seem to be suitably grateful? That's not fair!'

'Don't be too quick to judge us, Linda. In my heart I know how wretched she must feel. But if only she wasn't so determined to be so ... so...'

'Ungrateful?'

Florian looked perplexed. 'Don't let's quarrel, Linda. Gratitude is tricky, isn't it? You must know that, yourself. I mean, your guardian saved you from going to an orphanage. Were you grateful?'

'Yes, I was.'

'And yet you were not entirely happy, were you?'

'What makes you say that?'

'I remember you as a somewhat lonely child. That's why we became friends – and I hope we still will be – because, in spite of being part of this large and happy family, I was lonely, too.'

Mention of the family made Linda realize that Florian had left one member out when he was telling her of the way Pamela reacted to them. 'Your brother,' she said. 'You didn't tell me how Pamela behaves when Rupert is present.'

Florian looked perplexed. 'She totally ignores him. Even if he asks her outright to make him a cup of tea or fetch him the newspaper, she mumbles something with her head down and performs her duty as if she were a robot.'

'And how does Rupert react to that?'

'Most of the time he seems to find it amusing. To my knowledge, my elder brother has never been unkind to anyone unless they deserve it, but sometimes he loses patience with poor old Pamela and speaks sharply enough to make her cry. It's a mystery to me. But, hush, here she comes.'

'More coffee ... Sir?'

Linda noticed the pause and also Florian's amused reaction. If Pamela – or Hawkins, as she must learn to call her – had hoped to annoy Florian, she had not succeeded.

'No, thank you,' he said civilly. 'You may clear this away now.' As he spoke he smiled and indicated the trolley with a graceful gesture that made Linda remember how very attractive he was.

Linda had not quite finished her coffee but, not wanting to give Hawkins any cause for complaint, she replaced her cup and saucer on the trolley. The coffee set they had been using was quite different from the one Emerald Hylton had used earlier. These cups were plain white with a blue rim that matched the rim on the saucer. Linda recognized them as one of the lines that the Hylton pottery was famous for. Cafés, hotels and restaurants throughout the British Isles used this reliable everyday creamware, and she had read in a magazine that it was also used on ocean liners.

'Oh, do look,' Florian said as Hawkins wheeled the trolley away. 'I think Grandmamma has fallen asleep. She always sits too near to the fire, and this is usually the result.'

'What should I do?' Linda asked.

Florian looked puzzled. 'What should *you* do?' And then his face cleared. 'Of course, you have come here as the old dragon's companion. Well, we can't let her stay there, or she will wake later with a stiff neck and a foul temper. As usual, I must awaken her.'

'You?' Now it was Linda's turn to look surprised.

'Yes, me. Until now it has been my duty, with Cordelia's grudging help, to get our grandmother up to her room. Now I suppose Cordelia is off the hook and it will be your duty to assist me.'

'Or your duty to assist me,' Linda said with a smile.

Momentarily Hawkins was in the way as she collected the coffee cups from the table near the fire, but when she had placed them on the trolley and moved towards the door, Linda was startled to see that the elder Mrs Hylton was sitting forward in her chair and staring in their direction. A moment later her voice carried clearly across the room.

'I may be losing my eyesight, Florian, but I can make out enough of your amused expression to deduce that you have been talking about me in a disrespectful manner.'

'Me? Not respect you, Grandmamma? Never,' Florian replied, and he rose and began to walk across the room towards the trio by the hearth. Linda got up and followed him.

Emerald Hylton and her daughter smiled at Linda briefly and resumed their conversation.

'Come along, darling grandmamma,' Florian said as he proffered his hand. 'Linda and I will take you to your room where you can settle down and snore in peace.'

'I don't snore!' his grandmother said, sounding fierce; but Linda could tell from her indulgent smile that she was not cross with her grandson. It was obvious that there was a bond of affection between these two and Linda, even though she was inside the room she had so often observed through the window, realized that she might as well have been out in the garden again. She was still an outsider.

Chapter Three

Florian put one arm around his grandmother's waist and supported her as they climbed the stairs. Linda, going up behind them, noticed how strong he was. There was no disguising his limp, but he had learned to make the best of it, and she had learned that nothing angered him more than someone assuming that he needed help.

Linda remembered one day in the woods not long after she had first met him. She had come across him on the stepping stones again. His concentration was so great that he had not heard her approaching, and something made her stop and conceal herself behind the very tree she had been sitting in when they had first met the previous week. She watched his sheer determination as he balanced on one uneven, mossy stone after the other, the water glinting with sunlight, flowing swiftly round them. He gave a whoop of delight when he reached the bank.

Then he looked straight towards the tree. 'You can come out now,' he said. He had known all along that she was there. 'I hoped you would come today. That's why I brought this.' He turned so that she could see the knapsack on his back. 'Let's find somewhere warm to sit and have a picnic.'

When they had settled pretty much in the same place they had sat to dry themselves out the week before, Florian opened the knapsack and brought out a blue-and-white checked cloth and spread it on the ground. 'Cook gave it to me along with the grub. I didn't have to tell her that I wanted enough for two, because she spoils me rotten and always assumes that I have an enormous appetite. "A proper lad's appetite", she'll say. It's her way of trying to make me feel I'm no different from any other boy. That I wasn't born with one leg shorter than the other. And thank you for never asking about it, by the way.'

'Oh, I wouldn't! I mean, that would have been ill-mannered.'

'And your guardian has brought you up to be properly polite. But it's more than that. I sensed – and maybe I'm wrong – that it really doesn't matter to you that I'm different, does it?'

It had never occurred to Linda that Florian's limp made him different from any other human being. 'It doesn't matter at all,' she said.

She watched as he opened the knapsack and removed some greaseproof paper bags. He opened the bags to reveal cheese and tomato sandwiches, sausage rolls, flapjacks and an apple.

'Only one apple, I'm afraid,' he said, 'but I can cut it in two with my penknife. It's a Swiss Army knife.' He said this as if it were something to be proud of, so Linda tried to look impressed.

'And there's this.' He drew out a bottle of pink-coloured pop. 'Raspberry flavour. I hope you like it. Oh, no, I haven't even brought one cup, never mind two. We'll just have to drink from the bottle. I'll wipe it each time, of course.' He began to tear the bags open to make them into makeshift plates.

'What would you have done with all this if I had

not come today?' Until now Linda had not spoken, and Florian looked up and grinned.

'Eaten as much as I could and chucked the rest away, I suppose. But I knew you would come. I just sort of felt it in my bones. Is it silly to say that?'

'No, I don't think so. But maybe ... maybe...'

'Maybe what?'

'Maybe it was just wishful thinking.' She paused and looked embarrassed. 'I shouldn't have said that.'

'Why not?'

'I shouldn't have assumed that you would wish to see me.'

Florian laughed. 'Oh, you can assume all you like because it's true. I wished it most strongly. Now, let's start on this lot.'

Soon after that day Florian had gone back to boarding school, and they didn't meet again until the Christmas holidays. The village school had broken up the previous day. It was only mid-afternoon but the way through the woods was dark and shadowy. Linda wrapped up warmly and set out to trespass once more.

As she made her way along paths which had become familiar to her, dead leaves crackled underfoot. She saw a wavering light in the distance and stopped. The light was coming towards her and there was the sound of other footsteps. She didn't think it would be one of the servants from the house, but nevertheless she stepped back into the shadows. A moment later a voice called, 'Linda, is that you? Where are you?'

Florian! Linda emerged from the shelter of the trees and ran towards him.

65

'Hello, Linda, old bean, I'm so pleased to see you!' He was laughing.

'I'm not an old bean. That's a silly thing to say!' she exclaimed; nevertheless she joined in the laughter.

'They all say it at school. And it's better than calling you an old fart. They say that, too.'

After a moment their laughter died, and Florian held his arm out to the side then pointed the torch in their direction so that they could look at each other without being dazzled.

'I knew you'd come,' he said.

'And I knew you'd come to find me.'

'But what shall we do? We can't stand around here; it's far too chilly.'

Linda remembered all the dark, winter evenings she had peered through the windows of the Hall. She had never felt the cold.

'Why don't we just walk about?' she asked. 'Keep moving. And talk. You can tell me about school.'

Linda couldn't remember now how long they had spent walking and talking until the cold drove them to their separate homes. Neither could she remember what they had talked about. All she knew was that they had simply enjoyed being in each other's company. That was true when they were children, and even when they had grown a little older and become more self-conscious. In later years she had wondered if they had been on the brink of something deeper than friendship. However, they had not seen each other since Florian had been at university, for once Miss Taylor had had her stroke, Linda's trespassing days were ended.

'What is it, Florian? Have you come to escort me down to lunch?' Clara Hylton smiled questioningly at her grandson.

'No, my darling grandmamma. We have had our lunch. You looked a little tired so I – we – escorted you to your room.'

'We?' Clara peered at Linda, who was standing next to Florian, 'Oh, of course. Miss Bellwood. My companion. So we've had lunch, have we? Silly of me to forget. Perhaps it's because I'm tired. A little nap will put things straight.'

'Quite right,' Florian said. 'Now I'll leave you two girls and go and see to my packing.'

'Packing?'

Clara Hylton frowned. Linda tried hard to conceal her surprise. Then the older woman's face cleared and she smiled at Florian fondly. 'Ah yes, you are going away to visit a friend you made at university. Ian MacFarlane, isn't it? The young man with the very pretty sister.'

Linda was not prepared for the sudden surge of dismay.

'That's right, Grandmamma,' Florian said. 'Clever of you to remember.'

'Remember what? The name of your friend? The fact that you are going to stay with him? Or that he has a pretty little sister? Elspeth, isn't it?' Clara Hylton nodded and looked pleased with herself.

Florian laughed. 'I'm impressed. You have an amazing memory, Grandmamma.'

Clara's smile vanished. 'I know I have. The trouble is, it comes and goes. I mean, fancy forgetting that we had already eaten.'

'Don't worry. Just allow Linda to help you lie down and rest.' Florian leaned forward and kissed his grandmother on her cheek, then gave her shoulders a gentle squeeze and left the room.

'I was hoping to go for a walk after lunch,' Clara Hylton told Linda, 'but the boy is right, I should rest. What will you do?'

Linda was taken aback. 'I ... erm... I'm not sure what you mean.'

'I mean, what will you do when I'm lying in bed snoring gently? Do you think my daughter-in-law means you to sit here and keep watch over me?'

'I'm not sure. Would you like me to stay?'

Clara Hylton tilted her head to one side as she considered the question. 'Actually, I would,' she said after a slight pause. 'You could sort out some correspondence for me. Look – on that little writing desk over there – my escritoire. There's a heap of letters and postcards from friends. I am afraid I have neglected to keep up to date with them. Perhaps you could go through them and put aside the ones that should be answered.' She paused. 'What is it? You look mutinous.'

'No, not mutinous. Just troubled. I mean, surely you don't want me to read personal letters, do you?'

'Wait a moment.' While they had been downstairs, someone had made the bed, probably Vera Saunders, Linda guessed. Clara Hylton walked slowly over to it and sat down. 'Would you take my shoes off, dear? My old bones creak when I bend to undo them myself.'

'Of course.' Linda knelt down and undid the

buttons on the straps which arched over Clara Hylton's insteps, then she eased the shoes off gently. 'You like your heels very high,' she said.

'I do, and I'm reluctant to admit that I find them uncomfortable these days. It would be like surrendering to old age. Now, I won't get undressed. Perhaps I'll just take my skirt off and then lie on top of the bedspread. You can cover me with that rug.' She indicated a rug neatly folded and lying across the foot of the bed. 'You needn't close the curtains. You'll need the light to read my letters.'

'You haven't answered my question,' Linda said.

'What question? Oh, yes. You're worried about reading my personal correspondence. There's no need. You won't find anything scandalous, and even if you do, you're my companion, aren't you? We can enjoy the scandal together. It's much more fun to have someone to share these things with, isn't it?'

Linda arranged the rug over her charge, who smiled up at her before closing her eyes. Despite the grey hair and the wrinkles, in repose Clara Hylton looked almost childlike. Linda felt a pang of guilt when she realized that she would take more pleasure in looking after her than she had in looking after Agnes Taylor; the woman who had taken her in when she had been a homeless child.

Duty and gratitude, Linda thought. Miss Taylor thought it a duty to perform a charitable act, and although she was never unkind we never got close. And I, who was yearning for affection and for someone to love, felt only gratitude, an uncomfortable emotion, although on my part deeply sincere.

Is that why I was drawn to Fernwood Hall? I think it must have been. It wasn't just the excitement of exploring the woods; it was looking in on the family. The wonderful, vibrant people who not only led such an interesting life – I thought it a charmed life – but also seemed to love each other unreservedly.

Linda smiled as she remembered Florian's gentle teasing, for Clara Hylton did not snore; she breathed in and out peacefully and hardly moved from the position she had taken up when she first lay down. Linda settled herself at the writing desk as she had been bidden. It was an attractive piece of furniture; Linda guessed it to be an antique. Made from mahogany, it had two drawers at the front, and above them the writing surface was covered with dark red leather. At the back there was a series of drawers and pigeon-holes.

Linda stared in dismay at the jumble of cards and letters stuffed everywhere and anyhow. Most of the envelopes remained unopened. She decided first of all to separate the postcards from the letters, and then the unopened letters from the opened. After that she supposed the best thing to do would be to sort them chronologically. The date stamp on the envelopes would help her there.

She had just started on her task when she heard the door open. She turned her head to see Florian standing in the doorway. He raised a finger to his lips to signify that they must be silent, looked at the untidy desk and raised his eyebrows, then he beckoned her over. She rose and walked as quietly as she could to join him. He drew her outside and, leaving the door ajar, he indicated that they should walk along the wide passageway towards a long window. He stopped there, and for a moment he turned away from her and looked out at the grounds. In the not too far distance Linda could see the woods.

When he spoke he surprised her. 'I'm sorry,' he said. 'I should have told you before Grandmamma blurted it out.'

'What are you talking about?'

'The fact that I'm going to Scotland.'

'Scotland?'

'To stay with Ian.'

'Oh, your friend with the pretty sister.'

'That's right.'

Linda concealed a sudden surge of jealousy with what she hoped was an amused expression.

'Why are you smiling?' Florian asked.

'Because your grandmother was obviously teasing – or fishing, perhaps.'

'But I didn't rise to the bait, did I?'

'She probably didn't expect you to.'

'There's nothing in it, you know. Elspeth is certainly attractive, but there's nothing inside that pretty little head of hers except parties and balls and the latest fashions. Not my type at all.' Florian was looking at her intently. She didn't know what to say but became uncomfortably aware of the beating of her heart. 'This visit was arranged months ago. I'd never have accepted Ian's invitation if I'd known you were going to come here.'

'Why ever not?'

'Because, you are a much more interesting companion than Elspeth MacFarlane, and because we now have a wonderful opportunity to start again.'

'I am your grandmother's companion, not yours.'

'You deliberately misunderstand me – or at least you pretend to. You know very well what I mean, don't you?'

'Yes, I do. But, Florian. What do you mean by "start again"?'

'Start where we left off. We were friends for all those years, weren't we? All those years you came trespassing in our woods.'

Linda smiled. 'And you aided and abetted me.'

'Yes, I did.'

'Why did you do it?'

'Don't fish for compliments, Linda. It's not worthy of you.'

'And don't you start preaching at me. You know how I hate that.'

Florian took, her hand. 'See how easy it is?' he said. 'See how easily we slip into the old ways. I think we quarrelled as much as we agreed with each other, but we always remained friends, didn't we?'

'Yes.'

'And just as that friendship was beginning to develop into something more, you stopped coming.'

'I had to.'

'I know. And we couldn't even write to each other. You to explain, or me to ask. There was no way we could have explained how we knew each other.'

'You could have written to me when you were at university.'

'By then I thought you had forsaken me.'

'Forsaken? That's a funny thing to say.'

'Do you think so? Then you obviously didn't take our friendship as seriously as I did.'

'Are we quarrelling again?'

They looked at each other and smiled.

'You see how easy it is? How marvellous it's going to be? How I wish I didn't have to go away, but I can't let Ian down. Never mind, I can write to you.'

'You're only going away for a fortnight.'

'Well, that means at least two letters, doesn't it? Perhaps three. One to say I've arrived safely, another to say how much I'm enjoying myself, and another to say I'm coming home. I shall put them in the same envelope as my letters to Grand-mamma, then no one will know.'

Linda felt a twinge of disquiet. 'Why shouldn't they know?'

'If I started writing to you when I'm supposed to have only just met you, my parents would think it strange, wouldn't they?'

'I suppose so.'

'Then stop frowning and get back to your task. I don't envy you.' They walked back along the pas-sageway together and, as Linda slipped into the room, Florian said softly, 'I'll see you at dinner, but perhaps we shouldn't spend so much time talking together. We don't want to give people the wrong idea.'

Linda stared at the jumble of letters and cards. She found it hard to concentrate. She kept won-dering what Florian meant by 'the wrong idea'. And then, what had he meant when he said that their friendship had been about to develop into something more? From childhood companionship to romantic love? An inevitable playing out of the fairy tale? Had Florian Hylton from Fernwood Hall been on the verge of falling in love with Linda Bellwood, a girl from the village? And now that they had met once more, was the gap between their worlds too big to bridge?

She closed her eyes and let old memories play in her mind like the reels of a film. The sunny days when they had run through the woods and across the parkland. The competitions to see who could climb the highest in the old trees. The days they had splashed under the little waterfall and swum in the pool below it.

Florian had brought his swimming trunks and a big towel. The first time, Linda had completely unselfconsciously stripped to her vest and knickers and been soggy and uncomfortable on the way home. The next time and all the times that followed, she had smuggled out her swimming costume. She could do nothing about a towel; Miss Taylor would have noticed, but Florian's towel was big enough and thick enough for both of them.

Linda had friends at school. Or rather, there were one or two girls who would sit on the bench in the schoolyard and gossip with her at playtime. But she was never invited to their houses to play or to have tea. And Miss Taylor never suggested that she should bring anyone home. As she grew older, Linda realized that, as far as the village was concerned, she was different. She had been adopted by a stranger, an educated woman furthermore, who had little in common with the other village women. Maybe they believed Miss Taylor thought herself superior to them, and in a way they were right.

Agnes Taylor had been a good if strict teacher, but she had no social graces. She did not know how to make small talk, was not interested in village gossip, and was determined to bring Linda up to think herself a cut above the other girls. The result was that Linda had from an early age thought of herself as an outsider.

And then she had learned that Florian thought of himself as an outsider, too. At first Linda had imagined that this was because of his handicap, and that might have been part of his problem, but only a small part. Florian thought of himself as different from the rest of the family in many ways.

His father, William Hylton, was a businessman, and a very good one. He was enterprising and enthusiastic, and the Hylton pottery continued to flourish under his management. He expected his sons to follow him into the business, Rupert to take over eventually, and Florian to manage the overseas sales.

Rather pompously, Florian told Linda that his father's mind was not completely closed to culture, he did like to relax with a book, but he preferred the novels of Rider Haggard, Anthony Hope and John Buchan to those of Franz Kafka or John Dos Passos. Linda had no idea who the latter two authors were, and she didn't like to remind Florian that he had once told her that he had read and loved *The Prisoner of Zenda* by Anthony Hope and *The Thirty-Nine Steps* by John Buchan.

His older brother, Rupert, was the perfect son. Clever, sporty, hardworking and cheerful, he had done well at university but was not attracted to academia. He was perfectly happy to join the business and, once he had left his student days behind him, had never been seen to read anything more challenging than the *Field* or any other magazine to do with country life.

'Secretly he fancies himself as a country gent,' Florian told her. 'But that won't stop him knuckling under and doing his best for the business.'

As for his mother and his sister, Florian pretended to despair of them. 'Complete sybarites,' he had said dismissively.

Linda had had to look up the meaning of the word sybarite when she got home, and found that it meant somebody devoted to luxury and the gratification of sensual desires. She closed her dictionary and frowned. She could see why Florian thought his mother and sister were fond of a life of luxury, but perhaps he didn't know the meaning of sensual desires. After that incident she began to feel less intimidated when she was in his company. He spoke with great confidence, but maybe he wasn't quite as clever as he thought he was.

Linda and Florian became sparring partners and, as she admitted to herself now, along with their genuine desire to share their thoughts and opinions, they had probably talked a lot of rubbish. Precocious children, both of us, she thought, but only able to be our true selves when we were in each other's company.

Then, as they grew older, the way they talked to each other became a little self-conscious. Sometimes the conversation would dry up completely and they would sit in the sun-dappled meadow or shelter under a tree from a brief summer shower, thinking of nothing in particular, just happy to be in each other's company. If they walked through the woods Florian started holding her hand. This was to stop her tripping over exposed knotted roots, he said, and she didn't remind him that possibly she knew the pathways better than he did.

One early autumn evening, the last time they would meet before Florian went to university, he kissed her goodbye. A mist was rising from the stream and curling its way towards them, and the air was cooling rapidly. Linda shivered and Florian put his arm round her and drew her close. A sudden breath of wind loosened some leaves from the branches above them and one leaf landed on Linda's head.

Florian stood back from her, took the leaf and put it in his pocket. She wanted to laugh at what she thought a stagey gesture, but she saw that he looked quite solemn.

'"Know'st thou not at the fall of a leaf, How the heart feels a languid grief..."' he said softly.

Linda smiled. 'Rossetti!' she said. Florian was fond of quoting poems and challenging her to name the poet.

His answer was to take her in his arms and draw her close before kissing her very gently. 'Goodbye, Linda,' he said. 'We'll meet again when I'm home for Christmas, won't we?'

'Of course,' she had said, but there had been no of course about it. They had not seen each other again until today and now, incredibly, it seemed Florian wanted them to take up where they had left off. But where was that exactly? Linda wasn't sure.

'What are you doing sitting at my desk?'

Startled, Linda turned to see Clara Hylton sitting up in bed and blinking as she came slowly awake.

'I'm sorting your correspondence. You told me to, remember?'

'Did I?' Clara shook her head. 'Well, if you say so. It's certainly time it was dealt with. Have you made much progress?'

'Not much.'

'Well, don't worry, my dear. Take all the time you want. Now, how about ringing for Saunders? We'll have a pot of tea, shall we?'

Clara Hylton stayed where she was to drink her tea, and she told Linda to bring up a chair and sit closer.

'I used to have my own maid, you know,' Mrs Hylton said when Saunders had gone. 'When I first came here more than fifty years ago, houses like this were stuffed full of servants. The war put an end to that way of life. The younger men were conscripted, and many of the women went off to work in the munitions factories. They thought they ought to "do their bit".

'People like us had to learn to manage with fewer servants. And after the war was over the world had changed. And is still changing. Now my daughter-in-law manages with a couple of parlourmaids, a married couple who perform the duties of cook and handyman, a useful boy and a chauffeur. I believe some women from the village come in to do the rough work.'

'A useful boy?'

'In former days he would have been a footman

– and he still smartens up nicely to help serve at dinner parties – but now he's at the beck and call of just about everybody and would probably be worked to death if he hadn't perfected the art of going missing every now and then.'

Clara Hylton smiled when she said this, and Linda formed the impression that she was fond of the 'useful boy'.

'Now then,' Clara Hylton said when she had finished her tea, 'we had better sort out what you are going to wear for dinner.'

'Won't this do?' Linda asked.

'No, my dear. If you are to be one of us I can't have you sitting there in that very ordinary black dress. It isn't even stylish. Have you got a decent skirt?'

'Yes, I think it could be called decent.'

'By that I suppose you mean sensible. What colour is it?'

'Grey.'

'Flannel?'

'I'm afraid so. I told you my guardian favoured sensible clothes.'

Clara Hylton rolled her eyes in mock distress. 'So I suppose you're going to tell me that your blouses are smocked or sensibly pin-tucked?'

'Something like that.'

'Well, until we can go shopping in town we'll just have to make the best of things. You shall have to wear your sensible skirt, for even when I was a girl,' (she pronounced it 'gel') 'I wasn't as slender as you are. However, I think we can do something about your top half. Pass me my robe, Linda. It's on the chair over there.'

Clara Hylton, suddenly energized, slipped on her robe and felt for her mules; then she padded over to the wardrobe, flinging open both doors.

'Come here, child. You shall borrow a blouse. It may be a little large for you, but you'll just have to tuck it in. Hurry up. This is going to be fun!'

At dinner that evening Linda wore her flannel skirt and a smoky grey high-necked blouse with a darker grey chiffon bow at the neck. Rather than fashionable, she felt as though she was a child dressing up in her mother's clothes, but Clara Hylton had been insistent and Linda had not wanted to upset her. I shall have to be made of sterner stuff if I allow her to take me shopping, she thought. Perhaps I should have a look at Cordelia's fashion magazines.

Linda had been introduced to Mr Hylton and his elder son, Rupert, and it was Rupert who dominated the conversation at the table with general chatter and anecdotes taken from the working day. His father didn't say much but laughed at his jokes. So did his mother and his sister. Grandmamma Hylton gave the occasional appreciative chuckle. Only Florian remained silent.

When they were settled in the drawing room for coffee, Rupert came to sit beside Linda. He laughingly thanked her for being willing to take on his grandmother. 'She may appear fierce at first but she's not so bad when you get to know her,' he said.

'I don't find her fierce at all,' Linda told him.

Rupert raised his eyebrows. 'Really? Then she must have taken to you. But, nevertheless, let me warn you that she likes her own way.'

Linda smiled. 'I've already learned that.'

'Don't let her bully you.'

'I won't. I shall look upon it as a challenge.'

'Good for you!' Rupert said, and although his bonhomie was typical of a young man of his class, Linda thought it genuine. 'Now, if you'll excuse me,' Rupert said, 'I'll leave you to Florian's tender mercies. I'd better go and talk to my sister. I have a message from Charlie.'

He said this as though Linda would know who Charlie was. She turned to Florian, who had come to take Rupert's place beside her. 'Charlie?' she said.

'Meredith. Charles Meredith. The prospective bridegroom.'

'Oh, I didn't know.'

'You mean to say you haven't noticed the egg-sized diamond on the fourth finger of my sister's left hand?'

Linda glanced across the room at Cordelia. 'It's not egg-sized. It's quite modest.'

Florian smiled. 'I know. I've already told you that I exaggerate. I can't help it. But modest or not, it probably cost more than poor old Charlie can afford. But, look, let's not waste time talking about Cordelia's wedding plans. I'm sure you'll find out more than you want to know after I'm gone.' He gave a deep-felt sigh.

'You speak as if you are going away for ever. You're only going for a fortnight, aren't you?'

'It will seem longer.'

His smile was both rueful and humorous, and for all Rupert's charm and physical perfection,

Linda thought Florian the better looking of the two. He had a refinement and sensitivity totally missing in his elder brother.

'I'd better go and chase up the coffee,' Florian said. 'It seems Pamela has forgotten us.'

He limped across to where Pamela stood with the trolley, and when she had poured the coffee into two cups he came back with them. Linda could see how hard he had to concentrate if he was not to spill the coffee. She took both cups from him before he sat down.

'She's worse than ever tonight,' Florian said, glancing over at Pamela. 'I don't believe she looked me in the eye once when I was speaking to her. But I must learn to control my irritation. The poor girl looks utterly miserable, doesn't she?'

With a surge of sympathy Linda agreed that she did. Despite his irritation with her, Florian seemed to be sincerely sorry for Pamela. And Linda believed that kind-hearted Emerald Hylton had genuinely wanted to help the girl. Unlike her more worldly-wise mother-in-law, she had not foreseen the difficulties that would arise. Pamela's evident misery was tempered by a controlled rage which made her behave the way she did. Behaviour which the more forthright Cordelia could not understand.

And then, while Florian sipped his coffee, Linda witnessed something which startled her. Rupert rose from the seat beside his sister and, standing quite still, looked across the room at Pamela. Pamela returned his gaze, and for a long moment they simply stared at each other. Rupert's wary stillness and Pamela's pent-up anger explained everything.

She is in love with Rupert, Linda thought. And as for Rupert...? I'm not sure. There is something unresolved here. How can Florian, who is so clever and so sensitive, not have understood what is making Pamela so unhappy?

Chapter Four

When Linda went downstairs the next morning she saw Vera Saunders coming out of the dining room. Pleased that it was her instead of Pamela, she hurried across the hall. Vera heard her echoing footsteps and turned to greet her.

'Good morning, Miss Bellwood,' she said.

'What am I supposed to do?' Linda asked.

Vera looked puzzled for a moment and then her face cleared. 'Mrs Charles will have a tray in her room, but you will eat breakfast with the family in the dining room. That's what Mrs Aslett's been told.'

'Mrs Aslett?'

'The cook. She's the housekeeper, too, and as for her husband, Albert, he's handyman, steward, butler, all that's required of him. This household would never survive if the Asletts left.' She paused to let the information sink in then added, 'Don't worry, you'll soon learn who's who and what's what.' Then she asked, 'So what would you like for breakfast?'

Linda was surprised. 'The same as everyone else, I suppose.'

'They all have exactly what they want, and you can, too.' Seeing that Linda was still unsure of what to say, she said, 'For a start, would you like some porridge? Ivy Aslett makes good porridge. Oats and water and a pinch of salt stirred clockwise with a wooden spoon. No sugar, no milk, but you can add some cream if you like.'

'Sounds marvellous! I'll have porridge.'

'And then?'

Linda's eyes widened. 'There's more?'

'I told you, anything you like to follow. Bacon, eggs, sausage, black pudding, grilled tomatoes, fried bread, a bit of bubble and squeak, or you could have–'

'Stop!' Linda said and she laughed. 'Surely nobody can eat that much for breakfast.'

'The menfolk do, even Mr Florian. Mrs William and Cordelia have fruit juice or grapefruit and toast and some kind of preserve. Although Miss Cordelia sometimes has those American pancakes with maple syrup. As for Grandmother Hylton, she's easy to please, a soft-boiled egg, a pot of coffee, some fresh bread rolls and butter and her favourite Oxford marmalade. But she has that in her room, like I told you.'

'A boiled egg sounds nice. I think I'll have that.'

'Or you could have it poached.'

'Vera, what are you trying to do? Confuse me even further? Stop teasing me.'

'I'm not teasing you, pet. I mean, Miss Bellwood. Nor am I trying to confuse you. It's just that it was a joy to see your expression when I was telling you what was on offer here. I'm guessing your guardian Miss Taylor didn't set such a hearty breakfast table.'

Linda remembered that Agnes Taylor had a reputation in the village for being mean – not to say miserly. It was completely undeserved. Her guardian had not been mean. Linda had never gone without good food. It was just that Miss Taylor was careful with her money and almost puritanical on the subject of waste. The idea of food being cooked and then not eaten would have horrified her.

'Miss Taylor made jolly good porridge,' Linda said loyally. 'And she taught me to make it, too. And I've made up my mind about what I'll have to follow the porridge. I'll have a poached egg.'

'On toast?'

'Yes, please.'

'And will that be one or two eggs?'

'Vera!'

Vera Saunders smiled broadly. 'Go on in,' she said. 'I'll order two poached eggs, and by the time I come back with your porridge you can tell me whether you would like a pot of tea or coffee.'

The housemaid hurried towards the back of the hall, and Linda watched as she opened a door that appeared to have green baize covering the other side. When the door closed, she turned and had to get up her courage to enter the dining room. She had forgotten to ask who she would find in there, and she was still uncertain of the sort of welcome she would have.

There were only two people sitting together at one end of the table: Mr Hylton and his elder son, Rupert. They were enjoying a breakfast of bacon and egg and what looked like everything else Vera Saunders had mentioned. They were deep in a conversation that looked as if it were serious, but they glanced up distractedly and smiled as Linda entered.

'Ah, Miss Bellwood. What a pleasant surprise,' Mr Hylton said.

'Surprise?' In spite of Vera Saunders' reassurances to the contrary, Linda wondered for a moment if she should be there.

Rupert laughed. 'What my father means is that, except for Sundays, we do not usually have female company at the breakfast table. During the week we leave for the pottery very early indeed, and even on a Saturday, like today, my mother and sister barely have their eyes open by now. They will drift down later.'

'Oh, I'm sorry,' Linda said.

'No, no, there's nothing to apologise for,' Mr Hylton said. 'So long as you don't mind us discussing business while we eat?'

'Of course not.'

'Then do sit down and I'll ring for Saunders.' He half rose from his chair but Linda stopped him. 'It's all right. I met her on the way in. She knows I'm here.'

Linda sat at the other end of the table. She did not want to appear to be eavesdropping. As soon as they saw she was settled they resumed their conversation. They kept their voices low, but Linda thought that Rupert sounded annoyed.

Then she heard Mr Hylton say quite clearly, 'I'm sure that's the right thing to do.' He said it as though that was the end of the discussion.

Rupert raised his voice, sounding utterly exasperated. 'You're too soft with him,' he said. 'I mean, this holiday in Scotland – what will it achieve?'

Linda knew at once who they were talking about and she looked down at the tablecloth in embarrassment. She wondered if she should cough and remind them she was there. She decided not to, and knowing it was wrong to do so but not being able to stop herself, she strained to hear Mr Hylton's answer.

'It's the girl,' he said. 'If he's serious about her, he may want to settle down and take his place in the business.'

'And then I suppose it will be a matter of the fatted calf!'

'Don't worry, Rupert,' Mr Hylton said quietly. 'You are my heir and you must know how much I value you. All I want for Florian is to see him settled in some worthwhile occupation.'

'Working for Hylton's?'

'Of course.'

Vera Saunders returned with Linda's porridge and a jug of fresh cream. Both men looked along the table at her, but Linda tried to act as though she hadn't heard anything untoward. She thanked Vera and told her she had decided on a pot of coffee. Neither Mr Hylton nor Rupert spoke again, either to each other or to Linda. When they rose from the table they sent a brief smile in her direction and then headed for the door.

A moment later Vera Saunders came back and told Linda, 'Mrs William and Miss Cordelia have sent for trays, so you can relax and enjoy your breakfast in peace.'

'What do you mean, I can relax?'

'You seem rather edgy. I thought you might still be in awe of the Hyltons.'

'I've never been in awe of them!' Linda retorted defensively. Then, wanting to be candid, she added, 'Intrigued by them, perhaps, but I've never been in awe.'

Vera Saunders looked at her levelly. 'No, I don't suppose you have. You strike me as the kind of girl who wouldn't be in awe of anyone. Your Miss Taylor's done a good job rearing you. Perhaps she wanted something more for you than being an old lady's companion.'

'For heaven's sake, Vera, don't *you* start. I've had enough of that from Mr Sinclair.'

'I'm sorry. I didn't mean to upset you.'

Linda didn't reply and Vera left her alone to finish her porridge. When the maid came back with her eggs and her coffee, Linda had recovered her equilibrium and thanked her with what she hoped was a conciliatory smile. In truth she was pleased to be on her own. She wanted to think about the conversation she had overheard.

Those few short sentences told her that Florian was not interested in joining the family business and that his father was keen for him to do so. As for Rupert, she wasn't sure if Florian's elder brother wanted him to work with them or whether he was simply angry that his father was so lenient with him. She guessed that Rupert, like the dutiful son he was, had gone straight from university to work with his father, so it must anger him that Florian had not followed suit.

And what about 'the girl'? Mr Hylton must

surely mean Elspeth MacFarlane, the sister of Florian's friend Ian. Did Mr Hylton think Florian was keen on her? His grandmother had hinted as much the day before, but later Florian had told Linda that there was nothing in it. She remembered his words:

'There's nothing in it, you know. Elspeth is certainly attractive, but there's nothing inside that pretty little head of hers except parties and balls and the latest fashions. Not my type at all... This visit was arranged months ago. I'd never have accepted Ian's invitation if I'd known you were going to come here.'

Linda hoped fervently that this was true.

There had been no further instructions, so after breakfast Linda went up to Grandmother Hylton's room. She was greeted with a smile. 'There you are, dear. I was beginning to wonder if you were a dream.'

'Why should I be a dream?'

'You must know that my memory is playing tricks on me these days, and now and then I get a little confused.'

'Yes, I know.'

'Good girl, a more pusillanimous creature would have felt that I ought to be contradicted – and reassured. But you are not faint-hearted. You will speak the truth when it needs to be spoken. And I feel I can trust you to do your best for me.'

'So please explain why you thought I was a dream.'

'Because you are just the sort of companion I require, and maybe I thought I had conjured you up out of a subconscious need. But, here you are, and the sun is streaming through my windows and it's far too nice a day to stay indoors. When you have read the newspaper to me and then helped me dress, I propose to send for a light lunch for us to be brought up on a tray, then this afternoon you and I will go to the Autumn Fayre.

'And don't bother to hide how surprised you are. If you're wondering how I remembered about the Fayre, I didn't. Saunders reminded me when she came for my breakfast tray.'

'Pull up round the corner, Stevens. I don't want a crowd of curious children making sticky finger-marks all over the car. Linda and I can walk round to the village hall. You can wait in the car for us, or go for a walk. Whatever you like.'

The Hyltons' chauffeur parked the car in a narrow lane off the main street which led down to the river. This was not the car that Mr Hylton and Rupert took to work in Newcastle. William Hylton thought it ostentatious to take the Rolls to work, so he settled for a Lanchester, which, if the truth be told, was still rather grand. Father and son preferred to drive themselves, taking their turn, and leaving Paul Stevens, the chauffeur, at the behest of the womenfolk. He was also responsible for servicing the three automobiles they owned; the other car being Rupert's snazzy little MG.

Once Stevens had helped Clara Hylton out of the car, she smiled at him and said, 'Maybe you would like to come with us?'

Stevens shook his head. 'No thank you, Mrs Hylton.'

'Are you sure? There will be a refreshment stall. They serve tea and home-made cakes.'

'I'm sure the cakes are delicious,' Stevens said, 'but I'd rather go for a stroll along the river bank.'

'Very well, but don't let time run away with you. I shouldn't think Miss Bellwood and I will be long. Duty done we'll be returning to the Hall as soon as is polite.'

'Don't worry, Ma'am,' he said. 'I'll be waiting outside to help you carry all the things you've bought. I know you can't resist a bargain.'

He spoke with the easy confidence of a man who was good at his job, and furthermore a very good-looking man. His manner was one of old-fashioned deference diluted with an easier, less subservient manner. As Clara Hylton had told her, times were changing. But even so, Linda didn't think they had changed sufficiently for what she suspected Pamela Delafontaine, otherwise known as Hawkins, was hoping for.

'Very well, Stevens. Now, Miss Bellwood and I must be off.'

Stevens locked the car and set off for the river. Linda thought he was walking quickly rather than strolling, but maybe he just wanted to make the most of this short break. Perhaps he would sit quietly somewhere and smoke a cigarette and lift his face to the surprisingly warm sun.

If Linda had come on her own she would not have needed the car. The distance from the Hall to the village was not too great for young legs, but Clara Hylton, with her ridiculously impractical high heels, was already finding the short distance from where they had parked the car to the village hall difficult. Linda knew that pride would not let her admit it.

They passed a row of very old dwellings with drunken roofs and the sort of cottage gardens that appear on jigsaw puzzles.

'Oh, dear,' the old lady said when they reached the corner.

Two small girls and an even smaller boy stood there gazing at the car with eager eyes.

'What's the matter?' Linda asked.

'They're curious. They can't help it, poor little things. The minute we're gone they will go and look at the car.'

'Does that matter?'

'Of course it does. They will climb up on the running board to peer inside and leave dirty little fingermarks all over. They will look at their own endearingly grubby faces in the wing mirrors and twist them this way and that until the wretched things part company with the car.'

'Has that happened before?' Linda said.

Clara Hylton sighed. 'It has. I'd quite forgotten.'

'Perhaps you should have asked Stevens to stay.'

'Yes, I should have done. Why on earth did I think it would be safe if we simply parked around the corner?'

If village children were a known hazard, Linda wondered why Stevens hadn't thought of this, too. She looked back down the street but the chauffeur was already heading along the river bank. Perhaps he didn't mind the children leaving sticky finger-marks on the car. After all, he could easily clean them off. But he should have been worried about possible damage to the mirrors.

'These three look very small,' Linda said. 'I'm sure they couldn't do much harm. However, I have an idea.'

'And that is?'

'Why don't we ask them to guard the car? To stay and watch it, and if any other children come by one of them must run to the village hall and tell us.'

'We'll have to bribe them, of course. You realize that?'

'It will only take a penny or two.'

'To be paid before or after?'

'Oh, after, definitely.'

'Go ahead then. You negotiate, and don't break the bank!'

'I'm sure a penny each will be sufficient.'

'Really? That doesn't sound like very much. Let's make that tuppence each.'

Linda smiled and, imagining the delight they would take in spending their pennies in the village shop, she approached the children. As she drew nearer they looked uneasy, and she saw that like startled birds they were preparing for flight.

'Wait!' she said. 'We'd like you to help us.'

The children listened with round eyes and nodded vigorously as Linda explained. 'And remember,' she said finally. 'You mustn't touch the car, you must only watch it. If I find handprint marks Mrs Hylton will not pay you.'

They looked at Mrs Hylton, who tried to look stern, then back at Linda.

'All right, Linda,' one of the girls said. 'You can count on us.'

Mrs Hylton watched them walk towards the car

and shook her head sadly. 'Oh, dear, oh dear,' she said.

'What's the matter?' Linda asked.

'The girls forgot to curtsey.'

'Curtsey?' Linda was astonished. 'Did you expect them to curtsey?'

'Of course. We're gentry. It is our due.'

Linda realized that Clara Hylton had slipped back in time. Curtseying to the gentry was probably *de rigueur* for the villagers when she had first come to live at Fernwood Hall. Linda wondered what Clara Hylton's background had been. Perhaps she had come from a much grander family than the Hyltons.

The two of them turned to go, then Clara Hylton stopped and said, 'They knew your name!'

'I beg your pardon?'

'That child; she called you Linda. That is your name, isn't it?'

'It is.'

'Then please explain.'

'I come from this village, remember?'

'Do you? Do you really?'

Linda nodded.

The old lady looked her up and down. She frowned. 'Well, you don't dress very well, that's true, but you talk like a lady, don't you?'

'If you say so.'

'And yet you say you are a village girl. What a puzzle.'

'Puzzle or not,' Linda said, 'wherever I come from I don't intend to curtsey to anyone.'

Clara Hylton laughed out loud. 'Whatever you are, Linda Bellwood – see, I remembered your name – whatever you are, I like you a lot. Now come, *noblesse oblige,* we must represent the Hall and do our duty at the Autumn Fayre.'

When they entered the village hall, Linda couldn't help noticing the way some of the women nudged each other and put their heads together before gazing at them curiously. Clara Hylton, looking like a fashion plate in her fitted powder-blue coat and veiled high-crowned hat, smiled regally as she went from stall to stall. She bought a jar of home-made strawberry jam, an embroidered handker-chief case with a bag of dried lavender sewn inside, and a pair of hand-knitted gentleman's socks.

'I shall give them to Stevens,' she said to Linda.

Then she walked over to the table where Etta Crawford, a local farmer's wife, was selling raffle tickets for the Harvest Hamper. 'Give me a whole page of tickets,' Clara Hylton said, 'and then donate them individually to any deserving poor folk of your choice.'

Linda almost cringed at those words, but Etta Crawford kept her head down as she took the money and gave what could be interpreted either as a snort of laughter or of irritation. At this point Mrs Sinclair, the wife of the solicitor, came hurry-ing towards them and suggested they should find a table at the refreshment stall and have a cup of tea.

'Linda looked very well,' Muriel Sinclair was to tell her husband later. 'A little pale, perhaps, but that's probably the effect of the black dress.'

'And Mrs Charles?'

95

'Very gracious. I could tell she thought the tea foul.'

'What was wrong with it?'

'It was made in a giant tea urn rather than a dainty porcelain teapot. Nevertheless, she drank it and thanked me politely. She's not as dotty as some say, but definitely more eccentric than she used to be. Although she always was a little odd, wasn't she?'

'I think the word is forthright,' John Sinclair said. 'She would say whatever had to be said even if that caused offence.'

'She never was strictly conventional, was she? I've often wondered what her background was.'

'Oh, she came from a very grand family. Landed. Not aristocratic, but they could trace their Norman ancestors back to the Conquest.'

'So why did she marry into trade?'

'Because her own family's fortunes had been on the wane for some years. Her father was almost spent up. Her mother, as eccentric, I've heard, as Clara herself, didn't want her daughter to marry another penniless gentleman and live in a draughty old mansion. She wanted wealth and comfort for her daughter. Very wise of her.'

'And the marriage was happy?'

'I've heard so. But, tell me, how is Linda coping with her responsibilities?'

'On the evidence of the short time they spent at the Fayre, I should say very well. She is calm and kind and not at all intimidated by Mrs Charles's autocratic manner. In fact you could almost say the two of them were friends. They give every appearance of liking each other.'

John Sinclair did not know whether to be pleased or sorry. He certainly did not want Linda to be unhappy, but neither did he want her to be too content. He still cherished the hope that she would come to her senses and realize that for someone with her innate intelligence the job of a companion would not do at all.

As they walked back to the car, Linda and Mrs Charles were met by three disgruntled children.

'Why are you here?' Linda asked. 'We told you to stand guard over the car.'

'He told us to shove off,' the tallest of the girls said. 'He said we were something nuisances.'

'Something?'

'He used a bad word.'

'Who did?' Clara Hylton asked.

But Linda had already guessed. 'Do you mean the chauffeur?'

'What's one of those?'

'The driver ... a man with shiny buttons on his jacket and a cap with a brim.'

'That's the scoundrel,' the smaller of the girls said, and the little lad nodded vigorously.

'We said you'd told us to stay there but he didn't believe us,' the taller girl said.

'And he didn't give us a single penny,' the boy added.

Clara Hylton was already opening her hand-bag. She took out her purse and, to the children's amazement and joy, she gave them each a six-penny piece. 'There you are,' she said. 'I hope that will make up for the way that scoundrel has treated you.'

Their ringleader was suddenly much more confident. 'We told him you'd promised to pay us,' she said, 'and the lass wanted to give us something, but he just told us to clear off before he brayed the lot of us.'

Clara frowned. 'The lass?'

But the children had already turned tail and taken off. One of the girls turned and shouted, 'Ta-ra, Linda,' then they had rounded the corner and were gone.

'Who do you think they meant by "the lass"?' Clara Hylton asked Linda.

'We'll soon see. Look, there are two people sitting in the car.'

The lass turned out to be Cordelia Hylton. She was sitting in the front passenger seat, and she and Stevens appeared to be having an animated conversation, which stopped the moment Cordelia spied them approaching. She got out of the car and came smilingly towards them.

'Hello, Grandmamma, darling,' she said. 'I was strolling by the river when I met Stevens. I persuaded him to give me a lift back to the Hall. I hope you don't mind.'

'Of course I don't mind,' her grandmother said, 'but if I'd known you had nothing better to do, I would have asked you to accompany us to the Autumn Fayre. The villagers expect it of us. I believe you must have been keeping out of my way deliberately.'

'Oh, Grandmamma, apart from some of the old dears who are as antiquated in their ways as you are, I shouldn't think the rest of those sensible women care one way or another whether we go to their little Fayre. And as for keeping out of your way deliberately ... of course I was.'

Cordelia smiled and gave her grandmother a hug. Linda thought how attractive she looked. Her bright blonde hair had been plaited and wound round her head in Swiss braids. This was a fairly unsophisticated style for someone as fashion-conscious as Cordelia, but it went very well with her creamy complexion and intensely blue eyes. She was wearing a red cotton dress with a scattered pattern of white flowers. The cape collar almost obscured the very short sleeves.

'Still dressed for summer, I see,' her grandmother said with a hint of disapproval.

'It's such a lovely day.'

'Maybe so, but the evenings are drawing in, and you don't want to be ill when you've got so much to think about and plan.'

Cordelia's smile faded. 'Oh, yes, the wedding. Don't worry; Mother will make sure that all goes well. But now I'm sure you won't mind if I come home with you in the car. Or are you going to make me walk home as a punishment?'

Clara Hylton smiled, but Linda could tell she was not altogether won over by her granddaughter's cheery teasing. 'Get in,' she said, 'it's time I got home for a proper cup of tea.'

Chapter Five

Cordelia joined them for tea in the garden room. 'I've told Hawkins to bring a tray for the three of us,' she said.

'Good of you,' Clara Hylton said. 'I imagine there's an ulterior motive.'

Cordelia smiled and made sure that her grandmother had the most comfortable armchair, then found the footstool.

'Really, Grandmamma,' she said, 'those shoes of yours are stylish in the extreme but aren't they a little uncomfortable?'

'What are you suggesting? That just because I'm old I should settle for something more sensible? Some nice flat lace-ups, perhaps?'

Clara Hylton glowered at her granddaughter and Cordelia laughed. 'Of course not, darling, sorry I mentioned it. Now, where on earth is Hawkins with our tea?'

'I'm here, Miss Cordelia.' They turned to see Hawkins had just entered the garden room pushing the tea trolley. 'I'm sorry if I kept you waiting, but Mrs Aslett was busy so I made the sandwiches myself.'

There was a hint of mockery in her inflection. But if she had intended to annoy Cordelia she failed.

'Oh, how *good* of you,' Cordelia said with equal sarcasm. 'Now, please remember to tell Mrs Aslett that Miss Bellwood and I will not require an evening meal.' She waited until Hawkins had gone before she turned to her grandmother and said, 'Really, that girl! You would think she'd be grateful that Mother took her in, but instead she is full of resentment.'

'Emerald made a mistake. I told her so at the time. Expecting a girl who had been brought up in luxury to become a servant was foolish in the extreme.'

Cordelia frowned. 'To be fair, I'm not sure what else my mother could have done. She couldn't just have left the wretched girl to sink or swim, could she?'

'I don't see why not. She could have parked her at the YWCA or the Salvation Army and left her to get on with it. No good will come of this, you know.'

Linda was shocked and taken aback by Clara Hylton's apparent lack of sympathy for the unhappy girl. She hoped it wasn't because her father had been a criminal. Surely that had not been Pamela's fault.

Cordelia began pouring the tea. Her grandmother surveyed the trolley. 'Why the sandwiches?' she asked. 'And what do you mean by saying that Linda and you will not be dining at home this evening?'

'I have a favour to ask of you,' Cordelia said.

'Ah, the ulterior motive. Go on.'

'Do you think you could spare Linda tonight? Give her a night off?'

'She's only been here two days. Why should she need a night off already?'

'Because I want her to come with me to the cinema.'

'And have you already asked her if she wants to go to the cinema with you?'

'No, I haven't, I'm afraid. I just assumed she would.'

'Let's ask her, then. Linda, my dear, my grand-daughter would like you to go to the cinema with her. That's perfectly all right by me. But no matter what Cordelia assumed, please feel free to tell the truth.'

'I would like that very much. But I would also like to know what film we're going to see.'

'*Lost Horizon*. Ronald Colman's in it. Isn't he wonderful? Did you see him in *A Tale of Two Cities?*'

'I did.'

Linda remembered when the film had come to the village hall. She had paid Joan Lambert, the nineteen-year-old daughter of their neighbours, to sit with Miss Taylor. When she had come home there had been no sign of Joan. Linda had rushed next door and met Joan hurrying out of her house.

'Oh, you're back,' she'd said. She looked flustered. 'I just popped home for a cup of tea. Miss Taylor was asleep, so I thought it would be all right. I've only been five minutes. I mean, she's still asleep, isn't she?'

Linda had been too angry to say anything. She simply nodded and, turning her back on Joan, went home. The girl didn't follow her. She had told Joan she could make tea or coffee, whatever she wanted, and had left the tin of biscuits on the kitchen table. There had been no need for her to go next door. Linda had never had another night

102

out after that.

Cordelia was looking at her. 'You look a bit bleak,' she said. 'Are you remembering the ending? Tragic, wasn't it?'

'Yes, I'm remembering,' Linda told her.

'Wasn't he just wonderful as he waited to go to the guillotine? Comforting that poor girl? But don't worry; I don't think he dies in this film.'

'What nonsense you talk,' Clara Hylton said. 'It's only make-believe, child, and the charismatic Mr Colman is only an actor.'

Cordelia smiled. 'Don't pretend you're not partial to a certain actor yourself. You always had a soft spot for Douglas Fairbanks, didn't you?'

'Enough! Linda has agreed to go to the cinema with you, and if you're going to miss your evening meal you had better eat these sandwiches which Hawkins so willingly prepared for you.'

Cordelia picked up one of the sandwiches and screwed up her face as she pulled the slices apart. 'I don't believe it,' she said. 'Fish paste. Disgusting!' She looked at the other sandwiches. 'And they're all the same.'

Her grandmother frowned. 'Really,' she said, 'the girl goes too far. Ring for her and tell her to make some decent sandwiches.'

'No, I won't give her the satisfaction of thinking she's annoyed me. I'll give them to the birds.'

Cordelia rose and went to the door which led out onto a terrace. She opened it and threw the sandwiches out so forcefully that the plate almost went with them.

'But you must eat something,' Clara Hylton said.

'Don't worry, Grandmamma, we will. We'll nibble some of those biscuits now, and then after the show I'm going to treat Linda to fish and chips.'

'This is gloriously incongruous, isn't it?' Cordelia said. 'I mean, eating fish and chips in the back seat of a Rolls?' She grinned as Paul Stevens opened the car door, leaned in and handed her two newspaper-wrapped bundles. He kept another one for himself.

'You asked for extra batter, didn't you, Paul?'

'I did.'

'Then get in the car and drive us to a nice dark street in the respectable part of town. We're attracting glances, here.'

She nodded towards the queue of people which had spilled out of the fish and chip shop onto the darkened street. The bright lights inside illuminated curious faces turned in the direction of the car. Cordelia gave a moue of distaste. 'People are so rude, don't you think?'

'They're not being, rude,' Linda said. 'What do you expect when you park such a grand car in a street like this? It's quite natural that people should be curious.'

Cordelia's eyes widened and then she laughed. 'I stand corrected. You're a bit like my grandmother, aren't you?'

'In what way?'

'You say what you think. No matter who you're speaking to.'

Although Cordelia was smiling, there was something about the way she said that last sentence that told Linda she was being put in her place.

'Mmm,' Cordelia said a little later, 'there's nothing like fat, salty chips soaked in vinegar, is there?'

'Are you asking me or Stevens?' Linda asked.

'Oh, for goodness sake, you're still cross with me, aren't you? That's why you've hardly said a word since we picked you up from the cinema.'

'I'm not cross. What would be the point?' Linda said. 'But you might have warned me. That's all.'

'If I had, then you probably wouldn't have agreed to come.'

'So you decided not to give me the choice.' Linda smiled faintly.

The overhead light in the car was dim, but Linda could see Cordelia's face well enough to see that she looked contrite. 'I'm sorry. Truly I am,' Cordelia said. 'I thought you wouldn't mind. I mean, helping a friend out and all that.'

'Are we friends?'

'Oh, I hope so. But shall we talk about this later? Over a cup of cocoa, perhaps? I mean, it's awkward at the moment, isn't it?'

Cordelia nodded almost imperceptibly in the direction of Paul Stevens, who sat in the driver's seat apparently enjoying his fish and chips. He hadn't turned round to look at them or attempted to join in the conversation. Linda hadn't expected that he would.

They ate their fish and chips in silence, and when they had finished Cordelia licked her fingers and screwed up the newspaper. She leaned forward in her seat. 'Here, Paul, get rid of this, will you? And Linda's too.'

105

The chauffeur took the two crumpled newspapers and dropped them into the front passenger
well along with his own.

'Home now, Miss Cordelia?' he asked.

Linda marvelled at how formal and proper he
sounded, considering what had happened earlier.

But Cordelia was far from formal. 'Yes, home,
James, and don't spare the horses! Or should I
say horsepower?'

Stevens shook his head as if in despair at the
feeble joke, but Cordelia burst out laughing.
Linda thought there was a hysterical edge to the
laughter. In fact, she wasn't quite sure whether
Cordelia was laughing or crying.

With the interior lights turned off the car was a
small world of warmth and comfort as it travelled
through the city streets. Soon they had left Newcastle behind them and the headlights revealed
open country. Cordelia had sunk back into the
embrace of the generously padded leather uphol-
stery. Her voice, when it came, sounded distant.

'So tell me about the film,' she said. 'Did you
enjoy it?'

'Yes, I did.'

'Tell me about it.'

'Well, you probably know what it's about; I
mean, everyone is talking about Shangri-La.'

'No, I don't, actually. I thought Shangri-La was
a new perfume.'

'Are you serious?'

Linda turned towards Cordelia and peered at
her through the dimness. She saw that she was
smiling.

'No, I just enjoy teasing you. You take things so

106

seriously. But please, go on, tell me what happens when their plane crashes and they find themselves in this wonderful, mystical land where nobody ever grows old or dies.'

As the darkened countryside sped by, Linda told Cordelia the story of the film and also how it differed from the novel.

'You've read it?' Cordelia exclaimed.

'Yes.'

'Oh, you should talk to my brother Florian about it. He thought it was wonderful. But do go on,' Cordelia said. 'Did they ever leave that wonderful land?'

'Won't I spoil it for you if I tell you everything that happens?'

'Spoil it?'

'I mean, you might want to go and see the film yourself.'

'I can't. You forget; I've already seen it with you, tonight.'

Linda was silent for a moment. Suddenly the taste of fatty chips and vinegar, which had been delicious when the food was hot, came back to her and left a sour coating on her tongue.

'And that's why you wanted me to tell you about it, isn't it? So if anyone asks you about it, you will be able to pretend that you've seen it.'

There was a slight pause and then Cordelia said, 'I won't lie to you, Linda. I like you too much. We'll talk later, like I said.'

Linda was surprised to see a fire burning in the hearth in her bedroom. Someone must have decided that as the nights were drawing in it was

107

time to keep all the fires going. She wondered who had had the job of lighting the fire and decided it was probably the 'useful boy'.

Cordelia had told her she would ask Mrs Aslett to make cocoa and that she would be along in a minute or two. So Linda sat by the fire in her dressing gown and slippers, wondering who or what would arrive first: Cordelia or the cocoa.

They arrived at the same time. There was a knock at the door, then the sound of voices, and when the door opened Cordelia swept in, followed by Pamela Hawkins carrying a tray bearing two cups and saucers, a large jug with a lid and a plate of biscuits.

'Just put it over there on the little table,' Cordelia told the sullen-faced girl. Then she waited in silence until the maid had gone.

'Phew!' she said when the door closed with an unnecessarily forceful click. 'Sometimes her moods are too overpowering even for one of my sunny nature. You pour the cocoa, Linda. I'll just drag this pouffe over. No – stay where you are in the chair.'

Linda waited while Cordelia manoeuvred the large, velvet-covered padded stool into a suitably warm place by the fire and then handed her a cup of cocoa.

'Mmm,' Cordelia said. 'Delicious! This is like being back at school, isn't it? Hot drinks and a good old gossip just before lights out.'

'I wouldn't know. I didn't go to boarding school.'

'Oh, of course you didn't. But you look just the part sitting there in that old-fashioned flannel dressing gown. We must get you something a bit more glamorous. Like this, for example. It's Chinese silk. Don't you just love it?'

Cordelia put her cocoa down on the tiled hearth, stood up and posed like a model in a fashion parade. Her ankle-length dressing gown was smoky blue, and Cordelia turned round with both arms raised sideways to display the full-length pattern of a dragon embroidered in raised gold-coloured thread.

She turned round again. 'Well?' she said.

'It's lovely.'

'You look doubtful.'

'It's truly gorgeous, but dragons are evil creatures, aren't they?'

'Oh, no. In China dragons are regarded as divine mythical beasts that bring abundance and good luck. They're not at all malevolent.' She sat down on the pouffe again and picked up her cup of cocoa, but instead of drinking it she gazed wistfully into the fire. 'And I could do with some good luck.' She shot Linda an appraising glance. 'That's why I wanted to talk to you.'

'I imagine the purpose of this talk is to explain why you dumped me at the cinema and left me there all alone while you went off with Paul Stevens.'

Cordelia gasped. 'My, my,' she said. 'You're pretty direct, aren't you?'

Linda smiled at her. 'I thought we'd already established that.'

'Oh, Linda, please don't be cross with me. I thought you would understand and want to help me.'

'I'm not cross. It's just I wasn't given the chance to understand, was I?'

'No ... I suppose not.'

'Why? Why didn't you warn me before we set off?'

'I thought you might refuse to help.' She sighed. 'I behaved shoddily, I know. But I was desperate, you see.'

Cordelia suddenly looked so wretched that Linda found herself feeling sorry for her. 'Are you in love with Paul?'

'I'm not sure. I mean, I'm not sure I know what love is. I just know that I want to be with him all the time. And he wants to be with me. You must see what the problem is.'

Linda was uncomfortably reminded of the gulf between a servant and a member of the Hylton family. 'I think I do.'

Cordelia gave a bitter laugh. 'My parents would never allow Paul to come courting. He's our chauffeur!'

'Allow? This is the twentieth century and you're twenty-four years old. If you were determined to be with Paul, how could they stop you?'

'They could put me out. Cut me off without a penny. I have no money of my own – and before you say anything, Paul would lose his job and we'd be as poor as church mice.'

'Would that matter?'

'Of course it would. And even worse, my parents might never speak to me again, and I don't know if I could bear that. I do love them, you know, and I don't want to be estranged from them. And then there's Charlie Meredith.'

'Your fiancé.'

Cordelia flinched. 'Yes, my fiancé.'

'Don't you love him?'

'I thought I did. He's a good man. A decent man. I just couldn't put him through the humiliation he would suffer if I ran off with the hired help.'

'So what are you going to do?'

'My duty. I'll marry Charlie. But surely you can't blame me for snatching some happiness while I can.'

Linda shook her head.

'What is it?'

'I just don't know. I mean, it isn't very...'

'Very what?'

'Honourable.'

Cordelia's eyes widened. She looked angry. Then, after a pause, she said, 'I won't ask you to help me again.'

Linda remembered earlier that day when Paul Stevens had set off briskly to walk by the river and Cordelia was supposed to have met him there by accident. Of course it had been planned.

'It seems you've been managing up until now,' she said. 'So why the deception tonight?'

'We wanted more than a snatched meeting in the boathouse. We wanted nearly three whole hours alone together. We drove down to the coast and parked on the headland looking out at the lighthouse. We sat in the back together. You can't imagine how wonderful that was.'

Linda felt herself flushing. She was inexperienced, but she was not ignorant. She could imagine only too well how they had spent their

111

time together in the back seat of the car, and she didn't want those images invading her mind.

Cordelia drained her cup and put it back on the tray. 'I'd better let you get to bed.' She rose, but instead of leaving she stood there hesitantly. 'You won't tell, will you?'

She was chewing her lip nervously, and Linda thought Cordelia looked and sounded like an adolescent schoolgirl rather than a grown woman of twenty-four.

'Of course not. Why should I?'

'Oh, I don't know. A sense of honour?'

'It's not my place to judge you.'

'Oh, for goodness sake, Linda!' Cordelia's eyes flashed with anger.

'What is it?'

'Don't you know how self-righteous you sound?'

Linda was taken aback. 'I'm sorry. I don't mean to sound self-righteous. It's just... I think I may be out of my depth here.'

'Well, don't worry. I promise I won't involve you again.'

Cordelia turned and left the room, leaving Linda feeling utterly wretched. Her cocoa had gone cold. She felt the side of the jug to see if it was still hot, but it wasn't. Suddenly it seemed important to have a hot, comforting drink. If she had been at home she would simply have gone to the kitchen and made it herself. She couldn't do that here. In fact, she wasn't quite sure where the kitchen was or what kind of welcome she would receive if she ventured there. And to traverse the stately corridors of this grand house in her old-fashioned dressing gown was unthinkable. The thought of it almost brought a smile.

She glanced at the bell pull at the side of the fireplace and wondered if she should summon one of the maids. She shook her head. Pamela would be furious and she would not bother to hide the fact. Vera Saunders would ... would what? Would she take kindly to a girl from her own village summoning her and asking her to bring her a drink as if she were one of the family? How strange it was to choose to rely on other people to provide even the simplest things in life. Surely this restricted your freedom rather than adding to it.

Linda glanced at the clock on the mantel shelf. It was nearly midnight. That solved her problem. Surely everyone would be in bed by now? Even if she'd had the nerve to ring the bell, there would be no one waiting to answer it. She stared into the fire moodily. There was still a lot of life in it. The coals shifted and settled, sending out a shower of sparks. What was she supposed to do? Bank it up so that it would burn all night, or leave it for whoever saw to these things to start again in the morning?

She sighed. No doubt it would take a little time to learn the ways of the household. All she could do would be to live from day to day and try not to make any mistakes. She hoped she would be able to put things right with Cordelia. For although she had been shocked by what Cordelia had done, she realized that she felt sorry for her.

That brought a smile. Linda Bellwood, orphaned village girl, feeling sorry for the beautiful and privileged daughter of the wealthy Hylton family. Her smile turned into a yawn. She decided she was too tired to do anything about the fire, looked around for a cinder guard, found it, put it in place and went to bed.

'Do you go to church, Linda?'

The next morning Linda was surprised to find Cordelia already at the breakfast table. And even more surprised to find her smiling as though they had not quarrelled the night before.

'Sometimes. I'm afraid I don't attend regularly. In fact, after my guardian became ill I didn't go at all. Until her funeral, that is.'

Cordelia shivered. 'Don't talk of funerals. Not on a lovely day like this. Now, come and sit beside me, and why don't you try these pancakes? They're scrumptious dribbled with maple syrup.'

Mr Hylton and Rupert were sitting in exactly the same places as they had the day before and they still appeared to be talking business. Cordelia glanced at them and shook her head. 'No wonder my mother prefers to have a tray sent up,' she said. 'And if ever Rupert gets round to marrying someone, the poor girl will just have to get used to this.'

To Linda's relief it was Vera Saunders who served breakfast, and while they ate Cordelia kept up a flow of inconsequential chatter. Linda sensed that the older girl was nervous and keen to please, and her mind drifted as she tried to reply with an appropriate nod or two.

'And then there's the matter of the tableware,' Cordelia said. 'Would you mind?' She paused and Linda realized she was waiting for a response.

'I'm sorry?'

114

'I thought you weren't listening! I asked you if you would like to help me choose my dinner service.'

'Do you mean go shopping with you?'

'Go shopping? Really, Linda – remember who I am! Father's having one made specially for me as a wedding present. It will be unique. He's got his top designer, Graham Forsyth, on the job. The man's going to bring one or two designs for me to choose from. Would you like to help me?'

'I'd love to. But why ask me? Surely your mother or grandmother would be more suitable.'

'Heavens, no! – Grandmamma will go for something boringly traditional, and my darling mother is fatally fond of pretty flowers and all things sentimental. But you are young and I suspect your ideas are more twentieth century. Aren't they?'

'I hope so.'

'So that's settled then. Now, you'd better finish your breakfast, Grandmamma will be waiting for you.'

When they had finished Cordelia said, 'I'll come up with you. She'll want to know all about the film we saw. In spite of what she said, she's a bit of a film fan herself, and the only reason she hardly goes to the cinema now is because of her failing eyesight. Poor darling.'

So that's it, Linda thought. She's worried that I might say something that would give her away.

When they reached Clara Hylton's door, Linda placed a hand on Cordelia's arm. 'Wait a moment,' she said. 'I'm really sorry if I upset you last night, and I would never do anything to make life difficult for you. I want you to know that you

115

can trust me.'

Cordelia placed her hand over Linda's and squeezed it. 'Bless you, darling,' she said. 'I knew we could be friends.'

She opened the door and they went in together.

On Monday morning Linda had breakfast alone. Mr Hylton and Rupert had left for work earlier than usual, and Emerald and Cordelia were breakfasting in bed. She started with Ivy Aslett's special porridge, and then had a pair of Craster kippers. Vera Saunders had talked her into it. Linda had had kippers before, but never for breakfast, and never kippers that were quite as big as these were. They filled the plate; in fact their tails hung over the edge. Linda picked up her knife and fork and tried to ignore the glassy eyes staring up at her. After the kippers, which were delicious, she felt obliged to eat at least half the toast that Vera had brought her and she was grateful for the large pot of tea.

As she went upstairs she heard her name called and turned round to see a tall, rake-thin youth standing at the bottom. The 'useful boy', she conjectured. His fair hair flopped untidily over his forehead. As he grinned up at her, he pushed his hair back in what was probably a habitual gesture.

'The post,' he said, and he held his other hand out towards her. He was holding an envelope. 'This is for the old lady. Do you want to take it up?'

'All right,' she said. She waited until he came up the stairs to where she was standing then said, 'What's your name?'

'Robert. I get "Bobby" or sometimes just "lad", as in, "Come here at once, lad!"' His smile widened and Linda sensed that he had a lively sense of humour.

She took the letter from him. 'Thank you, Bobby,' she said.

'My pleasure, Miss Bellwood. Now I'd better go and find something to do.'

He turned and hurried down the stairs, taking two at a time. Linda remembered Clara Hylton telling her that the boy had perfected the art of going missing now and then, and she laughed out loud. She was still smiling when she knocked and entered Clara Hylton's room. She found her sitting up in bed with her breakfast tray.

'What is it?' Clara, said. 'You're smiling as if something has amused you.'

'I've just met Bobby.'

'Oh, the lad. Yes, he can usually bring a smile.'

'He gave me this letter.' Linda glanced at the postmark. 'It's from Scotland.' She walked over to the bed. 'Here you are.'

'No, you read it to me. And take this tray away; I've finished.'

Linda took the tray and put it on a small table by the fireplace. The fire was burning brightly. Vera Saunders must have come in early. Everyone knew that Clara Hylton craved warmth.

'There's a letter opener somewhere on the desk,' Clara said. 'I hate it when people just tear at the envelopes and mangle them, don't you?'

'Actually, yes,' Linda said. Miss Taylor had been just as fastidious and had taught Linda to be the same.

She sat down to search through the pigeon-holes for the letter opener. When she found it and opened the envelope, she was glad that she was there instead of being near the bed. Turning so that Clara did not have a clear view of what she was doing, she took out a single sheet of writing paper and, leaving the envelope on the desk, walked over to the bed.

'Bring up that chair,' Clara said. 'And read it to me. You said it's from Scotland so I suppose it's from Florian. Very dutiful of him to write so soon.'

Linda read her the letter and Clara Hylton stared at her in astonishment. 'Read that again.'

Linda obliged.

Dearest Grandmamma,
The journey was tedious, Scotland is cold. I can't wait to come home again.
Love,
Florian

'And that's it? There's nothing on the other side?'

Linda knew there wasn't but she turned the paper over anyway. 'No, nothing.'

'I don't know why he bothered.'

'I suppose it's because he promised he would write to you – and he wanted to let you know he'd arrived safely.'

'Humph.'

'Maybe he'll write another letter once he's settled in.'

'He'll be too busy trifling with the affections of the MacFarlane girl. At least, that's what his father hopes for. If he got married he would have to give up his silly idea of being a writer and take his place in the family business.'

'I didn't know Florian wanted to be a writer.'

'Why should you? You've only just met him.'

Linda changed the subject quickly. 'And what about Rupert? Surely his father would like him to marry, too.'

'Rupert doesn't need a wife to settle him down. He's quite happy to take his place in the family business. He'll find the right sort of girl and he'll marry when it suits him.'

'The right sort of girl?'

'Of course. Someone from a respectable family; a similar background. If not of wealth then certainly of breeding. He will marry someone who will fit in.'

Clara Hylton's unwavering belief in the old established hierarchy made Linda feel uneasy, and not just on her own behalf. She saw more clearly what difficulties Cordelia faced. And, as for Pamela, a girl whose father was a convicted criminal, she would never be considered 'suitable'. If what I suspect is true, that Pamela is in love with Rupert, she thought, then she will almost certainly have her heart broken.

It wasn't until she was in bed that night that Linda got the chance to read the other letter, the one Florian had intended for her. This letter had been in a separate envelope inside the one addressed to his grandmother, just as he had said it would be. Linda had been uneasy at the subterfuge, but she had had to agree with Florian when

119

he said that his family would think it strange if he wrote to her when, as far as they were concerned, he had only just met her.

Sometime in the afternoon the weather had turned from brisk but bright to cold and grey. After the evening meal it had started to rain, and now she could hear a worrisome wind rattling the window panes. A fire glowed in the hearth and her room was warm, but Linda could not settle.

Secrets, she thought. I've only just come to Fernwood Hall and already I have discovered so many secrets. Pamela is in love with Rupert and there is no way she could admit to it openly. Cordelia is attracted to Paul Stevens, even though she is engaged to be married to another man, and, as she intends to go ahead with the wedding, no one must ever discover that she is seeing Paul secretly. And now I have a secret. Florian has written to me and no one must know that we have known each other since we were children.

Linda frowned. Why should they not know? Because she would have to admit to having been a trespasser. Worse than that, she had actually spied on them. Gazed through the window and wished that she could be inside. But that was not all. Linda sensed there was another reason for Florian's discretion. For even though she had been made welcome and told to consider herself one of the family, no one would be pleased if they thought she and Florian were becoming close. She doubted if she would be considered the 'right sort of girl'.

But why shouldn't they be friends? That was all they were, wasn't it? That was all they had been.

At least, that was how she remembered it. But Florian had believed that their friendship had begun to develop into something more. If that were true, what might have happened if Miss Taylor had not had a stroke and Linda had been able to continue coming to meet Florian?

She had delayed the moment long enough. She had never received a letter before. There had been no one in her life who would have written to her. Wonderingly, she took the two sheets of notepaper from the envelope and, making herself comfortable against the pillows, she began to read.

My Dear Linda,

If only I had known you were coming to live in Fernwood Hall before I'd accepted Ian's invitation, I would have had time to think up some believable excuse to offer for not going to stay in his gloomy old castle. Actually it's not old, and it isn't even a real castle. His father, a third-generation ship owner – you know, the MacFarlane Line – had the place designed and built to look as if it had clung to that hostile hillside for centuries when, in fact, it is only about twenty years old.

From outside it looks like something in a gothic novel, but once inside it's not too bad. There's electricity and even central heating. Ian's father is so proud of the boilers – one for the radiators and one for the hot water – that he takes all guests down to the cellar to view them. He's even been known to stoke them himself. What a lark! I shall probably offer to stoke them for him in order to relieve the tedium.

I feel guilty that I am so discontented when

everyone is being so hospitable. Ian is jolly and kind and desperate to please. But now I'm not sure what we ever had in common. Except that he did like reading. That's where we first met, in the college library. And even if his taste in books veers towards the sensational, he can still appreciate a well-written story.

But as for Elspeth – I despair. I've never seen her with a book, and I'm not even sure if she *can* read. She is very, very pretty in a Scottish sort of way, and actually she is quite sweet and biddable. But oh, how boring it would be to face her over the breakfast table every morning.

You've probably guessed that that is what my family hope for. That I will propose to Elspeth MacFarlane. And there's no doubt that her family hope for it, too. At least her father and her brother do. I sense that her mother would rather she found a Scottish laird of some kind; it wouldn't matter if he were impoverished so long as he had his own, authentic castle. But let me assure you that, if Elspeth is also hoping that I will propose, the poor girl is going to be disappointed. But only for a very short while.

I believe it wouldn't be too long before she would breathe a sigh of relief and realize that I would make a rotten husband for a girl like her. She needs someone safe and conventional, someone who would consider himself lucky to have such a sweet, adoring little wife, not someone who would expect more of her than she could ever give.

Have I bored you with this Scottish lament? I know how unattractive it must be to seem sorry for myself. So from this very moment I shall resolve to be cheerful, to bear this period of exile with fortitude, and look forward to the day when I shall return to Fernwood – and to you.

Yours sincerely,

Florian

Linda folded the letter, put it back in the envelope and closed her eyes. Florian's letter was amusing and so well written that she could almost imagine herself there in that gloomy make-believe castle on the bare hillside. She felt as though she had met Ian and Elspeth and their parents. In just a few sentences Florian had brought them to life for her. His grandmother had said that he wanted to be a writer. Well, judging by this letter, he ought to be.

While reading it she had felt that he was actually talking to her. And that, she realized, was un-settling. The tone of the letter suggested an inti-macy between them that did not exist. At least, not in her mind. What was she to make of it? All she knew was that she hoped he had meant it when he had said that he would write two letters and perhaps three. She remembered his words:

'Well, that means at least two letters, doesn't it? Perhaps three. One to say I've arrived safely, another to say how much I'm enjoying myself, and another to say I'm coming home.'

Linda put the letter on the bedside table and switched off the pink-shaded lamp. She tried to settle but found sleep elusive. After a while, she reached out and picked up the letter, opened the little drawer, thought for a moment and then, still clutching her letter, closed it again. Smiling at her own adolescent behaviour, she slipped the enve-

123

lope under her pillows. Then, with the flickering light of the fire playing across the ceiling, she drifted off to sleep.

Chapter Six

William Hylton waited until Graham Forsyth had spread the sketches out on his desk, then he put on his spectacles and began to study each one closely. Graham felt as though he were back at school, standing in the headmaster's study and waiting nervously for another talking-to.

There had been many such days at school. He was constantly accused of neglecting his studies and reminded that he had taken up a valuable place at grammar school which some other more deserving boy or girl might have appreciated. Moments like this usually resulted in him being given extra homework, a punishment which he knew he deserved.

'You neglect all other subjects in order to concentrate on your drawing and painting,' the headmaster would say. 'And although your work is very good, you won't get into art school if you can't write a good sentence or pass a simple maths test.'

Usually at this stage Mr Wright's exasperation would give way to concern. 'You have genuine talent. There's no denying it. And I'll do my best to persuade your parents that the shipyards are not for you, but only if you make the effort to pay attention in your other lessons and to hand your homework in on time.'

It took the shock of failing the test papers for the School Certificate to make Graham take his studies seriously. If he failed the 'School Cert' he would not be allowed to stay on and take his Highers, and if he didn't have the Higher School Certificate he wouldn't get into art school. His parents would have their way and Graham would become an apprentice at Swan Hunter's drawing office, where his father was a senior draughtsman.

Thank God I came to my senses, he thought, as he waited for Mr Hylton's verdict. He was deeply satisfied with his job. He was both creative and innovative and Mr Hylton encouraged him to take risks. At the age of twenty-three he was the Hylton Pottery's senior designer.

At last Mr Hylton looked up and smiled his approval. He arranged the papers neatly into one pile. 'Good work, Forsyth,' he said. 'I think you've just about covered everything, from the traditional to the avant-garde. Surely my daughter will find something here that pleases her. Why don't you take them along now?'

'To Fernwood Hall?'

'That's right. You've got your car, haven't you?'

'Yes, sir.'

'Do you know the way?'

'I think I can find it.'

'It's very easy. Leave Newcastle by the West Road and then – wait a minute, I'll write some basic instructions.'

Graham gathered up his work and put it back in the large folder while Mr Hylton scribbled quickly on a notepad. When he had finished he tore the page off.

'Here you are,' he said. He glanced at his watch. 'I'll phone home and tell Mrs Aslett to give you lunch, and as I have no idea how long Cordelia will take to make her mind up, I suppose I'd better say you needn't come back today.'

'Thank you, sir.'

'You won't be thanking me after an hour or two of trying to persuade my daughter to choose the right design for her dinner service. And if her mother or mine want to be in on it, then God help you.'

The last few days had been wet and miserable, and the city streets were slick with rain. Once into the suburbs Graham caught the occasional glimpse of an old ruined wall to the left of the road: Hadrian's Wall, or the Roman Wall, as local people called it. Two figures, so wrapped up in waterproof clothing that Graham could not tell whether they were male or female, were walking heads down into the rain, along the route of the old stones. No doubt they were following the wall from coast to coast. Graham wondered if the huge rucksacks on their backs contained camping equipment. If so, good luck to them.

His father had always said they would do that one day. Just him and Graham, that was. Graham's mother had never been able to understand her husband's passion for antiquity. So on Sundays, when Dora went to church with her friend Ellen, Alec Forsyth and his son would set off to visit old castles and Roman forts.

His father would tell Graham the history of the places they visited: the battles, the alliances, the names of kings and bishops. But even as a small child, Graham was more interested in the way ordinary people lived. He would stare into glass cases, not just at old weapons, but at cloak-pins, necklaces, combs and bits of household pottery – objects that people who had lived in this place had used daily.

The pottery particularly caught his imagination. Some of it had been used for everyday necessities, but other pieces were finer, more richly decorated and glazed. Graham imagined that such a bowl or such a jug would only be set on the table when one of the kings or noblemen his father thought so important came to visit.

Whether they went to the ruins of a Roman settlement or to a medieval castle, there were always bits of earthenware to see. Maybe hundreds of years separated the making of them, but Graham understood that this was an ancient craft that would survive as long as humankind.

The rain grew heavier. Sometimes it looked as if buckets of water were being thrown across the windscreen. He had to drive very carefully, and by the time he reached Fernwood Hall he was worried about the reception he would receive. Not having the faintest idea where he should park his car, he decided to pull up as near the entrance as possible. Turning up the collar of his raincoat and grabbing his portfolio from the back seat, he slammed the car door after him and ran up the steps.

'Miss Hylton is waiting for you in the library,'

the maidservant who answered the door told him. 'I'm afraid you've missed lunch,' she said sympathetically. 'But I'll see you get something before you leave. Now give me your coat and I'll take it somewhere to dry off.'

This pleasant welcome did much to soothe Graham's nerves, for, in truth, he had been worrying about this visit to his employer's home. The Hyltons were very rich and very grand. At work he was accepted and valued, but here he might be judged by different standards. Rupert Hylton, William Hylton's elder son, gave every appearance of respecting Graham's talent, but there was always a hint of superiority. No matter how good your work and how much you contributed to the firm's success, you must never consider yourself Rupert's equal socially. Cordelia was Rupert's twin sister. She was probably cut from the same cloth. Graham, confident in his skills, was not sure if he had the patience to deal with a young woman who might treat him as an inferior.

There were two young women waiting in the library. One was tall and fashionably slim with bright blonde Eugene-waved hair. She had obviously been pacing up and down, and when he was shown in she turned and glared at him with cold blue eyes.

'You are late, Mr Forsyth,' she said. Her tone was cool.

'I'm sorry but the rain–'

She cut him off with an impatient gesture. 'Shall we sit over there?' She indicated a large table. It was a command rather than a request.

Graham put his portfolio down on the highly

polished surface, and as he bent forward his hair fell wetly over his forehead. He thrust it back quickly before any raindrops fell onto the table.

'Oh, for goodness sake!' Cordelia Hylton said, but her words were tempered with laughter. 'You are like the proverbial drowned rat. Linda, get the poor man a towel.'

'No, really, it's all right.' Graham took a large handkerchief from his pocket and began dabbing at his forehead.

'I insist,' Cordelia Hylton said. 'I shall feel guilty if you catch a cold. Now, just sit down and wait for Linda.'

Graham sat as he was told. The other girl, whom he had barely noticed, had left the room as soon as Cordelia told her to. Graham wondered if she was some kind of servant.

'Look, I'm sorry I snapped at you just now,' Cordelia said while they were waiting. 'But, such a chore, I have to go out this afternoon with my mother and grandmother. We're going to look at a house.'

Graham hadn't expected an apology, and when Cordelia smiled at him he began to warm to her. She was all right, he decided, but she was obviously edgy. Something was bothering her. He hoped she would be able to concentrate on choosing a design for her dinner service.

'Here you are, Mr Forsyth.'

The other girl, Linda, Cordelia had called her, had returned as silently as she had left them. She was standing next to him offering him a thick white towel. When he took it he discovered it was warm. Linda stood beside him as he dabbed at

129

his face and hair, and took the towel from him when he had done.

'Just put it over a chair,' Cordelia told her. 'I want you to help me choose a design as you promised.'

'You mean, as you told me to,' the other girl said, and Graham glanced at her appraisingly.

Not a servant, then. The way she spoke to Cordelia suggested that she did not regard herself as a social inferior. And yet she was dressed like a servant in plain and not very stylish black. He realized with a start that she was beautiful. How could he not have noticed her as soon as he entered the room? He had been too taken up with the imperious Miss Hylton. Linda was not quite as tall as Cordelia, but she was just as slender. She was as dark as the other girl was fair, and her short hairstyle emphasized her rather waiflike features. But he sensed that this was no helpless urchin. She had an air of confidence and resourcefulness, and it was she who asked him if he would open his portfolio and show them the sketches.

Graham stood to spread his work out before the two young women who were sitting opposite.

'So many!' Cordelia said.

'I've never met you. How could I know what you would like? I thought I'd better give you as wide a choice as possible.'

'But don't you see that just makes it more difficult?' She turned to Linda and swept an impatient arm over the sketches. 'I have no idea where to start!'

'Start by putting aside any that you don't like. That's easy enough, isn't it?'

130

'I suppose so.'

She's like a spoilt child, Graham thought. But it's more than that. If I allowed myself to be fanciful, I would say she's behaving like a trapped animal. Certainly her heart isn't in this. He watched as Cordelia tried to concentrate on her task.

She gave a heartfelt sigh and said, 'Well, what have we here?' Her glance skittered over the drawings. 'For a start I don't favour flowers, leaves, vines or creepers. Nothing that my darling mama would choose, in fact.'

Linda pushed the offending designs over to Graham. Their eyes met and she smiled as if to say, 'Be patient with her. She's not bad really.'

Graham sat down. He watched both girls as they pored over his work. One so blonde and brittle – that was the word that sprang to mind – and the other so dark and intense. Was she intense? No, that wasn't quite right. She had too much of a sense of humour to be one of those tortured young women who take life too seriously. *Passionate.* That was the word he'd been looking for, and as he looked at her dark head bent over his work he was startled by the sudden tug of attraction.

As if she had sensed his shock, she looked up at him questioningly. Her eyes widened momentarily as if some deep but wordless message had passed between them; then her curiosity turned into embarrassment. He was relieved when Cordelia tugged at Linda's sleeve and said, 'You're not concentrating!'

'I'm sorry,' Linda said. 'Where were we?'

'Nowhere! Nowhere at all.'

'Cordelia, we've established that you don't want

anything floral. What about landscapes or sea-scapes?'

'Ugh!'

'Something formal, then? Plain with a blue or gold rim? Look at this one; it has your initials intertwined. C and C. Cordelia and Charlie.'

Cordelia smiled briefly. 'Grandmamma would like that one, wouldn't she? Very posh. Hinting at a coat of arms. Was that the idea, Mr Forsyth?'

'I'm afraid so.'

'Afraid?'

Graham risked a smile. 'Your fiancé is from an upper-class family, isn't he?'

'He may be so, but they're not that grand these days. He's as poor as the proverbial church mouse. I don't think he looks to the past at all. And I respect him for that.' For a moment Graham thought she looked almost sad – regret-ful – and then mercurially, her mood changed again. 'What's left?' she asked briskly.

Linda rearranged the sketches on the table in front of them. 'You don't want traditional, so how about something modern? Look at this one. I think it's what you call abstract. Is that right, Mr Forsyth?'

'Graham, please. But yes, that's right.'

'I love it,' Cordelia said. 'All splashes and dabs and bright merging colours!' For a moment her smile was almost carefree, but then she frowned. 'The trouble is, that is something that might go out of fashion. Just think, in years to come, guests at my table might think it quaint – or worse, passé. No, Linda, I know I'm being difficult, but what-ever I choose must never go out of fashion. So

132

sadly that rules out the geometric shapes as well.' She shook her head. 'It's just as well I banned my mother and darling Grandmamma from helping me choose, isn't it? We would have been here all day.'

Graham remembered what Mr Hylton had said and was truly grateful that the two older ladies were not there.

'What are we left with?' Cordelia asked Linda.

'A pastoral scene with shepherds and shepherdesses?'

Cordelia hooted with laughter. 'Mr Forsyth, I'm surprised at you!'

Graham laughed with her. 'That sort of design is very popular,' he said. 'The Hylton potteries have been producing something like this since–'

'Since prehistoric times!'

Something had caught Linda's attention. She was smiling. 'Anything with animals?' she asked.

'Positively not!'

'Not even these gorgeous dragons?'

'Dragons?'

'Mmm. Look.'

Linda pushed the sketch towards Cordelia, whose eyes opened wider as she gazed at it with pleasure. A beautifully drawn dragon covered the centre of the plate while five smaller dragons crawled around the rim.

'They're magnificent! But do they have to be black?'

'No. I just wanted to show you the detail,' Graham said. 'You can have red, pale or dark blue, green, amethyst – anything, within reason.'

'Oh, I'd like red,' Cordelia said. 'The Chinese

133

think it's the happiest of colours. Or, wait a moment, green is for health and prosperity. I want Charlie and me to be happy, but I'd like us to be healthy and rich, too. Linda, what shall I do?'

'Your dragons aren't real creatures, you know. They're mythical, and the colours are only symbols. I can't help you choose because I don't believe in it. And, in any case, if I say one colour and years later you think it a mistake, you'll blame me.'

Cordelia frowned. 'Mr Forsyth?'

'I can't help you. For the same reasons.'

Cordelia sighed. She closed her eyes for a moment and then opened them and said solemnly, 'Red. I've decided on red.'

Intrigued enough to want to know her reasoning, Graham said, 'May I ask why?'

Cordelia smiled disarmingly. 'Well, whatever the colours symbolize, I think red will be the most attractive. Thank you, Mr Forsyth. I think Mrs Aslett has prepared something for you to eat, but I'll leave Linda to take care of you. Now I must go and view this wretched house.'

She swept out of the room, leaving a drift of sophisticated perfume. Graham thought he recognized it; Prince Matchabelli's Infanta – supposed to be dangerous – and definitely expensive, as he knew to his cost. He concentrated on putting his designs back into his folder, then looked up to find Linda smiling at him.

'That went well,' she said.

'Do you think so?'

'Well, she made a decision, didn't she?'

'Eventually.'

They both laughed.

'And now she is going to see a house?'

'Mr Hylton is buying it for Cordelia and her fiancé. Apparently it is – or was once – very grand but fell into disrepair after the son and heir died during the war. If Cordelia likes it, everything necessary will be done to make it a pleasant home for her.'

'And yet she refers to it as "wretched".'

Linda's smile faded. 'There are reasons. I think she is beginning to feel pressured by everything that must be done before the wedding.'

'That's not until June, is it?'

Linda's smile returned. 'And that's not nearly long enough for Cordelia and her mother and grandmother. I am so glad I was not required to go with them to see the house this afternoon. You've met Cordelia. Her mother and grandmother will have decided views of their own. Can you imagine the discussions that will go on before any decisions are made?'

'Excuse me, Miss Bellwood.'

They turned to see that a maidservant had entered the room. She was carrying a tray covered with a clean linen cloth. Linda smiled at her. 'What is it, Vera?'

'I've got these sandwiches for Mr Forsyth. And I can fetch a pot of coffee for two if you like.'

'Yes, please. I'm ready for coffee!' Linda said.

'Do you want to stay here? I can put a cloth on the table.'

'No, I think we'll go to the garden room.'

'Very well.'

The maidservant vanished, and once Graham

135

had tied the strings on his folder Linda led the way to the garden room. By the time they got there the sandwiches were already on one of the small tables and their coffee was on another.

They were good sandwiches; cold roast beef and horseradish. And it seemed there were enough for two, although Linda ignored them and simply drank her coffee.

'I wish you'd join me,' Graham said. 'I feel awkward eating these alone.'

Linda shook her head.

'Couldn't you manage just one?'

'Not even one. I had a good lunch. They eat very well here.'

'Are you...?' Graham faltered. He did not know how to ask the question that had been bothering him since he had first set eyes on her.

'Am I what?'

'Are you one of them? One of the family? Or are you a–'

'Servant? Is that what you wanted to say?'

'Yes. I'm sorry if I've offended you.'

'I'm not offended. I'm a sort of servant. I'm here as companion to the elder Mrs Hylton. But I live as one of the family. Or so they try to insist.'

'Are they good to you?'

'What a strange question. Of course they're good to me. Why on earth should you doubt that?'

Graham saw that he had gone too far. 'I'm sorry. I don't doubt it. It's just that Miss Hylton – I mean, the way she speaks to you...'

'Oh, that. That's just the way she is. In fact Cordelia and I are quite good friends. But in any case, why should it concern you?'

136

Why indeed? Graham had no idea why the happiness of this girl should be important to him, and if he couldn't answer the question for himself what on earth could he say to her? He stared at her for a moment and when his wits returned he smiled.

'Forgive me,' he said. 'Curiosity, I suppose. My mother would tell me I should mind my manners.'

'And your mother would be right. Would you like some more coffee?'

Her abrupt change of subject signalled that she meant to put the awkwardness behind them.

'Yes, please.'

While he drank his coffee Graham stared out across the rain-drenched garden. Linda, whose chair was positioned slightly behind his, looked at him surreptitiously. She guessed him to be about her own age, perhaps a little older. He was tall and spare and he looked as though he could do with several good meals. Perhaps from the way he was enjoying the sandwiches it was some time since he'd had one.

He had dark hair and a good profile. Tall, dark and handsome, Linda found herself thinking just as he turned to look at her.

'What is it?' he asked.

'I didn't say anything.'

'I know. It was the way you were looking at me. What were you thinking?'

'That you have an annoying habit of asking personal questions. I wasn't thinking anything in particular, except perhaps wishing that the rain would stop.' Suddenly she smiled.

'Why are you smiling?' he asked. 'And before

you scold me I think that's a perfectly reasonable question.'

'Yes, it is. I was smiling at the thought of Paul escorting the Hylton ladies one by one from the car to the house. I hope he remembered to take the biggest umbrella.'

'Paul?'

'The chauffeur.'

'The chauffeur, of course.'

'Don't look so critical. It's perfectly reasonable that the Hyltons should have a chauffeur.'

'I know. It's just that this whole way of life is strange to me.'

'If you were rich wouldn't you live like this?'

'I'm not sure.' He grinned. 'But I'll probably never be rich enough to find out. And now I suppose I've taken up enough of your time. I should go.'

Linda would have liked him to stay but didn't know how to tell him. Instead she said, 'We'd better find out where Vera put your coat.'

Chapter Seven

The windscreen wipers were losing the battle. Linda sat forward, peering through the rain, and instructed Graham which way to go. A wind had sprung up, and as well as buffeting the car from side to side it was hurling leaves and even broken branches across their path. She glanced at him and he gave her a quick smile. She still wasn't sure why she had allowed herself to accept his offer of help.

When Vera had brought Graham's coat she had asked Linda if she still intended to go to the village.

'I'm not sure,' Linda had said. 'Maybe I should wait until the rain stops.'

'Pity,' Vera had said. 'This would have been a good opportunity for you while their ladyships don't require your services.'

Linda, realizing that Vera was prompting Graham to give her a lift, was embarrassed. However, he had insisted, and now they were boxed up together in his small car.

'It looks like the rain is set in for the night,' Graham said. 'How will you get back? Do you want me to wait?'

'Vera will tell them where I am. They'll probably send Paul.'

'Of course, the chauffeur. And then I imagine you'll be taken back to the Hall in a much grander vehicle than this.'

She glanced at him quickly but saw that he was smiling. 'Yes, indeed. The Rolls, no less.'

'And won't that set the villagers talking?'

'Of course not. They know I work at Fernwood. They'll be much more likely to gossip about the fact that I've arrived home in a stranger's car.'

'Home?'

'It's the house I lived in since I was a small child. So, yes, I guess it's home. And we're nearly there. Pull over to the left ... now.'

When the car stopped Linda made no move to get out. 'What's the matter?' Graham asked.

'I don't know. It feels strange. This is where I

lived in another life. Do you know what I mean?'

'I think I do.'

'And I'm not sure if it feels like home any more.'

'But your family will be there.'

'I have no family. I lived here with my guardian, Miss Taylor, and when she died she left the house to me.'

'Why did you want to come here today?'

'To check if everything's all right. Do a bit of dusting. Put a fire on and warm the poor old place up for a while.'

'You look reluctant.'

'Not reluctant. Just memories, I suppose.'

'I'll come in with you.'

'No, I couldn't impose on you further, Mr Forsyth.'

He grinned. 'Do you know how formal that sounds? You are not imposing, Miss Bellwood. I want to come in. You know I'm as curious as the legendary cat.'

'First a rat and now a cat.'

'I beg your pardon?'

'Cordelia said you were like a drowned rat when you arrived at the Hall, remember?'

They looked at each other and laughed, and after that it seemed natural to invite him in.

'I don't have an umbrella, I'm afraid,' Graham said. 'We'll have to make a dash for it.'

The house was cold and unwelcoming. Linda shook their coats and hung them in the scullery. As soon as she had put the kettle on, she went through to the front parlour, where she found Graham looking for a socket to plug in the two-

140

bar electric fire that stood on the hearth.

'There it is,' he said, and when the bars came reluctantly to life he frowned. 'There's not much heat in that.'

'It will have to do. I won't be staying long enough to light a real fire, and besides, the coal house is across the yard. I'm not braving the rain until I have to.'

'Is there anything else I can do?'

'Go and make a pot of tea, if you like. I'm just going to have a look around upstairs.'

Linda knew she would have to come to the house regularly during the winter months in order to keep it aired. Also to dust and clean a little, as she had told Graham, although she did not intend to do so today. The upstairs windows were small and the rooms were dark. Linda switched on the lights. The single light bulbs with their saucer-shaped glass shades somehow made the rooms look even more dreary.

What am I looking for? she wondered. Rainwater on the window sills? Soot, or worse, dead birds on the hearths? Each room was as clean and tidy as she had left it; her guardian's so much so that it looked as if no one had ever slept in there. Linda was expecting to feel sad when she entered her own bedroom. She had been happy here. Miss Taylor had not denied her toys and books, and if there had been no bedtime stories, Linda had discovered the joys of reading by torchlight long into the night.

The toys were long gone. As she outgrew them Miss Taylor had encouraged her to give them away to charity sales. The bookcase was empty

141

because Linda had taken her precious books with her to the Hall. There was nothing here. No worldly goods nor any lingering memories. The room was strangely sterile.

Linda remembered her distress when Mr Sinclair had advised her to sell the house. It was the only home she had known and she had been determined to keep it. Now she wondered why. I feel like a traitor, she thought. Miss Taylor took me in and was as kind to me as she knew how to be. I should be grateful. I am grateful. But gratitude is different from love.

She switched off the lights and closed the doors. She stood for a moment on the landing and tried to control the treacherous emotions which threatened to overcome her. I must not be maudlin, she thought, but nevertheless she had to brush a tear from her eye before she hurried downstairs.

When she entered the front parlour she found Graham had put a tray with a teapot and cups on the table. 'Do you like tea without milk?' he asked.

'Milk! I meant to get half a pint at the village shop.'

Graham glanced towards the window. 'Do you want me to run across?'

Linda smiled. 'I think we'd better manage without. You've had enough soakings for one day.'

The view outside was so gloomy that Linda switched on the light and drew the curtains before they took their tea to sit by the fire. It wasn't giving out much warmth but the glow was cosy enough, and for a while they sat in a silence which was only disturbed by the beat of the rain on the windows and the occasional fizz and crackle of a worn element.

'Do you mind if I ask you a question?' Graham said.

'Is there any way of stopping you?'

'You could order me to leave your house forthwith.'

Linda sighed in mock resignation. 'Go on, then. What do you want to know?'

'Are you related to the Hyltons?'

'What makes you ask that?'

'Well, I know you told me you are employed as a companion, but you are not at all afraid to stand up to Cordelia and you seem so at home there.'

'More than I do here, you mean?'

'Yes, actually.'

'I do feel at home at the Hall. I haven't worked there for very long at all, but ever since I was a small child I watched the Hyltons and wished I was one of the family.'

'You watched them?'

'Yes. Oh, dear...'

Graham was looking at her curiously, and maybe it was something to do with the fact that she'd never sat here by the fire so intimately with anyone before, or maybe it was because coming here today had stirred up old emotions, but she found herself telling him about the child she had been. The child who had wandered through the woods one summer's day and found what she took to be a castle from a fairy story.

'I shouldn't have been in the woods, of course, but I was always an adventurous child, and I had a head full of fairy tales. I'm not sure who I imagined I was that day when I was pretending to be lost in an enchanted forest. Was I Goldilocks or was I Red Riding Hood? I couldn't have been Gretel, because there was no Hansel. When I reached the end of the wood and saw Fernwood Hall for the first time, it looked like an enchanted castle. It took a moment or two for me to realize it was a real house. And that the children playing on the expanse of grass that lay between the woods and the Hall were real children.'

'Cordelia and Rupert?'

'And their younger brother Florian. I didn't know their names then, of course. I wanted to join them, but I remembered in time that I shouldn't have been there. There were signs up at the village side of the woods saying "Trespassers Will Be Persecuted".'

'*Prosecuted,* surely?'

Linda smiled. 'Of course. But my reading skills were still pretty basic. I hid behind a tree and watched them until a beautiful lady came out of the house and walked towards them calling, "Rupert! Cordelia! Florian! Time for tea."'

'The names are a little pretentious, don't you think?'

'Maybe so, but at the time I thought them perfect storybook names. Anyway, they ran towards her. She hugged Cordelia and held out her hand for Florian. They went back to the house together and oh, how I wished that Cordelia was my sister and Rupert and Florian were my brothers and that beautiful lady with the silvery voice was my mother. And that I could go with them into that magic castle and stay with them forever.'

Linda sat back in her chair and closed her eyes, lost for a moment in the memory of that day that she had never spoken about before.

'After that, I take it you became a regular visitor to the enchanted woods?'

She opened her eyes to find Graham smiling at her. 'Yes, I did. And as autumn came and the days became shorter I grew more bold. One shadowy day, drawn on by the lighted windows, I crept across the grass and actually looked in. That's how it started.'

'And now that you're living in the magic castle, is it everything you want it to be? Are you happy there?'

'I'm not a child any more. I know they are not people from a storybook. And that's all the better, isn't it? They are real human beings and they treat me like one of the family. Of course I'm happy.'

Graham stood up. 'I suppose I'd better go,' he said. He looked uncertain. 'Are you sure you don't want a lift back?'

'I'm sure.'

Linda brought his coat from the scullery. When he'd put it on he stood near the door looking awkward. 'Perhaps we'll meet again,' he said

'I'm not sure how.'

'Maybe Cordelia will come to the pottery to check up on the progress of her dinner service. If she does, you could come with her.'

'Only if Grandmamma Hylton doesn't need me.'

They looked at each other for a moment and then Graham turned abruptly to open the door. He gripped it forcefully as the wind pushed against it and hurled rain into the hall. 'I'd better go,' he said again.

He edged round the door, and Linda stepped forward to take hold of it. She pushed it shut. She stood there for a moment, wondering if she would see Graham Forsyth again. And wondering if she wanted to.

Very soon after she'd washed the cups and tidied up a little, Paul arrived to take her back to Fernwood. He had a large umbrella which he juggled awkwardly while he helped her to close the door and lock it. Then he held the umbrella over both of them and joked, 'Your chariot awaits you, madam.' They made a dash for the car and he said, 'Sit in the front and keep me company, won't you?'

On the way back to the Hall he talked about the rotten weather, the state of the roads – some of them had become mud tracks – and the fact that it would probably take all day tomorrow to get the poor old car washed and polished.

He's talking for the sake of talking, Linda thought. He doesn't really expect me to answer him. She glanced sideways and was shocked to see that he looked utterly miserable. Then she remembered how he had spent his day. He had taken Cordelia to see the house she would live in with her husband. No wonder Cordelia had called it a 'wretched' house. It must have been miserable for both of them. She wondered what Cordelia's mood would be tonight.

If Cordelia was miserable she was making a determined effort not to show it. When Linda was getting changed for dinner she burst into her room carrying an armful of clothes. She dumped them on her bed.

'Here you are,' she said. 'Sort through this lot. I know you are dark and I am fair, but there must be some things that will suit you. No – don't refuse me – anything you choose you must keep. You're my friend, aren't you? I'm sick of you looking like a poor relation.'

Conversation at the dinner table was all about Green Leas, the house that Cordelia had gone to see. Her grandmother deemed it suitable; her mother said they would have to get the best interior designer to have a look at it before they started any major work; and Cordelia... To Linda's surprise, Cordelia seemed quite cheerful. The 'wretched' house had become 'just the ticket' for a young couple. Smaller than Fernwood, of course, but large enough for entertaining.

She and her mother began a lively discussion about interior designers, and Clara Hylton, after telling her son that if the building and renovation work was to be done properly it would prove costly, withdrew from the discussion and let the talk flow over her. Linda could see that she was tired and was not at all surprised when, after dinner, Clara told her that she would go straight to her room.

'Be a darling and order some cocoa for both of us,' she told Linda. 'I'd like you to read to me.'

Florian was still in Scotland, so Rupert got up to help his grandmother. He put his arm around her waist to support her as they climbed the stairs, and when they reached her room he said, 'We're very pleased to have Linda here, aren't we, Grandmamma?'

'Don't talk as if I were a child, Rupert. But, yes, it was a brilliant idea of your mother's to engage Linda. She is already becoming indispensable. Now, please go back and rein your sister in before she has your father promising a nabob's fortune to put her house right.'

Rupert lingered. 'So it's pretty definite, is it?' he said. 'Cordelia likes the house?'

'Yes. And I was surprised. She had shown no great enthusiasm before we got there, but the place really is charming, you know. I think as she walked around she began to see herself living there, having charge of her own household, her own servants, her own husband.'

Rupert smiled. 'Poor Charlie. You put him at the end of Cordelia's requirements.'

'I'm afraid I do. I've never thought this a love match – at least, not on Cordelia's side – but she's twenty-four, all her friends are married. It's time she flew the nest. And speaking of that...'

'Oh, no, Grandmamma, don't start on that. It's different for men. You won't be hearing wedding bells for me for a year or two yet.'

'If at all.'

Rupert's smile faded. 'What do you mean by that?'

'I mean that if you don't get a move on your poor old grandmother might not be here when those wedding bells ring out. I could be six feet under. Time's winged chariots are drawing nearer, you know.'

'Darling, don't talk like that.' Rupert took her in his arms. 'You're going to be with us for years yet.'

'Hmm. Not if I don't get enough rest. Goodnight, Rupert. You're a good boy. I know how hard you work for your father, and I'll just have to trust that one day, in the not too distant future, there will be another generation of Hyltons to carry on the name and the business.'

When Clara was settled in bed, Vera Saunders brought cocoa and biscuits and Clara asked Linda to go and fetch a book from the small bookcase. *'The Good Earth,'* she said, 'by Pearl Buck. It's set in a village in China. Have you read it?'

'I haven't.'

'I think you'll like it.'

'You've already read it?'

'It's the sort of book you can read again. That's right. Come and sit beside me. Now drink up your cocoa and begin. The story starts with a wedding.'

Linda soon became absorbed in the story and she did not realize that Clara had fallen asleep until she heard the gentlest of snores. She closed the book and placed it on the bedside table, then eased the pillows down a little and pulled the bedclothes up. She placed the cinder guard over the fire and went to her room. She knew that Cordelia would probably want to talk to her, but she had a lot to think about and decided to have an early night.

When she was ready for bed she took her embroidered handkerchief case from her top drawer. This was where she had decided to keep Florian's

149

letters. He had jokingly promised three, but in fact after the first letter there had only been one more. As before, there were two letters in the envelope, one for his grandmother and one for Linda.

Clara Hylton was better pleased with his second missive. In it he told her about the scenery – grand but gloomy – the food – ghastly but plentiful – and the people. Here he was more tactful. 'Elspeth is a very nice girl,' he wrote, 'but I need someone more cerebral.'

'Cerebral!' Clara Hylton had snorted. 'He does like to use big words for effect. Showing off, that's what it is. What he needs is a girl who will bring a little reality to his life and not encourage him to think of himself as a writer.'

Linda had thought this cruel but had not said anything. Later that day, when she read her own letter, her belief that Florian should indeed be a writer was reinforced. His descriptions of people and places were vivid and humorous, although sometimes verging on the clichéd. When he expressed his own feelings the writing was heartfelt.

Tonight she reread the second letter briefly, expecting to experience a rush of pleasure when he told her that he would be home very soon. But instead of pleasure, she felt strangely flat. Disconcerted, she put the letter back in the envelope, returned the handkerchief case to the drawer and went to bed.

As she listened to the rain on the windows, she found herself imagining Graham Forsyth driving back to Newcastle along wet, leaf-strewn roads. He would be home by now. She wondered what that home was like. He had mentioned his mother.

Did he live with her and would she have a good meal waiting for him? He certainly needed one.

She smiled when she remembered his unashamed curiosity. Under his probing questioning she had revealed so much about herself. It was only now that she realized that she knew next to nothing about him.

On the way home the country roads were dark, and when the car crested a hill Graham could see the pattern of the street lamps in distant Newcastle. He gave a brief thought to the two hikers he had seen on the way. He couldn't imagine them pitching a tent in this weather and hoped they'd had the good sense to find a hostel. He would love to tell Linda about the resolute pair and how his father had always hoped that the two of them would one day walk from coast to coast, following the route of the Roman Wall. 'We'll do it when I retire, lad,' he'd said. 'You'll be at art school by then and you'll have a long summer break. That will be the time to do it.'

Sadly Alec Forsyth's retirement lasted little longer than a week. On the first Monday morning when he would not have to go to work Dora woke up to find that he had died in his sleep. There was no known cause and no suspicious circumstances. It seemed that at the age of sixty-five his time had come.

Graham often wondered whether his father had had some kind of premonition. After his funeral it was discovered that he had made a will leaving the house to Dora, who would also receive the pension he'd been paying for. But there had also been a letter saying that on no account was Graham to leave art college, and that he'd opened a savings account precisely to deal with this contingency. The money in the account was Graham's and it should see him through. His mother hadn't been pleased. She thought he should get a job and contribute more to household expenses, but her husband had tied the savings account up neatly and there had been nothing she could do about it.

Of course, once Graham had completed his course and got a job at Hylton's, he made sure that his mother had everything she needed. The trouble was, she was never satisfied, and when she decided to go and live in Darlington, with her sister, Graham's Aunt Edna, he bought the house from her and breathed a sigh of relief. His mother thought it her duty to visit now and then, but they got on better now that they didn't have to see each other every day.

Graham's thoughts kept returning to Linda Bellwood. He wondered what the story was behind her being orphaned so young, and what her guardian, Miss Taylor, had been like. She had obviously thought enough of Linda to leave her the house, but he wondered if she had ever appreciated how lonely Linda must have been as a child. Surely only a lonely little girl would have wished so intensely that she could become part of another family? Clearly those dreams still lingered, even though she was now a grown-up, intelligent and beautiful young woman.

It had been both impetuous and foolish of him to suggest that they might see each other again.

How could they without giving people the wrong idea?

By the time he reached the respectable avenue in Heaton where he lived, the rain had eased off a little. He parked outside the house and sat in the car watching raindrops meander down the windscreen. Street lamps shone on privet hedges and light escaped round the edges of curtains; including those in his own house. Graham sighed, wishing he felt happier to come home.

He decided to leave his portfolio in the car. Although the next day was Saturday, he would be going into work until lunchtime. Then he might stay after the others in his office had gone home and work for an hour or two on Cordelia Hylton's dinner service.

As he opened the gate, a gust of wind shook the branches of the lilac tree and a shower of raindrops descended and drenched him. He smiled and wondered what Linda would say if she could see him now. He was still smiling when he unlocked the door and stepped into the hallway, but his mood changed abruptly when the door of the front parlour jerked open.

The woman standing there glared at him. 'You promised to come home early tonight,' she said.

'Did I?'

'We're going to the pictures, remember?'

'Oh.'

'Don't stand there looking as if you can't remember. The truth is, you don't want to take me.'

'No, I'm sorry. I do want to take you, really I do. I had to work late. It couldn't be avoided.'

'Well, you could have warned me. What's the

153

use of having a telephone if you don't use it when you should?'

'Look, I've said I'm sorry. Is it too late?'

Her scowl eased. 'Not if we hurry. We'll catch the second house. But you can forget about anything to eat before we go. If you're hungry we'll get some fish and chips on the way home.' She surveyed him critically. 'For goodness sake, go and dry your hair. You look like a drowned...'

Graham was halfway upstairs before she had finished the sentence. As he towelled his hair dry, he tried to suppress rumbles of hunger. Then he cheered up a little as he contemplated that the fish and chips would, in any case, be better than anything Sonya, his beautiful wife, could prepare for him.

Chapter Eight

Next morning, when Linda looked out of her bedroom window, she saw two figures wrestling with a large stone urn which must have been blown over during the high winds of the day before. She recognized Bobby, the useful boy, and she presumed the other, older and more substantial figure was Albert Aslett. She hadn't met him yet, or his wife Ivy, and she was beginning to wonder whether anyone would mind if she ventured into the staff quarters and introduced herself.

Suddenly there was a cry as the urn escaped their grasp and toppled over again. She saw

154

Bobby jump out of the way, slip on the wet grass and fall flat on his back. Albert Aslett had not moved quickly enough, and although the urn had missed him, its contents, a large rose bush, had not. The thorny branches must have caught his face, for after yelping with pain he fished a large handkerchief from his pocket and began mopping at his brow and cheeks. Bobby was still on the ground. Linda focused her gaze on him and saw to her concern that he was shaking. She was about to run down and see if she could help when she saw him pull himself into a sitting position. He was still shaking – with laughter.

Then, as she watched, two other figures appeared on the lawn. William Hylton and his son must have seen the incident through the dining room windows. They had removed their jackets and rolled up their shirtsleeves. The four men then righted the massive urn together. They were all laughing as they strolled back to the house, and Linda found herself wishing she could tell Graham Forsyth about it. He would enjoy the humour, but also it might prove to him that although the Hyltons were very grand, they were not afraid of getting their hands dirty.

None of the Hylton ladies came down for breakfast, and as Mr Hylton and Rupert had left for the pottery by the time she was dressed, Linda ate alone. When Vera brought her breakfast she told her that Mrs Hylton senior did not need her. The trip to Green Leas the day before had tired her out and she had decided to stay in bed until lunchtime.

'Then what am I to do?' Linda asked.

'Why don't you find a cosy corner to sit and read? There's a nice fire going in the drawing room and Mr Florian has left a pile of books on the table there. You might find something that suits. I'll bring you a cup of coffee when I have a chance.'

'I could make my own coffee.'

Vera drew in her breath and shook her head emphatically. 'Mrs Aslett wouldn't be best pleased. The kitchen is her domain, and if any of the family is brave enough to venture there she thinks they've come to spy on her. No, get along, but you can keep the fire going if you like. Pamela Hawkins is sickly this morning and Mrs Aslett has given her permission to stay in bed. Most reluctantly, I can tell you. But the lass really did look bad.'

Linda looked through the books on the table. She had not heard of most of the authors and the classics she did recognize were in their original language. She was impressed; Florian must be able to read Russian and French. She looked through a copy of *Madame Bovary*. All she knew about it was that it had caused a scandal when it was first published and that the author, Gustave Flaubert, had been charged with immorality. She had learned French at school but she wasn't proficient enough to tackle a novel. She replaced the book on the table and looked around to see if there were any magazines lying about.

When Vera brought her coffee Linda was sitting in Grandmamma Hylton's favourite armchair by the fire flicking through a copy of *Vogue*.

'I feel guilty,' Linda said.

'Goodness, what have you done?'

Linda smiled. 'Nothing – it's just that it doesn't

feel right having you wait on me like this, especially when you're so busy.'

'You mean because Pamela has taken to her bed?'

'Yes, it means you have twice as much to do.'

'Not quite. The lad has been pressed into housemaid duties. Mrs Aslett set him on laying the table in the dining room. If that Pamela hasn't got herself up and dressed by the time Mr Hylton and Rupert come home, Bobby will have to help me serve the lunch. But, don't worry, he's done it before and he scrubs up quite nicely. And at least you get a smile from him.'

Linda poured her coffee. 'It sounds as though you don't like Pamela very much.'

'I neither like nor dislike her; it's just that she isn't easy to get on with. Does as she's told but keeps herself to herself. It's like she thinks she's too good for the rest of us. I sometimes wonder where she came from.'

Linda remembered that Florian had told her that no one apart from the family knew the truth about Pamela – that she was really the daughter of the disgraced financier Jack Delafontaine. The servants had been told that she had been supplied by a domestic agency in London.

'Perhaps she's just unhappy,' Linda said.

'Then she has no right to be. This is a good place to work, and if that young madam doesn't pull her socks up I can see her getting her marching orders.'

'From Mrs Hylton?'

'No, from Mrs Aslett.'

Linda wondered what would happen if the

157

housekeeper did want to give Pamela the sack. Would Emerald Hylton agree? She had brought her here because she was sorry for her, but if Pamela was causing discord in the household she might have to think of some other plan.

Vera knelt down and began sweeping the hearth.

'Oh, I'm sorry. Did I make a mess?' Linda asked her.

'Not at all, lass. I'm just delaying going back to the kitchen for a few more minutes. On top of everything else there are going to be guests for dinner tonight, Miss Cordelia's fiancé and his parents. They'll be wanting to discuss the house. Paul the chauffeur doesn't think much of it, but no doubt he has his reasons. And, of course, Mr Florian will be home by then.' She laughed. 'Bobby will have a lot of potatoes to peel. Now, you drink your coffee and read your magazine. No doubt they'll find something for you to do after lunch.'

Linda didn't have much time to enjoy her coffee and magazine. Cordelia swept into the room just as Vera was leaving. 'Ah, Saunders,' she said. 'Please tell Mrs Aslett that my grandmother would like a tray sent up at lunchtime. Something light, a bowl of consommé and maybe a poached egg, that should do. And bring me some coffee, will you?'

'Very well, Miss Cordelia.'

Behind Cordelia's back Vera raised her eyebrows and shot Linda an amused smile, as if she were inviting her to imagine Mrs Aslett's reaction to these orders when she was already coping with the loss of Pamela and the preparations for tonight's meal.

158

'Does your grandmother want me to go up to her?' Linda asked when Vera had gone.

'Yes, sorry about that. You'll have to have your own lunch quickly. Or we could ask Mrs Aslett to arrange a tray for you.'

'No! Don't do that,' Linda said. 'I think they are extra busy in the kitchen this morning.'

'So?' Cordelia looked surprised. 'That's what they're here for, isn't it?' As she said this she smiled at Vera, who had returned with her coffee. She gestured towards the small table near the fireplace. 'Over there,' she said. 'With Linda's.' Then she sat in the armchair at the other side of the fireplace and looked at Linda brightly.

'You were saying?'

Linda realized that it would be pointless to explain her feelings about causing extra work for the staff, so she simply said, 'I'd rather have my lunch with you.'

'How sweet. And listen, once my grandmamma has settled for her afternoon nap, I want you to meet me in the library. There's something I want you to do for me.'

'What's that?'

Instead of answering, Cordelia made a show of pouring her coffee from the fresh jug Vera had brought, then adding the cream and sugar.

'What do you want me to do?' Linda repeated.

'Mmm? Oh, I'll tell you later.' Then Cordelia turned the conversation to other matters. 'I think you'd love Green Leas,' she said. 'I was reluctant to go – you know that – and it was really painful having Paul drive us there. I sat in the front passenger seat and I looked at him now and then and

'... and ... he just looked so unhappy.'

'Are you surprised?'

'No, of course not. But with my mother and grandmother sitting behind us, there was absolutely nothing I could say, was there?'

'I don't suppose there was. And even if they hadn't been there, what could you have said to him? *Stop! Turn the car round. Let's go away together – right now.*'

'Don't, Linda. You know that's impossible and I've told you why.'

Cordelia looked so distressed that Linda felt guilty. 'I'm sorry,' she said. 'I really am. And I do understand.'

But she wondered if that were true. She wondered what *she* would do if she loved one man but married another. She hoped she would never find herself in that position.

Cordelia reached into the pocket of her Chanel cardigan and brought out a packet of cigarettes.

'I didn't know you smoked,' Linda said.

'I didn't until recently. It helps calm the nerves, you know.'

She put a cigarette in her mouth and, taking a box of matches from the same pocket, lit it clumsily. It was obvious that she was just getting the hang of these things. She tossed the match into the fire and inhaled, coughed, picked a bit of tobacco off her lip and then smiled at Linda through a haze of smoke.

'Does that really make you feel better?' Linda asked.

'Well, I have to admit the first time I inhaled I felt sick, but you soon get used to it and it's really worth persevering. Believe me. Would you like to try?'

She waved the packet of cigarettes in Linda's direction. Linda shook her head. 'No, thank you,' she said.

'Suit yourself.' Cordelia gazed into the fire for a moment and then said brightly, 'I wonder what mood my little brother will be in when he returns from wooing the fair Elspeth.'

'Will he have been wooing her?'

'Goodness, no. I'm being sarcastic, or ironic, or something like that. But that's what the family want. Poor Florian's heart isn't in it at all. Do you know, I've often wondered whether he's been hankering after someone else – someone he met at university perhaps? And if that's the case, why hasn't he done something about it? Either she turned him down flat or she's someone completely unsuitable. Anyway, he'll be home tonight and the parents will increase the pressure.'

'For him to marry?'

'That, but even more important for them, they want him to give up his bohemian ideas and join the business like a good son should.'

'And what do you think?'

'Me? I actually feel sorry for the poor lamb. He has never given way to his physical disability. He gets positively angry if anyone is foolish enough to offer help, and if he's totally different from Rupert, that's not his fault. Our parents could easily afford to give him some kind of allowance to enable him to get on with his writing, but that's not the Hylton way. The girls have to marry well and the boys have to damn well work for a living.'

161

'And what about you?' Linda asked.

'What do you mean?'

'Have you ever wanted to work for your living?'

'Goodness, no, although it's not unheard of. One of our great aunts had an artistic flair and she actually worked at the pottery. She was responsible for the Hylton dragon. You know, the green dragon breathing orange fire as he rampages round the lovely pale green teapot. And the cups that have dragons inside which look as though they're going to jump out at you.'

'I don't think I've ever seen one.'

'No? Hylton's was quite famous for it at one time, but they don't make them any more. Not since Great Aunt Edith married a missionary and went off to live in China. A family story has it that she only married him because he was going to China. I hope the poor old thing didn't expect to find real dragons there.'

'Is that why you're so fond of dragons, do you think? Do you take after your great aunt?'

Cordelia looked thoughtful. 'Maybe I do. I've never really thought about it. I just know I've always loved dragons. But – hey – the old Hylton dragon! Do you think that's what gave the gorgeous Mr Forsyth the idea for my dinner service design?'

'*Gorgeous?*'

'Oh, come on, Linda. You must have noticed those dark brooding looks. And furthermore I think he took quite a shine to you.'

Linda was saved from responding to this startling notion by the ringing of the bell to announce luncheon was served.

162

Clara Hylton didn't look well. Her eyes were puffy, her nose was red and she was having to breathe through her mouth. The symptoms of a head cold. She had forbidden her daughter-in-law to call a doctor.

'I need to rest in bed, have chicken soup at teatime and a hot toddy right now,' she told Linda. 'It's that damned house that did it. Green Leas. Damp and draughty. Any chair or sofa that was left there was far too grimy to sit on, so I just had to wander about after them and let the cold get into my bones.'

'Why didn't you wait in the car?' Linda asked.

'I should have done. Wrapped up cosy and warm in a nice big travel rug, but I'm a curious old woman and I had to see the house where my granddaughter will set up home.'

'And of course you wanted to be able to give them your opinion.'

Clara raised her eyebrows, gave Linda a cool look and then hooted with laughter. Unfortunately the laugh turned into a sneeze followed by a coughing fit.

'Linda–' she gasped when her cough subsided, 'you see right through people, don't you? And you're not afraid to speak as you find.'

'I'm sorry.'

'Sorry for telling the truth? Don't be. It's very refreshing. Now, can you tell me, should I send for another hot water bottle or open all the windows? Opinion seems to be divided on this.'

'I think you should dispense with the hot water bottle and pull the blankets up. Keep warm without getting too hot. And open one window just a little way to let some fresh air in. That's what my guardian would have done.'

'Really? Well, I've heard Miss Taylor was a very sensible woman, so we'll do just that. And, Linda, stay with me for a while.'

'Of course I will. Would you like me to read to you?'

'No, dear, my head's full of fuzz. I wouldn't be able to concentrate. Just stay until I'm safely in the land of nod and then you can go and see Cordelia. I think there's something she wants you to do for her.'

Linda was uneasy about leaving the old lady alone. Although Clara had fallen asleep quite quickly, it was an uneasy sleep, her breathing was laboured and she tossed and turned restlessly. Eventually Linda decided to go and find out what Cordelia wanted and then come straight back.

Cordelia was waiting in the library. 'Oh, good,' she said. 'Here you are. I think he'll be home from work by now.'

'Who will be home and what do you want me to do?'

'I want you to make a telephone call for me.'

Linda was puzzled. 'Why can't you make it yourself?'

Cordelia didn't answer her. She had opened a drawer in the desk and brought out a telephone directory. She began to leaf through it. 'Ah, here we are. Forsyth, G.'

'You want me to phone Graham Forsyth?'

'That's right. I want you to tell him that I've

164

changed my mind about the dragon.'

Linda was surprised. 'You don't want a dragon?'

'Yes, I do, but I want it to be green, not red.'

'But I thought you said red was the colour of happiness?'

'It is. But to tell the truth, I chose it because I thought it would be the most attractive.'

'And now you don't?'

'Maybe it is, but green is much more appropriate. Can't you guess why?'

Linda stared at Cordelia for a moment and then she smiled. 'Of course. Green Leas. The name of the house. Green Leas must have a green dragon.'

'A green dragon breathing fire! So there will still be some red in the design. And I don't want any smaller dragons going round the rim. That will be too fussy now. You can explain all this to Mr Forsyth.'

'Why can't you explain it to him?'

'I'd feel foolish.'

'I can't see why.'

'Well, you know, I think I made a bit of a fool of myself yesterday. I was so grumpy when he arrived and then took so long to make my mind up. And now I'm going to change it. He probably thinks I'm spoiled and ungrateful.'

'I'm sure he doesn't.'

'Well, at least inconsiderate. And it's vain of me, I know, but I don't like people to think badly of me.'

'How does it change things if I telephone him, not you?'

'I think he respects you. He'll listen when you explain my reasons. I mean, I hadn't seen the

165

house when we were looking at designs. The truth is, I'm a bit embarrassed. Graham Forsyth is Hylton's top designer and he's gone to so much trouble, but it's important to get this right before he does any more work on it. And another thing – I'm sure he'd rather talk to you than to me!'

Cordelia pushed the phone across the desk towards Linda and then dragged up another chair so that they could sit next to each other. 'This phone has a dial,' she said, 'although you'll still have to get the operator because Newcastle doesn't count as a local call.' She paused. 'I say, don't think me rude, but have you used a telephone before?'

Linda smiled. 'Of course I have. There's a phone box in the village and I've made calls for Miss Taylor. To the doctor, the dentist, the butcher and the coal merchant.'

'What an exciting life you've led!' They looked at each other and laughed. 'Here's the number.' Cordelia placed a manicured finger on the page of the open directory. 'Go on – pick the receiver up and dial–'

'O for operator, I know.'

While they were waiting for the operator to answer, Cordelia leaned towards Linda and whispered, 'They listen, you know.'

'Who listens?'

'The operators in the local exchanges. It's a well-known fact. And you can't even tell when it's happening. So never say anything you don't want other people to know about.'

Linda nudged Cordelia to let her know the operator had answered, and they were both giggling when she gave Graham's telephone number. Linda held the phone away from her ear so that Cordelia could listen to the ringing of the bell in the distant house.

The ringing stopped and Linda held the receiver close again. A woman's voice said, 'Hello, Mrs Forsyth speaking.'

So Graham did live with his mother, Linda thought. Although her voice sounded surprisingly young.

'Could I speak to Mr Forsyth, please?'

There was a pause then a distinct coolness. 'Who may I say is calling?'

'Linda Bellwood.'

'And who exactly are you? And what do you want?'

Cordelia could see Linda's growing discomfort and mouthed 'What's the problem?'

Linda shook her head then continued, 'I'm phoning on behalf of Miss Hylton. Cordelia Hylton. It's about her dinner service.'

'Then why didn't you say so?'

Linda wanted to scream, *Because you didn't give me the chance!* But she forced herself to remain polite and say, 'I'm sorry. I should have done.'

'Wait a mo,' the voice said. 'He's not been home from work for very long but I'll call my husband to the phone.'

Linda gripped the receiver as she listened to the voices at the other end. She could imagine the woman holding the receiver away from her mouth but making no attempt to cover it with her other hand. 'Graham!' she shouted. 'It's someone called Linda Bellwood. She's phoning on behalf of the

167

Hylton girl. It's about the bloody dinner service. As if you haven't wasted most of the day on the damn thing already.'

When Graham came to the phone he sounded subdued. 'What is it, Linda?' he asked.

Linda explained about the dragon. How Cordelia wanted only one dragon on each plate and that it should be green but breathing out red flames. Cordelia was pulling at her sleeve. Linda turned her head to look at her.

'Apologize,' Cordelia said. 'Tell him I hope this won't be a problem.'

Linda did so.

'Tell Miss Hylton that it's quite all right,' Graham said. 'At this stage it's only my time that has been wasted.'

Then there was silence. It seemed that neither of them could think of anything else to say. Linda put the receiver down without saying goodbye.

'What's the matter?' Cordelia asked. 'Was he cross with you? If so, I'm really sorry.'

'No, he wasn't cross with me – although maybe he was a tad cross with you.' Linda forced a smile and tried to make a joke of it.

'Whoever it was who answered the phone seemed to be giving you a hard time,' Cordelia said. 'Who was it?'

'Mrs Forsyth.'

'His mother?'

'No, his wife.'

'Oh, poor you!'

'Why do you say that?'

'Because I think as well as him taking a shine to you, you were rather stricken, too.'

'You're mistaken. I definitely wasn't stricken. What a silly word.'

'If you say so.' But it didn't look as though Cordelia believed her.

'I'd better go back to your grandmother. I'm quite worried about her.'

'Are you? Do you think my mother should risk the old girl's wrath and call a doctor?'

'I do.'

'I'll tell her. But do you think we could leave it until tomorrow?'

'I suppose so. Why?'

'Because Florian will be home. In fact he's coming back tonight.'

'Is he?' Linda immediately forgot her puzzling sense of disappointment when she had learned Graham Forsyth was married. Her spirits lifted as she asked, 'What difference will that make?'

'Grandmamma pretends not to have favourites, but she adores Florian. He stands a better chance of persuading her to see a doctor than any of us, even you.'

Linda paused outside Clara Hylton's door when she heard voices. Two voices talking quietly and then a burst of laughter. She opened the door to see Florian sitting by his grandmother's bed. The old lady was smiling. She was breathing easily and her complexion was normal.

'You see, Linda, I am quite better,' she said. 'Young people make too much fuss these days.'

'You're home,' Linda said to Florian.

'I caught an earlier train. I couldn't stay away from you any longer.'

When he said this he took his grandmother's hand and smiled at her. But Linda knew to her joy that the words had been meant just for her.

Chapter Nine

Thursday, 23rd December 1938

Hark the herald angels sing...

The carol singers' young voices carried through the frosty air as Muriel Sinclair walked home from the village hall. The streets were dark and she took each step carefully. A heavy snowfall the week before and a partial thaw followed by icy temperatures had made the pavements treacherous. Muriel was cold and tired and beginning to regret having volunteered to organize the old folks' Christmas party.

Not that it hadn't gone well. Everyone seemed to have enjoyed themselves. But that scare at the end had drained her of any remaining energy. Perhaps next year she would go to the party as a guest, sit down at the trestle table nearest to the old coke stove, and have some nice young people like Florian Hylton and Linda Bellwood wait on her. It would not be her responsibility to make sure that everybody got their fair share of sandwiches, jelly and fruit, and mince pies.

Most of the old folk were not averse to complaining if they thought some tasty titbit had passed them by. Even Clara Hylton, who was the

170

last person to need the generous bounty provided by the ladies' committee, had kept a very sharp eye on what was on her neighbour's plate and looked positively indignant when she saw that Mrs Morris had a piece of Christmas cake with icing on the top and one side, whereas her slice only had a thin strip of icing on the top.

Clara Hylton had been coming to the Christmas party since she was a young bride, as a helper then, of course. There were those who remembered how hard she had worked and what fun she had been, even though she never quite managed to shed her air of being a grand lady. When her son William had married she brought her new daughter-in-law along, too, but Emerald Hylton had stopped coming to help the first time she had been pregnant and huge with the twins she was carrying. People forgave her because she still gave generous contributions, providing a magnificent hamper of food for the raffle, for example. And, of course, she had her little tea parties at the Hall now and then.

Mrs Hylton senior had gone on helping at the Christmas party until only a year or two ago, and it was because of her long service that the ladies' committee thought she now ought to come as a guest. This year she had brought her youngest grandson, Florian, and her companion, Linda Bellwood, and offered their services. Linda had done everything asked of her – buttered the bread for the sandwiches, warmed the mince pies, and filled up the teacups again and again.

Florian had helped people to their seats and then vanished. Muriel wondered where he could have gone. The puzzle was solved when Ted Crawford appeared dressed as Father Christmas, carrying his sack full of presents. Florian had rummaged through the collection of theatrical costumes kept in a wicker basket behind the stage and dressed himself up as a Christmas elf.

Florian laughed and joked with everyone as he dived into the sack to find the presents, and made a big show of getting the names right. When the sack was empty, he and Ted led the singing of the Christmas carols. Muriel herself played the piano.

Linda, although perfectly amenable, hadn't said very much. Muriel wondered if it was because she felt awkward. Most of the people at the party had known her since she was a small child. They knew where she had been born, in a rundown cottage in the poorer part of the village, and how lucky she had been to be adopted by the schoolteacher. Although they thanked her politely when she filled up their teacups, there was an air of reserve. It was as if they didn't quite know whether to regard her as one of their own, a village girl, or now that she was so smartly dressed, one of the gentry from the Hall.

She really did look stylish, Muriel thought. Her grey skirt hugged her slender hips and flared gently towards a mid-calf hemline. Her short-sleeved sweater was cherry-red with a black bow knitted into the contrasting neckline; it had shoulder pads to give that fashionable square look. She wore patent black Cuban-heeled shoes and a matching leather belt that emphasized her enviable waistline. Her dark hair was softly waved and she wore just a hint of make-up. How different she looked from the unsophisticated girl who had come to the Autumn Fayre.

And how naturally she communicated with both Clara Hylton and Florian. She was perfectly at ease with them, and they with her. Muriel thought Linda was more like part of the family than an employee such as Paul Stevens.

The Hyltons' chauffeur had been invited in and had made straight for the kitchen. Each time Muriel had cause to go there, she found him sitting glumly at the table with both hands round his mug of tea and with a truly miserable expression on his face. However, he helped to clear up when the party was over and the guests had gone. While Linda and Muriel washed dishes and Florian swept the floor, Stevens took off his jacket, rolled up his shirtsleeves and began stacking the chairs and folding the trestle tables, something John should have been doing if he hadn't caught that beastly cold.

Muriel noted with cynical amusement that Etta and Ted Crawford and the remaining members of the ladies' committee had vanished almost as soon as the guests did. Some gave the excuse of seeing the more doddery old folk safely home along the icy pavements, and Muriel supposed that was fair enough. But not so Ted and Etta.

'I've seen to the stove,' Ted called from the doorway. 'So we'll be off now. Etta and I are going to call into the Old Fox on the way home. I think we deserve a nip of something to preserve us from the cold.'

'Besides, we'd only get in the way if we stayed,' his wife said. 'You seem to have plenty of helpers.' And then she added, perhaps a touch shamefacedly. 'And well done, Muriel. We do appreciate your efforts, you know.'

Yes, Muriel thought, you appreciate the fact that I'm so foolishly willing to take on far too much. Thank goodness for the contingent from Fernwood. And then, when they were all busy, someone had noticed that Clara Hylton was nowhere to be seen. Her present from Santa, a bar of carnation bath soap, was lying on the chair where she had been sitting. The paper it had been wrapped in was on the floor. Worryingly, so was her mink-brown Persian lamb coat.

Linda looked stricken. After all, it was her job to look after Clara Hylton. 'She was there just a moment ago,' she said. 'I told her we wouldn't be long and that we'd be going home soon.'

'She may have gone to the cloakroom,' Florian said.

Linda shot off without saying anything, and only a moment later returned. Her face was drained of colour. 'She's not in the cloakroom and not in the kitchen,' she said.

'Behind the stage? Sorting through the theatrical costumes?' Florian asked, but Muriel could see that he thought this unlikely. Nevertheless, she hurried away to make sure.

When she came back, shaking her head, Paul Stevens said, 'She's probably gone out to the car.'

'Without her coat?' Linda said. 'She's only just shaken off a head cold.'

'Did you lock the car?' Florian asked.

'I did. She'll just be standing there waiting for me.' The chauffeur hurried out of the village hall and returned immediately, shaking his head.

'I'll get my coat,' Florian said. 'You, too, Stevens.'

'I'm coming, too,' Linda said.

'No, Linda,' Florian said. 'You stay here with Mrs Sinclair in case Grandmamma comes back.'

Muriel was surprised by the expression on his face. He looks as though he's more worried about Linda than about his grandmother, she thought.

The two men hurried out, Stevens shrugging his jacket on as he led the way, and Florian trying to keep up, although his limp had become more noticeable as the evening wore on.

'Do you think she's followed one of the guests home?' Linda asked.

'Is she likely to do that?' Muriel said.

'It's possible. She forgets where she is sometimes or what she's supposed to be doing. Oh, I shouldn't have told you that.'

'Don't worry, dear. It's hardly a secret that Clara Hylton is getting ... what shall I say? A little absent-minded.'

'It's so unfair!' Linda exclaimed.

Muriel was taken aback. 'Do you mean the Hyltons expect too much of you?'

'I don't mean that at all. I mean it's so unfair that she should become like this. She's always been so intelligent and witty and kind, and it must be torture for her to be so muddled at times.'

'Just at times?'

'Yes, sometimes whole days go by without incident and then ... then something like this happens.'

'You mean she goes missing?'

175

'A few weeks ago we were in Fenwick's in Newcastle. She was perfectly all right in the French Salon. She knew exactly what she wanted, although perhaps she was a little too generous.'

'The clothes were for you?'

Linda looked embarrassed. 'I couldn't refuse.'

'Don't worry, dear. I know how formidable that lady can be. But go on. After that something went wrong?'

'She had insisted I try everything on, and when I was getting into my own clothes again she wandered off. When I came out there was no sign of her. The assistant who'd been serving us said that Mrs Hylton had arranged for our purchases to be delivered to Fernwood and that she'd gone to the powder room. I was to wait for her in the Salon. So I did. I waited for ages, and finally I decided I'd better go along to the powder room. I couldn't see her, so I knocked on the cubicle doors and called her name. Very embarrassing! But she wasn't there. Finally I went to the Tivoli.'

'The restaurant on the first floor?'

'Yes. She'd said we might lunch there, although it wasn't definite. Emerson's had been mentioned, too.'

'And was she there? In the Tivoli?'

'Yes. Getting crosser by the minute. A waitress was hovering by the table. "You took your time!" Mrs Hylton said when she saw me. She was almost shouting. Diners at the other tables looked round. That didn't stop her. "I was just about to order and eat without you. And you know very well that I can't read the bloody menu!" She thrust the menu into my hands.'

'Did you tell her what had happened? That she'd left a message for you to wait in the French Salon?'

'No. I didn't want to embarrass her in front of the waitress. And in any case, it wouldn't have done any good. She obviously believed that she'd told me to meet her in the restaurant.'

'And after that?'

'Everything went smoothly. She couldn't have been sweeter. We had a lovely meal, then took a taxi to the Haymarket where we'd arranged to meet Stevens. On the way home she took my hand and told me she hadn't enjoyed herself so much for a long time.'

Linda was frowning and Muriel said, 'There's something you're not telling me.'

'It was the way she got so angry. I hadn't seen her like that before. And although I haven't known her long, I believe it was completely out of character.'

'Has this kind of thing happened again?'

'A few times. She shouted at Pamela, one of the housemaids, that the cocoa she had brought her was cold, when the truth was that the cocoa had been brought at least an hour earlier and she'd forgotten about it.'

'And the housemaid's reaction?'

'Cold fury. I thought she was going to yell back at her, so I hurried her out of the room and told her I would come to the kitchen and make a fresh cup of cocoa.' Linda smiled. 'Actually it was the first time I'd ventured into the kitchen. Vera Saunders – you know Vera?'

'I do. Her parents live in the village.'

177

'Well, Vera thought Mrs Aslett – she's the cook/housekeeper – might object to my presence.'

'And did she?'

'Not at all. For all Vera thinks I ought to be treated as one of the family, Mrs Aslett and her husband, Albert seem to regard me as one of the staff. It's a funny sort of existence, being neither one nor the other.'

'Does it make you unhappy?'

'No it doesn't. In fact I feel privileged.'

'So you made the cocoa?'

'I did.'

'But that didn't do anything for Pamela's ruffled feathers, I imagine.'

'Sadly, no. And there have been other small incidents with Mrs Hylton, but the worst thing is that she has no memory of them.'

'I should think that's just as well.'

'When she gets into a state only one person can cope with her. Florian. She adores him and he's devoted to her.'

Linda shivered. Ted Crawford had damped down the coke stove before he'd gone, and the radiators were almost cold. Muriel brought their coats from the cloakroom and they put them on. Neither of them felt like speaking further, and they sat near the rapidly cooling stove with their hands in their pockets.

Once in Royal David's city...

Suddenly the carol singers started up nearby.

'Goodness, those children are still out there,' Muriel said. 'I don't know what their mothers are thinking of. The poor lambs will catch their death of cold.'

'Maybe not,' Linda said. 'If they're lucky, some people invite them in and give them hot drinks and a mince pie each.'

Muriel smiled. 'John and I have done that sometimes. I'd forgotten. Did your guardian invite the children in?'

'She would have done. Many a year she had a plate of mince pies waiting, but they never called at our door. I think they were too much in awe of her.'

'Oh, poor thing. How sad.'

There was a draught of cold air as the outer door opened, and they turned to see three people coming into the hall; Paul Stevens, Florian Hylton and his grandmother, Clara. Muriel and Linda rose to their feet and hurried towards them.

'Thank goodness!' Linda said.

'Where did you find her?' Muriel asked.

'Find me?' Clara said. 'Find me? I'm not a parcel, you know. They didn't go to lost luggage!'

For a moment Muriel thought Mrs Hylton was angry. And perhaps she was, but she was also laughing; her expression changing from outrage to amusement and back rapidly.

'My darling grandmamma was singing carols,' Florian said.

Muriel looked at the older lady anxiously. She had dressed for the Christmas party and was wearing a beige silk crêpe de Chine day dress. Hardly the best garment to wear outside on a bitter winter's evening. Florian had given her his coat and she was wearing it over her shoulders like a cloak. She looked rather grand.

'Too, too sweet,' she said. 'Enthusiastic but a

179

little out of tune. Do you think we should invite them in and give them mince pies like those two dear old ladies did?'

'No, Grandmamma,' Florian said. 'It's time the children went home. And you, too. Now put your nice warm coat on.'

Linda helped Clara Hylton into her coat and Florian reclaimed his. Paul Stevens hurried outside and came back to say that the car was ready. Florian led his grandmother out, and Linda was about to follow when she had turned and said, 'Will you be all right? Is there anything I could help with?'

'Don't worry, dear,' Muriel had told her. 'It's all shipshape. All I have to do is lock up and get home as quickly as I can.'

John was looking out of the window when Muriel got home. No sooner did the gate clang shut behind her than she saw the curtain of the sitting room being pushed aside and his anxious face appear. Then the curtain fell back into place and a moment or two later the front door opened. He stood there in his dressing gown.

'John! You'll get a cold!'

'I already have a cold.'

'Then your cold will get worse.' Muriel hurried in and shut the door. She pushed her husband gently into the sitting room where a good fire was blazing.

'I was worried about you,' John said. 'You're later than I expected. I've been keeping the soup warm.'

'Well, why don't we pour it into a couple of

mugs, add a dash of sherry, and sit here by the fire,' Muriel said 'I'll tell you all about it.'

While they drank their soup Muriel told John what had happened when the party was over. How Clara Hylton had slipped away and had been found singing carols with some of the village children.

'I imagine the two dear old ladies she mentioned would be the Forbes sisters,' John said. 'And she actually went in with the children to have mince pies?'

'It seems so.' Muriel sighed. 'Imagine what the village gossips will make of that.'

'Oh, I don't know,' John said. 'Violet and Rose are a little, shall we say, eccentric themselves. There's a chance they'll forget all about it.'

'I'm not so sure, and I'd hate it to get back to the Hall for Linda's sake.'

'Won't they know anyway?'

'No. As they were leaving I heard Florian tell the chauffeur that there was no need to mention what had happened. He tried to make it sound as though he was protecting Stevens, but I could tell he was really concerned about Linda.'

'You think he's sweet on her?'

'It looks that way.'

'And Linda?'

'It's hard to tell. They get on well together, but as far as Linda is concerned there is a slight air of reserve, as if she can't allow herself to believe what is happening, much as she would like to.'

'Oh dear.'

'What's the matter?'

'I hope you're wrong about their being attracted

181

to each other. I hope they are nothing more than friends, for no matter how twentieth-century the Hyltons have become, I cannot see them welcoming Linda into the family as a daughter-in-law.'

Once back at Fernwood, Clara Hylton decided she was too tired to go down to dinner. 'Tell Saunders to bring a tray up,' she said. 'I don't want Pamela Delafontaine anywhere near me.'

'Hush, Grandmamma, you must call her Pamela Hawkins now,' Florian said.

Clara Hylton frowned and looked puzzled for a moment and then said, 'Oh, yes, of course.' She paused then turned to Linda and said, 'Will you stay with me?'

'Of course I will.'

'Shall I stay, too?' Florian said. 'The three of us together. It will be like a midnight feast in the dorm.'

'Don't be silly, Florian,' his grandmother told him. 'First of all, it is nowhere near midnight and secondly it would be scandalous for you to be in the dormitory with us!'

Clara said this with such conviction that Linda could not tell whether she was joking or not. Florian responded as though it was a joke, or rather that they were playing a game of pretend.

'You're quite right,' he said. 'I'd better go before the headmistress catches wind of my presence here. We don't want to have you expelled, do we?'

Clara burst out laughing. It had been a joke. But they had been kept guessing for a moment. Linda wondered sometimes if Clara Hylton did this kind of thing on purpose; whether she was playing games with them. But if that was the case she must be fully aware of what was happening to her. And that was very sad indeed.

Florian waited until Vera Saunders had brought the first course of barley cream soup then kissed his grandmother goodnight. Turning to Linda, he said quietly, 'Come down to the drawing room when you can. No matter how late I'll wait up for you.'

Vera had set a table for them near the fire. Clara enjoyed her soup and was halfway through the second course of mutton and kidney hotpot when she started coughing. At first it was just niggly little coughs which she tried to ease with sips of water, but the bouts grew longer and she began to look distressed.

'What a nuisance,' she said at the end of a particularly tiring burst. 'I love hotpot, but this damn cough won't let me enjoy it.' She pushed her plate aside, looking as miserable as a child who has been denied a treat. 'Damn it, Linda, I'm hungry but it's not just the cough, my throat is sore. What can we do?'

Fortunately Vera Saunders came into the room at that moment bearing their dessert. It was orange jelly and ice cream, and Clara tucked into it enthusiastically. Her cough subsided and Linda was relieved. It was probably caused by something that went down the wrong way, she decided.

'Do you want to go downstairs for a bite of supper?' Vera asked Linda about two hours later. 'They'll be having sandwiches in the drawing room. They're listening to the wireless. There's a programme of Christmas Carols from the concert hall in Broadcasting House.'

'No, I'd better stay here a little longer.'

Clara had gone to bed straight after the meal they had shared and it hadn't taken her long to fall asleep.

'Do you think so? I mean, she looks all right to me. And anyway, why wouldn't she be?'

Linda felt uneasy. When they had first arrived home, Florian had taken her aside and told her quietly not to tell anyone that his grandmother had gone carol singing without her coat on and that they'd had to search the village for her. He made it sound as if they would all be in trouble, Stevens, Linda and Florian himself, but Linda believed the burden of guilt was hers alone.

'And in any case,' Florian had added, 'you would only upset my parents, and they've got enough to worry about lately. An elder son who has become almost totally uncommunicative, a daughter who is insisting on a grand wedding and yet has whole days when she gives the impression that she doesn't want to marry at all, and then there's me.'

'What's wrong with you?' Linda asked.

'Everything, as far as my parents are concerned. I don't want to join the family firm and I want to be a writer. In fact I'm more like a changeling than a real Hylton. Not very satisfactory at all.'

They had had no time to discuss this further, and now Linda felt that she must comply with Florian's wishes.

'I'm a little tired,' she told Vera and that wasn't altogether untrue. 'It will be nice to sit here

184

quietly for a while. And I'm not hungry – really.'
'Well, if you change your mind just ring for me.'
'I will, I promise.'

Chapter Ten

Linda made sure that Clara Hylton was sleeping, then she sank into one of the armchairs by the fire. She stretched out one leg to hook her foot round the curved leg of the little footstool and pulled it towards her. Then she put her feet up, leaned back and closed her eyes. She would have liked to have gone down to listen to the Christmas carols on the wireless, but her enjoyment would have been spoilt by worrying about Clara. No, it was better to stay here.

There was a sudden spit and sizzle from the fire and Linda opened her eyes. The fire sparked again and Linda realized it must be raining. Or more likely, snowing, and stray snowflakes were finding their way down the chimney. The first fall had been in early December and had been deep enough to cause all kinds of problems. Mr Hylton and Rupert had had great difficulty getting into Newcastle to work, so on some nights, particularly if they'd been working late, they had stayed in a hotel. The builders who had been hired to renovate Green Leas had not been able to get there, and Emerald and Cordelia began to fret and worry that the house would not be ready in time for the wedding.

Cordelia had insisted that she wanted to go to Green Leas to make sure that the heavy falls of snow had not damaged the roof or brought the guttering down. Her mother had tried to dissuade her, even though Cordelia was obviously fretting. One morning when the sun was visible in a hazy sky and there was no sign of snow clouds, Emerald capitulated. Paul Stevens had put a snow shovel in the boot of the Rolls, made sure there were rugs, a hamper of food and a thermos flask of hot tea, and they had set off after breakfast, not to return until late that night.

Emerald had been out of her mind with worry. She was convinced that they had ended up in a snowdrift. When she could bear waiting no longer, she hurried into the library with Clara and Linda trailing in her wake and she had telephoned the hotel in Newcastle where William Hylton and Rupert were staying. She was told that they were not there, that they had gone to the cinema; the receptionist didn't know which one. Emerald was seriously considering phoning every picture house in Newcastle when her mother-in-law took charge.

'Sit down, Emerald,' she said forcefully. Most reluctantly, Emerald allowed herself to be led away from the desk in the library and gently pushed down into a chair by the fire. 'What would you achieve by phoning the cinemas?' Clara asked her.

'They could put a message up on the screen,' Emerald said. 'They do that, don't they?'

Clara remained standing. 'And what would that message say?'

'It would tell William to phone home.'

'And then?'

'It's obvious, isn't it? I'd ask him to come and look for Cordelia.'

Clara sighed. 'Darling, you're not thinking straight. Tell me, why are William and Rupert staying in Newcastle?'

Emerald stared up at her. Her eyes filled with tears. 'Because the roads are too bad for them to come home.'

'Exactly. And that's probably why Cordelia isn't home yet. But don't worry. It won't help anyone if you get into a state, will it?'

'No,' Emerald said miserably.

'Deep breathing, darling. There's a good girl. Now remember, Stevens is a very good driver. I'm sure he won't take any risks, and I'm sure he'll get our girl home safely.'

Before sitting down herself, she pulled the bell rope, and when Vera appeared she ordered a pot of tea for three. Then she looked across at Linda, who was still standing by the desk. 'If you open that second drawer on the right-hand side you'll find a bottle of whisky. A teaspoonful in each cup is just what we need. Bring it over and pull up a chair for yourself. The three of us will sit this out together.'

Soon the three became four. Florian, who had been writing in his room, came downstairs to see if there was any supper on the go, and when he found them sitting in the library he joined them.

'Why don't we stay here and eat by the fire?' he said.

'You don't really think I could eat anything at a time like this?' Emerald said.

187

'The boy's right,' Clara told her. 'We'll get Saunders to bring some cold cuts and the rest of that game pie, and with any luck Cordelia will be home before we've finished it.'

Clara Hylton was right. Not much later the door opened and Cordelia hurried in. The fur collar of her coat was pulled up to frame her face. Her cheeks were flushed and her eyes were sparkling. She looks like a Russian princess, Linda thought. Or like Greta Garbo in the film *Anna Karenina*. Anna's face glowed with rapture like that when she had been with Count Vronsky.

'Oh, it's so cold out there!' Cordelia gave a mock shudder. 'But how cosy you four look. Shall I come and join you?'

'Thank God you're home,' Emerald said. 'We've been so worried about you.'

Cordelia looked penitent. 'You must have been, and I'm sorry. But the driving conditions are foul – almost impossible. If Stevens wasn't such a good driver we wouldn't be home yet.'

'I suggest you take your coat off and come and sit by the fire,' Clara said. 'Your mother has fretted herself into a state of exhaustion and I'm weary too, so we'll go to bed. Linda and Florian will stay with you while you have something to eat. There's plenty of food left, but you might like to ring for a fresh pot of tea or coffee.'

Cordelia shrugged off her coat, tossing it carelessly over the back of a chair. When Clara and Emerald rose to go, Cordelia kissed them goodnight. 'Why don't you go off to bed too, Florian,' she said. 'Then Linda and I can talk girl stuff.'

'Girl stuff?'

'Oh, you know, wedding dresses, floral arrangements, all that sort of thing.'

'I surrender,' Florian said. He grinned. 'In the face of such an onslaught I shall beat a hasty retreat!'

The brother and sister smiled at each other affectionately, then Florian said, 'Goodnight, ladies,' and he left the room.

Cordelia pulled the bell rope before flopping into one of the armchairs.

After a minute or two it was Pamela who answered the summons.

'You took your time, Hawkins,' Cordelia said.

The answer was a tight-lipped grimace.

'Bring me a pot of hot coffee – enough for two.'

'You could have said "Please",' Linda told her when the unhappy housemaid had gone.

'I know, but her attitude brings out the worst in me, whereas you, my darling, bring out the best.'

'Do I?'

'Why the frown?'

'We were very worried about you tonight.'

'Please don't scold.'

'I'm not scolding, but I wonder if it crossed your mind how concerned we would be.'

'I couldn't help the weather or the state of the roads, could I?'

'No, of course not, but I don't believe that you could not have been home sooner.'

Pamela came back with the coffee and they both remained silent until she had cleared the used cups and plates onto a tray and left the room again. Cordelia took her time before she responded.

'I won't lie to you, Linda. I respect you too much. Paul and I stayed at Green Leas as long as we could. We wanted to be together.'

'You must have been freezing!'

'No. Paul had smuggled logs into the car. He lit a fire in the drawing room and we spread a blanket and had a picnic. It was so romantic. We lay in each other's arms. Oh, Linda, I didn't want to come home.' There was a catch in her voice and tears began to stream down her cheeks. Suddenly she got up and knelt down on the floor beside Linda's chair. She reached for Linda's hands. 'Don't look so shocked. I couldn't bear to have you disapprove of me.'

Linda was at a loss. 'I don't disapprove. At least, I don't think I do. I just think you're being unwise.'

'Unwise? What sort of word is that? Oh, Linda, don't you sympathize with me just a tiny bit?'

'Yes, I do. But you've made your mind up to marry Charlie and yet you still want to spend time with Paul. And in the house where you will live with your husband. That's why I looked shocked.'

Cordelia let go of Linda's hands and knelt back. 'Yes, and no doubt I shall feel thoroughly ashamed of myself once I'm a respectable married woman, but until then I can't promise you that I won't do it again.' She looked utterly drained.

'You don't have to promise me anything,' Linda said. 'I'm not your mother or your grandmother, nor even your sister.'

'But you're my friend, aren't you? At least I hope you are.'

'Then let me tell you as a friend that I think you

should stop seeing Paul immediately.'

'Immediately? That's harsh.'

'But better in the long run.'

Cordelia sighed deeply. 'I know.'

'For Paul's sake as well as your own.'

'You're right, and I'll try to put an end to it, really I will. But thank the Lord I have you to talk to. If I didn't I think I would go crazy.'

They hadn't talked much after that, but both of them, it seemed, were reluctant to leave the comfort of the fireside. Cordelia retreated to her armchair again and drank whisky as she stared moodily into the fire. When the fire began to die down she would have rung for someone to make it up again, but Linda stopped her.

'It's after midnight,' she said. 'They'll all be in bed. The only person who will hear the bell will be Bobby in his little room next to the kitchen. Let him sleep. If you want to stay here any longer I'm perfectly capable of putting more coal on the fire.'

'No, it's all right. We should go to bed.'

They both rose and Cordelia kissed Linda's cheek before saying goodnight.

Later, lying in bed, Linda remembered those days when as a child she had looked in through the windows and marvelled at the lives of the people who lived in what to her was an enchanted dwelling. She had longed to be able to step through the window like Alice had stepped through the looking glass and become one of the family. Well, now she was here, and although she was not a Hylton they had made her welcome as naturally as if it had been meant to be. As if they had been wishing for her to arrive, she thought fancifully, as much as she had wanted to be there.

It was only a moment or two before she drifted off to sleep that night that it had crossed her mind that Cordelia had not, at any point, thought to consider Paul's feelings.

'Linda, are you still here?'

Linda came back to the present to see Clara Hylton struggling to sit up in bed.

'Yes, I'm here.' She rose and went over to the bed. 'Can I get you anything?'

'Yes. Water. A glass of water. I feel awfully hot.'

'Do you?' Linda poured some water from the carafe and Clara drank it thirstily. 'Slow down,' Linda said. 'It's not good to gulp it like that.'

'I know, Nanny, I'm sorry. It will make me sick.'

Linda glanced at her quickly. Did Clara really think she was a child again, speaking to her nursemaid, or was she having fun?

'Got you!' Clara said and burst out laughing. The laughter soon turned into a ragged cough. Clara reached out and grasped Linda's hand.

'Should I go and get Mrs Hylton?' Linda asked when the coughing subsided.

'Why? What could Emerald do?'

'She may wish to call the doctor.'

'Poor man. Drag him out on a night like this? No, Linda, ring and ask the kitchen for some warm milk and honey. And there are some Beecham's powders in the bathroom cabinet. That should bring my temperature down and ease my throat as well. Why are you looking at me like that?'

'I really think you should see the doctor.'

'And I forbid you to call him.'

They glared at each other for a moment and then Clara said, 'Shall we at least give the Beecham's powders a try? I promise you, if I'm no better in the morning you can call whoever you like.'

Clara was getting agitated, so Linda decided not to quarrel with her. Thankfully it was Vera rather than Pamela who answered the bell, and she came back in next to no time with the warm milk. Meanwhile Linda had found the Beecham's powders. Clara took the medication and drank her milk like an obedient child. It wasn't long before she was asleep.

Without being asked, Vera returned with a plate of sandwiches and a cup of cocoa for Linda. 'I thought I'd better,' she said. 'It doesn't look as though you're coming down tonight.'

Linda sat with Clara for nearly an hour, and when she saw that she was breathing evenly decided she could go to bed herself. Once in her room she remembered that Florian had said that he would wait up for her. She checked Clara again and then went quietly downstairs and into the drawing room.

At first she wasn't sure if Florian was there. The overhead light and the lamps had been switched off, and the only illumination came from the dying fire and the Christmas tree. The tree, standing by the bay window, was very tall. The upper point of the shining star on its apex touched the ceiling. Tree lights glowed from the branches; the acorn-shaped bulbs of red, blue, yellow and green reflecting on the tinsel streamers and the glass baubles. The wonderful smell of fresh pine pervaded the room, drawing Linda towards the tree.

'Linda,' a voice said softly.

She stopped where she was and drew her breath in. 'Florian?'

'Did I startle you? Sorry.'

'Where are you?'

'Behind the tree, on the window seat.'

As he spoke, she saw his figure emerge and start walking towards her.

'What were you doing there?' she asked, but she was smiling when she added, 'Were you hiding in order to frighten me?'

'No, just hiding.'

'I don't understand. Who else would you hide from at this time of night?'

'No one in particular. Just the world, I suppose. Wondering what all this is about and what I'm doing here.' He laughed. 'Don't worry, I'm not going to go all metaphysical on you. Can't have you thinking I'm a pretentious little twerp.'

'I don't think that at all.'

'No, you don't, do you? I think you are the only person in this house that takes me seriously. The only person who believes that I can succeed as a writer.'

'I believe you should be given the chance.'

'Dear Linda. Always honest. That's not exactly an endorsement, is it?'

'I don't know whether you could succeed or not. How could I? I know nothing about the world of publishing. But in my opinion you are a very good writer, and that's why I think you should be given the chance. Although...'

'You're going to say something I don't like.'

'Not all writers who have succeeded have been free from having to earn a living.'

'You think I should buckle down and join the family firm, and write when I come home at night and all day Sunday?'

'Some people do.'

'I know. And if needs be that's exactly what I will do. But you can't blame me for wanting to take the easier option, can you?'

'No, I don't blame you.'

'Then come and sit behind the tree with me. Let us both escape from this cruel world for a moment or two.'

'Is there room there for two of us?'

'Come and see.'

Florian took her hand and pulled her towards the tree. As they brushed past it they made some of the branches tremble and set the little silver bells tinkling. Florian sat on the velvet cushioned window seat and drew her down beside him. She shivered.

'Are you cold?' he asked.

'There's a draught from the window.'

Florian moved the curtain aside. 'The window's closed,' he said. 'But the glass is cold. That's what it is.' He closed the curtains again and put his arm around Linda. 'I'll keep you warm,' he said. 'Snuggle up.'

Here in this enchanted world of fairy lights and sparkling tinsel it seemed quite natural to snuggle up to Florian, even though they had never been so close before. Since he had returned from Scotland, Florian had sought her out whenever he

195

could, and it hadn't taken long for them to slip back into the old easy relationship they'd had as children.

But they had hardly ever been alone together. They had talked at the dining table, in the drawing room after meals, and in Clara's room where he would come in the pretence of wanting to talk to his grandmother. This was not entirely dishonest because, once there, he devoted himself to Clara so much that she had no idea that it was Linda he really wanted to be with.

Now they were completely alone together in a house where everybody else was sleeping, and it seemed that the novelty of it had rendered them both speechless. Linda sensed that Florian, usually so self-confident, was feeling unsure of himself. This was unfamiliar ground for both of them.

'It's magical, isn't it?' he whispered at last.

'Magical?'

'Being here together in this little world of fairy lights and silver bells. Please say you feel the same way.'

Linda thought for a moment. 'I think I do.'

'Only think so, Linda? What is it you're not sure about? Don't you like being here?'

'I do.'

'Then perhaps you don't like being here with me.'

'Oh, I do, really I do. It's just that ... just that ... oh, I don't know...'

Florian held her more tightly for a moment and then let her go, but only to take her face in both his hands. Then, moving towards her, he kissed her, softly, gently, lingeringly, and long enough to

196

arouse in Linda a nameless and unbearably sweet yearning for some kind of mysterious fulfilment.

When they drew apart she told him reluctantly that she would have to go, to see if his grandmother was all right.

'I'll come with you,' he said. 'But I must put these lights out. Go on ahead.'

Halfway up the stairs he caught up with her, and when they reached Clara's room he stayed only long enough to make sure that his grandmother was sleeping soundly. 'Goodnight, Linda,' he whispered and, making no attempt to kiss her again, he closed the door quietly behind him.

Linda went to her own room but she left both bathroom doors open so that she would hear if Clara called out to her.

The fire was burning low and the bed luxuriously comfortable. As Linda pulled the bedclothes up, the smell of fresh pine and the tinkle of silver bells seemed to surround her and take her once more to that magic world behind the Christmas tree. A world in which Florian had taken her in his arms and kissed her lingeringly and tenderly. Perhaps dreams really could come true.

Next morning she woke to hear the sound of Vera seeing to the fire. 'I didn't knock,' Vera said. 'I was hoping not to wake you. My goodness, you look dreadful.'

'Thank you.'

Vera laughed. 'No, you're as bonny as ever. I meant that you look as if you've hardly slept a wink.'

'I did sleep. But I kept waking up thinking I'd

197

heard Mrs Hylton coughing.'

'And was she?'

'No. I went in at one stage and she was sleeping peacefully.'

'As she is now. I've already seen to her fire. Look, why don't you treat yourself to a lovely deep bath? I've got to stay up here and see to the other fires, seeing Pamela hasn't deigned to get up yet.'

'Is she ill again?'

'So she said last night. An excruciating head-ache. That was her way of putting it. If only she knew what a headache she is to the rest of us.'

'You didn't believe her?'

'Actually, I did. The lass looked dreadful. All pasty-faced and baggy-eyed. I knocked on her door when I got up this morning and when she didn't answer I went along to the kitchen for breakfast. Mrs Aslett said to leave her a little longer, that she would go and wake her up when she started on breakfast for the family.'

Linda grinned. 'I didn't think Mrs Aslett was so soft-hearted.'

'She's not. Not really, but even she has noticed that Pamela has been suffering lately, and it's her job to look after the staff as well as the family. But we're wasting time. You go for your bath and I'll keep popping along to have a look at Mrs Charles.'

'Would you?' Linda threw the bedclothes aside and got out of bed. 'That's marvellous but I'd rather go out for a walk.'

Vera looked astonished. 'In this weather?'

Linda pulled her curtains open. 'Look – the sun is shining and there's not a snow cloud in sight. Fresh air is what I need.'

'Rather you than me. But if you've made your mind up, then wrap up warm. You'll find plenty of wellingtons in the boot room. Something there should fit you.'

'Are you mollycoddling me, Vera?'

'Maybe I am. Someone should.'

'What do you mean by that?'

'Never mind. Just go and clean your teeth and whatever else you do and get yourself out from under my feet.'

'Thanks, I will.' Linda grabbed her clothes and hurried into the bathroom. Within minutes she was heading downstairs to the boot room and then out into a world made pristine by snow.

Linda headed for the woods. The wellington boots she had borrowed sank into the un-trampled snow almost to their rims. The dark, leafless branches of the trees ahead contrasted starkly with the snow. At first glance the wood appeared to be dead, but Linda knew that it was merely sleeping; like the hibernating woodland animals, it was waiting quietly for the spring sun to bring it into leaf again.

While she was walking a blustery wind sprang up, lifting the surface flakes of snow and hurrying them ahead of her. When she reached the trees there was no real shelter. Linda remembered a poem she had learned at school.

When winter winds are piercing chill,
And through the hawthorn blows the gale,
With solemn feet I tread the hill,
That overbrows the lonely vale.

199

She recalled how that poem had made her aware of how lonely she was and how sad it had made her feel. This morning, although the wind was certainly chill and the air cold enough to coat the hawthorn trees with ice, Linda was far from sad. She looked at the one splash of colour visible just a short walk into the wood: a holly tree. Still green and heavily berried, to Linda this was the very symbol of Christmas. She turned and looked back at Fernwood, its silhouette bold and confident against the winter sky.

She laughed as she retraced her steps by stepping into the imprints she had made on the outward journey. Linda hurried back towards the house she could now call home.

'For God's sake, Graham, do you have to go to work on Christmas Eve?'

Graham had just got the fire going in the breakfast room when his wife appeared behind him. Sonya had been sleeping when he got out of bed and was still asleep by the time he had finished in the bathroom. He didn't expect her to get up and lay the fire. She didn't have a clue how to do it. Nor did he expect her to make his breakfast. He was perfectly capable of brewing a pot of tea and burning a slice of toast in their new de luxe automatic toaster which had cost him twenty-seven and sixpence at Parrish's on Shields Road.

The trouble was that he hadn't mastered the art of cutting the bread into slices thin enough to fit into the pop-up mechanism, so usually all that popped up was a haze of blue smoke and the smell of burning bread. He would fish this out

200

with a knife – remembering to turn the toaster off first – and then scrape the blackened bread until it resembled something that could be spread with butter and marmalade.

On the days that he burnt the toast he was careful to hold the toaster upside down over the sink in the kitchen and shake the crumbs out. Then, like a guilty schoolboy, he would turn the tap on and wash them away. Then he would enjoy his breakfast as much as he could, hoping that Sonya would never know.

This morning she would be here to watch him. If there's enough milk left, I'll settle for a bowl of cornflakes, he thought. He went through to the kitchen to wash his hands and Sonya followed him.

'It's like something from Dickens,' Sonya continued her complaint. *'A Christmas Carol.* Old Mr Hylton is Scrooge and you're Bob Scratchit.'

'Cratchit,' Graham said. 'The character's name is Cratchit.'

Sonya scowled and pulled her pale green satin robe more tightly round her body then retied the sash, pulling it viciously. 'Know-all,' she said sulkily.

'Want a cup of tea?' he asked as he spooned tea into the teapot.

'I suppose so.'

He filled the pot with boiling water and they returned to the breakfast room, where Sonya sat and waited while Graham got the cups and saucers and the milk and sugar. She reached into the pocket of her robe for a packet of Craven A. 'Light me,' she said.

'I wish you wouldn't.'

'Wouldn't what?'

'Smoke so early in the morning. Smoke at all if it comes to that.'

'Oh, Graham you're not going to scold me, are you? Not on Christmas Eve.'

Graham laughed at the way she pouted, giving the impression of a little girl who has been unfairly scolded. No matter how unreasonable Sonya could be, how impossible to live with, there were still moments when he responded to her charm. She was beautiful, and her tawny hair and green eyes, her tall, voluptuous figure, made her almost unbearably sexually attractive.

He lit her cigarette using the box of matches from the kitchen bench, placed the cut-glass ashtray on the table before her and then poured her a cup of tea. 'Join me in some cornflakes?' he asked.

She shook her head and said with a grin. 'Too scared to make toast?'

They both laughed.

At moments like this it was easy to remember how happy they had been. How much in love and how much pleasure they had taken in each other's company; in each other's bodies. When had they stopped loving each other? For although they hadn't acknowledged it yet, that was the state of affairs. There had been no one moment when Graham had looked at this beautiful woman and thought that she was no longer the woman he wanted to spend the rest of his life with.

And what about Sonya? Had she woken up one morning and realized in the cold light of dawn that no matter how tumultuous and satisfying their lovemaking had been the night before, this man had disappointed her, that the sort of life she wanted to live was slipping away from her day by day and leaving her more and more frustrated?

'I'll try to come home early,' Graham said placatingly.

'Humph!'

'Why humph?'

'Your idea of early and mine are far from similar. I don't see why they couldn't let everybody go home at lunchtime today. That's what some firms do.'

'Maybe not at lunchtime, but I'm sure I'll be able to leave soon after.'

'Mind you do, because you've got to pop into town and collect your dinner suit from Moss Bros.'

Graham stared at her uncomprehendingly.

'You've forgotten, haven't you? You've forgotten that we're going to the Dinner Dance at the Grand.'

'The Grand?'

'As in Hotel. As in Tynemouth. Margery and Ken are coming too, and you're giving them a lift.'

'Oh, yes. I remember.'

'Well, try to look more enthusiastic. The food will be good and they've got a terrific dance band.'

'But I can't dance. As you never fail to remind me.'

'You're not that bad. But in any case, it doesn't matter. I shall dance with Ken and you can keep poor Margery company.'

'Why poor Margery?'

'Two left feet. It's a wonder Ken ever got hooked

203

up with her.'

'She's very attractive.' Graham was moved to defend Margery for no other reason than that Sonya had been so dismissive of a woman who was supposed to be her friend.

'I suppose so,' Sonya said, narrowing her eyes as she breathed out a cloud of tobacco smoke. 'And she's stylish, I'll give her that. But then Ken encourages her to spend as much as she likes on her clothes and her hair. Since his promotion to head sales rep, he likes them to be seen as a classy couple.'

'Anywhere but on the dance floor,' Graham said. 'Still, he'll have you to partner him tonight, and I'll be quite happy to sit and talk to poor Margery.'

Sonya took one last drag of her cigarette and then stubbed it out in the ashtray. 'Good.' She headed for the door and then turned to face him. 'Oh, and while you're in town, grab a sandwich or a snack, will you? I won't have time to make a meal before we go. That would be pointless, anyway, seeing we'll be having a four-course dinner later.'

Graham took the dirty dishes through to the kitchen and was just about to wash them but decided not to. Give her something to do, he thought. God knows she does little enough. Mrs Slater comes in to clean and do the washing and ironing, and Sonya's idea of cooking a meal is to open a tin. So when she said she won't have time to make a meal tonight it's because she will happily spend hours bathing and doing her hair and her make-up.

And the result will be sensational. Glamorous and fashionable and much more stylish than her friend Margery or any other woman at the Grand Hotel that night. Every man there will think I'm the luckiest chap in the world. I used to think that once. Sonya hasn't changed. I have.

So it's up to me to make the best of it. To go cheerfully to the Christmas Eve ball and enjoy the four-course meal, the complimentary bottle of wine, the party hats, the streamers and the dance music. I'll talk about the latest movies to Margery and I'll even join the drunken line doing the conga. And when the time comes I shall insist on dancing the last waltz with my wife, no matter how poor a partner she thinks me.

Completely unbidden, the thought of Linda Bellwood sprang to mind. Graham remembered how at home he had felt with her in her house in Redesburn and how he hadn't wanted to leave her. I wonder what Linda will be doing tonight, he thought. For even though I have no right to feel so protective, I couldn't bear the thought of her being disappointed, or of anyone hurting her or letting her down. I can only hope that Christmas at Fernwood Hall, with the family she so obviously adores, will live up to her expectations.

Chapter Eleven

Linda stood on the doormat and held the wellingtons at arm's length in front of her then knocked them together to dislodge the snow. Immediately the wind blew it back in her face. Laughing at herself and blinking furiously in order to dislodge the snowflakes from her eyelashes, she stepped back and closed the door. She returned the wellingtons to the boot room and started along the passage that led to the grand entrance hall, but as she passed the closed kitchen door she heard raised voices. Curious, she paused and listened.

'Why didn't you tell me earlier, you stupid boy?' Ivy Aslett scolded. Linda guessed the stupid boy would be Bobby.

'I thought you must know. I mean, no one goes anywhere without your say-so, do they?'

'It seems they do!'

'Calm down, Ivy,' that was her husband, Albert. 'You know what they say. It's no use crying over spilt milk. We'll just have to manage without her.'

'I don't know what Mrs. William will say,' Ivy continued. 'I wouldn't be surprised if this sets off her palpitations, and we don't want her having a heart attack. Not on Christmas Eve.'

'We don't want her having a heart attack at any time, do we, Ivy love, but that's not going to happen. She's had this condition all her life and she hasn't had a heart attack yet, has she?'

This was the first Linda knew about Emerald Hylton having a heart condition. Then she remembered following her upstairs when she had first arrived at Fernwood and being surprised that a relatively young woman had had to stop and grip the banister rail. And the night Cordelia had come home so late, Clara had told Emerald to sit down and take deep breaths. These were signs she should have noticed.

'I'll tell her if you like,' that was Bobby's voice.

'You?' Ivy was scornful. 'And will you also tell her that you watched the young madam drive away early this morning and never thought to come and let us know?'

'Don't be hard on the lad,' her husband said. 'Let's carry on as best we can. Starting with breakfasts.'

'Right-ho. But don't just sit there. Vera is still upstairs seeing to the fires. One of you had better go and tell her that Hawkins has done a bunk. And all those guests coming here for dinner tonight!'

Linda heard a chair scrape over the stone-flagged floor and, feeling embarrassed about having eavesdropped, she hurried along the passage and through the green baize covered door into the hall.

'There you are.' Vera had just come downstairs and she hurried towards her. 'I looked out and saw you coming back to the house. The old girl's still asleep, so I wanted to catch you and tell you to have a proper breakfast before you go up to her. Now hurry along to the dining room. I'll see if Ivy's got the porridge ready.'

'Wait – Vera...' It was too late.

The door to the domestic area had opened and Bobby was standing there beckoning Vera towards him. The older woman hurried away and the door closed behind them. Linda wondered what she should do. It didn't take her long to realize that she could do nothing at all. Although she would be willing to help in any way she could, she must wait until she was asked. Vera had told her to go to the dining room, so that was where she went. There was no one there. Mr Hylton and Rupert had stayed in Newcastle the night before and it was too early for anyone else to appear, except maybe Florian.

Vera hurried in with a bowl of porridge. 'Sorry if I've kept you waiting, pet, but Ivy Aslett's in a right state. Would you believe that little madam, Pamela, has done a flit? First thing this morning she drove off in a taxi and never even left a note of explanation.'

Linda knew all this but was reluctant to admit to it. She asked, 'Did anyone see her go?'

'The lad. He thought he heard something and looked out of his bedroom window. The taxi had come to the back door and Pamela must have been standing in the doorway waiting, because Bobby didn't hear a knock. Anyway, she passed a couple of cases to the taxi driver – hope she didn't take the family silver!' Vera laughed. 'As I said, gave the driver her cases then closed the door and got in herself. And that was that. Well, she won't be getting any references, that's for sure.'

'I wonder what she will do if she can't work?'

'God knows. She must have friends that we don't know about. She doesn't strike me as the type who would settle for a life of hardship. Anyway, you eat your porridge before it gets cold. Do you want bacon and eggs?'

Remembering Mrs Aslett's harassed tones, Linda said, 'No thank you. Toast and coffee will do very nicely.'

Linda enjoyed her breakfast even more when she realized that Vera had called her pet rather than Miss Bellwood.

'I said no good would come of this.'

Clara Hylton was sitting up in bed drinking coffee. Once her breakfast tray had been removed she had asked Linda to comb her hair, but her face was free of make-up and Linda thought she looked unnaturally pale.

'Would come of what, Grandmamma?'

'You know very well what I mean, Florian. Taking Jack Delafontaine's daughter in and expecting her to be happy in service. Your mother is very unworldly sometimes, you know.'

'She means well.'

'Yes, I know she does, and I'm very fond of her. That's why I'm so upset about the girl leaving us in the lurch on the day of the Christmas Eve dinner party.' Clara sipped her coffee and spluttered as she began to cough. Linda took her cup and offered her a large clean handkerchief. 'Don't look at me like that,' Clara said crossly.

'Like what?'

'As if I'm some sort of invalid. I've got a foul head cold, that's all it is.'

'Of course it is, Grandmamma,' Florian soothed. 'And there's no need to worry about the dinner party. Saunders has a friend living in the village, a married woman who likes to earn a little extra now and then doing domestic work. Stevens was sent for her and she's downstairs already polishing the silver.'

Clara frowned. 'That doesn't reassure me. I mean, what sort of domestic work has she done? She could be a charwoman.'

'Don't fret,' Florian said. 'Ena Johnson has helped out at the house of the Lord Lieutenant himself. She won't let us down.'

'How do you know all this?' his grandmother asked. 'You always know the gossip, don't you?'

'It's because I'm a writer. It's a writer's business to know about people and what they do.'

'Well, off you go and write something, darling, because I'm tired and I must get some beauty sleep before the party tonight.'

'But–' Florian began.

Linda held up a hand to silence him. 'That's right,' she said. She leaned over the bed and made the pillows more comfortable. 'Try to have a good rest.'

Clara settled down and then opened her eyes wide. She reached for Linda's hand. 'Nanny – will you stay with me?'

'Of course I will. Florian, would you draw the curtains?'

A few moments later Clara was asleep. Linda and Florian went to sit by the fire, the only source of light.

'What's this about going down for dinner to-night?' Florian asked. 'Surely she's not well enough?'

'No she isn't, but it would have upset her to tell her so. Hopefully she will forget about it.'

'And she called you "Nanny". Was that a joke?'

'Sometimes it is and she knows very well what she's doing.'

'And what *is* she doing?'

'Teasing me. But sometimes I wonder if she really has gone back to her childhood.'

'Poor Grandmamma. And poor Linda.'

'Why do you say that?'

'If my grandmother can't come to the party you

will have to stay here and look after her.'

'I don't mind that at all.'

'You might have found our guests interesting.'

'Tell me about them.'

'Well, you've already met Charlie and his parents, but not the Lord Lieutenant and his wife, or Alma Arness, the esteemed and decidedly eccentric poet, or Stanley Carson, the American businessman who made a fortune selling liver powders and bought a castle in Northumberland.'

'And does he have a wife?'

'Most certainly. He's had two or three, in fact. The present Mrs Carson was a dancer – a Goldwyn Girl – can you believe that?'

'Why shouldn't I?'

'It's such a cliché, isn't it? Self-made millionaire on trip home to America goes to a show on Broadway and falls hook, line and sinker for a beautiful blonde dancer.'

'What happened to whoever was Mrs Carson at the time?'

'Loretta? No need to grieve for her. Stanley can afford to be very generous to his ex-wives. I've heard she's living in the South of France, happily married to her tennis coach.'

Linda burst out laughing and immediately looked over to the bed to see if she had disturbed Clara.

They stayed quiet for a moment and Florian got up and tiptoed over to the bed. After a moment he returned and said quietly, 'It's all right. She's still in dreamland.' He knelt down and, using the tongs, he carefully placed more coal on the fire. Then he sat back on the hearthrug and leaned back against the chair he had been sitting in. 'Why did you laugh just now?'

'It's like a cast of characters in a detective novel, isn't it?'

'What do you mean?'

'The guest list for tonight's dinner party. The Lord Lieutenant and his wife, the poet, the rich businessman and Goldwyn Girl wife–'

'Not forgetting the young engaged couple and two sets of doting parents!' Florian entered into the spirit of the conversation. 'And there's an older brother who has been acting rather mysteriously of late.'

'Do you mean Rupert?'

'I do.'

'In what way mysterious?'

Florian frowned. 'It's hard to say. Nothing in particular. Just that he's been a little withdrawn ... acting as though he had something on his mind. What do you think?'

'I don't know him well enough to be able to form an opinion.'

Florian was silent for a moment and then he shook his head and smiled. 'Well, whatever is bothering him I'm sure he will sort it out as efficiently as he always does. But the question that should concern us is, who is going to murder who?'

'Murder?'

'In this detective story. And who will the detective be?'

'Oh, you had better be the detective. The handsome young writer who solves crimes and then writes bestselling novels about them.'

'Do you really think that, Linda? That I'm handsome?' Florian looked at Linda intently.

'Of course you are, and you must know it.' Linda suddenly felt shy.

'Perhaps I do. It's just that I've always been somewhat overshadowed by Rupert, who looks rather like a film star, don't you think? What you call a hearthrob. And is athletic and clever to boot. He's the perfect son, isn't he?'

'Is that what you think?'

'I do.'

'And would you wish to be more like him?'

'Never!'

'There you are then. There's no need to be at all envious of him.'

Florian laughed softly. 'You're very wise, Linda, and very good for me.'

He stood up and, leaning over, he took her hands and pulled her up into his arms. This time when he kissed her he was more assured. Linda found it natural to put her arms around him and return his kiss. When the kiss was over they stared into each other's eyes wonderingly.

'I think I'm in love with you,' Florian said.

'No! No! No! What is happening here?' They turned, startled, as Clara struggled to sit up and fumbled to switch on her bedside light. 'How dare you?' she said. 'How dare you try to entrap my brother? The son of the house. He can never marry you. You are only a servant. I shall tell Papa and have you dismissed immediately.'

Gasping for breath, Clara took hold of the bedclothes with both hands and gripped them tightly. Florian hurried over to the bed.

'Grandmamma,' he said, 'it's me, Florian. I'm not your brother, I'm your grandson and this is Linda.' He turned and beckoned Linda to join him. He took her hand. 'Look,' he said. 'This isn't your nanny. You are not a little girl any more. This is Linda, your companion.'

Clara stared at them uncomprehendingly for a moment and then sank back into the pillows. Her breathing became less erratic and she closed her eyes. Linda and Florian waited anxiously until they thought she had gone to sleep again. They were just about to walk away when Clara Hylton said, 'A companion she may be, but she's still a servant.'

Linda turned and fled through the interconnecting bathroom to her own room. Florian followed her.

'Don't be upset,' he said. 'She's old and she's muddled. She's living in a different age – the last century.'

'Do you think so?'

'Of course I do. Now, I'm going to get Ena Johnson to come and keep an eye on her, and you and I are going down to lunch.'

'They won't thank you for it.'

'Won't thank me for what?'

'For tearing Mrs Johnson away from polishing the silver.'

'I'll set the lad onto that. Now, come on, no excuses. And I guarantee when Grandmamma wakes up she'll have forgotten all this nonsense about servants not marrying the son of the house. And if I was to tell her that I wanted to marry you, I'm sure she'd be delighted.'

214

Linda wanted to believe him. When she had arrived at Fernwood the whole family had welcomed her. Clara more than anyone had treated her like a friend. Did she mind being thought of as a servant? She realized that she did. But not because of any snobbish reasons; she felt just as much at home with the Asletts and Vera and the lad. No, it was because she had come to feel that she was one of the family, something she had dreamed about since she was a child.

Lunch had been an informal affair of sandwiches in the drawing room because the dining room was being prepared for the dinner party. Not long after the plates had been cleared away, Mr Hylton had arrived home from Newcastle and he had sought Linda out.

'Florian, I want to talk to Linda. Would you go up and sit with your grandmother,' he said. 'Apparently Mrs Aslett is making a fuss because Mrs Johnson is needed in the kitchen.'

When Florian had gone he turned to Linda and said, 'I'm sorry that your position here is proving so difficult.'

'It's all right, really.'

'No, it isn't all right. We didn't employ you as a nurse. We thought that all my mother needed was a companion.'

'I don't mind, really I don't.'

'Of course you're used to looking after an invalid, aren't you?'

'Yes. My guardian. But do you see your mother as an invalid?'

'I don't know what I see her as.' William Hylton

looked perplexed. 'All I know is that it's obvious that she will have to have proper nursing care. Maybe sooner than we thought.'

'And then you will no longer need me.' Linda made it a statement of fact, but William Hylton must have sensed her dismay.

'Do you like living here?'

'Very much.'

'And we like having you. When the time comes, perhaps you would consider staying on as a companion to my wife.'

'Your wife?'

'Yes. You see, Emerald has always attempted too much. She ... she isn't strong, but it's no use at all telling her to take things easy. She has a sort of nervous energy which compels her to do what she considers her duty. Until now we have coped but – and she will hate me for saying this – she is getting older and her health problems have become more pronounced. Until Cordelia got swept up in the plans for her wedding and her new home, she was some sort of help for her mother, although not always entirely satisfactory.'

William Hylton smiled ruefully and Linda realized, as she had not fully until now, what a kindly man he was.

'From now until the wedding my wife and my daughter will be swept up in a frenzy of preparations, and I would be really grateful if you were to stay and try to instil some calm into the situation. Would you like that?'

'I would. But when the wedding is over?'

'When Cordelia has gone Emerald will be bereft. She will need you more than ever. In the short time you have been here, you have become like one of the family. So what do you say? Will you stay with us? Please say you will.'

'I'll stay for as long as you want me to.'

'Good. I'm glad that's settled. So now would you go up and tell Florian to come down and put his coat and boots on? We're going to clear the drive of snow to make satisfactory parking places for our guests. It will take the four of us – Aslett, the lad, Florian and me.'

'And Rupert?' Linda was surprised that the elder son hadn't been mentioned.

'Rupert took his own car in today and he's stayed in town to do some last-minute Christmas shopping. He promised to be home in time to get ready for the dinner party.'

Florian looked very handsome in his dinner suit and Clara told him so. 'Shall I stay here with you?' he asked his grandmother.

'Stay here? Of course not. I'm just going to have a little nap and then I'll come down and join you. Now off you go.' Clara closed her eyes and seemed to settle down. Then suddenly she opened her eyes wide and sat bolt upright. 'Don't pretend you came here to see me,' she said. 'It's that girl, isn't it? I've told you to stay away from her.'

She was staring in Florian's direction accusingly, but neither Florian nor Linda knew exactly who it was she saw.

'All right, I'll go now.' Florian, usually so self-assured, looked thoroughly disconcerted and uncharacteristically unsure of what to do.

Clara nodded, as if pleased, and settled down

again. Florian and Linda walked to the door. 'Are you all right?' he asked.

'Don't worry. She's old and confused like you said before.'

'All the same, I think I'd better not come to her room for a while.'

'She'll miss you.'

'Who will she miss? Her grandson or her brother?'

'I think this cold she has is making her more confused than usual. Perhaps when she's better...'

'What? What will happen when she's better?'

Linda sighed. 'I don't know. We'll just have to wait and see. Now off you go and enjoy the party.'

'I would enjoy it better if you were coming.' He took her hands and pulled her out of the room.

'What are you doing?' Linda asked.

'I'm going to kiss you. And we mustn't let little Clara see her big brother kissing the nanny, must we?'

Chapter Twelve

Emerald Hylton stood by the bed and looked down at her mother-in-law. 'Let her sleep,' she said. 'If she wakes up and she's hungry you can ring for a tray.' She turned and gave a nervous smile. 'I'm so sorry that this is the way you must spend Christmas Eve. You might have found our guests interesting.' She laughed and for the moment the worry lines eased away.

218

'What's funny?' Linda asked.

They moved away from the bed so that their talking would not wake Clara up.

'This is a duty guest list,' Emerald said. 'Apart from Charlie and his parents, the people who are coming tonight are not close friends of ours. But they are amusing – even if it's not their intention to be.'

'Yes. Florian told me about them.'

'Did he?' Emerald looked mildly surprised.

She looks beautiful, Linda thought. Her evening gown of white silk jersey clung to her figure. The neckline was square and the shoulders were padded. Across the left shoulder there was a spray of blue and black glittery embroidery, and the pattern was repeated at the ends of the sash tied around her waist and falling almost to the hemline.

'Cordelia is disappointed that you won't be joining us. The vain creature thought that as you are so dark and she is so fair the two of you would make a pretty picture in your party clothes.'

Linda thought wistfully of the simple black skirt and beaded velvet evening blouse hanging in her wardrobe.

'You'll have to have something suitable for dinner parties,' Clara Hylton had told her that day in the French Salon.

Linda had never had the occasion to wear an evening gown. In fact, the only time she had glimpsed such exotic apparel was on the screen when she went to the film shows in the village hall. And those impossibly glamorous frocks were all make-believe, weren't they? Confronted with reality in Fenwick's, she had been bewildered by the assortment of shimmering silks and floaty chiffons, crisp, shiny taffeta and luxurious draped lace.

Then she had seen the black velvet blouse, or was it a jacket? It closed at the front with a zip, so she decided it could be worn as either. The short sleeves were slightly puffed and the front of the blouse was covered with a beaded design of tiny coral and turquoise beads. The skirt was quite plain. Clara had been delighted with her choice and had insisted on buying a coral and turquoise necklace to fill in the square neckline and, on discovering that Linda's ears were not pierced, a pair of matching clip-on earrings.

'What is Cordelia going to wear?' Linda asked. 'She wouldn't tell me. She said I had to wait and see.'

'Well, wait no longer! Here I am.'

Cordelia floated into the room in a cloud of white organza. The huge puff sleeves and the entire bodice were scattered with tiny, sparkling crystals. Not a princess now, but a queen, Linda thought. The Snow Queen in the fairy story. All she needs is a diamond headdress. Somehow Cordelia's next words were no surprise.

'The diamonds,' she said to her mother. 'Do you think I could borrow Grandmamma's diamonds? Will you ask her or shall I?'

Emerald looked across at her mother-in-law, and shook her head. 'I don't want to wake her up. Not when she's sleeping so peacefully.'

Cordelia looked disappointed. 'No, I suppose not. But, you know, I don't think she would mind one little bit if I wore them, do you, Linda?'

'I'm not sure. I didn't even know that she had a diamond necklace.'

'Oh, not just a necklace. She's got the earrings to match, and a brooch and a bracelet, too. They're all a little old-fashioned, of course; when I inherit them I shall have them reset.'

'Cordelia!' Emerald was shocked. 'You mustn't talk like that.'

'I don't see why not. Grandmamma has made it quite plain that her diamonds come to me, just as she will leave money to each of my brothers. Remember when I was just a little girl she used to let me put them on.'

'I know. But now...' Emerald glanced at Clara again, 'It's as if you're expecting her to...'

Cordelia's eyes widened. 'Oh, no. Don't say it. And I'm not expecting that at all. I mean, all that is wrong with her is a cold, isn't it? Linda, what do you say?'

'About your grandmother's state of health or the diamonds?'

'Both.'

'I don't think she's desperately ill, but I do think that she should see a doctor. She doesn't want to, but if she's still like this tomorrow–'

'Christmas Day,' Cordelia said.

'Never mind what day it is, if Linda thinks your grandmother should see a doctor I will call Dr Phillipson tomorrow,' her mother told her. 'And as for the diamonds, she has always indulged you so I imagine she would be pleased to let you wear her necklace tonight.'

'And the earrings.'

'Very well.'

Cordelia opened a drawer in the dressing table and took out a leather-covered jewellery box. When she had put on the necklace and earrings she turned to Linda and said, 'What do you think?'

'Lovely.'

'The necklace or me?'

'Both, you vain creature.'

The girls laughed, and, glancing over at the sleeping form in the bed, Emerald shushed them. 'We'd better go,' she said. 'Linda, I'll send you up a tray.'

'Wait a moment.' Cordelia had found her grandmother's scent bottle and sprayed herself liberally. 'Mmm, Narcisse Noir. It's hard to believe that Grandmamma ever favoured something so voluptuous.'

'She still does,' Emerald said. 'And although I'm sure she would not mind your borrowing her diamonds, she may not be so pleased at your extravagant use of her favourite scent.'

After they had gone the fragrance lingered. The room was warm and suddenly peaceful. Linda sat by the fire with a book, *Poirot's Early Cases* by Agatha Christie. The great detective was about to reveal who had killed Lord Cronshaw when Vera arrived with her tray.

'How are things going?' Linda asked her.

'Probably better than if Pamela was here. Ena Johnson actually smiles instead of scowling at folk when she's serving them. The food's as good as ever, Mr Hylton has served some of his best wine, and the guests are suitably impressed. Only fly in the ointment is Mr Rupert. He's very quiet, not his usual self at all. I hope he isn't sickening for something. Now then, eat this up. And by the way, that wine is the same as they're drinking downstairs. I didn't think you should be left out. Just ring when you're ready for your dessert.'

Before leaving, Vera glanced at Clara Hylton. 'What do you think?' she asked quietly. 'Should I bring something up for her?'

'I think we should leave her sleeping. I'll ring if she wakes and is hungry.'

Clara didn't wake up, and when Vera came for the tray she put some more coal on the fire and Linda got back to her book. However, replete with good food and wine, she very soon began to feel drowsy. She pushed the small table aside, pulled up the footstool and lay back in the chair. She tried to continue reading but the book soon slipped from her hands and she fell asleep.

It gave Pamela great satisfaction to summon the maid and tell her to put more coal on the fire. It was late and the girl looked tired.

'Will that be all, madam?' she asked.

'No. I might want a hot drink later. I'll let you know when you can go to bed.'

When the girl had gone, Pamela stared into the flames. There would be no more getting up at uncivilized hours and ruining her hands making up fires. No more 'Fetch this, Hawkins,' and 'Carry that, Hawkins', in fact she would never have to answer to the name of Hawkins again.

But neither could she have reverted to her old name. Pamela Delafontaine was too unusual, too uncommon. It wouldn't be very long before some keen-nosed reporter found her and the headline in the paper would scream: 'Swindler's Daughter Found In Hideout By The Sea!'

So it had been decided that she would be known as Mrs Wade. Why Wade? Pamela did not know or care; he had simply picked the name from the telephone directory. She had left everything to him. She had had to trust him, and he hadn't done too badly. The semi-detached house in an anonymous but pleasant enough street was large enough to accommodate a live-in maid-of-all work, was furnished comfortably, even tastefully, and was not too far from the railway station so that she could get into Newcastle to visit a good hairdresser or to do some clothes shopping.

Or London. What was to stop her going to the capital now and then to visit the shops or the theatre? She could stay at a nice hotel. After weeks of squabbling, the allowance he had agreed to give her had been generous enough to allow a few luxuries. Of course, they would never be luxuries on the scale of those she had enjoyed when living with her father. Poor Father, no matter what they said she knew he couldn't be a crook. He had just been unfortunate, had made some unwise investments, and nobody had been prepared to give him a chance to sort things out – not even those whose fortunes he had made in the past.

And now where was he? Locked up in a prison cell on Christmas Eve. And then the disloyal thought came to her that at least there would be other men there to wish her father Happy Christmas and sit down with him to enjoy whatever meal would be provided on Christmas Day.

Whereas she would have only Polly, a miserable little housemaid, to cook for her and wait on her and no doubt ask to go and visit her family as soon as the washing-up was done.

At least he'd provided a hamper. If the girl ruined the joint of beef and overcooked the vegetables, Pamela would have her make up a plate of cold cuts and cheeses with coffee and mince pies to follow. And she supposed it was a nice little touch to have ordered the Christmas tree and the box of glass baubles. They'd dressed it together before he had to leave, and she had pretended to be surprised when he placed the tempting little parcels round the crêpe paper-covered tub.

'Oh, no,' she'd said. 'You shouldn't have!' When in truth she would have been livid if he hadn't bought her any presents.

The door opened and a cold draught made the fire flare up. 'You should knock before you enter,' she told the girl.

'I'm sorry, Mrs Wade. I did knock but I don't think you heard.'

'Well, next time knock louder.'

'Yes, Mrs Wade.'

'Well, what do you want?'

'I was wondering if you'd like your drink now.'

'Because you want to go to bed, I suppose?'

The girl didn't answer and Pamela suddenly saw she was exhausted. She had been working here for days getting the house cleaned and ready for Pamela to move in.

'It's all right. You needn't make anything. Just bring me a glass of wine – no, bring the bottle – and then go up.'

225

When Polly returned with the wine Pamela told her to wake her up at nine the next morning with a cup of tea. And with a sudden burst of fellow feeling she added, 'As long as you see to the fires you needn't get up too early. After all, it will be Christmas Day.'

'Thank you. Goodnight, Mrs Wade. I hope you know I'll always do my best for you.'

After Polly had gone Pamela turned on the wireless and listened to a programme of carols being broadcast from a cathedral somewhere. She poured a second glass of wine, even though she wasn't sure if she should be drinking it in her condition, and she tried not to think of Christmases past.

At least she would not have to spend another Christmas waiting on the Hylton family. That batty old woman had disapproved of her from the start, although she had never been as rude to her as that stuck-up cow Cordelia. And as for Emerald Hylton, supposedly an old school friend of her mother's, did she really think that giving Jack Delafontaine's daughter a job as a housemaid was the best way of helping her?

No, thank God she had got away from Fernwood, never to return until the day he finally saw sense and married her, when she would return as Mrs Rupert Hylton. Then they would have to forget all their airs and graces and treat her as an equal. And as far as she was concerned, that day couldn't come soon enough.

Clara couldn't understand why they hadn't come for her. Had they forgotten that she was supposed to be going to the party? Or was she being punished for something she couldn't remember doing? She moved the bedclothes aside and slid out of bed. Someone had put the lights out, but a warm glow from the fire revealed a sleeping form in the armchair. She would have to be quiet.

She frowned. There was no one to help her dress and there were no clothes laid out ready. She tiptoed over to the wardrobe and opened it, wincing when the door squeaked. She held her breath and glanced over her shoulder, but the figure in the chair had not moved.

What on earth should she wear? She took out garment after garment, stared at each one and then let it slip to the floor. Were these really her frocks? Of course they were, otherwise they wouldn't be here in her room. Finally she came across one that pleased her: a black lace full-length dress with a jagged hem and a little matching bolero. She tossed it on the bed and then knelt before the wardrobe to find a suitable pair of shoes.

The shoes puzzled her. They all had high heels. How long had she been wearing high heels? Never mind, she had just come across the perfect pair to go with the dress: black suede with a pattern of little silver beads and very high, slim heels. She loved high heels.

It didn't take her long to dress, but her hair was a problem. She would need a better light to do it properly. In the end she took the comb from the drawer in her bedside table and combed it through. Clean and untangled, that was the best she could do. As she put the comb back in the drawer she noticed something shining. She reached in and her fingers closed over a powder compact. Of course, she should powder her nose – and add some lipstick! Luckily there was also some lipstick in the drawer, and she peered into the compact's mirror while she applied it. The light was dim, and for some reason her vision seemed to be blurred, but she did her best. There, that should do.

Clara rose from the bed, confident that she looked attractive. Feeling very grown up in her sophisticated gown and high-heeled shoes, she walked quietly across the room towards the door. She had forgotten about the clothes she had strewn on the floor, and her heel caught in the folds of one of the dresses and knocked her off balance. She gasped as she righted herself, then froze when the figure in the armchair sighed and changed position.

Her heart was thumping and she felt a trickle of sweat run down her brows and into her eyes. She blinked to clear them. Why was she so hot? She seemed to remember that she had a cold, a rotten stuffy head cold. That must be why they hadn't come for her. They would want her to rest. Well, sod that for a game of soldiers, as her brother would say, she was going to the party whether they liked it or not.

When it became obvious that the person in the armchair was still sleeping, Clara freed her heel from the clinging fabric, edged towards the fire and looked down at her. Was it Nanny or was it someone called Linda? Where did that name come from? But whoever it was, if she woke up she might make her go back to bed, and that wouldn't do.

She stepped out onto the landing. The only light came from the moon shining through the tall window at the end of the corridor. She stood still while her eyes adjusted to the shadows and then, drawn by the sound of talk and laughter, she headed for the stairs. She gripped the banister rail and looked down into the brilliantly lit hall. Then she drew back when she saw a woman she didn't know crossing the black-and-white marble tiles carrying a tray. On the tray were jugs of coffee and hot milk, and the woman was walking towards the dining room. But who was she? Clara did not recognize the grey, severely permed hair or the way the woman walked so quickly in flat, sensible shoes. Was she someone they'd hired in to help with the dinner party?

Just before the woman entered the dining room she stopped to talk to another woman who had just emerged, holding an empty tray by her side. Ah, that was Saunders. She recognized her tidy brown hair and her comfortable figure. But then confusion overcame her. The scene below was recognizable and yet wrong somehow. Familiar and yet unfamiliar. Were those black-and-white tiles on the floor? Shouldn't there be a Turkey carpet? She blinked in an attempt to clear her vision.

And then she began to shake as the realization came over her that she was not sure who she was. She glanced at her left hand resting on the banister. It was old and wrinkled. That couldn't be right. Bizarrely there was a wedding ring on the fourth finger. But she couldn't be married, could she? She was just a little girl. And if she was a child, what was she doing in a black lace gown and high-heeled shoes?

Then to her relief an explanation presented itself. She'd been dressing up in her mother's clothes. That was it. They had told her that she was too young to go to the party, but when they saw what she had done they would smile and laugh and say how clever she was. The ladies would say, 'How sweet,' and the men would say, 'She's going to be a beauty!' Feeling more cheerful, she straightened her back and decided to ignore the puzzle of her wrinkled hands.

The maidservants were no longer in the hall. There was no one to stop her before she got to the dining room and surprised everyone. She took hold of her skirt with both hands and raised it a little so that she wouldn't catch a foot in the jagged edge. She began to hurry down the stairs.

It happened so quickly that she had no time to fling out her arm and grasp the banister to save herself. These shoes were not made for hurrying. One of the slender heels twisted sideways. She went over on her ankle and the pain shot up her leg. Clara shrieked in pain and terror as her knee gave way and she toppled down the stairs, banging her head on each step as she went down. A terrifying blackness swooped in and claimed her long before she had reached the bottom.

Chapter Thirteen

February 1938

John Sinclair had a sense of déjà vu. A few months ago he had sat at this very table and talked to Linda Bellwood about her plans for the future, and now, after another funeral, here they were again. The first time, that day in autumn, she had been dressed in black as she was now, but today there was a subtle difference in her demeanour. He was sure that she had genuinely mourned Agnes Taylor, but her feelings had been a mixture of gratitude and respect, whereas today she looked as though grief had overwhelmed her. However, well mannered as ever, she had made him tea and managed to produce a plate of biscuits, although John was pretty sure there was not much in the larder.

'I think she's neglecting herself,' Muriel had told him. 'I saw her in the village shop the other day and there wasn't much in her basket. Do you think the Hyltons have cast her out without a penny?'

'I'm certain they have not,' he had assured his wife. He would have liked to have told Muriel of the generous settlement they had insisted she take when they asked her to leave, but that was a matter of confidentiality.

This morning he had come to see Linda to find out what she planned to do. He intended to ask

231

her whether she had changed her mind about selling the house, but the first thing she mentioned was the money the Hyltons wanted to give her.

'I don't want it,' she said.

'Why ever not?'

'What have I done to deserve it?'

'It's not about you, Linda, it's about them. They feel responsible for you.'

'I don't see why they should.'

John tried to hide his exasperation at her confrontational attitude. He sensed it sprang from both hurt and anger. 'Don't you? Well, I do. They asked you to leave without giving proper notice, without giving you the chance to find another position. This is normal under the circumstances.'

'One hundred pounds is far from normal; especially as I was responsible for Mrs Hylton's fatal accident.'

'You were *not* responsible, and the Hylton family don't think so either.'

'I fell asleep and she fell down the stairs and died.' Linda stared at him bleakly.

'You were not hired as a nurse. They know now that they should have got more specialized help. They are the ones who feel guilty.'

Linda thought for a moment then said, 'Yes, that's what Mr Hylton told me.'

'And in my opinion – in confidence – I think that's why they could not keep you on as a companion to Emerald Hylton. Your presence would have been a constant reminder. Can't you see that?'

'I suppose I can.'

'And I don't wish to be cruel, but surely staying

there would have been painful for you?'

Linda looked at him thoughtfully. She sighed. 'It would. But families overcome these tragedies together, don't they?'

John Sinclair was aghast. 'Families do, but...'

'I am not one of the family. Go on, say it.'

'I'm sorry, I don't know what to say.'

'It's all right.' She gave a faint smile. 'I'm the one who should be sorry; subjecting you to these self-indulgent ramblings when all you want to do is help me. But I felt I belonged there – that I was part of the family. When you told me that I could go and live there I was overjoyed. You see, ever since I was a little girl I have admired them. I was drawn to how warm and close they were.'

'But how could you know that?'

Linda looked down at the table. 'I used to play in the woods. One day I saw the house and the children playing on the lawn. They looked so happy. After that I went there many times just to watch them. I ... I got bolder.'

'Bolder?'

'I used to creep across the lawn at dusk and watch them through the windows. I used to imagine that one day I would live there with them.'

'So that's why you were so keen to take the job of companion.'

'Yes. And I don't regret it. For a while it was wonderful. I know in my heart that I wasn't responsible for Clara Hylton's death, but I can see why I can't stay there. Really, I can. And now you must make me a promise.'

'If I can.'

The tone of her voice was lighter. 'Promise that

233

you will never report me for trespassing. I don't want to be persecuted.'

'You mean prosecuted.'

'Yes.'

'Why are you smiling?'

'I'm just remembering the first time I met Florian.'

'While you were trespassing?'

'Yes, we became friends. And he didn't report me.'

John smiled at her. 'And you may rest easy, for neither shall I.'

'And now, no doubt, you will try to persuade me to sell the house and go to college.'

'Would you at least consider that?'

'I'm just not sure what to do.'

'Take your time. Don't be too hasty in making a decision one way or the other.' He smiled at her. 'The money that you don't want to accept but definitely deserve, will give you breathing space.'

'You are very kind to take so much trouble. Why do you do it?'

'It's because I like and admire you. My wife and I knew your mother, you know.'

'Of course you did. She was your cleaning lady.' Linda's smile was rueful.

'She was a good woman. Life was not kind to her but she worked hard and did her best for you. If she could see you now, she would be very proud. And please, now that you have come back to the village, my wife said that I must tell you to call and see her whenever you feel like talking – and even if you don't. She could talk enough for both of you.'

Linda promised him that she would, and when John Sinclair took his leave he was filled with a sense of deep regret that he had dissuaded Muriel from taking Linda into their home when Joan Bellwood had died, leaving her only child an orphan. Even though they had four children of their own to raise, they would have managed somehow, and Linda might have had a happier childhood with them rather than the one she'd had with that good but emotionally deficient woman, Agnes Taylor. He was sure that Linda would have been happy to fit in with his own children – she would have become part of the family – and would never have become fascinated by the Hyltons, who had obviously broken her heart.

When Mr Sinclair had gone, Linda sat listlessly by the fire and replayed in her mind everything that had happened since Clara Hylton's fatal accident. The funeral had been on New Year's Eve. The old church in the village had been full of mourners, some of them having travelled a long way. Many of the villagers attended, although they would not be going back to the Hall for the funeral tea. The family had gone to the church in the funeral cars and Linda, the Asletts, Vera and Bobby had been driven there by Paul.

Caterers had been hired to provide the food, which had not pleased Ivy Aslett, but Mr Hylton explained that he wanted them to feel part of the family on this saddest of days. It was a kind gesture, but when they got to the church Linda couldn't help noticing that their places were far behind those of the Hyltons. And that she had been relegated to sitting with the staff.

Back at the Hall there was no segregation, and Linda observed Bobby talking to one of the young cousins as if he were one of the family. The girl was staring up into his face adoringly, and if she had noticed that his bony wrists outshot the sleeves of a well-worn jacket she must have thought that was due to the eccentricities of the rich.

The food was set out as a buffet in the dining room and guests filled their plates and carried them through to the drawing room or the library, whichever they preferred. Vera encouraged Linda to help herself.

'I'm taking mine along to the staff sitting room,' Vera said. 'Cosier there. You can join us if you like. But suit yourself.'

Vera left Linda at the table. Conscious of impatient remarks behind her, she put some food on her plate without really seeing what she was taking and turned to come up against two middle-aged women, the source of the impatient remarks. Their coats were black, as were the coats of all the mourners, and they had fox fur stoles draped around their shoulders. Both wore the full fox-pelt with head, sharp-clawed feet and bushy tail still attached. The eyes of each animal – surely glass? – glinted on each foxy head.

Stopping and moving her plate aside just in time to stop the contents tipping onto their patent leather shoes, Linda apologized and would have moved on when one of them spoke to her.

'Miss Bellwood, isn't it?'

Linda nodded.

'Cat got your tongue?' the other woman asked.

236

'No ... I'm sorry ... I...'

And then she felt a hand in the small of her back. 'Linda,' Florian said, 'I need to sit down. My leg's hurting. Would you keep me company?' He steered her through the assembled guests, out of the dining room.

She couldn't help glancing over her shoulder and saw that the women were staring at her malevolently. They blame me, she thought. Everyone here will know that Mrs Hylton would not have fallen down the stairs if I had looked after her properly.

Florian took her across the hall and into the living room. He said, 'The window seat, I think.'

The Christmas tree had been taken down, as had all the decorations. In fact Mr Aslett and Bobby had removed them on Christmas Day, even though Florian had protested that it was the last thing his grandmother would have wanted. 'She was never a spoilsport,' he said. 'She would have wanted us to enjoy Christmas just as if she were here with us.' He had been ignored, and Christmas lunch had been a snatched affair fitted around the doctor's visit and urgent phone calls.

'That was kind of you,' Linda said.

'What was? Rescuing you from those two harpies?'

'Yes. And the way you did it. Mentioning your leg. I've never heard you do that before.'

He grinned. 'Desperate times call for desperate measures. If I'd left you with those two harpies, they might have devoured you. Harpies are half women and half birds of prey, you know, and they definitely had you lined up as their next good meal. I had to act quickly and that was the first thing that came to mind. I hope you noticed how I exaggerated my limp as we walked away from them.'

'I did, and I don't deserve such kindness.'

'Yes, you do.' He paused and looked at her plate. 'Oh, for goodness sake, that wouldn't feed a sparrow!'

'I'm not hungry.'

'Well, I am.' Florian looked across the room and saw Bobby, who was still talking to the young cousin. He waved to catch his attention. When Bobby joined them – reluctantly – he told him to go to the dining room and fill up another plate with as much as he could pile onto it. 'Then bring it back, sharpish, and you can go back to making googly eyes at young Flora.'

'You've embarrassed him,' Linda said.

'No, I haven't. Not our Bobby. He's as confident as they come. If he survives the next few years he'll go far.'

'Why shouldn't he survive the next few years?'

'The war. It can't be long now. We'll have another year of peace, maybe two. But when the war starts young Bobby will be cannon fodder, just like generations of good lads before him,' he paused and sighed. 'And I suppose my brother and Charlie will have to fight, too.' Florian was silent for a moment then he grinned puckishly. 'But we shouldn't be talking like this,' he had said. 'We shouldn't be gloomy. After all, this is a funeral.'

When the guests and the caterers had gone, it had been left to the Hall's own staff to finish

238

tidying up. The family retreated to the library and Linda was left alone in the drawing room. Vera found her there and invited her to come along to the kitchen, where Ivy Aslett was taking possession of her territory again.

The conversation was about the events of the day and speculation about the new maidservant who would be starting work on Monday, in three days' time. No one knew anything about her except that Mrs Hylton had got her from an agency in Newcastle. The opinion was that she was bound to be better than Pamela had been.

'I wonder what she's doing now,' Vera said. 'Pamela, I mean. Did she find another job or did she go to friends?'

'I can't say I care one way or the other,' Ivy told her. 'Stuck-up little madam. I'd hate to work for her!'

'Well, that's not very likely, is it?' Albert Aslett said. 'She's hardly likely to be able to afford servants.'

'Unless she's found a rich admirer,' Bobby put in. 'I mean, that's what happens in the novels and the movies, isn't it?'

They all laughed at this. Not because what he had said was particularly funny, but because they were beginning to wind down after a difficult day.

'Are they staying up to see the New Year in?' Vera asked. Everyone knew who she meant.

'Yes, but there're no guests coming,' Ivy said. 'And they want Albert, here, to be first foot. What about you, Linda?' she added. 'Are you going to see the year in with the family or would you like to stay here with us?'

'I think I'd rather just go to bed.'

'You'll do no such thing,' Vera said. 'Make your mind up one way or the other, but you're not going to bed before we see the New Year in.'

A bell rang and Vera looked up at the panel over the door. 'The library,' she said. 'I wonder what they want.' She got up wearily.

It wasn't long before she returned. 'Mr Hylton wants to see you, Linda. He asked me to find you. He seemed quite worried.'

Linda wasn't sure whether she believed that, but she was aware of the silence as she left the room. The others would be wondering, just as she was, what exactly Mr Hylton was going to say.

When she entered the library she found him sitting there alone. He was at his desk and he had obviously been going through some papers. He looked up and smiled wanly. Linda felt desperately sorry for him.

'So much to do,' he said, and he waved an arm over the mass of papers. There was also a bottle of whisky and a tumbler on the desk. Mr Hylton poured himself a drink and rose from his seat. 'Let's sit by the fire.'

When they were seated either side of the hearth he wasted no time. 'Do you remember the conversation we had the day ... on Christmas Eve?'

'I do.'

'I said that once we got a nurse for my mother we would like you to stay here and be a companion to my wife.' He stared into his drink. Light from the fire flashed on the facets of the crystal tumbler. 'This is difficult,' he said.

'Are you trying to tell me that as the circum-

240

stances have changed so dramatically that will no longer be possible?'

'That's right, Linda. I'm sorry.'

He had gone on to explain why it would be too difficult for her to stay, and why it would be difficult for the family, too. He had offered her a settlement, which she had been unwilling to take. So Mr Hylton said he would leave it to John Sinclair to convince her and to sort things out. Eventually he had risen and told her that he was going to join the family to see in the New Year. He didn't invite her to come with him, and it was only after he had left the room that she realized that, even though he had told her that she would probably find it easy to find another job, there had been no mention of a reference.

Linda went miserably to bed and the next morning she didn't go down for breakfast. She began packing her clothes. Vera appeared with coffee and toast.

'What happened to you, last night?' she said. 'We thought you were with the family until Mr Florian came looking for you. By then it was after midnight, so I told him you'd gone to bed and not to disturb you.'

'Thank you.'

'And what have we here?' Vera asked as she surveyed the two piles of clothes on the bed. One large and one small.

'I'm just taking what I came with,' Linda said.

'And what do you suppose will happen to the other things? They'll just give them away, you know.'

'Good.'

'No, it's not good. The old lady really enjoyed herself going shopping with you, and it's like you're throwing her generosity back in her face if you don't take her gifts when you leave here.'

'Do you think so?'

'I know so. And if your case isn't big enough, I'll find one for you. There's some old luggage up in the attics. No one will mind if you take one. Paul's going to drive you home, by the way.'

Vera helped Linda with the rest of her packing and then, to her surprise, she hugged her. 'Nobody blames you, you know. Ivy and Albert, Paul and Bobby and me. What happened wasn't your fault and we're really sorry to see you go. But perhaps it's for the best. Get away from here and get a life for yourself. You're too intelligent to live your life through other people; no matter how glamorous they seem.'

Linda looked at her in surprise.

'There, now, you didn't expect such words of wisdom from me, did you? Well, I'll have you know I'm not so daft either, and although I won't deny this is a good job, the only reason I'm working here is because there's nothing else for women like me. Come the war and the world will change.'

This was the second time someone had mentioned the possibility of war. Perhaps it was because the beginning of the year often presaged change, and the news from Europe had been more and more troubling.

When they had done, Vera asked Linda if she wanted to say goodbye to the family.

'I don't think they want me to,' Linda said, hoping she didn't sound too forlorn. Miserably she wondered if Florian knew she had been asked to leave. Ought she to seek him out and tell him? But what if she were to meet one of the family? She flinched at the thought of how awkward that might be. Feeling utterly wretched, she told Vera, 'I think I'll just slip away.'

'Well, come to the kitchen and say goodbye to the rest of us. I'll tell Paul to bring the car to the back door.'

As Linda handed her luggage to the chauffeur she smiled wryly.

'What is it?' he asked.

'I'm going home in style, aren't I? It's different from the day I arrived when I walked from the village carrying one old suitcase.'

They had not driven far when they heard a shout and Paul, glancing in the rear-view mirror, stopped the car. 'What is it?' Linda asked.

'Someone to see you.'

As he said this, Florian pulled open the door and got in beside her. 'Were you going to go without saying goodbye?' he asked. He sounded angry. 'Silly question. It's obvious you were. Don't you care for me at all?'

Paul turned and slid the glass partition into place, dividing the car so that those in the back seats could not be heard by the chauffeur. Florian glared at Linda.

'Well, don't you?' he asked.

'I thought it best just to slip quietly away.'

'I notice you haven't answered my question. Is it because of those ridiculous things my grandmother said when she thought I was her brother and you were her nanny?'

Linda stared at him bleakly.

'It is, isn't it? Look, I haven't time to talk about this now. Father has called a family conference to discuss my grandmother's will. But I'll come and see you as soon as I can. And Linda?'

'What?'

Florian took her in his arms and held her close. He kissed her tenderly and then he whispered. 'Happy New Year, my darling. And don't despair. I know this year is going to be wonderful for both of us.'

'Is it?' she asked, wanting fervently to believe him.

'I promise you it is.' He took her face in his hands and looked into her eyes. 'Trust me.'

He had left her hurriedly, slamming the door, hard enough to make Paul wince. Keeping the partition in place, Paul drove her home. When they reached Linda's house he helped her in with her luggage and then said, 'Do you mind if I give you a piece of advice?'

'What is it?'

'Don't get involved with them, Linda. You can't trust them. They take you up and then drop you when it suits them. They'll only break your heart. As I know only too well.'

Linda looked up into his face and saw the anguish there. 'Why do you stay?' she asked.

'God only knows.' He gave a crooked grin and then got into the car and drove back to the Hall.

That had been more than a week ago, and still Florian had not been to see her. Linda was beginning to believe that Paul was right.

Pamela stood by the small table in the oak-panelled hallway and stared at the telephone. She had insisted that Rupert have one installed and he had insisted that she was never to use it to call him, either at work or at Fernwood Hall. He would call her, he said. So why hadn't he? Surely things had settled down enough by now for him to tell her what they were going to do.

He had phoned on Christmas Day as he had promised he would. It must have been about six o'clock in the morning, and she had leaped out of bed and hurried downstairs without pausing to put on her robe. She snatched up the receiver as she sat down on the chintz-covered seat that was part of the table. Speaking very quietly, Rupert had told her he didn't have long before the others would be getting up. He sounded subdued.

'Rupert, darling! Merry Christmas!' She tried to sound light-hearted, but she could sense something was wrong.

'Merry Christmas, Pamela. Did you like your presents?'

'Yes. Lovely. The charm bracelet is sweet and the perfume is heavenly. But what about you?'

'Me?'

'Yes, you. Did you like the driving gloves?'

'Oh, sorry, I haven't opened your present yet.'

Pamela began to shiver and she hunched her shoulders against the cold. 'And now I've spoilt it by telling you what it is.' She paused. 'You haven't lost it, have you?'

'No, Pamela, I haven't lost your parcel. It's just that things are chaotic here.'

'Have they found out about us? Is that it?'

245

'It's nothing to do with us. It's my grandmother. She... I'm afraid she died last night.'

'Oh, Rupert, I'm sorry.'

Rupert went on to tell her how Clara Hylton had been resting in bed but had decided to come down to the dinner party. How she had fallen on the stairs. Pamela wasn't really listening. She murmured things like, 'How dreadful!' and 'I'm so sorry.' But all the time her mind was racing as she tried to work out what this might mean to Rupert and herself.

She knew that Rupert would inherit some money. He had told her that he was mentioned in his grandmother's will. But he had also said that he had no idea how much his inheritance would be. 'Perhaps then it will be easier for us to marry,' he had told her. 'When I have money of my own.'

'For goodness sake!' Pamela had said. 'Your grandmother could live for years yet.'

She had always suspected that Rupert had just been making excuses and had no intention of marrying her. That was why she had allowed herself to become pregnant. But even that hadn't had the desired effect. He had had to find somewhere for her to live so that she could leave the Hall before her pregnancy showed, but this was as much to protect himself as to protect her.

She had decided that what was stopping him from making a commitment was fear of what his parents' reaction would be. And his grandmother's, too. Those bloody Hyltons, she had often thought. Behaving as though they were some truly grand family rather than jumped-up tradespeople.

Well, now he would have some money of his own, and Pamela determined even before the telephone call was ended that he must marry her before their child was born.

'I'm sorry, I don't know when I'll be able to come and see you,' he said. 'I'll phone and let you know.'

That had been more than a week ago and he still hadn't called her. She picked up the receiver and her hand hovered over the dial. But where would he be? At work – after all, the business must go on – or at home? She decided to call the pottery first. She would give a false name to whoever answered. It would work, because no one knew her there. She had worked out a story about being a buyer for a department store. But the story wasn't needed. The young woman who answered the phone, no doubt impressed by her upper-class voice, put her through straight away.

'I thought I told you never to call me,' Rupert said.

'I wouldn't have had to if you had kept your promise and phoned me.'

There was a long silence and then she heard Rupert sigh. 'I'm sorry, Pamela, but there's been so much to do. Look, I'll come and see you to-morrow evening. Get the girl to cook something nice and I'll bring some good wine.'

'Why don't we go out to dinner? We could try the Waverly on the promenade. Polly's aunt is a waitress there, and in Polly's words it's very posh!' She laughed, trying to lighten his mood.

'You know we can't dine out, Pamela.' He sounded exasperated.

Her laughter died. 'Of course we can't. How silly of me. I'll see you tomorrow, then.' Pamela slammed the receiver down.

She took her coat from the rack at the bottom of the stairs, pulled it on and tied the belt. She left the house, slamming the door behind her. Most of the snow had gone but the wind was keen, and as she strode along the deserted promenade she felt tears of rage and frustration streaming down her cheeks. She turned to look at the sea. It was as grey as the winter sky, and the waves churned and crashed down on the shore angrily.

When she had started the affair with Rupert Hylton she had imagined that her days as a housemaid would soon be over. That, if not as fabulously wealthy as her father had been, Rupert was more than comfortable. That her life would soon change for the better. So what had she achieved? She was living in a semi-detached house in a second-rate seaside resort, with one maid-of-all-work to clean the house and see to her needs. And what am I supposed to do with my life? Pamela thought. Listen to the wireless? Read magazines? Take up needlework?

She wore a wedding ring but that was only to keep up a facade of respectability. The story for the neighbours who might become curious about the new resident was that her husband had to travel for his work. And what of this 'husband'? He came after dark and he never took her out anywhere because they couldn't afford to be seen together. Until now Pamela had felt no shame, but today she realized that she felt utterly humiliated.

Linda was about to go to bed when the doorbell rang. She couldn't imagine who would call at this time of night. Switching off the light in the front parlour, she pulled the curtain aside a little and peered out. The moonlight revealed the Hyltons' Rolls Royce, but the interior was too shadowy to see whether there was anyone inside it. It must be Paul at the door, she thought. But why should he call at this time of night? Had something happened?

Convinced that the chauffeur must be bringing bad news, Linda opened the front door. It wasn't Paul who was standing there. It was Florian, and he was smiling.

'Oh it's you,' she said offhandedly.

Momentarily taken aback, Florian's smile faded. 'Aren't you going to invite me in?'

'I suppose so.'

Linda stood back to allow Florian to enter. Over his shoulder she caught a glimpse of curtains twitching across the street. There goes my reputation, she thought, but it was too late to change her mind. Florian came in and shut the door behind him.

'Why are you here?' she asked coldly.

'Can't we go and sit somewhere? I have so much to tell you.'

Linda didn't move, so Florian led the way into the front parlour. He gave a mock shiver. 'It's chilly in here,' he said. 'Why have you let the fire die down?'

'Because I was just about to go to bed. And if you're cold in here, what about Paul?'

Florian frowned. 'What do you mean?'

249

'Are you just going to leave him sitting in the car?'

'Stevens is a chauffeur. He's used to sitting in the car and waiting for people. But in any case, he's not cold. He's got the heater on and he's perfectly happy listening to a dance band programme on the wireless. Carrol Gibbons and the orchestra at the Savoy, no less.' Florian reached for her hands. His eyes were shining. 'Would you like to dine at the Savoy, Linda?'

She withdrew her hands and stuffed them in the pockets of her cardigan. She frowned. His air of exuberance was puzzling. Surely he didn't expect an answer to such a silly question?

Florian's smile faded. 'Aren't you pleased to see me?' he asked.

'I don't know that I am.'

'What on earth is wrong? Why are you being so hostile?'

Even though she was aware that she sounded pettish, she couldn't stop herself from saying, 'You promised you'd come and see me.'

'I'm here, aren't I?'

'You made the promise weeks ago. What kept you?'

He looked contrite. 'I know, and I'm sorry. I should have written, but there was so much to do and I wanted it all arranged before I told you. And it's much better to tell you in person, isn't it?' His excited smile had returned. The front parlour suddenly seemed to be too small to contain his exhilaration.

'I can't answer that until you've told me. Florian, please sit down. You're making me nervous.'

He moved obediently towards one of the fireside chairs and perched on the edge as if he were about to spring up again at any moment. He looked up at her. 'All right, but don't stand there looking down at me so crossly. Sit opposite me and I'll tell you everything.' When she was sitting he said, 'My grandmother left me some money. Not a great fortune, but quite enough to keep my head above water until my novel is published.'

Linda sighed. 'Then I can understand why you're so excited.'

'There's more to come. I've told my parents that I won't be joining the family firm.'

'And what did they say?'

'There's no need to go into that.'

'It was that bad?'

'It wasn't good. So I decided the best thing to do was to get right away from the situation. I mean, how could anyone concentrate on writing with all that anger seething around him?'

'You're leaving home?'

'I am.'

'Where will you go?'

'I've been! I mean, it's all arranged. The reason I haven't been to see you is because I've been to London. I've bought an apartment in one of those new mansion blocks in Putney. There are three bedrooms and wonderful views. You'll love it!'

'*I* will love it?'

Florian stood up. Reaching for her hands, he pulled her up into his arms. 'You didn't think I'd go without you, did you?'

'But how could I possibly come with you?'

'Haven't you realized, darling? I'm asking you to marry me. You will come to London with me as my wife.'

Part Two

Chapter Fourteen

Summer 1938, London

Florian was arranging chairs in a circle in their sitting room when Linda told him that she was going for a walk. He turned towards her. 'Are you sure you don't want to stay for the meeting, darling? You know you're very welcome.'

'I don't know why. I haven't written anything, so I've nothing to read out.'

'That doesn't matter. Your opinions are greatly appreciated.'

Linda smiled at her husband. 'By you, perhaps, but some of the others have hinted that I don't know what I'm talking about.'

'Who precisely?'

'Doreen and Reginald. Once when Doreen disagreed with my opinion she said, "Well, of course you haven't been to university, have you, my dear?"'

'That was perfect!'

'You agree with her?'

'Of course not. You are twice as intelligent as Doreen Lamb, despite her university degree. No, it was the way you reproduced her pained little voice. You ought to be an actress!'

'No, thank you. One actress in the group is sufficient.'

'Nadine is very intelligent and the revue

sketches she writes are not at all bad, but I sense that she comes to the meetings only because Gerald can't bear to come without her.'

'Can't bear to, or doesn't like to let her out of his sight for too long?'

Florian grinned at her. 'What are you suggesting? That if left on her own the lovely Nadine might stray from the straight and narrow?'

'If she hasn't already strayed.'

'Really? Do you think so? Have you any proof?'

'Of course I haven't, and I shouldn't be saying this because she may be totally innocent, but she's obviously bored to death with poor old Gerald. Sometimes I think she's going to explode with frustration.'

Florian looked at her with amused surprise. 'How observant you are. But then I already knew that. Perhaps I should get you to make notes about all the members of our little group and I could use them when I'm creating characters in my novels.'

'Would that be an honest thing to do?'

'Oh, entirely honest.'

'But what if they recognized themselves?'

'People never do. But what about Reginald? You mentioned that he was unkind to you.'

'Not exactly unkind. It's simply that he adopts an extremely patronizing air when he talks to me. I sense that in his opinion I am only half educated, and on top of that I'm much too young to be allowed an opinion at all.'

Florian frowned. 'Reginald Lamb is a pompous ass and pretentious to boot. I had no idea you were so upset. I'm sorry. I shall make it quite plain to one and all that my wife is both intelligent and perceptive, and if they don't go along with that they can leave the group.'

'No, please don't. I'm not upset. It doesn't matter at all what they think of me and I should hate to be the cause of discord, especially when you enjoy your meetings so much.'

'Yes, I do. And thank you for being so understanding. In fact, thank you, thank you, thank you, not only for encouraging me to write but also for being my inspiration.' Florian moved aside the chair that stood between them and took her in his arms. 'Thank goodness you agreed to marry me.'

'Did you think I wouldn't?'

'I was afraid that you were so cross with the entire Hylton family that you wouldn't want anything to do with me. We were meant to be together, weren't we, Linda? Right from the moment we met in the woods.'

'Perhaps we were.' Linda smiled as she remembered those enchanted, carefree days.

'Perhaps! Is that as far as you'll go?' He pretended to be outraged. 'Then let me prove it to you.' He drew her closer and was about to kiss her when there was a discreet cough from the doorway. They drew apart breathlessly and turned to see their maid, Rosa, standing there.

She gave an embarrassed smile. 'I'm sorry to interrupt you, Mrs Hylton,' the young woman said, 'but I would like you to scrutinize the table.'

'That's all right, Rosa.' It was Florian who answered her. He dropped a light kiss on Linda's forehead. 'My wife will come and scrutinize the table as you put it, although I'm sure it will not need such careful examination as your vocabulary suggests.'

Rosa sighed and pretended to be sad. 'You are making a joke of me, Mr Hylton.'

'No, I would never do that. Your grasp of the English language is improving every day. I am very impressed.'

Rosa observed him levelly and then, obviously deciding that he was sincere, she smiled. 'It is good to work in a house with so many books. I have been lucky.'

'And we are lucky to have you. But now we had better call a halt to this session of mutual admiration. I want to go over my script before my guests arrive.'

Florian picked up a sheaf of papers that had been lying on one of the chairs and sat down. He began reading and it was clear immediately that he had entered another world. Linda followed Rosa to the dining room.

Rosa had covered the table with a white linen cloth, and at one end there were teacups and saucers, teaspoons, plates, napkins, sugar cubes, and lemon slices. At the other end she had placed the coffee cups and a bowl of brown sugar cubes.

'I shall bring in the milk and the cream with the tea and coffee when the guests arrive,' Rosa said. 'Do you think I should make some iced tea as well? You have a nice pitcher and some tall glasses.'

'No,' Linda said. 'What you have done is sufficient. You shouldn't have gone to so much trouble.'

'It is no trouble. I am very pleased to make a good table for your guests.'

'You've certainly done that,' Linda surveyed the

serving trays containing savouries and finger sandwiches in brown and white bread with their crusts cut off. There were also plates of iced cakes and buttered scones. 'What a feast. And you've even made a tray of devilled eggs.'

'Mr Hylton. He likes them so much.'

'He does, and you're spoiling him.'

'Spoiling? I have not done them properly?'

'No, Rosa, I'm sure they will be perfect. I meant that you – how shall I put it? You indulge my husband as if he were a child.'

Rosa smiled. 'That is my pleasure. But it is almost time for the meeting. I shall go and boil the kettle. Would you like a cup of tea before your guests arrive?'

'No tea, thank you. I haven't time. I'm not staying for the meeting.'

'No?'

'I'm going for a walk.'

'Another walk?'

'I need fresh air rather than hot air.'

Rosa frowned. 'You are making another joke?'

'I am.' Linda smiled at her. 'And I have no intention of explaining it.'

Shaking her head, Rosa hurried through into the kitchen.

Linda knew that Rosa was impressed by the writing group. She had been about to go to university when her family had fled Nazi Germany. Her parents, both teachers, had no alternative but to leave when Jews were banned from many professional occupations. They had also known intuitively that there was worse to come.

In England Rosa's father, who had taught mathematics, was the caretaker of an office block and her mother, an accomplished artist, was working in a flower shop. Rosa, only seventeen, had found work as a housemaid and she thought herself lucky to have found employment with people she thought of as intellectuals. Linda did not want to disappoint her by telling her that the people she had made such a marvellous tea for were not intellectuals, although at least two of them probably thought of themselves as such.

Linda went to the bathroom and splashed her face with cold water before combing her hair. It was so hot. Perhaps she ought to have agreed to Rosa's suggestion of making iced tea for the writing group. Too late now. She wanted to escape before any of them arrived.

In the bedroom she sprayed herself with the perfume Florian had given her. It had a lovely green floral fragrance, and Linda thought its name, Cocktail, was most misleading. She slipped on the matching jacket to her red-and-white Swiss cotton frock and glanced quickly in the mirror. She decided that the cut of the jacket would allow her to take off the red leather belt of her dress, allowing it to hang loosely. She picked up her shoulder bag, making sure that the letter that had arrived that morning was inside it.

Before leaving she looked into the sitting room. Florian was intent on his script, so, not wishing to interrupt him, she left their apartment and made her way along the geometrically tiled corridor to the bank of lifts.

She could hear one of the lifts ascending and she pressed the button quickly to summon another.

Luckily the lift was on her floor and the door opened straight away. She hurried in thankfully but feeling rather guilty. Florian enjoyed the meetings of the writing group so much that she wished she could share his enthusiasm. He had discovered the existence of the group when he came across a notice at the library. They met after work on Fridays in a draughty church hall. Florian had gone along eagerly, only to discover that the group was on the point of breaking up because the room they used was needed for confirmation classes.

'Oh, but you must come to my apartment,' he had told them. 'There's plenty of room and it will be much more comfortable. And you won't have to bring your own sandwiches. I can give you a proper tea.'

That had been in March, not long after they had moved into the brand-new mansion block, and Linda was still coping with Nina Bernard, the overbearing interior designer that Florian had insisted on hiring. Linda really couldn't see why they needed someone else to tell them which furniture to buy, or what colour they should paint the walls, or what sort of rugs they should put on the floors. But Florian convinced her – almost – that it was part of the fun of moving into a new home of your own.

This had made Linda think of the house she owned in Redesburn, which was full of Miss Taylor's solid old-fashioned furniture. Mr Sinclair had found tenants for it: a married couple, both archaeologists, who were to start work on a nearby Roman site. They had been working in Syria with Max Mallowan, and Linda wondered what they would think of Northumberland and whether they would deem it necessary to employ an interior designer to liven up the staid old house.

Fortunately Nina Bernard's tastes were not too eccentric. She favoured a plain, uncluttered look with pale washes on the walls and simple stream-lined furniture, much of it made from blond Italian walnut. She recommended floor and table lamps in chrome with frosted glass shades. Linda agreed but was doubtful about the lamps' sculptured shape of a woman holding an illuminated globe.

'Oh, but it's fabulous,' Florian had said. 'Everyone has one.'

'That's no reason for us to follow suit,' Linda told him.

'I know. But it's such fun, isn't it?'

And Linda had agreed that it was.

Linda approved of the checkered tiled floors for the kitchen and bathroom and simple gleaming wood for the other rooms. She loved the large rugs with bold, bright, geometric patterns, but when it came to pictures she drew the line at scenes from ancient Egypt, fashionable or not. For a moment it looked as if Nina would have a tantrum, until Linda opted instead for some still life paintings of weird but cheery looking fruit and two Paul Klee prints.

'Super, darling,' Nina said approvingly. 'Especially Sinbad. And if you can afford them...?'

The interior designer left the question hanging but Florian immediately said, 'Of course we can.'

At that point Linda had begun to worry about how much money Florian was spending, but he

262

assured her there was plenty and that, in any case, they would not have to depend on his inheritance once his novel was published.

Linda had no idea who she might have avoided by diving so quickly into the lift, but when she reached the ground floor she was not so lucky. The lift doors opened to reveal Reginald and Doreen Lamb.

'Going out, Mrs Hylton?' Reginald asked. He looked down at her from his great height like a short-sighted vulture surveying its prey and smiled condescendingly.

'Yes.'

'Somewhere special?'

'Just for a walk.'

'Very wise, Linda,' Doreen Lamb said. 'There's no need for you to sit and listen to work you don't understand.'

Linda gasped. This was the most insulting re-mark yet. Enraged as she was, she might have responded with something truly disparaging about Doreen's poems – Doreen's twee little poems – when the lift doors, tired of standing open, at-tempted to close. Linda hurried out and watched as Reginald shepherded his wife in. She made no attempt to control her laughter when she saw that the doors had closed on Doreen's cheap print skirt, and as the lift rose she could imagine the inelegant attempts the woman would be making to pull it free.

Despite their unpleasantness, Linda realized she felt sorry for them. Was it disappointment that made them look older than their years? They were only in their forties. But whatever it was it had not affected their arrogant manner. Linda reflected that perhaps they needed to feel superior to other mortals, otherwise they would have to admit that they were failures.

Each carried a briefcase. During the school term the briefcases would be bulging with work they had to take home from school, but this evening they looked as if they were almost empty. Reginald's novel and Doreen's poems, Linda thought. Once the meeting started they would read extracts to the group, hoping for encouragement and praise. She had learned they did not want criticism, no matter how constructive.

Florian had realized this straight away and he was always kind to them. 'But that's not helping them,' Linda had told him.

'I know, darling,' he had responded, 'but those two are never going to get published so it doesn't matter.'

After only a few meetings Linda had realized that none of them stood much chance of being published, except perhaps for Amy Purvis, a secretary at the Home Office, and of course, Florian. The passages he read out were so very much better than anyone else's that it was almost embarrassing. So why did he continue holding the meetings? Linda decided that it was partly vanity. It is because they admire him, she had decided. The women for his looks, the men for his wealth, and all of them for his talent. He can't resist their praise. And I would be cruel to deny him that.

The sun had shone all day from a windless sky, and when she stepped out onto the pavement Linda discovered a hot and dusty world. She decided she would walk by the river. Her chosen path took her along an almost rural part of the embankment. In fact, on quiet days it was hard to believe that she was in one of the largest cities in the world. At this time of day, when children would be going home for tea and the working population was not yet ready to go out for the evening, Linda had the path to herself. But not the river. She was followed as usual by an ever hopeful band of ducks, and this part of the river being popular with rowers a steady procession of large and small boats paddled by.

Today she turned back sooner than she usually would have done and headed for the café near Putney Bridge. She was out of breath. The book she had borrowed from the library had informed her that, although breathlessness was most common during the latter part of pregnancy, it was not unusual to experience it earlier on and if it occurred there were several things she must do.

She must take it easy. Well, that wasn't difficult. She did no housework, hardly any cooking, and didn't have to carry much shopping home because Florian insisted they have most of their household needs delivered. She must eat a balanced diet and take gentle exercise. Again, easy. Red meat, leafy greens, lots of fruit; all she had to do was give Rosa a menu for the week and the young maid delighted in having such an abundance of good food to prepare.

The book also said she must never slouch but should sit up straight with her shoulders back. That amused her, as it was exactly what Miss Taylor had told her to do all the time she had lived with her. And she must focus on her breathing. She must spend a few minutes each day inhaling and exhaling to her lungs' full capacity. That was not so easy. Florian might be working in the room he had turned into a study and Rosa might be cooking or doing housework, but Linda could never be sure that one or other of them would not have a question for her. With Rosa it might be something about a recipe, whereas Florian might want her to listen to something he had written. So Linda had taken to going for walks whenever she could. She would sit by the river or on the heath and do her breathing exercises unobserved. Because telling Florian that she was pregnant was not going to be easy at all.

All thoughts of a balanced diet fled when Linda entered the café and smelled the bacon frying. A pot of tea and a bacon sandwich. Heaven. This was her guilty secret, although she tried not to indulge herself more than once a week. Well, twice. She had been lucky to escape morning sickness, or sickness at any time of the day, and she was young and healthy. She had no qualms whatsoever when she gave the waitress her usual order and settled back to read the letter which had arrived this morning. The letter from Vera.

Chapter Fifteen

16th July 1938

Dear Mrs Hylton,

Don't be annoyed, I couldn't resist writing that even though in your letter you said I must call you Linda. Your apartment sounds lovely but, like you, I might have got a bit fed up with the lady designer. Fancy being able to make a living by telling people how to decorate and furnish their own homes! The new Mrs Meredith employed an interior designer as well. A man. And that fancy gentleman had some right old flare-ups with both Cordelia and her mother, I can tell you.

But Green Leas looks marvellous, if perhaps a little too grand for the size of it. Do you know what I mean? The new maid here at Fernwood, Brenda, and I went along with the lad to help the new staff get the house ready for the young couple while they were on honeymoon. They went to Biarritz, which I'm told is on the Bay of Biscay and has a famous casino. Albert Aslett says the casino might have been the attraction because he's heard that Charles Meredith likes a bit of a gamble now and then, and in that he takes after his father. Maybe that's why the Merediths are always hard-up. Are you shocked by this below-stairs gossip?

Servants always know a lot more than their employers think they do. Your little maid sounds nice. It must be funny to have to leave your own country and start anew somewhere else, but Rosa and her parents are not the only ones, are they? What troubled times we live in.

Here's a bit of news. Albert has taken over driving duties until Mr Hylton engages a new chauffeur, because Paul Stevens gave his notice and went off to join the army. He said he would rather join up before he's called up, because conscription's bound to come if and when war is declared. He joked that pretty soon he might be driving a tank instead of a Rolls Royce, but Albert told him Rolls Royce make tanks, too. At least, they make the engines for them. Poor Paul. He thought we didn't know about his pash on Cordelia. We never said anything, but we all knew it was hopeless. That young madam was just playing with him. She would never have defied her family like Florian did.

You might not have had a big posh wedding like Cordelia and Charlie, but what you and Florian did was very romantic, wasn't it? Running off together and defying the lot of them. He must really love you. But why shouldn't he? In fact, he's very lucky to have found you. Are you blushing furiously? Sorry.

And talking about pashes. Young Bobby is in love! Yes, he is. He's getting letters that he's very secretive about. The envelopes are a pretty pink and they smell of roses. But who on earth can the girl be? I mean, Bobby never goes anywhere where he could meet a girl. He came here from an orphanage, so he has no family to visit, and until recently he would spend his days off just lazing around with a book. Mr Hylton gave him free rein in the library. But then the lad started going to Newcastle to go to the pictures. He says the films are better on the big screen than on the portable screen in the village hall. Maybe that's not the only attraction. Likely he's met another film fan!

Now that the wedding is over you would have thought that everything would settle down here, but the Hyltons aren't the happy family they used to be. I don't know why. Mr Hylton is just as considerate, but Mrs Hylton seems to suffer badly from her nerves. She always was fine-tuned but now she's more skittery than ever. Ivy thinks it's because she misses Cordelia, and I suppose that could be true. I think she's lonely. She never made any real friends, you know. Those little tea parties for the village women are just a sort of game. She was a good wife and mother, and a good daughter-in-law, too. She was quite happy just being part of a family. She visits Cordelia but has the good sense not to go too often, and otherwise she just sits here on her own reading magazines. Mr Hylton doesn't seem to notice.

And as for Rupert, we hardly see him these days. He doesn't come straight home from work; he goes to some gentlemen's club to play billiards. At least, that's what he tells his parents. His mother asked him why he's not content to play at home – after all, there's a perfectly good table at the Hall – but he told her he can't expect his pals to come all the way out to Redesburn, and I suppose he's got a point there. Now and then he stays at his club for the night, and when you think about it, it's natural that he should want to spend his time with his pals going to the theatre and the like. He works hard, so why shouldn't he play hard, too?

You needn't worry about your house, Linda. Your tenants, Mr and Mrs Millard, seem very respectable and they've told people how happy they are living there. Apparently this thing they're working on – a dig, that's what they call it – could be a lifetime job, and I've heard on the village grapevine that Mrs Millard has been asking questions about hospitals and schools. Now, of course, everyone is watching the poor woman keenly.

And what about you? Are you happy living in London? Is Florian getting on with his book? I'm sure he will do well now that he has you to encourage him. Bobby said he once found some of Florian's papers in the library and that in his opinion he was a first-class writer. It was a short story and he said it was very funny and it reminded him of the stories of P.G. Wodehouse. I said I'd take his word for it. I prefer a book by the likes of Georgette Heyer. You know, olden times, arranged marriages, romance, fashion and a bit of mystery thrown in.

I'd better stop these ramblings before I bore you silly! Do write again and let me know how you're getting on.

Ivy and Albert and Bobby send their love.

Love,
Vera

Linda folded the closely covered pages then put them back in the envelope. She looked around and blinked as the little café came back into focus.

While she had been reading Vera's letter she had been transported back to Redesburn and Fernwood Hall: the village she had grown up in and the house that had seemed so enchanted to her as a child.

How happy she had been when she had gone to live at the Hall, and how moved when the family she had been entranced by for years had made her so welcome. For far too brief a time she had been able to pretend that she was one of them; one of the fabulous Hylton family, but when tragedy had struck they had drawn together and there had not been room for her within the magic circle.

And they had cast Florian out too. Florian had remained tight-lipped and silent about his family's reaction to the news that he and Linda were to be married. Linda could only assume they had been very angry indeed and that Florian had not revealed the depth of their outrage because he had not wanted to hurt her.

Although he had written to his mother several times since they had come to London, there had been no reply. Linda could not make her mind up whether this was because he had displeased them in choosing not to go into the family business or whether it was because he had married her. She had decided it was probably a combination of both. There had been no letters of condemnation but neither had there been a letter welcoming her into the family. Just a chilling silence.

While she had been reading Vera's letter the waitress had brought her order to the table. Linda peeled back the top slice of bread and added a liberal dab of HP Sauce. She waited for a moment

271

to allow the tea to brew and then filled her cup. She looked down at her plate and thought: ambrosia! Before taking a bite, she paused and visualized the tasteful spread Rosa had provided for the writing group and decided that, delicious as it was, it could in no way compare to a bacon sandwich.

As she enjoyed her guilty feast she thought about Vera's letter. So her mother's old friend thought that what she and Florian had done had been romantic. Linda smiled. She supposed it had been. She remembered the evening when Florian had asked her to marry him.

Even before he had given her time to answer him he had pulled her close and kissed her. Consumed by the sorrow and misery of Clara's death and what had happened afterwards, the sheer joy of having someone love her and want her had overwhelmed her.

'I'll get a special licence,' he said. 'We can get married within the next few days.'

Linda pulled back a little. 'But your parents?'

'What about them?'

'What do they say?'

'It doesn't matter.'

'They don't approve!'

Florian looked uneasy. 'Well, not exactly. They think I'm too young.'

'Is that the only reason?'

Florian looked uncomfortable.

'They don't like me, do they?'

'You mustn't think that! Of course they like you. Given time I'm sure they'll come round to the idea.'

'Then why don't we wait?'

'Because I couldn't bear to! Linda, I love you and the idea of going to London without you is intolerable. Please say you will marry me. Don't torture me like this.'

Linda smiled. 'I'm not torturing you. I'm just trying to be sensible.'

'Sensible? Sensible when you're deciding whether or not to break my heart!'

He put his hand over his heart when he said this and declaimed the words like an actor in a melodrama. Then he smiled, and it was that smile that caught her up in the romance of the moment.

'Yes, I'll marry you,' she said and gave herself up to his kiss.

That night in bed she did not regret her decision, but she wondered why she had not had the courage to ask Florian why he thought his parents needed time to come round to the idea of their marriage. She could accept that at twenty-two they might think him too young, but she knew in her heart that that was not the only reason.

Could it be that they would never get over the fact that she had been looking after Clara the night she died? Or in addition to that, did they not want their son to marry a girl from the village, and the wrong end of the village at that? Whatever the reason, she decided there was nothing she could do about it. Florian loved her. He wanted her to marry him and go to London; to leave this place and its memories behind them. By the time the sun rose the next morning Linda was sure that that was what she wanted, too.

Their wedding day had been a crazily joyful affair. 'Put your best bib and tucker on and leave it all to me,' Florian had told her the night before.

'But how...? Where...?'

'I've told you. Leave it to me, but please be ready at nine o'clock tomorrow morning. All packed and ready to go.'

'But how will we cope with all the luggage?'

'Stevens will take us into town. My parents can hardly deny me that.'

When the Rolls Royce drew up at her door the next morning, Linda was aware that it had attracted attention. One or two of the villagers actually braved the cold wind and stood on the pavement to watch her go. That will give them something to talk about, she thought. Not one of them was aware that this was her wedding day.

Paul took Linda and Florian into Newcastle, where the first call was to the Central Station to leave their cases at the left luggage office. When he dropped them off at the registrar's office he wished them well, thanked Florian for what was no doubt a generous tip, then drove away. Linda wondered if she would ever see him again.

It was bitterly cold and Linda shivered. 'As soon as we get to London I'll buy you a fur coat,' Florian said. 'It will be my wedding present.'

'You're supposed to be a struggling writer. I can't let you be so extravagant.'

'Thanks to my darling grandmamma, we won't have to struggle quite so hard, if at all. So just try and stop me!' They smiled at each other. 'Do you feel like a runaway bride?' he asked her.

'I do. Although I had no stern parents to

outwit. Only Mr Sinclair, who kept asking me if I was sure I was doing the right thing.'

'I hope you assured him that you were.'

'I think so. He wished me well.' Then it occurred to Linda that they were the only people standing there. 'Where are the witnesses?' she asked. 'You said you'd arrange that.'

'Look over there,' Florian told her. 'What do you think?'

Linda looked across the street. Two bowler-hatted gentlemen carrying briefcases were standing chatting to each other. They showed no sign of turning to come across the road, although they must have seen Florian and Linda waiting there.

'Are they...?' Linda began.

'Or what about those two?' Florian pointed to an elderly couple who were coming down the street towards them. The man and woman were respectably dressed, if a little threadbare. The woman held a shopping bag in one hand and with the other was hanging onto the man's arm, no doubt to save herself from slipping on the treacherous pavement. 'Which do you prefer?'

'I don't understand.'

'The old couple, don't you think? They look as if they would enjoy themselves.'

Florian patted her hand and hurried towards them. Linda watched him stop them and saw the surprised expressions on their faces. All three heads turned as he pointed towards Linda, and she watched the couple's eyes widen in surprise before they smiled and nodded their heads.

Florian shepherded his new friends back to where Linda was standing. 'Meet Mr and Mrs

Talbot,' he said. 'Our witnesses.'

'You mean you hadn't already arranged it?' Linda asked him.

'I thought it would be more fun to do it this way. Don't you agree?'

'I suppose so,' Linda said doubtfully. And then, caught up in Florian's infectious mood of enjoyment, she said, 'Of course I do.'

'Then let us go and get married.'

After the ceremony Florian insisted that the Talbots accompany them to the Royal Turk's Head for the wedding breakfast – or rather, a splendid four-course lunch. When offered the menus, Mr and Mrs Talbot looked at each other uneasily and Linda guessed that they did not know what to order. 'Why don't I order for everyone?' Florian asked, and they agreed thankfully.

After the meal their new friends stayed for coffee and Florian insisted on buying Mr Talbot a cigar, although he didn't take one himself. They had moved through to the lounge where there was a roaring fire, and Linda realized that their witnesses were reluctant to go. Florian told them that he and Linda would be staying at the hotel until later that night and asked them if they would like to take afternoon tea with them. Mrs Talbot explained that they had come into town to do some shopping and had better get cracking before the shops closed.

'All the very best, Mr and Mrs Hylton,' Mr Talbot said. 'This has been a day my wife and I will never forget.'

Mrs Talbot, made sleepy by the large meal and

the warmth of the fire, rose a little unsteadily. 'It's been a lovely day,' she said. 'The champagne was a real treat.' Then, perhaps emboldened by the mood of friendly intimacy, she added, 'But if you don't mind my saying so, what a pity the bride didn't have some flowers.'

Florian was stricken. 'I forgot the bouquet!'

'It's all right, really,' Linda said.

'No, it isn't. All brides should have a bouquet. I promise I'll make it up to you.'

So that was why, when they arrived at the Central Station some hours later, Florian signalled for a porter and sent him on an errand. By the time they had arrived at their first-class sleeper compartment, it was full of flowers.

Linda glanced at her watch and ordered a fresh pot of tea. It was too soon to go back to the apartment. Some of Florian's writing guests would linger after the meeting was over and finish eating whatever was left on the table. At least, Reginald and Doreen Lamb did. When they arrived they would fill their plates hungrily and before they left they did so again. Linda guessed that they were not very well paid in their council schools, and this probably added to their ill-disguised air of resentment.

When she arrived home she heard voices coming from the sitting room so she went straight to the kitchen. Rosa had finished washing the dishes and was putting everything away.

'Are Mr and Mrs Lamb still here?' she asked.

'No, it is Mr and Mrs Grey.'

Linda was surprised. These two, with such a

277

busy social life, were usually the first to go.

'Mr Hylton is discussing Mr Grey's work with him. I think he is writing a play – a drama. For the stage,' she added.

'What makes you think that?'

'Mrs Grey gets up and walks about and – what do you say? – she declaims. She speaks theatrically.'

'She used to be an actress.'

'I know that. And Mr Grey, he wants her to have success again. He blames himself.'

'For what?'

'For interrupting her career when she could have been so great a star. He will write a play and he will put his money into a production.' Rosa's eyes were shining.

'Rosa, how do you know all this?'

'Because when I walk in to clear away and tidy I am wearing this–' she looked down and with a downward motion of her hands indicated the clothes she was wearing. 'This black dress and the little white apron. This makes me invisible. People talk as if I were not there. I listen. Why should I not? Oh, Mrs Hylton, I am fortunate to be with such interesting people.'

As they spoke they heard voices in the hall and then the sound of the front door closing. A moment later Florian walked into the kitchen.

'You're back,' he said, smiling briefly at Linda. Then, 'Rosa, I need coffee.'

'It's time for Rosa to go home. I'll make the coffee,' Linda told him.

'No, I will do it,' Rosa said. 'Please go and sit down, Mrs Hylton.'

278

'Yes, darling, come and talk to me.'

In the sitting room the chairs were still arranged in a circle. On the chair next to the one Florian usually sat in there was a fat folder of papers. Florian looked round at the chairs and said, 'I'll see to this later. Or perhaps Rosa...'

'No.'

'She wouldn't mind.'

'I know she wouldn't, but we mustn't impose on her. I'll help you when you've had your coffee.'

Rosa brought in a tray with the coffee and set it on a small table. 'For your evening meal there is a dish of salad in the refrigerator and some slices of ham,' she told them. 'Also, the cakes which were not eaten I have put in the cake tin. Shall I pour the coffee?'

'No, I'll pour,' Linda said. 'And now you must go home before your mother starts worrying about you.'

Rosa said goodnight and left reluctantly. Florian smiled. 'I think she'd be happy to move in here,' he said. 'And sweet as she is, that would be dreadful.'

'Why do you say that?'

'Because I like being here alone with my wife. Perhaps when we move to something larger than this, but this apartment isn't suitable for live-in staff.'

Linda poured the coffee, taking care to pour very little for herself. She was still full of tea and bacon sandwiches, but she couldn't tell Florian that.

'I didn't realize you intended to move,' she said.

'Oh, it won't be until I've had a novel or two published. Meanwhile we shall have to make do with this.'

He laughed as he said this and it left Linda wondering whether he was serious or not. He seemed to think that once his novel was published fame and fortune would come his way. Possibly they would. But it was also possible that they wouldn't. She had no idea how much money novelists earned but she thought it very unlikely that they would all be able to live in luxury.

Florian sipped his coffee and sighed with contentment. When they heard the front door closing he said, 'Alone at last!'

'Rosa said the Greys stayed on after the meeting,' Linda said. 'They usually hurry away.'

'I know, and Reginald and Doreen Lamb were most put out. They hovered over the dining table, had a sausage roll or two and went on their way feeling very disgruntled.'

'Why did Gerald and Nadine stay?'

Linda felt awkward. She didn't know if Florian would be annoyed with Rosa if he knew she had listened to some of the conversation. She thought she had better act as though she knew nothing at all. Luckily Florian was quite happy to tell her.

'Gerald wanted to show me his work.'

'Another little anecdote for a motoring magazine?'

'They're not that bad, actually. I'm sure he could get one accepted eventually. But he didn't bring one tonight. He's writing a play.'

Linda pretended surprise. 'A play? That's a strange project for a motor magnate, isn't it?'

'He used to be an actor.'

Now Linda really was surprised. 'Gerald?'

'Yes. He's tall and dark, and in his youth he must

have been very handsome. Quite an imposing presence on the stage.'

'But I've never heard of him. Or of Nadine, come to that.'

'He was never very successful, and when an uncle died and left him the motor dealership he retired from the stage gratefully. He proved to be a very good businessman.'

'What about Nadine?'

'Nadine Temple, she was then. She was just starting her career when she was swept off her feet by an older, handsome fellow thespian who had just inherited a successful business. Being a rich man's wife obviously appealed to her. But she never intended to give up her career.'

'So why did she?'

'Gerald wanted a son.'

'They have a child?' Linda was astonished.

'Not just one. The first was a girl and then they had the boy. The perfect family. At least as far as Gerald is concerned.'

'But not Nadine.'

'No, poor Nadine.'

'Why do you say that?'

'She's talented, she's extremely beautiful, and I'm told she showed great promise, but by the time the children were packed off to school and she was ready to go back to work the world had moved on. The casting directors had forgotten about her. So now Gerald believes the only way to relaunch her career is to invest his own money in a production. God knows he has enough.'

'I can understand that, but why does he want to write the play himself?'

'Because he believes he knows what she's capable of better than any stranger could. Only he can do her justice.'

'And can he?'

Florian frowned. 'I'm not sure. When he asked me to look at the script I was terrified that I would have to offend him. But the idea is a great one and his writing isn't too bad. However, it needs a bit of editing and tidying up.'

Linda suddenly understood. 'That's why he has shown it to you, isn't it? He wants you to help him.'

'That's right.'

'And will you?'

'I'm not sure. It's an interesting project, and he said I would be credited as co-author and have a share of the profits.'

'What have you told him?'

'I said I'd think about it. I said, even if I agree I want to finish my novel first.'

'That was wise.'

Florian picked up the folder that was on the chair next to him. 'Do you want to read Gerald's play? I'd like to know what you think of it.'

'All right. I'll start reading as soon as you start writing in the morning.'

Suddenly Florian looked serious. 'Are you happy, Linda?'

'I am. Why do you ask?'

'Because I want you to know that I'm blissfully happy. I have you and my writing, and there is nothing to interfere with the peace of my days or destroy my concentration. I can't help feeling that life is perfect.'

Chapter Sixteen

October 1938

Linda stared at the pamphlet in dismay. It described the various characteristic smells of the gases which might be used against the civilian population and there was a terrifying warning about mustard gas. It said that one spot of mustard gas falling on your boot or shoe could rapidly penetrate to the foot and prove sufficient to cause death. Children had already been issued with gas masks, and warnings had been issued that masks were not to be tested by putting one's head in a gas oven as they were not designed to deal with coal gas. Apparently some poor souls, unaware of this warning, had done so with fatal consequences.

'I sometimes wonder what sort of world I am bringing this child into,' she said.

'You must try not to dwell on these things.'

While the writing group occupied the living room Linda was sitting in the kitchen with Rosa, drinking iced tea. A dry spring had brought an early fall of autumn leaves, but the warm air lingered over London like an impenetrable dome. The weather in early October was more like late summer than autumn.

'I try not to,' Linda said. 'But it is very hard when any minute we may be at war.'

'No, your Prime Minister Mr Chamberlain has

saved us. Just last week you heard the crowds cheering on the wireless when he went to Buckingham Palace.'

'Where he stood on the balcony and waved his bit of paper and said he had got peace with honour ... peace in our time.' Linda shook her head.

'You don't believe this?'

'I think Mr Chamberlain believes it, but I also think Herr Hitler will do whatever he wants.'

'And what does Mr Hylton think?'

Linda pushed her hair back from her damp forehead and smiled tiredly. 'Mr Hylton does not listen to the news these days. Nor does he read the newspapers. He is completely taken up with wondering whether his novel has been accepted.'

Rosa grinned. 'I know. He waits in the hall each morning and watches the letters coming through the letterbox. He snatches them up and he even seems relieved if there is no letter from his publisher. That is strange.'

'No, it isn't. Florian thinks no news is good news and also that the longer they keep his manuscript the more likely it is that they will accept it.'

'Do you think that is true?'

'I'm not sure, but I hope it means that someone is reading it.'

'And then they will see how good it is.'

Linda laughed gently. 'You haven't read it, Rosa, so why are you so sure?'

Rosa was silent. She suddenly busied herself getting more ice cubes from the refrigerator.

'Rosa!' Linda said. 'Look at me. You *have* read it, haven't you?'

'Yes – well, not entirely. Sometimes when I

cleaned Mr Hylton's study I could not help glancing at the papers on his desk.'

'You shouldn't have done.'

'I fell to temptation.'

'Oh, Rosa, not even I was allowed to read his finished draft. He must never find out.'

'He won't. Unless you tell him.'

'I won't.' Linda leaned across the table and lowered her voice conspiratorially. 'If you tell me what you think about it.'

Both girls laughed but Rosa was spared from replying when Amy Purvis, one of the writing group, came into the kitchen. 'Sorry to interrupt, Mrs Hylton,' Amy said, 'but the meeting is not yet over and we are all parched with talking. Mr Hylton suggests we have a short break and he asked me to tell Rosa to make another pot of tea.'

It was typical of Florian, Linda thought, to send someone else rather than come himself. He couldn't help it. That was the way he had been brought up. And of course that someone else would have to be a woman rather than a man. He would not ask the beautiful Nadine, everybody spoiled her, and he would probably have been wary if not scared of asking Doreen Lamb, so that left Amy Purvis.

Amy just missed being attractive. She was tall and slender and her skin was good, but she wore ugly wire-framed spectacles over pale, washed-out blue eyes. Her dark blonde hair was greying and carelessly pinned into an untidy bun which would have suited a much older woman rather than one in her forties, which Linda guessed her to be. The sensible clothes she wore did her no favours.

Linda sensed that she simply did not care how she looked, had given up caring years ago, perhaps when some tragedy had marked her with a permanent air of regret for what might have been.

She wore a ring on the fourth finger of her left hand, a very small diamond set in white gold, but there was never any mention of a fiancé. Florian and Linda had guessed that Amy Purvis must have lost the man she was going to marry in the last war. The war that was supposed to end all wars, but instead had laid the foundations of turmoil which was catapulting the world into another one.

Instead of going straight back to the sitting room, Amy surprised Linda by joining her at the table.

'May I sit for a moment?'

'Of course, but Rosa will take the tea in.'

'It's not that, Mrs Hylton. I just wanted to ask...' Amy Purvis hesitated and then said with a rush, 'to ask how you are.' She coloured slightly.

Amy seemed embarrassed, and Linda thought it might be because her generation thought it indelicate to refer openly to pregnancy. But she dismissed this thought immediately when she sensed that the secretary had been going to ask a different question entirely and had lost her nerve.

'I'm well, thank you. Please call me Linda.'

Amy brushed a stray tendril of hair from her brow. 'Hot days must be trying for you.'

'They are. But that's not what you want to talk about, is it?'

A delicate pink flush began to suffuse Amy's face. 'No... I...' She glanced at Rosa, who although she had her back to them was obviously

286

listening keenly.

Rosa turned to face them. 'I shall take the tea in now, and I will stay to fill up their cups and encourage them to fill up their plates.' The look she gave Linda clearly meant, *I'm giving her the chance to talk. Tell me later!*

When the maid had gone Amy said quickly, 'I wanted to ask you for your advice.'

'*My* advice? About your writing, do you mean?'

Amy smiled. 'Don't look so surprised. I remember that you made some very intelligent comments before Doreen and Reginald's appallingly rude attitude stopped you from coming to the meetings. At the time I thought your husband ought to have insisted that you stay.'

Sensing criticism of Florian, Linda hurried to defend him. 'He did. In fact, he wanted to take it up with the Lambs, but I asked him not to. He enjoys the meetings so much that I didn't want to spoil things for him.'

'He's a lucky man to have someone so understanding.'

She said this so wistfully that Linda was prompted to ask, 'And you don't?'

Amy's smile was rueful. 'I live with my mother, who loves me, there's no question of that, but she cannot understand why I want to shut myself away and write when I come home from work. She tells me I should get out more. She arranges for friends to ask me to dinner, she demands that we go to the cinema or the theatre together. She thinks I should have what she calls, "a proper life". I think she is ashamed that someone once as beautiful as she was should have an old maid for a daughter.' She sighed. 'It was quite a battle to get my novel finished.'

'You've finished it?'

'Some weeks ago.'

'But you didn't tell the group, or I'm sure Florian would have told me.'

'No, I didn't say anything.'

'And now you are asking me whether you should have done?'

'Yes.'

'I don't understand what the problem is.'

'Florian was so excited when he told us that he had sent his manuscript off, and everyone wished him well and assured him that he would be successful. There didn't seem to be an opportunity for me to tell them I had sent my manuscript to a publisher, too.'

'I think I understand.'

'But that's not all of it.'

'What do you mean?'

'I didn't think – I still don't – that they would be as encouraging to me as they were to your husband. I do have some pride, you know.'

'Florian would have been – encouraging, I mean. More than once he has told me that your writing shows promise.'

'Has he?' Amy's eyes widened with pleasure. 'However, the others don't share his opinion. You know, once when I was leaving, I was hardly out of the sitting room when I heard Mrs Lamb say to Florian that she didn't know why that dreary little secretary bothered to bring her sentimental scribblings to the group.'

'How dreadful. I don't think your work is sentimental at all – at least, not in a maudlin way. What did Florian say?'

'He told her that in his opinion she was wrong to dismiss my work and that she obviously had missed the point of it.'

'Good for him.'

'But I didn't wait to hear her response. I fled like the poor little mouse that awful woman thinks I am, and I very nearly didn't come back.'

'I'm glad you did.'

'And it's thanks to your husband. He really is an inspiration, isn't he?'

'He's dedicated to the cause!'

They both laughed.

'It's obvious that he stands head and shoulders above the rest of us,' Amy said. 'We are all expecting that he will hear any day now that his novel has been accepted.' She looked troubled again.

'Amy, what's the matter? You said you wanted to ask my advice. Is something wrong?'

'Yes, my novel–'

Suddenly Linda thought she understood. 'Oh, no, it's been rejected and you don't want to tell the group because of what Doreen Lamb might say? Is that it?'

'Not quite. *The Lost Years* has been accepted.'

'But, that's marvellous!'

'Yes, it is, isn't it?' Amy smiled nervously.

'So what's the problem?'

'I feel I can't tell the group while Florian is still waiting to hear about his novel.'

'Why ever not?'

'I don't want to steal his thunder. He should have been the first to hear.'

'Please don't worry about that. Florian will be delighted for you. He'll probably try and take credit for the fact he's encouraged and advised you.'

'But that's true, he has. And I shall say as much. In fact, I'm going to dedicate the book to him.' Amy paused and looked embarrassed. 'If you don't mind, that is.'

'Of course I don't mind. Now go in there and tell them the wonderful news.'

'You think I should?'

'I do.'

'Will you come with me?'

'Definitely not. Stand up straight, square your shoulders and stand on your own two feet!'

Both women burst out laughing at this absurd mishmash of clichéd commands, but when Amy had left the kitchen and Linda was alone, she admitted to herself why she had not wanted to accompany Amy. It was because, although she sincerely believed it was the right thing to do, she didn't want to be there to see Florian's reaction.

Although she could not see his face, a few moments later she heard him say, 'But that's marvellous, Amy.' There was a pause – a stunned silence? – and he added, 'Isn't it, everyone?'

Nadine Grey, bless her, was the first to respond. 'Yes, it's absolutely marvellous, darling. Well done, our little Amy.'

Linda wasn't so sure about that last bit and was pleased when Gerald immediately said, 'Jolly good, old girl. That's one up for our group, isn't it?'

Rosa had lingered in the dining room and when she returned to the kitchen she told Linda that the Lambs had uttered no words of congratulation but that Mrs Lamb had asked Miss Purvis which publisher she had sent her manuscript to and that she had been very surprised at the reply.

'Why was that, do you think?' she asked Linda.

Linda told Rosa that it was because the publisher in question had a very good reputation. Amy Purvis had done very well.

The meeting broke up quite soon after, and as soon as Rosa had gone home Florian surprised Linda by saying that he wanted to take her out to dinner. 'Don't worry,' he said. 'You needn't put your evening dress on; we'll go to Stefano's.'

Florian knew very well that Linda could no longer zip up any of her evening dresses, and she thought it might have been kinder of him just to say that they would go to Stefano's.

'Are you sure you want to go out?' she asked him. 'All the way to Soho when there's a beef and beetroot casserole all ready to go in the oven? Rosa gave me the recipe.'

'I'm sure it will be delicious, but pop it in the refrigerator and save it for tomorrow. I want to go out tonight. We should go out while we can, we agreed on that, didn't we?'

Linda said, 'Yes, we did,' although she had never actually agreed in so many words to any such thing.

Sensing that she was not entirely enthusiastic about the idea, he said, 'You know, once the baby is born we won't just be able to go out on the spur of the moment like this, will we?'

291

Although he was smiling, Linda could sense an underlying air of reproach – as if it was entirely her fault that she had become pregnant. She had put off telling him until she could no longer conceal her condition, and she didn't think she would ever forget his totally unguarded expression of dismay. At first he had been speechless.

'Aren't you pleased?' she had asked him.

'Pleased? Why?' He looked bewildered.

'Pleased that we are going to have a child?'

To do him justice, he had recovered quickly. 'Of course I am. A son ... a daughter ... I don't mind which. Another little Hylton. Perhaps then my parents will take me back into the fold.'

Linda was surprised. 'Do you want that?'

He looked thoughtful. 'No, not literally. I love my life here with you. You are the perfect wife.' He grinned. 'In my bed, in my kitchen, in the ordering of my days, no man could want for more. It's just that I didn't think my parents would cut me out completely. I thought that my mother might at least write a letter or two.'

And then he had become serious again. 'I'm sorry if I didn't whoop for joy just now like the prospective fathers do in the romantic films, but I suppose I had never imagined that our way of life would change so suddenly. Silly of me, I know.'

That conversation had taken place in August and Florian had asked her when the baby was due. Late January or early February, she told him, and he did his best to hide his relief.

'I'll have my novel finished long before that,' he had told her. And then, 'We must make the most of our time together, darling. Once the baby is

292

born our lives will never be our own again.'

So this evening, although she would rather have stayed at home, Linda agreed to go out and tried to look happy about it.

'Why don't you wear that pretty floral thing?' he said.

'You mean the smock? I thought you hated it.'

'It doesn't look like a smock if you keep your jacket on, and that dusky rose and moss green pattern is very pretty. Now, who's first for the shower? Or shall we squeeze in together?'

It seemed to Linda that Florian was having to make an effort to be cheerful and she wondered if this had anything to do with Amy's announcement. So far he hadn't mentioned it, but maybe it had unsettled him. He was nervous enough waiting for news of his own novel, so it must have cost him to have to congratulate another member of the group.

Linda suddenly felt ashamed of herself. Florian was a good husband and a good friend to the members of the writing group. He deserved a bit of consideration. If he wanted to dine out the least she could do was to be happy about it.

'Oh, together, definitely,' she said, and refrained from saying that they wouldn't be able to do that much longer.

They hadn't been in London very long before Florian had discovered Stefano's. It wasn't so much the food – which was excellent – as the sort of people who ate there: writers, people who worked in the film industry and in the BBC, as well as chorus girls from the Palladium. An

293

eclectic mix from the world of the arts, he told Linda, as well as the flotsam and jetsam washed up on England's shores by the turmoil in Europe, the refugees who had had to flee their homelands.

'What stories they have to tell!' Florian said. 'What inspiration to be found on the menu at Stefano's!' He had laughed self-consciously. 'I go over the top sometimes, don't I?'

'Perhaps.'

'Then it's just as well that I have you to rein me in.'

'Oh, Florian, I hope I don't do that.'

Florian looked thoughtful. 'No, you don't, but you do help me to keep a sense of proportion. You're good for me, Linda. We make the perfect couple, don't we? Me and my flights of fancy and you so level-headed.'

Linda had not been sure that she liked to be thought of as level-headed. She wondered if that might be interpreted as boring.

Florian had ordered a taxi to take them into London and so they avoided the crowded buses and trains of the rush hour. When they arrived at the restaurant Stefano's wife, Marina, greeted them with a smile and showed them to their table. She gave them the menu and left them to decide.

Florian leaned across the table towards Linda and said quietly, 'She's magnificent, isn't she?'

Linda looked around at the diners on the other tables and frowned. 'Who do you mean?'

'Marina, of course. So regal, such a classical profile, her hair swept up and back to reveal those extravagant gold earrings. If you picture her in sandals and a stola you could just imagine that she has stepped down from one of those ancient Greek friezes in the British Museum, couldn't you? The caryatids, for example.'

'Chiton.'

'I beg your pardon?'

'It was Roman ladies who wore stolas. Greek women wore chitons.'

Very briefly Florian looked irritated but then he shrugged and smiled. 'Of course, chitons. I knew that, but it's easy to get them muddled up, isn't it?' Without waiting for a reply, he began to study the menu. 'Shall I order for both of us?'

'Please do.'

'Then I think we'll have beef stifado for the main course, shall we?'

'What's that?'

Florian laughed. 'It's a beef casserole.'

Linda wondered whether Florian would mention Amy Purvis's success, and to his credit he did. 'She learned a lot from coming to our meetings,' he said. 'Her problem was that she had no confidence in herself.'

'Then it can't have helped her to have had to endure the comments of Doreen Lamb.'

'In a way it did. I told Amy that she must accept criticism but that she must also have faith in her own judgement. In the end she did.'

'I love you, Florian.'

He raised his eyebrows in surprise. 'What brought that on?'

'I love you because of the way you want to help others even though your own work is so important to you.'

The moment she said that Linda wished she

hadn't. Mention of his own work reminded him that he still hadn't heard from the publisher. What an idiot I am, she thought. Coming out tonight was probably a way of taking his mind off things and now I've spoilt it.

Nevertheless Florian made an effort to be cheerful and when he suggested they should end the night out by going to the cinema to see *The Lady Vanishes*, Linda agreed enthusiastically, even though she was desperately tired. They both enjoyed the rather harebrained story (Florian's description) of a rich young woman travelling home to be married trying to trace a fellow passenger who had been kidnapped from their train somewhere in Europe.

When they got home Florian insisted on making them cups of Ovaltine and bringing them to bed along with a mound of hot toast and butter. After finishing their midnight feast and attempting unsuccessfully to brush all the crumbs from the bed, they fell asleep in each other's arms.

Linda slept late and when she woke up she was alone. The wet towel on the bathroom floor showed her that Florian had already been in there. Early morning noises coming from the kitchen told her that Rosa had started work, so she pulled her robe on and went to the dining room expecting to find him at breakfast. On the table there was a half-eaten plate of bacon and eggs and a cup of coffee that looked as if it hadn't been touched. It's like the *Marie Celeste*, she thought.

Puzzled, Linda left the dining room and went to the study. He wasn't there. The typewriter on the desk was covered and a neat pile of unused foolscap lay beside it. The little bookcase behind the desk contained the usual array of dictionaries and reference books. At first Linda thought that everything was as it should be until she saw the large, empty envelope lying on the floor next to the wastepaper basket, which had fallen on its side because it was stuffed full and overflowing with typewritten sheets of paper.

Oh, no, she thought, because she knew at once what it was. Florian's novel. The publisher had rejected it. Not being able to bear seeing his work discarded like this, she knelt down and took the manuscript from the basket, gathering up some loose pages that were scattered on the floor. She got up too quickly and almost fell down again; clutching the manuscript to her body in one hand, she reached out with the other to grab and hold onto the back of the chair. When the world stopped spinning she sat down and placed the pile of papers on the desk in front of her. She felt like crying.

'Shall I bring you a cup of tea?'

Linda looked up to see Rosa had come into the room.

'Have you seen Mr Hylton?'

'He has gone out.'

'Where?'

'I don't know. He was eating his breakfast when the postman came. The postman rang the bell and Mr Hylton hurried to answer the door himself. He didn't go back to the dining room. He came in here and it seemed only a moment or two later I heard the front door slam. I think the news is bad, yes?'

'Yes, I think it is.'

Linda couldn't say this with any certainty because she had not been able to find a letter of rejection. But there could have been no other reason for Florian to have acted the way he did.

'I am sorry to hear that.'

'But I won't let him throw it away. Not after all that hard work. He must send it to another publisher. That's what people do.'

'And perhaps he should go through it and maybe make some changes?'

'I don't need editorial advice from my housemaid, Rosa.' Florian was standing in the doorway.

Rosa's eyes widened in shocked surprise. 'I am sorry, Mr Hylton, I should not have presumed...'

'No, you should not. Now please go and make Mrs Hylton's breakfast. What would you like, darling? Nothing to say? Can't make your mind up? Then I'll decide. Go and make scrambled egg for Mrs Hylton, Rosa, and bring a fresh pot of coffee and a clean cup for me.'

Linda thought that their young maid actually flinched when she passed Florian in the doorway. As soon as they were alone she said, 'That was cruel of you.'

'What was?'

'To talk to Rosa like that. She respects and admires you, and she is just as upset as I am that your novel has been rejected.'

'Oh, you've worked that out, have you? Perhaps it was because you found it in the wastepaper basket. That would be it. And you and our little housemaid are upset?'

'Of course we are. And I know how wretched you must be feeling, but I would never have imagined that you could be so unkind.'

'Is this your way of consoling me?'

'Stop it, Florian. This isn't you talking. You're upset and I understand that. You're angry, that's obvious, but don't vent your anger on people who love you. Be angry with the stupid people who rejected your book!'

Florian's eyes widened in surprise. 'You're angry, too.'

'Of course I am. And I really believe you should try again.'

'Darling, I'm so sorry. You're right. I've been a monster. I must go and apologize to Rosa, mustn't I?'

Linda nodded. Her throat was aching with unshed tears.

Florian hurried out of the room and a moment later she heard subdued voices in the kitchen. Linda did not ask him what he had said but he must have made a good job of the apology, because when Rosa brought the scrambled eggs into the dining room she was smiling. Florian looked at the plate and said that it looked delicious and asked Rosa if she would mind doing some more for him. She said she would be very pleased to.

'Bless you for that,' Linda said.

'No, I'm really hungry.'

He grinned and looked so like his old self that Linda believed his terrible mood of despair had eased. Neither of them mentioned the rejected novel, but when they had finished eating Florian poured himself another cup of coffee and rose from the table.

'I'll take this into the study with me,' he said. 'I'd better start work. I'd be grateful if you just left me alone for a while. Tell Rosa no coffee break. I need to get my thoughts in order.'

Florian closed the study door behind him, put his coffee on the desk and walked to the window. He lit a cigarette and half closed his eyes as he stared out over the communal garden, eleven acres of manicured grounds. He remembered how thrilled he had been when he had bought this apartment. How much he had wanted everything to be perfect for Linda and for their new life together. He had no idea how long he stood there – long enough to finish the cigarette and leave a scattering of ash on the polished floor. When he sat at the desk he saw the wrinkled skin on his coffee and pushed it aside in disgust.

He pulled the manuscript towards him. He had promised Linda that he would start work. But what exactly was he going to do? He pulled the crumpled letter out of his pocket. The letter that had arrived with the manuscript, the letter that he did not want anyone else to see. Then he tortured himself by smoothing out the expensive sheet of paper and skimming through it all over again.

Thank you for sending us your novel ... we read it with interest ... you have a certain style ... however... Ah, those 'howevers', therein lay the sting. *Derivative ... unoriginal ... perhaps too slick ... we don't think it would profit you to revise this work ...* and then another 'However': *If you start afresh and come up with something more original we hope you would let us have a look at it.*

Florian was not so ignorant of the world of publishing that he did not realize that this was a 'good' rejection. No matter how hurtful it had been, the letter had at least praised his style and asked him to submit another novel. But how long would that take him? The truth of it was, he didn't have time to start afresh. He had been so sure that his novel would be accepted and that by now he would have been offered some sort of advance, that he had cheerfully squandered his inheritance.

Not completely. He reckoned there was enough left in the bank to see them through until the baby was born in the New Year. He couldn't possibly get another novel written before then, and even if he did there was no guarantee that they would take it. What about sending it to another publisher, as Linda had suggested? He considered this for a moment and sighed. Perhaps he should, but whether he did or not he knew that he could no longer assume that his novel would be published. He lit another cigarette.

When Linda knocked on the study door at lunch-time Florian called for her to come in. He sounded cheerful enough, and she was pleased to see that he was writing in pencil in a large note-book. He looked up and smiled.

'I'm going to send the poor thing out again,' he said. 'I shall visit bookshops and libraries and make a list of the most likely publishers. Would you like to come with me?'

'I'd love to. Are you making some revisions?'

'No. I'm starting work on something new.'

301

'Another novel?'

'I will write another novel, but not yet. I think I got too intense about it all. I need a break. I need to do something entirely different. I've decided to take Gerald up on his offer and write a play with him. A play for the lovely Nadine. But instead of waiting for my share of the profits, I shall ask him to pay me some sort of salary. After all, a labourer is worthy of his hire.'

Chapter Seventeen

June 1939

'Do you want me to stay a little longer? Perhaps I could take the baby for a while and let you rest.' Rosa raised her voice so that she could be heard over the angry screams.

'No, it's all right. She must stop soon or she'll have no breath left in her body.' Linda tried to make a joke of it but she felt nearer to crying than laughing. There was absolutely nothing wrong with her daughter, both the doctor and the nurse had assured her of that. Imogen was just one of those babies.

Just? One of those babies? Easy for them to say. For all their experience of such things, they didn't have to live with a baby like this. Be with her twenty-four hours of every exhausting day.

'I don't mind, you know,' Rosa said. 'I could watch her while you have a shower. Or better still, you could relax in a perfumed bath.'

'A perfumed bath?'

Linda smiled at the concept. Rosa's English was almost perfect, indeed better than some who had been born here, but sometimes her language was engagingly poetic; influenced no doubt by the books she devoured whenever she had time to read.

'Yes. I shall prepare it for you. Which bath salts shall I use? The rose or the carnation?'

Holding her daughter close and attempting to rock her to sleep, Linda was tempted. She closed her eyes and imagined sinking into the warm water, imagined the rose-scented steam rising to surround her and form a temporary barrier between her and the everyday world.

'Rose,' she said and for a moment did not realize she had spoken aloud.

'Very well. Rose it shall be. I shall fill the bath and I shall take charge of the baby. Then I shall stay until it is time to give her her next bottle. You will have a rest.'

'But what about your parents? Won't they be worried about you if you get home late?'

'It was my mother who suggested I should stay and help, but if you don't mind I shall telephone the flower shop and tell her.'

'Of course.'

Rosa hurried to the bathroom and Linda sank down onto the nursing chair and began to rock, knowing that the gentle motion was more to soothe her own ragged nerves than to encourage Imogen to sleep. But it did at least turn down the volume. The screams became angry sniffs and

303

gulps of reproach, as if Imogen was telling her mother and the world in general that she was very hard done by. Linda looked down at her daughter's flushed angry face and was met with a hostile stare. Its intensity was shocking.

'Do you hate me, baby?' Linda whispered. 'How can you hate me when I love you so much?'

Linda felt hot tears scald her eyes and then begin to stream down her cheeks. This is wrong, she thought. I mustn't cry. The nurse told me that would only upset the baby more if she sensed my distress. *As if she would care!* The subversive thought took Linda unawares. Then she told herself, *Remember, it isn't personal.*

Rosa came back to tell her that her bath was ready and took Imogen from her. This brought on renewed screams of fury and Linda fled. Once in the bathroom she closed the door.

By the time she emerged, Rosa had performed a minor miracle: Imogen was swaddled and sleeping, albeit uneasily, in her cot.

Rosa came towards Linda, turned her round and propelled her out of the nursery. 'Go and lie down,' she whispered. 'I shall bring you tea and while the baby sleeps I shall make sure the meal is ready for when Mr Hylton returns.'

When she brought Linda a cup of tea she said, 'I could stay here tonight. The divan bed in the nursery would be very comfortable and I would be there if the baby awakes.'

'*When* she awakes, you meant But no, that won't do. I couldn't impose on you.'

'I have told you this before. You would not have to pay me any extra. I would have my meals here.

That would be enough, and my parents would have more to share!' She smiled when she said this, but it reminded Linda that the Balkels were struggling to get used to a much more modest way of life than they had been used to in Germany.

Linda knew there was no way she could take advantage of such a generous offer. If Rosa worked more hours she would have to be paid a fair wage. But she had been sorely tempted by the idea of having an uninterrupted night's sleep. Uninterrupted in so far as she wouldn't have to leave her warm bed when Imogen started crying, for she knew instinctively that she would wake up. And Florian would wake up, too. He would turn over and pull the bedclothes up over his ears. He seldom spoke, and when he did it was to mutter something like: 'For pity's sake, go and see to your daughter.' *Your* daughter, not *our* daughter, Linda noted.

Once after a very bad night Linda had broached the subject of Rosa living in.

'Like a nursemaid?' he'd asked.

'I suppose so.'

'And who would clean the house and prepare the food?'

'Rosa, of course.'

'You're not thinking straight. If she is looking after Imogen all night, she would not be fit to do much work in the morning, would she?'

'I don't suppose she would.'

'So we would have to engage a maid-of-all-work. No, Linda, we can't afford it.'

And that had been the end of the conversation. Florian had made up his mind and when Linda was able to think logically about it she knew that he was right.

It seemed like no time at all, but when Linda glanced at the clock on her bedside table she saw that she must have slept for nearly an hour and a half. She had left her tea to go cold and Rosa tutted as she removed the cup. A moment later she was back with another one.

'I shall watch you as you drink this,' she said and sat down on the dressing table chair.

'Imogen...?'

'I have made the next bottle. You will just have to warm it.'

'Well, at least that's one mercy.'

'I don't understand.'

'The fact that I had to give up the idea of feeding her myself. She might have died if I had persisted. At least I know how much nourishment she is getting from the bottles.'

'You are a good mother.'

Linda looked at Rosa in surprise. 'I am a dreadful mother. Even my husband thinks so. If I were a good mother Imogen would not behave the way she does.'

'You are wrong. You really care about your daughter. You want things to get better and I'm sure they will. My mother says so.'

Linda smiled at Rosa. 'Then it must be true.' Impulsively she added, 'You are lucky to have such a mother. My mother died when I was quite small and the good woman who brought me up was not wise in the ways of motherhood.'

They looked at each other awkwardly for a moment and then Rosa said, 'While you were sleeping Mr Hylton telephoned to say that he would be staying with Mr and Mrs Grey for the evening meal and that afterwards they would go on working on the play. If it gets too late he will stay the night there.'

'I see.'

Florian had been coming home later and later from his working sessions with Gerald and Nadine. Once or twice he'd had dinner with them, but he had never stayed there all night before.

'But you must eat even though he does not come home. I have made potato soup and a mutton hotpot. Do you want to come to the dining room or shall I bring a tray?'

Linda suddenly remembered all the trays that had been taken up to the bedrooms in Fernwood Hall for Clara, Emerald and Cordelia. For them that was a way of life. A way she did not want for herself.

'No tray, thank you. I'll get up now, and Rosa, don't bother with the dining room. The kitchen table will do, and I would very much like you to stay and eat with me.'

Rosa had been only too pleased to stay and they sat companionably enveloped in the warmth and the comforting aromas coming from the oven. The nourishing meal was rounded off with apple dumplings made to Mrs Balkel's recipe. Linda had barely finished when an angry screaming started in the nursery.

Why can't she just cry like other babies? Linda thought. Why does she have to sound so enraged? Wearily she set about the task of changing and

307

feeding her daughter while Rosa washed the dishes and made a pot of coffee.

Rosa appeared in the doorway of the nursery. 'Coffee is like mother's milk to me,' she said, 'but maybe I should make you tea instead.'

Linda was sitting in the nursing chair with Imogen. She looked up. 'Why?'

'It is getting late. The coffee might keep you awake.'

Linda laughed then with a movement of her head indicated the baby in her arms. 'As if this one needs any help to do that, you mean? No, coffee will be fine. Hot and strong and an extra spoon of sugar.'

Later she regretted that decision. Rosa had gone reluctantly homewards and Imogen, after the usual battle of the bottle, as Linda called it, had actually fallen asleep. Linda should have been able to sleep as well but she couldn't because of the coffee. She lay back against the propped-up pillows and surrendered to the headache that had been threatening all day. Or maybe all week ... or maybe ever since Imogen had been born.

At midnight she accepted that Florian would not be coming home. She considered whether she should be hurt or traitorously relieved. Probably the latter, she decided. Thinking how she usually slipped out of bed as soon as Imogen started crying, painfully aware of Florian's unresponsive back and silent complaint, she was thankful that tonight she would not be made to feel guilty as well as wretched when Imogen fought with the bottle and yelled her protests in between angry sucks.

Florian was putting all his energy into writing this play. It seemed as though he had quite forgotten about his novel. Linda had thought him very brave to admit to the writing group that his work had been rejected. They had been genuinely astonished. The Lambs had immediately come up with examples of other writers who had been rejected many times before finally being published and Florian had assured them that he would not give up.

The writing group had limped on until Christmas and then Florian had used Linda's condition as an excuse to say that they would not be able to meet here again. At first Linda had tried to persuade him that it would still be possible, but once Imogen was born she realized that Florian's decision had been right, even though it might have been made for another reason altogether.

After Christmas there had been half-hearted attempts to find another venue. Linda had wondered why Gerald and Nadine did not offer to have the meetings in their house, apparently it was big enough, but she decided that Gerald had simply lost interest in the group once Florian had agreed to work on the play.

Reginald and Doreen Lamb were never heard of again; whereas Amy Purvis had written to Florian thanking him for the way he had encouraged her and went on to tell him that he was too good a writer to fall at the first fence. Florian tore the letter up and said to Linda, 'Who the hell does she think she is? She's had one trivial little novel accepted and she thinks that gives her the right to patronize me.'

Linda was sure that Amy was not being patronizing in the slightest but she kept her counsel, hoping that Florian would calm down and do something about the manuscript that was languishing in the bottom drawer of his desk. In spite of his promise to do so, he had not sent it out again. She had mentioned it once or twice, but he had told her impatiently that as Gerald was paying him good money the play must come first. And furthermore he was thoroughly enjoying himself.

'Perhaps I am a playwright, not a novelist,' he'd said. 'It's wonderful how my words come alive when Nadine reads them aloud. She's a very good actress, you know.'

'And what about Gerald's words?' Linda had asked a trifle waspishly.

Florian had not noticed her mood. 'There won't be any of those. It's amazing that someone who used to be an actor is so bad at writing dialogue.'

'So what exactly does Gerald do?'

'Provides the ideas, outlines the scenes, that sort of thing.'

'And you write them to order?'

Florian raised his eyebrows, perhaps at last becoming aware that Linda was not entirely enthralled. 'Not at all,' he'd said. 'We discuss everything and if I don't agree with something I tell him so.'

'And that's all right with Gerald?'

'Absolutely. He respects my judgement. And so does Nadine.'

'Nadine takes part in the discussions?'

'Of course. She knows instinctively what will work and what will not. She was born to act. I'm determined that she shall have the chance to become a star.'

Linda had not mentioned his novel again.

At two o'clock, still sleepless, Linda remembered the letter that had arrived the previous morning and which she had only had time to skim through. She slipped out of bed, pulled on her robe and crept through to the kitchen. She held her breath, worried that the slightest noise would disturb the sleeping child. She warmed milk, poured it into a mug and spooned in some honey. Then she collected the biscuit barrel and went back to bed.

Sipping her drink and eating chocolate biscuits, she felt like one of the pupils in the Chalet School having a midnight feast. Mr and Mrs Sinclair had first given Linda *The School at the Chalet* as a present on her tenth birthday, and each year until she was fourteen had given her another Chalet School book. Then Miss Taylor had asked them to stop, saying Linda was too old for such frivolous fiction. She had made her give her books to the church jumble sale.

Linda took Vera's letter from the drawer of her bedside table and, hoping that Imogen would remain sleeping a little longer, she began to read.

17th June 1939

Dear Linda,
Mr and Mrs Hylton have gone to Green Leas for the day, Rupert is goodness knows where, and the Asletts have gone into Newcastle. It's their

311

day off and they decided to go to the Sunday market on the quayside. There's a chap there who ties himself up in chains, locks them with a padlock and then jumps in the river. When he pops up again he's freed himself of the chains. Then he takes a collection, and they say the longer he stays under the water the more money people give him. Ivy and Albert are going to have a meal in town and then go to the pictures. So that means I'm all alone for the day.

Where are Brenda and the lad? I hear you say. They've gone. They've left Fernwood Hall and they probably won't be coming back. As soon as Bobby turned twenty he was called up to do six months of military training. They say we've got to be prepared. If we go to war, as seems more than likely now, the lad will be sent God knows where. And Brenda has joined the Women's Land Army. They've started that all over again, because if war comes we'll have to grow more of our own food. Brenda will live on a farm and get thirty-two shillings a week, which is very much better than the fifteen shillings she got here!

Do you think there will be a war, Linda? We've been working up to it for so long now that some had stopped taking it seriously. If the balloon goes up, as they say, I hope you and Florian and baby Imogen will leave London and come back home. Surely Mr Hylton wouldn't turn you away in the circumstances. In fact, I should think he'd be glad to have his youngest son safe and sound under his roof because Rupert will almost certainly be called up. Charlie Meredith will have to go as well, and I imagine, old pals that they are, that they will want to go together.

Rupert will be missed at the pottery, and Hylton's will probably lose all the healthy young men of call-up age. No doubt they'll be calling back men who have retired, like they did in the last war.

I hope Florian doesn't think less of himself because he will not be fit to serve. I can't help remembering all those poor boys during the last war, the halt, the lame and even the blind, who could not serve king and country whether they wanted to or not, and who were driven to despair and worse by evil people who called them cowards.

Albert Aslett won't be going. He's still got a bullet in his shoulder from Passchendaele. You wouldn't think so to look at him, would you, but apparently he wouldn't be able to hold his rifle properly, and if the bullet started moving it could kill him. So it looks as though if anything happens it will be me and the Asletts holding the fort.

Thank you for sending the snaps of Imogen. I can't decide who she looks like. What do you think? I've shown them to Ivy and Albert, I hope you don't mind, but I really wish I could show them to the little mite's grandmother. Honestly, it's unnatural the way she never mentions the baby. What's the matter with the woman? You would think that when Florian wrote to tell her about the birth of her first grandchild she would have been on the first train to London. But not her. All she does is read her magazines. She's even given up on her little tea parties. By the way, Cordelia's had no luck yet if you know what I mean. If she had, I'm sure we should have heard about it.

Well, Linda, pet, I'd better bring this letter to an

end. No doubt you have a hundred and one things to keep you occupied now that you have your darling baby. I only wish I could be there to help you.

Love,
Vera

Linda's eyes were moist when she folded the letter and put it back in the envelope. While reading Vera's letter it was almost as if her old friend was in the room and talking to her, bringing to life the people she had left behind.

Linda tried to imagine Fernwood Hall without its useful lad. Bobby, cheerful and gangling in his ill-fitting clothes, would now no doubt be stiffly smart in uniform with his cowlick hair severely disciplined into a short back and sides. So many men preparing to go to war. Rupert Hylton and his brother-in-law Charlie would answer the call along with others of their generation. Did that mean Graham Forsyth, too? Of course it did. Without warning Linda had a vision of Graham's tall, dark frame defined in uniform. The image was disturbingly clear and she had no idea why it had come to her.

Hands shaking slightly, she put the envelope back in the drawer and closed her eyes. When normality returned she picked up the other letter. It was from John Sinclair and had arrived just a few days ago. He and his wife were de- lighted with the photographs she had sent and were putting them in the album along with snaps of their own grandchildren. Mr Sinclair went on to say that the Millards had asked him whether she would sell them the house and he had promised to pass on the enquiry. He urged her not to be hasty but to think about it carefully.

Should I sell my house? Linda thought. We could do with the money, but what if I wanted to go back and live there one day? She smiled. If I did I would have to be a wicked landlady and turn the Millards out.

She returned the letter to the drawer and lay back amongst the pillows. She yawned. The effects of the caffeine had worn off and she was drowsy at last. But just as her eyes closed and sleep beckoned, Imogen woke up and began to cry. Feeling infinitely weary, Linda got out of bed and went to see to her daughter.

Earlier in a large, comfortable villa in West Putney Florian had spread his papers out on Gerald Grey's magnificent mahogany desk. Gerald said it was Victorian but Florian thought it might be Georgian and worth quite a lot of money. But he didn't say anything because he didn't like to contradict the man who was paying him a decent wage, and in any case, Gerald certainly didn't need any more money.

Florian could not understand why Gerald was content to live here when he could have afforded something more luxurious. But this was where Gerald had been born and where he had lived happily with his parents for most of his life, save only for his absences during the war and later with a travelling stage company. He had inherited the house when his parents died in a car crash, the same accident claiming the owner of the car,

315

his mother's bachelor brother. His uncle had bequeathed Gerald the motor dealership, thus putting an end to his career on the stage.

So Gerald stayed in his childhood home but was happy to make any improvements that Nadine demanded; such as installing central heating, and also to allow her to redecorate and refurnish whenever she felt like it. He also acquiesced in sending the children off to boarding school. Much as he loved them he loved their mother more.

'Would you like to take a break now and have some dinner?'

Florian looked up to find Nadine smiling down at him. He saw with surprise that she was no longer wearing the tailored slacks and Fair Isle sweater she'd had on when he first arrived. Now she wore an emerald green crêpe de Chine wrap-over frock that wasn't exactly an evening gown but certainly a little too chic to be called a day dress. It was what his mother and sister would have termed a cocktail dress, he supposed. She had unpinned her shoulder-length hair so that it fell down in gleaming coppery wings to frame her fine-drawn face and, as always, the musky scent of her perfume filled his senses.

Florian frowned. 'Dinner?'

Nadine laughed softly. 'You were in a different world, weren't you? It is always the case when you are writing.'

'Not always.'

'What do you mean?'

'It's difficult to leave the everyday world behind when I am at home. That's why it's so much better to do my writing here.'

316

The moment he had said this he felt guilty. He knew he was betraying Linda and he knew in his heart of hearts that the fact that their daughter was a difficult baby wasn't Linda's fault. He wished he could take his words back but it was too late. Nadine's smile was both understanding and sympathetic.

'Poor Florian. But you can't expect Linda to put your work first now that she has a child, can you? Nor see to it that a meal is waiting for you.'

Florian should have said straight away that there was always a meal waiting for him and that Linda and their young housemaid Rosa together made sure that it was delicious, but he let the moment pass.

'So now we must eat,' Nadine said.

Florian shuffled his papers into some sort of order and rose to his feet. 'Are we going out?'

'No, why do you ask?'

'Because you have changed your clothes.'

'Oh, that. No, I always change when we have guests for dinner. Gerald likes me to impress our guests.'

'But Gerald isn't here – he's in Coventry having meetings in some car factories, and you have only one guest.'

'Yes.'

They looked at each other wordlessly then Nadine smiled. 'Come, eat. I have told Mrs Harker she may leave as soon as we have finished our meal and she has seen to the dishes.' She paused. 'And I have given her a list of things I want her to sample in Fortnum and Mason's in the morning before she comes to work.'

Nadine looked at him meaningfully and Florian experienced a delicious sense of guilt. Nothing explicit had been said, but they both knew why Nadine had suggested that he should stay the night. He knew he should not have agreed but he also knew that he could not resist her.

After the meal they made a show of going back into the study to work on the play. Nadine picked up some of the pages and read the dialogue out loud, stopping to ask Florian questions about it every now and then. They left the door open. When Mrs Harker knocked and came in to say she was leaving they looked up as if they could not quite tear themselves away from their work.

As soon as the front door closed behind her and they could hear her footsteps hurrying up the path, Nadine let the pages she was holding fall to the floor. 'Are you coming?' she said.

Florian stood up. He realized he was shaking. For a moment he stayed where he was, keeping the antique bulk of Gerald's desk between them. Nadine raised her eyebrows then backed away from him. Her hands moved to the diamanté clasp on her hip and she pulled it apart. Her dress fell open, revealing her voluptuous silk-clad figure. She shrugged her shoulders and the dress slithered to the floor.

She stood a moment longer then said, 'Well, I'm going up. I don't know about you.'

He didn't need any more prompting. He followed her upstairs.

When Florian woke up the next morning he was immediately aware of the blessed silence. No screaming baby, only the gentle breathing of the woman lying next to him. Nadine. Rather than the lingering sour smell of spilled baby milk which clung to Linda, Nadine's exotic perfume scented the air. Sunlight edged round the curtains and fell across the bed. Florian propped himself up on one elbow and looked down on her. Her long hair, usually so fashionably coiffed, was tousled and her ivory skin faintly flushed.

He was in Gerald's bed, and this woman was Gerald's wife. He examined those words and wondered why he did not feel guilty. He knew he should. Gerald was a decent chap who further-more was paying Florian good money, money that was desperately needed to keep his little household going. But instead of remorse he was fired with exhilaration.

Why on earth had he rushed into marriage with Linda? It was true that she encouraged him, that she believed in him, but he never felt that she was altogether appreciative of his work. Her comments were intelligent and intuitive but sometimes he sensed that she was holding back; that she was not as enthusiastic as she should have been. Now and then she had tried to hint at changes and that had tried Florian's patience. What could a village girl of limited experience know of writing style?

Whereas Nadine, although not a graduate, had gained a classical education in the theatre and had an instinctive feeling for dramaturgy. Work-ing with her was marvellous. She even brought out the best in Gerald, but then Gerald was deeply in love with her and entirely in her thrall.

Nadine stirred and opened her eyes. When she

319

saw him looking at her she sighed and turned away from him.

'What is it?' he asked. 'Are you regretting what we did?'

'No. Are you?'

'Of course not.'

'You will.'

'Why do you say that?'

'I am older than you are.'

Florian moved closer and put his arm around her. 'So what?'

'Don't you mind?'

'Of course not. And in any case, you don't look a day over forty.'

Nadine's face suffused with outrage. 'I'm only thirty-four!' She stared at him and saw that he was smiling. 'Florian! You didn't mean that. You were teasing me!'

He pulled her into his arms. 'Forgive me?'

'I might. If you show me how sorry you are.'

'How can I do that?'

She moved closer and whispered in his ear, 'Use your imagination.'

Am I in love with Nadine? Florian wondered as her mouth opened to his kiss. And then, as their passion flared all over again he knew the answer.

Part Three

Chapter Eighteen

1st October 1939

Pamela and Rupert had taken their coffee into the sitting room and were sitting at opposite sides of the hearth where a fire flickered comfortingly. Baby David had fallen asleep on a rug on the floor with some of his toys scattered around him. Sunday lunch had been roast veal and braised vegetables followed by plum tart and custard. Polly had turned out to be a reasonable cook and was devoted to the recipes to be found in women's magazines. Glancing at Rupert and then at their child, Pamela felt as much at peace as was possible in the circumstances. Then Rupert made his announcement and spoilt it all.

She stared at him in dismay. 'Why,' she said. 'Why have you volunteered? Only men aged between twenty and twenty-three have to register.'

'That's just the beginning. They're going by age. I'm twenty-six. It wouldn't have been long before I got my call-up papers. I didn't want to wait. Didn't want to prolong the agony.'

'I believe you want to go. To get away from me – from us,' she added and regretted it immediately when she saw his usual look of controlled impatience.

'That's not it at all. You must know that I would rather not go. But this war has to be fought and

323

our island has to be defended.'

'Don't we mean anything to you?'

'Of course you do. You and David. That's why I have to go. Can't you see that?'

'But what if ... what if...?'

'I don't come back?'

'Yes.' Pamela was gripped by fear. Her throat constricted, making it difficult for her to talk. 'What would happen to us, then?'

'Don't worry, Pamela. I've seen to it that you will be provided for. I have money and shares of my own and I haven't touched the money my grandmother left me. If I should die it will all come to you and David. I've made my will.'

'And how would I know?'

'What do you mean?'

'How would I know if anything happened to you? If you were taken prisoner ... or worse. Presumably your family would be told and I would be left wondering why your letters had stopped coming. You are going to write to me, aren't you?'

'Of course I will. And as for the other thing, I shall name you as next of kin. That's possible, you know.'

'But marrying me isn't possible. I'll never understand that.' She stared accusingly at him. 'You're supposed to love me.'

'I do.'

As always, Pamela wasn't sure if she believed this. She was honest enough to acknowledge that if she had not set out to seduce him, Rupert might never have approached her. And if she had not become pregnant the affair might not have lasted. At heart Rupert was a good man and in looking after her he was doing the decent thing. And he still wanted to come to her bed. But was this love?

'And yet you tuck me away in this miserable little seaside town,' she said. 'You haven't even told your parents that they have a grandson, while your younger brother cocks a snook at all of you and marries his little village girl.'

Rupert sighed. 'Pamela, you must be patient. We'll have to wait a while longer.'

'Haven't we waited long enough?'

'No, we haven't. You father is still in jail. He still has questions to answer about what he did and how he did it. There are people that he ruined who are waiting to confront him and who will not let the scandal die down.'

'The sins of the fathers!'

'That's sad but true. My father is a respectable businessman. The family firm has a first-class reputation. It just wouldn't do if it became general knowledge that I was connected to someone like your father.'

Pamela gasped and she gripped the arms of the chair until her knuckles whitened.

'I'm sorry if that sounds brutal,' Rupert said, 'but I will not risk destroying what generations of Hyltons have achieved.'

'But have you considered this? You *are* connected. You have made me your mistress and you have a son. A son who is Jack Delafontaine's grandson. What if that became general knowledge?'

'And how would that happen?'

'If I got sick of waiting and ... and...'

'If you were so foolish as to tell anyone I would

simply deny it. Who would believe the daughter of a fraudster as opposed to the son of a respectable family? That's the way of the world, Pamela, and I'm afraid you'll have to accept that.'

'You would deny your own son?'

'I would. And furthermore you and David would never inherit one penny of Hylton money.'

'That would be utterly ruthless.'

'As you were utterly unscrupulous when you set out to seduce me. And now that we're being honest with each other, tell me, do you love me at all or did you just see me as a way to have an easier life?'

Pamela felt the tears welling up. 'However it began,' she said, 'I do love you, now. You and our son.'

'And I love you. Perhaps we deserve each other.'

'What do you mean?'

'You may have set out to tempt me into an affair, but I'm big enough and old enough to realize that I was taking advantage of you. I'll do my best for you, Pamela, but you must believe me that I would do anything to protect my family.'

'So how long must we wait? When will we be able to stop this hideous charade and get married?'

'I don't know. I really don't. The world is changing, rapidly. Perhaps when this war is over...'

Pamela rose to her feet, clenching her fists, and almost screamed in frustration, 'Over! It's only just begun!'

Their son, who had been sleeping the sleep of an exhausted but happy child, opened his eyes in alarm. Raising himself to a sitting position, he looked from one parent to the other, and began to cry.

Charlie and Cordelia had been to lunch at Fernwood Hall and they were on their way back to Green Leas. They could not afford a chauffeur but Charlie enjoyed driving. As they sped through the country lanes, the downdraught from the car sending the fallen leaves swirling in their wake, his spirits began to lift. The atmosphere at the Hall had been depressing. Cordelia hadn't spoken since they had taken their leave of her parents and he glanced at her and smiled. She didn't respond. He thought he knew why.

'Will you miss me, Cordelia, my darling?' he said.

'Of course I will.'

'Are you angry with me for volunteering?'

'No. It's been a month now since war was declared and I've been expecting it. In fact I would have been disappointed if you had not volunteered.'

This was not what he had been expecting. 'But you are angry with me about something. I can tell.'

'It's not you, it's Rupert.'

'What has he done to make you angry?'

'Isn't that obvious?'

'No. Tell me.'

'For goodness sake, Charlie, haven't you noticed how miserable my mother is? And Father's not much better. Rupert hardly spends any time at home now. He goes into town and stays at his club or goes to stay with his other bachelor friends. At least, that's what he says.'

Charlie looked at her in surprise. 'Don't you believe him?'

'I'm not sure if I do.' Suddenly she laid a gloved hand on his knee. 'Charlie, you would tell me if you knew anything, wouldn't you?'

'Knew anything about what?'

'About Rupert and why he is neglecting our parents like this.'

Charlie took one hand from the steering wheel and laid it over Cordelia's hand. 'Rupert is my friend,' he said.

She snatched her hand away. 'So you wouldn't.'

'Let me finish. Rupert is my best friend but you are my wife. Of course I would tell you.'

'He hasn't said anything to you?'

'No, he hasn't. To tell the truth, my old friend has been neglecting me, too.'

When they arrived home Cordelia hurried into the house ahead of him. She shed her coat, handing it over to the waiting maidservant. 'Isn't it wonderful to be home!' she said.

Later, in bed, she came into his arms and whispered, 'How much longer do we have?'

'I'm not sure. The papers will probably arrive this coming week. And then I'll have to go.'

'Well, then, my darling, we had better make the most of the time we have left.'

Later, when Charlie was sleeping, Cordelia got up and pulled on her robe. She pushed her feet into her feather mules then padded through to the dressing room, closing the door behind her. She crossed over to the window and opened the curtains then stood for a moment looking out across

328

the moon-silvered lawn towards the sheltering trees. They had shed most of their leaves and those that were left clung to the branches precariously, fluttering in every breeze.

Where is he now? Is he waiting in some miserable, overcrowded camp, in a draughty billet or under canvas, or has he already been shipped to France? How could he just leave like that without saying goodbye?

Cordelia realized how unreasonable she was being. Paul loved her. He had told her so many times. Had she really expected him to stay once she was married to Charlie? He had too much pride to do that and, much as she desired him, she knew she wouldn't have respected him if he had been content to settle for another man's wife.

Charlie... When they made love he was exasperatingly tender and when it was over so very grateful. He had never stopped telling her what a lucky dog he thought he was to have bagged a prize like her. Those were his words: irksomely adolescent and far from romantic. Not when you had become accustomed to the overwhelming lovemaking of two people who were equally passionate and equally confident in their sex appeal.

Cordelia went to the dressing table. Sitting on the velvet-padded stool, she opened a drawer and took out her cigarette case. Behind her the room was shadowy and when her lighter flared it revealed her own face in the mirror, ghostlike and insubstantial. She gazed at herself through the blue spiral of cigarette smoke and wondered how hurt Charlie would have been if she had told him that she couldn't wait for him to go. It was not that she wanted any harm to come to him. She had only a vague idea of what he would face, but he would come through it just like her father had come through the last war. Rupert would, too. Her brother and her husband, who had been at school together, had volunteered together and they would see each other through. Wouldn't they...?

Florian wouldn't have to go. It wasn't that he wasn't as brave as the next man; it was just with one leg shorter than the other he would make a hopeless soldier. But he was so bright... In some ways brighter even than Rupert. Cordelia wondered if there was some way the government could make use of his intelligence, of his writing ability. For example, in the last war someone had to make all those films and those posters that were supposed to make people hate the Hun and go off to war willingly. All these years later some of the faded and tattered remnants of the posters could still be seen on billboards in neglected parts of town or on the gable ends of shops.

Women of Britain say GO!

Be Ready. Join Now!

Florian... Cordelia realized that she missed him – and Linda, too. She had always loved her younger brother and she had really liked Linda. She had treated her like a friend, even though she was only a village girl. Maybe what had happened was her own fault. Linda must have thought she was truly one of them and forgotten that there was a huge social gulf between her and the Hylton family.

Well, Linda was Mrs Hylton now and furthermore she and Florian had a child. Florian had written to tell their parents of the birth. What was

330

the child's name? Imogen? Yes, that was it. So Florian had made sure there would be a new generation of Hyltons as she and Charlie had not been able to do. So far at least. And even if they did manage to conceive a child, that child, like Florian's, would not bear the Hylton name. So everything depended on Rupert, and he showed no sign of wanting to marry anyone.

Poor Father and Mother. What an anxious time this was for them. Cordelia ground the stub of her cigarette into the bowl of a porcelain trinket pot that was not meant to be used as an ash tray.

'Couldn't you sleep, darling?'

Cordelia was dismayed to find Charlie wide awake when she went back to bed.

'Did I disturb, you? Sorry.'

'That doesn't matter.' He pulled her close. 'Tell me what the matter is.'

She wanted to scream at him, *Everything is the matter!* But, instead, she put her arms around him and laid her head on his chest. 'Can't you guess?' she said. 'I can't sleep for thinking that you will be leaving me soon.'

'Poor pet,' Charlie said. 'It must be dreadful for you. I promise you I'll think of you every day and I'll do my level best to come home to you as soon as I can. Cordelia? Did you hear me?'

For an answer Cordelia kept her eyes closed and pretended to be asleep.

The next day Graham Forsyth asked to see Mr Hylton and told him that he had volunteered.

His employer sighed but looked as though he had been expecting it. 'I'm sorry to lose you,

Graham, but you can rest assured that your job will be waiting for you when this war is over.' Mr Hylton looked up at him wearily and for a moment he seemed at a loss for words. Then he blinked and said, 'And of course your wife...' his sentence trailed away.

'My wife?'

'Oh, yes, tell her that if she needs help of any kind she must come to me. This is a family firm and for generations now we have looked after the welfare of our employees.'

'Thank you, sir. I'll tell her.'

'Good.' He nodded and turned to look out of the window.

Graham wasn't sure whether he'd been dismissed or not so he stood there uncertainly. Without turning his head, Mr Hylton said, 'Rupert has volunteered, you know, and my son-in-law, Charlie Meredith. It's no more than I expected of them and they would have been called up soon, anyway, but it still hits hard.'

He continued to stare out of the window. A light rain had no effect on the ever-present pall of soot that hung over the city.

'Well, then,' Graham said. 'I'd better go.'

William Hylton seemed to make a supreme effort in order to turn and face Graham. 'Have you had your papers yet?'

'No, sir. I'm expecting them any day.'

'Then don't waste the days you have left by coming in to work. Leave clear instructions for ongoing work with your team; tell them they'll have to learn to manage without you. Then go home. Spend the time with your wife. Make the most of every moment.'

'Thank you, sir, but if you don't mind I'd rather come in to work.'

Mr Hylton looked surprised. 'Why is that?'

Graham was at a loss how to answer him. 'It's because... I'd like life to be as normal as possible for as long as possible.'

'I think I understand that,' Mr Hylton said. 'But whatever you do, I wish you well, and I shall pray that along with Rupert and Charlie it won't be too long before you come home again.'

Graham's team of decorators were mainly women. There were only four young men, and two of them had already been called up while of the other two one was waiting for his papers and the other said he was going to declare himself a conscientious objector. He would face a tribunal and most likely end up in the Non-Combatant Corps. This meant the girls would be taking over at the pottery. Graham was confident that they would manage. Particularly Caitlin. She had started as a gilder when she left school at fourteen and she was showing promise as a designer.

His team were sorry that he was leaving them but they had been expecting it.

'What with Master Rupert going and now you, who is going to run this place?' Caitlin asked.

'Mr Hylton, who else? As far as I know he's not going anywhere,' Graham said.

'You know as well as I do that he's been leaving more and more of the decisions to Rupert, and even you.'

Graham smiled. 'Yes, even me.'

'You know what I mean. When was the last time he turned down one of your designs? And when was the last time Mr Hylton left the office to meet any business contacts? Rupert is the face of this business, isn't he?'

'The face of the business? My goodness, Caitlin, I think you have the makings of a business-woman yourself.'

'Don't laugh at me.'

Graham felt contrite. 'I'm sorry. I'm not laughing. I really do think that you could go far. Maybe you'll be a second Clarice Cliff.'

Caitlin flushed with pleasure. 'She's my hero! But that doesn't mean I want to copy her work. I have my own ideas.'

'I know you have, and maybe while I'm away you'll have a chance to put them forward.'

'Now you've made me feel dreadful.'

'Whatever for?'

'It sounds like I can't wait for you to go off to war just so that I can advance my career.'

'It's all right. I know that isn't so, Caitlin,' Graham said. But he wasn't so sure. Caitlin was not just talented, she was ambitious. He didn't know how long this war was going to last, but when he came back – if he did – he wondered whether his job really would be waiting for him.

On the way home Graham reflected that Caitlin had not mentioned Florian Hylton. When he had left home and gone to London with his new bride there were those who criticized him for not wanting to go into the family business.

'It's that woman,' someone had said. 'Probably wanted a taste of the bright lights. Little gold digger. Got herself a rich husband and wanted to live it up in London. All I can say is that young Florian will regret this one day.'

Graham had kept quiet. He did not believe for one moment that Linda was a gold digger. If she had married Florian it must be because she loved him. He hoped and prayed that Florian would not let her down and give Linda cause for regret.

That evening after their evening meal – a tired-looking pork pie and some elderly tomatoes – Graham told Sonya that he was joining the army. He was not expecting her to be pleased and her first question, although breathtakingly insensitive, did not altogether surprise him.

'And how am I supposed to exist on whatever miserable pay you'll get from the army?' she asked.

'You won't have to. I've put some money in a savings account for you. The house is paid for, so all you'll have will be the usual bills and living expenses.'

'But I bet there won't be much left over for fun!'

'Fun?'

'Yes, fun. The world isn't going to stop turning, you know. I'll still want to go to the pictures or a variety show, or maybe a dance or two.'

'And who exactly will you go dancing with?'

'Margery, of course. I'll teach her how to dance properly.'

'I see.'

'For God's sake, Graham, don't look so hurt.'

'I'm not hurt.'

'Yes, you are, and there's no need to be. It doesn't mean I won't miss you. The opposite, in

335

fact. But it's better to keep myself occupied so that I won't be moping around, isn't it?'

'You could always get a job. That would solve two problems. You wouldn't be sitting around moping, and you'd be earning some money of your own.'

'I thought when we got married you said with all my worldly goods I thee endow. I'm your wife. I shouldn't need to make any money of "my own" as you put it.'

'Wouldn't you want to do something? Something to help the war effort?'

Sonya stared at him as if he had taken leave of his senses. He didn't press her for an answer.

Florian was furious. 'They didn't even tell me that my brother had gone to war. I have to learn the news from a servant.'

He was sitting with Nadine in the darkened auditorium of a theatre. On the stage the director, Max Hulbert, a tall, handsome man, was talking to the set designer. A few of the actors who had been auditioned that morning were making their way to the exits reluctantly. It was obvious that they would have liked to know whether they had got the part they auditioned for, but Max had told them he would get in touch with their agents as soon as he had made up his mind.

In fact it wasn't just a matter of making a simple decision. Gerald had made it plain to Max that the last word should go to Nadine. After all, the play had been written for her and, more importantly, it was Gerald's money that was paying for everything – including Max's services as director.

Nadine had had a marvellous day. She was in a theatre again and furthermore she was the star of the show and the director was properly respectful. She chose to believe that this was because of her acting ability rather than her husband's money, and she could have been right. Max Hulbert was the best money could buy and he hadn't earned his reputation by being a pushover.

Florian had been sitting there all day watching the auditions and guarding his script jealously. It was also part of the deal that he had the say-so if Max wanted to make any changes to the directions or the dialogue. However, Nadine had sensed that he hadn't been entirely attentive and now he told her why. It was because of a letter from home. She tried to quell her feelings of elation and offer Florian the sympathy he was so obviously asking for.

'Do you mean one of your father's servants wrote to you?' Nadine asked him.

'No, not to me. One of the housemaids wrote to Linda.'

'Linda corresponds with servants?'

'Apparently. It is obvious if you read the letter that it is not the first one.'

'How did this come about?'

'Linda told me that the woman knew her mother and that she befriended her when she came to work at the Hall.'

'Oh yes. Your wife was also a servant.'

Florian looked away uncomfortably. 'Not exactly a servant. A companion for my grandmother.'

'Florian, darling, companions are servants, just like governesses were. It's very sweet of you to try to elevate her. But it is not the fact that this maid-

337

servant has written to your wife that has made you angry, is it? I sense there is something more.'

'No, you're right, although I was vexed that Linda had never told me of the correspondence. No. I am angry because if this woman had not written to Linda I might never have known that my brother has joined the army.'

'Surely you knew that he would?'

'Yes, I might have known that Rupert would be quick off the mark, but you would think that my mother and father would write and tell me. Obviously, they're still angry with me because I wouldn't go into the family business, because I wanted to be a writer instead.'

'Well, then, Florian, when this play is successful, as I am sure it is going to be, and when you are being hailed as a wonderful new talent, they will surely forgive you. Although perhaps it should be you that forgives them.'

Florian was silent.

'What is it?' Nadine asked.

'It's not just my wanting to write that angered them. It was my marriage, too.'

'They did not approve of Linda?'

'No ... and I didn't anticipate that. Linda got on so well with my mother and my sister. I thought they would be pleased.'

'Poor darling. Your marriage has made it even harder to be reconciled with your family. Ah ... there's Gerald.' She tried to sound disappointed, but in truth she was relieved to bring their conversation to an end. She loved Florian as much as she could love anybody, but he should have had the sensitivity to know that this was not the time

338

to bring his problems to her.

Florian looked up to see that Nadine's husband had just walked on to the stage from the wings.

'Were you expecting him?'

'Not really, but I'm not surprised. He's so thrilled that this is going ahead that I think it's reminded him of his own acting days. Look at him standing centre stage and looking quite at home there. It's a wonder he hasn't asked for a part. In fact, that may be what he's talking to Max about now.'

'He wouldn't, would he? What part?' Florian sounded appalled.

'The butler. He would look good in a starched shirt, a tailcoat and pinstripe trousers, don't you think?'

Florian frowned. 'There isn't a butler in the play.' Then his brow cleared. 'You're teasing me!'

Nadine laughed softly. 'Yes, I am. But nevertheless Gerald is going to be a problem. He'll want to come to rehearsals and once we open he'll probably come to every performance. It will be very difficult for us to be alone together.'

'What can we do?'

'I've thought about it and I'll have a word with Max.'

'What good will that do?'

'Max is the director. He can say that he doesn't want the cast distracted by having family and friends around.'

'Will Gerald go along with that? After all, he put the money up.'

'He'll go along with it if Max insists. He'll want to be professional.'

'Then what about me? Will Max have to ban me as well?'

In the semi-darkness Nadine moved closer to him and reached for his hand. 'Don't worry, darling. He can't ban you from rehearsal. You wrote the play, he might want you to do some rewrites. But after the first night the playwright usually vanishes. Maybe he'll drop in occasionally, for instance if there's a change in the cast, but he ought to be getting on with writing the next play.'

'The next play... I hadn't thought of that.'

'Well, please start thinking. And make sure you write it for me.' Nadine withdrew her hand and moved away from him. 'Gerald's looking at us,' she said.

Gerald had moved to the front of the stage and was shielding his eyes as he peered down into the auditorium. Nadine stood up and waved. 'Here I am, darling. How good of you to come along.'

'Still here, Florian?' Max Hulbert had come down from the stage and he began to walk up the central aisle to where Florian was sitting in the stalls. 'Haven't you got a home to go to?'

Florian sighed. 'Yes, I suppose I should get along.'

'What's the matter? You look utterly miserable.'

'No, I'm not miserable.'

'Worried, then? Anxious?'

Florian shook his head.

'Look, old man, you don't have to pretend with me. I know all about it.'

'You do?' For a horrified moment Florian thought that Max was going to tell him that he knew about his affair with Nadine. Nobody must

340

know about that. If it got back to Gerald he might pull out of the production, and without his backing there wouldn't be a play.

Max was looking at him compassionately. 'This is your first play, isn't it?'

What on earth was the man talking about? 'Yes.'

'I've worked with many playwrights, the brilliant, the mediocre and the ones who only just get by, and believe me, they all feel the same way as you do. It's even worse if it's their first play. You've been carried along by sheer enthusiasm until this moment. Now everything is beginning to take shape. The theatre, the cast, the director. Your play doesn't belong to you any longer. It belongs to all of us and you're terrified that it's not going to be a success, aren't you?'

'Yes... I suppose I am.' So that's what Max was on about. Thank God.

'Well, stop worrying right now. I'm the best director money can buy. The leading lady is both beautiful and competent, and I'll make sure that the rest of the cast is strong. And to crown it all the script is bloody brilliant. Don't worry, old man. *The Shadow Wife* is going to be a success. It will run for years.'

Max persuaded him to go for a meal with him. 'Our leading lady and her husband have gone off to the Ritz,' he said. 'I suggest we go to somewhere less stuffy. Do you know Stefano's?'

'I do.'

'Well, then, let's go there. And after we've eaten I know a nice little club we can go on to. Do you like the sound of that?'

'Very much.'

341

It crossed Florian's mind briefly that Max had called Nadine 'competent' rather than something more extravagant but, cheered and flattered by the director's assessment of his play, he thrust all thoughts of his previous grievance about Linda's letter behind him and set off to enjoy a night on the town.

Chapter Nineteen

December 1939

The morning newspapers were spread out on the kitchen table. Rosa held Imogen on one hip while she made toast. Imogen, keenly interested, watched round-eyed and silently while her mother opened one newspaper after another and read bits out aloud.

'More coffee?' Rosa asked.

Linda nodded. She closed the newspaper she had been reading, made a pile of all of them and pushed them aside.

'They are all wonderful, are they not?' Rosa said.

'They're pretty good.'

'Then why do you not look more cheerful? The theatre critics have all agreed. It is a wonderful play and – what do they say? "The playwright Florian Hylton is a bright new talent – a shining star."'

'No. It's Nadine who is the shining star.'

'They shine together. Listen.'

Rosa leaned over the table and sorted through the newspapers with one hand, found the one she wanted and then turned the pages over until she found the theatre reviews.

She read aloud, 'Nadine Temple returns to the stage in triumph in this intriguingly magical tale of a wife who is determined not to be forgotten. *The Shadow Wife* is Florian Hylton's first play and in him the theatre has found a major new talent.' Rosa looked up and smiled. 'And it says here that the play will run forever! That is wonderful, isn't it?'

'Yes, wonderful.'

Rosa poured coffee for both of them then sat down, making sure her own cup was pushed well away from Imogen's curious fingers. She used the baby's bib to wipe the dribble that emerged from her mouth and then gave her a rusk to chew on.

'Here, let me take Imogen,' Linda said.

'Certainly not. She might spoil your beautiful evening dress. You have already crumpled it by sleeping in it. I think perhaps you should go at once and take it off.'

'Please, Rosa, don't scold. I was tired when I came home. I sat down on the bed to take my shoes off. Then I thought I would just lie back for a minute. The next thing I knew it was morning, but I couldn't understand why I was under the coverlet.'

Rosa smiled at her. 'I looked in when Imogen woke up for her early bottle and covered you up. I did not want to disturb you but also I did not want you to catch a cold. So now you must leave Imogen with me. And if you won't go and

343

change, drink your coffee and eat some toast. You look tired.'

'You must be tired, too, after spending all night looking after a teething baby.'

'No. It was not bad. It is strange that a little baby who never seemed to stop crying when there was nothing wrong with her should now be so good when she really has something to cry about.'

'I don't deserve you, Rosa.'

'Yes, you do. Now tell me – are you going to make a scrapbook?'

'A scrapbook?'

'Of the theatre reviews and the photographs.'

'Should I?'

'Of course you should. Maybe you should make two and send one to Mr Hylton's parents. They will be so proud of him.'

Linda shook her head. 'I'm not so sure.'

'Well then, you must ask Mr Hylton what you should do when he comes home. Oh, my goodness! You are crying. What is the matter?'

'Nothing... I'm tired ... exhausted, that's all.'

'But of course. You must be. The theatre, the party, the wondering how the play would be received. But now you know that is all right and you are reacting. You must go and have a warm bath. Now you are laughing. What have I said that has amused you?'

'A warm bath seems to be your cure for everything. But you are right. I will do as you say. No, don't get up. You have your hands full with Imogen. I shall fill the bath myself and be totally extravagant with the bath essence.'

Trying to smile, but with her throat aching and

her eyes smarting with unshed tears, Linda fled to the bathroom. Once there she closed the door, put the plug in the bath and turned on the taps. When the water was gently steaming she took the new bottle of bath essence from the glass shelf – Floris's Rose Geranium, and very expensive. Florian had brought it home for her the day his play went into rehearsal.

When she expressed surprise he said, 'You deserve something luxurious for putting up with me. I must have been a pain to live with, lately.'

'Yes, you have.'

They smiled at each other and for a moment Linda thought everything was going to be all right, that they would rediscover the happiness that their marriage had brought them. She had expected that now that Florian had finished writing the play he would spend more time at home with her and Imogen, but instead, if it were possible, he absented himself even more.

When Linda asked him why he had to go every day he explained that he had to be at the rehearsals in case Max wanted some rewrites, and it was important to go to the Greys' home when rehearsal was over to go over the next day's scenes with Nadine. Linda asked him why Gerald couldn't do that. After all, he had once been an actor. But Florian explained that Gerald didn't know enough about the play.

'I thought Gerald co-wrote the play,' Linda said.

'Oh, no. It soon became obvious that our ideas for Nadine were too different. Gerald dropped out quite early on.'

'I didn't know that,' Linda said.

345

'Why should you?'

'I'm your wife. I would have thought you would discuss your work with me. You used to. Florian, when was the last time we had a proper conversation?'

'That's easy,' he said. 'It was just before Imogen was born.'

They had stared at each other, appalled by the realization that Florian had crossed some kind of line and that the nature of their relationship had changed forever. For a while after that Florian had made every effort to be kind to her; he even spent more time at home, but when he did, it was obvious that he would rather be somewhere else, and when he gradually slipped back into his old ways, Linda had made no comment.

Now she unscrewed the cap of the stylish glass bottle and, holding it carefully, she allowed a few drops to fall into the running water. After a moment the luxurious fragrance rose up to embrace her.

When the bath was full Linda turned the taps off and then reached around to unzip her evening dress. Too weary to pull it up and over her head, she let it slither down over her hips onto the tiled floor. Heedless of its cost, she kicked the jade-green chiffon into a corner and then took off her underwear and threw everything into the laundry basket. She stepped into the bath and sank down into the warm scented water then lay back and closed her eyes.

Far, far away she could hear Imogen begin to cry. Then Rosa started to sing and the baby's cries died away. Thank God Imogen didn't take so long to settle these days. She must have gone to sleep, because a short while later Linda heard music coming from the wireless – the sort of music that was supposed to keep all housewives happy. A housewife? Was that what she was? The sort of woman who stayed at home and made the place comfortable for her husband as well as bringing up a child. Well, it seemed that she wasn't making a very good job of it.

For months now she had been prepared to believe that the reason Florian was hardly ever at home was because of the play. He had needed a more peaceful environment when he was writing, and then when the play went into rehearsal it was natural that he should want to be there. But even when he was at home he had been distant.

And then, two nights ago, he had come home from the final dress rehearsal in a jubilant mood. Linda was already in bed, reading. She looked up from her book to see him standing over her carrying a large flat box.

'You've got your dress sorted out for the first night, haven't you?' he asked.

She told him that she had.

'And an evening coat of some sort?'

'I thought my black velvet would do.'

'Very nice. But I'd rather you wore this.' He put the box down on the bed. 'Go on. Open it.'

Linda lifted the lid and pushed aside the tissue paper. 'A fur coat!' she said.

Florian smiled and sat down on the bed. 'Not a coat, sweetheart, although I know I promised you one. And I'll keep that promise one day, I really will. But meanwhile this is a fashionable little cape. The latest thing.' He grinned. 'Or so I'm told.'

They looked at each other and smiled. It was so long since they had shared such an intimate moment that Linda felt as if she was going to cry. She blinked the tears away and looked down at the silvery fur. She was about to pick it up when Florian said, 'Silver fox. Isn't it lovely?'

Linda drew her hands back quickly. 'Fox?'

'Yes, what's the matter?' He looked puzzled for a moment and then his eyes widened and he laughed softly. 'Oh, Linda, my love, it's not a stole complete with head and tail. And those dreadful little glass eyes. And the claws! Something like that is entirely suitable for those two harpies at my grandmother's funeral, but not for my beautiful young wife.

'Here, sit forward.' When she did so Florian lifted the cape out of the box himself and draped it round her shoulders. 'See, it's just a little cape. And you will look marvellous in it at the theatre tomorrow. Are you excited?'

'Excited?'

'About the first night of my play. Don't say you've forgotten it's tomorrow.' His smile faded.

'No, of course not. And yes, I am excited. Rosa is going to help me get ready and then she's going to stay and look after Imogen. How could you think that I would forget something so important?'

'I don't know. You've been so distant lately. Detached. You haven't asked me about my work for ... oh, for ages.'

'Florian, that's so unfair. If I've been detached it's because you've kept me at a distance. You come home late and when you do you are too tired to talk to me. Sometimes when I asked you how things were going you gave the shortest answers. I felt excluded.'

'What do you mean by excluded?'

'You and Nadine and Gerald ... the three of you were working on the play. You didn't need me. When we first got married you would discuss your ideas with me. I used to love listening to you.'

'Did you?'

'You know I did.'

'Yes. I'm sorry. It's just that everything changed when Imogen was born, didn't it? The reason I didn't discuss things with you when I came home was because you were tired – worn out, sometimes. And on the occasions when we did manage to have a conversation we would be interrupted by her eternal screaming.'

Linda looked at him helplessly. It was pointless to try and refine the truth. 'I know,' she said. 'I'm sorry.'

Florian looked stricken. 'Linda, darling. It's me who should be sorry. You were doing your best to look after our daughter and I didn't help you at all, did I?'

'You had your work. I understood that.'

'And you never complained.'

Surprised and pleased by Florian's changed mood, Linda regained some of her old confidence. 'No, I didn't, did I?'

'I've been a perfect beast.'

'I won't deny it.'

'I'll be a better husband from now on. I promise.'

Linda could hardly believe they were having this conversation. Suddenly she seemed to have the old Florian back.

'Do you like my present?'

'I do.' Linda stroked the fur with both hands then grasped the cape and pulled it up to her chin. The fur was soft against her skin and there was a pleasant if puzzling aroma. She wondered if they kept furs in mothballs, but if they did the mothballs must be soaked in an exotic perfume.

'So you will wear it tomorrow night and look absolutely stunning. Everyone will say what a lucky chap I am to have such a beautiful wife.'

Florian reached for the cape and hung it up in the wardrobe. When he joined her in bed, he took her in his arms and made love to her gently and tenderly. It had been months since they had come together like this, and Linda found herself weeping with happiness. When it was over Florian held her close, and when she reached up to stroke his cheek she found traces of tears. He had been crying, too.

The next morning they awoke to the smell of coffee and the amazing realization that Imogen had slept through the night – and they had slept through Rosa arriving. They pulled on their robes and went into the kitchen to have breakfast together. Rosa had already brought Imogen from the nursery and put her in her high chair.

Florian insisted on giving Imogen her cereal. His daughter looked at him with round, surprised eyes and when he raised the spoon to her mouth it looked for a moment as if she might refuse it. But then, to Linda's joy and Rosa's delighted relief, Imogen gave her father a dazzling smile and her breakfast went without incident.

Florian could hardly eat his own breakfast, he was so nervous and excited. Rosa chided him gently and told him that he must eat something or he would be ill. He managed a slice of toast and two cups of coffee. 'You make the best coffee in the world,' he said to Rosa and she flushed with pleasure.

His good mood continued while he went for his shower, and afterwards Linda found him in the bedroom packing his evening clothes into a suitcase. He looked up and answered her question before she could ask it. 'I won't have time to come home and change,' he said.

'Are you going to the theatre now?'

'Yes. There are all kinds of last-minute arrangements to be made. I'll have some lunch with Gerald and Nadine and then save myself for the party.'

'There's going to be a party?'

'After the show at Max's house in Fitzrovia. Apparently it's surprisingly grand, but, of course, as well as being a successful director Max is independently wealthy. I would quite like to live there myself.'

Florian was talking so quickly that Linda was having a job keeping up with him.

'In Fitzrovia?'

'Yes, it's terribly bohemian.'

'Bohemian? Is that what you are now?'

Florian's smile faded. 'Are you teasing me?'

'Yes, I am, but only very gently. As a matter of fact, Fitzrovia would be a good place for a successful playwright to live. After all, George

Bernard Shaw lived in Fitzroy Square.'

'Did he? How do you know that?'

'My guardian, Miss Taylor, was a fan of his plays – and of his politics, too. I think she knew so much about him that she could have written his biography.'

Florian didn't respond. He looked distracted.

'What is it?' Linda asked.

'I can't remember whether I ordered the relevant newspapers to be delivered here tomorrow.'

'Relevant?'

'All those that might have a review of the play.'

'Of course. Don't worry. I'll slip along to the newsagent this morning and make sure he knows.'

'Of course, Max will be having the papers delivered, too. Hot off the press, as they say!' He closed his case and looked around the bedroom. 'I think I've got everything.'

'Then off you go.'

She walked with him to the door and he turned and kissed her. 'I've ordered a taxi for you – to take you to the theatre. You mustn't be late, you know.'

'Don't worry. I won't be. And you know I've arranged for Rosa to stay the night with Imogen. It's just as well if we're going to a party.'

At the theatre Florian had not joined Linda and Gerald in their seats in the stalls. He told them he would be too nervous to sit there and watch as his work was put before the public for the first time.

'Where will you go?' Linda asked him.

'I'll wait in the green room.' He squeezed her hand and was gone.

Gerald explained to Linda that the green room

352

was a sort of rest room for members of the cast who were waiting to go onstage. 'It's where the party will start after the performance,' he added.

'I thought Max was having the party at his house,' Linda said.

'I said the party will *start* there, then we'll go on to Max's house to wait for the papers.'

'Of course – to read the reviews.'

When the house lights dimmed and the curtain rose Linda gave herself up to the experience of being in the theatre. She had never read Florian's play and once the curtain went up she was glad of the fact, because she could watch the story unfolding before her. She loved stories, and this play told an enchanting story which kept you guessing until the very last moment whether there would be a happy ending. It was whimsical but not cloyingly so, and Linda soon found herself wishing desperately that this woman – the shadow wife – was going to be able to save her marriage. The writing was razor-sharp, witty and yet sensitive. Florian's novel had been funny and the characters had been sharply drawn but there had been no depth to them. She was glad now that he had abandoned it. Perhaps he would never get back to it now; he had already mentioned that he had an idea for the next play.

As the curtain came down on the final scene, the audience rose to its feet, clapping and cheering. The cast were called back for several encores, the greatest cheer going up for Nadine. Then someone in the audience started shouting, 'Author! Author!' Several people took up the cry and Florian appeared on the stage, brought

353

forward by the director Max Hulbert. There was no sign of the nerves he had suffered before the play began. He bowed and smiled confidently, then turned to Nadine, took her hand and raised it to his lips. The audience cheered anew.

Linda heard a muffled sob and turned to see that Gerald had sat down again and was quietly weeping. She sat down and reached for his hand. 'I know,' she said. 'It's wonderful, isn't it?'

'This is what I want for her. This acclaim. This is what she deserves.'

'And you have made it possible.'

'I owed it to her. But I couldn't have done this without Florian. He seems to know exactly what she's capable of. It's as if he has looked into her soul.' Gerald took a clean white handkerchief from his pocket and wiped his eyes. He laughed. 'Listen to me,' he said. 'You must think me a sentimental old fool.'

'No, I don't. You have every right to be proud of her.'

'And you of Florian. But look, the safety curtain is being lowered. The first night is over.'

Chapter Twenty

The house lights had come up and the audience was leaving the theatre. 'What are we supposed to do now?' Linda asked.

Gerald stood, picked up Linda's fur cape from the seat behind her and draped it round her

354

shoulders. 'Come along. We're going backstage.'

Linda was surprised to see how shabby the green room was, with its faded old carpet and sofas and armchairs that looked as if they might have been there since the previous century. Max Hulbert, his mane of white hair brushed back and looking as handsome as any Hollywood film actor, was already holding court, surrounded by important-looking people in evening dress. Florian and Nadine each had their own circle of admirers and the excited voices were gradually rising to a shrill crescendo.

Food and drinks had been set out on a table at one end of the room and a couple of formally dressed waiters were circulating with drinks and trays of titbits. Gerald took two gasses of champagne, handed one of them to her and then, murmuring that he wouldn't be long, he slipped away, soon to be gobbled up by the excited throng.

Linda sipped her champagne and looked around her. She recognized two of the cast standing nearby. One of them had played the part of 'the other woman', an enchanting young creature who had lured the husband away from his wife. The other was the young man who adored her and who was determined to win her back. In real life and without their stage make-up they were disappointingly ordinary. And tonight they were obviously very excited.

'Are you going on to Max's house?' the girl asked.

'You bet I am.'

Linda was surprised to hear that the young man had an American accent. In the play he took

355

the part of an Englishman and you would never have guessed that he wasn't.

'Have you been there before?' the girl asked.

'Never. Have you?'

'Oh, yes,' she said carelessly. 'Heaps of times.'

'Really?'

'Well ... once. I had a bit part in his last production.'

Linda realized that she was staring and turned away. But not before the young American had seen her.

'Who is that attractive woman?' she heard him say.

There was a pause when she could imagine the girl turning to look and then the answer, 'I saw her arrive with Gerald Grey so I imagine that's Mrs Hylton.'

'Florian Hylton's wife? But she's lovely!'

'Why shouldn't she be?'

'Well ... you know.'

'Oh, that. You shouldn't believe backstage gossip, darling.'

Linda realized that her hand was shaking. They had made no attempt to lower their voices and the noise around them was such that they probably didn't realize that Linda could hear every word. She knew very well where this conversation might be going and she was torn between staying to hear the worst or fleeing now and remaining in ignorance. She decided to flee. She began to push her way through the crowd although she had no real idea where she was going.

At one point her cape slipped from her shoulders and was retrieved by a tall, thin gentleman whom

Linda recognized as the actor who had played the doctor. He draped it round her shoulders, took her empty glass from her hand, and asked her if she would like him to get her another drink.

'Yes, please,' she said but when he returned, obviously hoping to talk to her, she took the drink, thanked him and dived into the crowd once more.

Soon, without having planned it, she found herself not far away from Florian and Nadine. They had disentangled themselves from their separate circles of well-wishers and were talking only to each other. She was startled to hear her own name mentioned.

'You'd better go and devote yourself to Linda, darling,' Nadine said. 'And I must rescue poor Max before Gerald bores him to death.'

'You're right,' Florian replied. 'But I wish we could escape this melee and find somewhere to be alone together.'

'Oh, no, darling. You and I must enjoy our triumph. I hope it will be the first of many. By the way, I hope you made a fuss of Linda last night like I told you to.'

'I did.'

'Good. We must allay suspicion. We can't afford a scandal, not yet.'

'Whatever you say.'

'And did she like the cape?'

'Yes, she did. I ... I didn't say it was from you. I let her believe I'd bought it for her.'

'Well, it's as good as new. I've hardly worn it.'

Linda felt herself burning. Burning with embarrassment, shame and anger. She slipped the cape off and clutching it in one hand she called out,

357

'Actually, I don't like the cape, Nadine.' Florian and Nadine turned towards her, their eyes widening in horror. 'I don't like accepting cast-offs, even if you do.' The way Linda glanced at Florian when she said this made her meaning quite clear.

'Linda–' Florian began. 'Please don't...'

'Don't what, Florian?' A moment ago she had been burning up, but now Linda was icy cold. 'Make a fuss? Risk a scandal? Don't worry; I merely want to return Nadine's property.'

Linda dropped the cape on the floor at their feet, and when both Florian and Nadine instinctively bent to retrieve it she emptied her glass of champagne over their heads.

Only a few people in the crowded room had witnessed the incident, but of those who had, some gasped with surprise and others laughed. Those who had no idea what was going on turned and looked curiously as Linda pushed her way none too gently through the crowd. She became aware that someone was following her but she didn't look back. When she reached the door and stepped out into the darkened passage she stopped and looked around her. She realized that she did not have the faintest idea how to leave the theatre.

'Let me help you,' a voice said.

She turned round to find Max Hulbert standing there. Still shaken, she didn't protest when he led her gently back into the auditorium.

'Sit down,' he said, indicating seats in the front row of the stalls. The house lights were on and Linda was aware of the cleaners who had started at the back and were working their way forwards.

'I'd rather not,' Linda said. 'I want to go home.'

'Very well. I'll get a taxi for you, but first please sit and talk to me. I need to ask you something.'

Linda sat next to him unwillingly. 'What do you want to know?' she asked.

'What are you going to do?'

'About what?'

'Don't play games, Linda. I saw what you did and I can guess why.'

'So everyone knows about my husband and Nadine?'

'No, not everyone. Hardly anyone, in fact.'

'Does Gerald?'

'No. Are you going to tell him?'

Max relaxed back into his seat as if the matter was of no importance to him. Linda turned her head and looked at him. She couldn't read his expression.

'Are you asking me not to?'

'I have no right to do that. It's entirely up to you. But I'd rather you didn't.'

'Because you need his money.'

'We don't. Not now. This play is going to be an enormous success.'

'Then why shouldn't I tell him?'

'Because it would be cruel, and I don't think you are a vindictive person.'

'You've only just met me. You don't know what I'm capable of.'

Max's smile was gentle. 'I'm a good judge of character, Linda. That's why I'm such a good director.'

Linda couldn't help smiling. 'And modest about it, too.'

'It's no use being modest in this business. But

you haven't answered me. Are you going to tell Gerald what you think you've discovered?'

'*Think?*'

'You can't know for sure. I mean, you can't know if they have actually started an affair.'

'That's beside the point, isn't it? Florian has betrayed me in thought if not in deed.'

'So I ask again. Are you going to tell Gerald?'

Linda sighed. 'No, I'm not. He'll find out sooner or later, won't he?'

'I expect so.'

'Max...?'

'What is it?'

'I heard Nadine say that they can't afford a scandal yet. But if they don't need Gerald's money, what are they frightened of?'

'It's a matter of what Nadine is frightened of. She's just returned to the stage. It's obvious from the reception the audience gave her tonight that she's going to get good reviews. Her career is about to take off. She can't have people thinking that she only got the part because she's sleeping with the playwright.'

Linda gasped.

'I'm sorry, that was brutal,' Max said.

'No, don't be. In a way it's a relief to have it put into words.' Linda rose to her feet abruptly. 'I want to go home.'

'You're not coming to the party at my house?'

'What do you think?'

'And you don't want to speak to Florian before you go.'

'If Florian wanted to speak to me he would have followed me out.'

'He's probably too scared to do so.'

'Or too reluctant to leave Nadine's side. No, I won't lower myself by chasing after him.' Linda left her seat and began to walk up the aisle.

'Wait a moment, Linda, the doors will be locked. You'll have to leave by the stage door. I'll show you the way.'

Max told the stage door keeper to hail a taxi, and when it arrived he insisted on paying the driver in advance.

'I could have asked him to wait and paid him when I got home,' she said.

Max shook his head. 'Will you be all right?' he asked. 'I mean, you wouldn't do anything foolish, would you?'

'Of course not.'

As the taxi made its way through darkened war-time streets Linda sank back and closed her eyes. She felt like crying but she knew that if she started she wouldn't be able to stop. She shivered in the cold air when she left the taxi and hurried across the entrance hall towards the lifts. The building was quiet, and as she made her way along the corridor she suddenly realized that she had never felt so alone.

She had gone to bed fully clothed just as Rosa had found her the next morning. For a while she lay awake wondering whether Florian would come after her and what she would say to him if he did. Eventually it became obvious that he must have gone on to the party at Max's house. And then, through sheer exhaustion, she slept. The next thing she knew was Rosa coming in to awaken her.

'Mr Hylton is not here?' Rosa asked.

'Not here? Oh, no. He wanted to stay with the others to read the morning papers at Max Hulbert's house.'

Linda tried to sound as if everything was fine by her, and in fact what she had told Rosa wasn't a complete untruth. Max had explained this was something of a ritual on the morning after a first night, and he had promised all those who stayed a breakfast of scrambled eggs and Buck's Fizz.

'And you did not want to stay with him?'

'Oh, Rosa, I was so tired. I knew that I would only spoil the fun, so I came home.'

'Then I shall make you breakfast, but you will have to be content with coffee rather than champagne and orange juice.'

And so they had breakfasted together, with Imogen proving to be quite amenable to the arrangement. She had been much more manageable of late. Perhaps bewildered by the discomfort of teething, she had decided not to grizzle about it. Linda already knew that her daughter had a will of iron, and now it seemed that when she had every right to complain, she had decided to demonstrate great fortitude. Linda loved her daughter more with every day.

Linda did not know how long she had been lying in the bath. She realized that she could no longer hear the sound of the wireless or indeed any kind of sound. The bath water was almost cold. She raised herself up and, dripping, stepped onto the bath mat and reached for the giant towel that was warming on the heated towel rail. If anything, she felt even worse than she had when she had eased herself into the expensively scented water. Rosa's recommended cure-all had not worked. Linda doubted if there was anything that would.

Florian turned the key in the lock and opened the door quietly. He was hoping that Linda would still be asleep. He needed time to prepare himself. Although he knew what he was going to say to her, he had not worked out the best way to say it. I'm a writer, he thought. I'm supposed to be good with words, but it seems that is only when I'm writing fiction. I can tell the characters I've created what to say, but when it comes to real life I have no idea what I'm going to say to my wife.

When he stepped into the hallway he saw Rosa putting Imogen into the pram. His daughter was dressed warmly in her teddy bear coat and hood. As Rosa eased her back onto the pillow and tucked a blanket round her, the baby smiled at her father, causing a rush of guilt and shame.

'Are you going out, Rosa?' he asked quite unnecessarily.

'Yes, we are going for a walk.'

'It's cold out there.'

'I have wrapped the little one warmly and we will not be long. Only to see the ducks on the river and back.' Rosa held up a paper bag. 'See, I have some crusts to give them. I am going so that Imogen will have some fresh air but also because Mrs Hylton looked tired. And you must be tired also. You stayed at the party.'

Florian wasn't sure if this was a rebuke but decided it wasn't when he saw Rosa was smiling. 'I wanted to read the morning papers with the others.'

'Yes, Mrs Hylton told me that was why you didn't come home with her.'

'Did she?' Florian was grateful that Linda had made the effort to present his actions as reasonable.

'And now you will want to read the reviews all over again! You must be so pleased.'

'You've read them?'

'Mrs Hylton and I read them together.'

'Where *is* my wife?' he asked, and he hoped that the slight tremor in his voice would be taken for fatigue rather than trepidation.

'She is in the bath. I don't think she will be much longer. Shall I make some coffee for you? I have seen to the fire in the sitting room. It is nice and warm in there.'

'No. I can make coffee. You go for your walk. Come, I'll see you to the lift.'

Florian walked with them along the corridor and helped Rosa manoeuvre the pram into a lift. 'Shall I come down and help you out?' he asked.

Rosa shook her head and the lift doors closed. Florian went back to his apartment.

Linda, wearing her towelling robe, opened the bathroom door and a slight draught told her that the front door was open. She looked into the hall and saw that the pram had gone. Rosa had taken Imogen for a walk. The door was ajar. Linda frowned. It was not like Rosa to be careless. She took one step towards the door when it opened further and Florian walked in.

'Linda, I...' he began before his voice faltered and died away.

His topcoat was open to show his evening clothes and his loosened tie. He looks like a character in a film, she thought. He's good-looking even when he is so obviously tired. And then she saw that the fatigue was mixed with anguish.

'I have something to say,' he said. 'But can we go and sit down?' He turned and closed the door behind him.

Wordlessly Linda led the way to the sitting room. He's going to tell me that he is in love with Nadine, she thought. That our marriage is over. She sat down in the armchair nearest to the fire, but no matter how brightly the coals burned she felt as cold as ice.

Florian looked wretched. 'Would you...? Can I get you anything? Coffee? A cup of tea?'

'For God's sake, Florian, get on with it,' she said. 'I don't want coffee or tea, I just want to know what is going to happen to us.'

Florian shrugged off his coat and laid it over the back of the settee and then he took the chair opposite her. 'Happen to us?' he said nervously. 'What do you mean?'

Linda looked at him scathingly and then, despite her own torment, she responded to his utter misery. 'I mean,' she said quietly, 'are we going to have a divorce?'

'God, no!' Florian said. 'That's not what I want and I hope you don't want it either.'

Linda was puzzled. 'But Nadine ... you and Nadine. Don't you want to be together?'

'I want to stay with you.'

Linda was aware that this was not a satisfactory answer. 'Do you mean you want to stay married

365

but at the same time carry on with your affair? You don't deny that you have been having an affair?'

Florian shook his head, and although this was the answer she was expecting, Linda felt a pang of almost inconsolable grief.

'No, I don't deny it,' he said. 'But it's over.'

'Nadine agrees with that, does she?'

'Don't, Linda. Don't talk like that. I want to put things right between us.'

'That might be difficult. Things haven't been right for a long time, have they, Florian?'

'Then I shall have to try all the harder. I don't want to lose you, Linda. You and Imogen, you mean the world to me.'

'Do we?'

'Yes. And I've realized what I've risked. Please forgive me and let us start again.'

Linda burst out laughing.

'What is it?' he asked. 'What do you find so amusing?'

'You. If only you could have heard yourself just now. You sound like a character in a play. Imagine the scene. The errant husband comes home to his wife, begs her forgiveness and swears that if only she will stand by him he will never betray her again.'

Florian flushed. 'I'm sorry if I sound insincere, but I meant every word.'

'Did you? Did you really?'

He looked so genuinely unhappy that Linda's anger faded. 'All right, Florian,' she said. 'We must try and mend our broken marriage for the sake of our daughter. No, don't come near me.' Florian had risen from his chair. 'I'm not ready for the reconciliation scene. Not yet. You'll have to be patient with me.'

'Nadine?'

'Where are you, Florian? I hope you are not telephoning from home.'

'Of course not. I came out to do some shopping. I'm in a phone box.'

'You? Doing the shopping?'

'Rosa was making a list. It started to snow, so I offered to go. I had to speak to you.'

'Why? We've agreed it's over.'

'Only because you insisted.'

He heard her sigh. 'Florian, darling, it's not what I want.'

'Then why?'

'Because the time isn't right. If Linda divorced you Gerald would have to know. He's not stupid. I think he already suspects something, and if he knew for sure he would divorce me. Then what would you do? You would still be responsible for Linda and Imogen financially. Could you afford to keep me?'

'But you are working.'

'Yes, I am, but I'm not earning nearly enough for us to live comfortably. And besides, you wouldn't want people to think that you were being kept by a woman, would you?'

'No, but it won't always be like that. This play is going to be a success. I'll write another – I already have an idea.'

'So we'll wait until then. We'll just have to be patient, darling. And meanwhile, remember to be good to that little wife of yours, just as I will have to be nice to Gerald. We've already agreed to this, haven't we?'

'Yes, we've agreed.'

'Then do your shopping like a good boy and go back to your family. Goodbye, Florian.'

'Goodbye.'

Florian replaced the receiver and stood hunched inside the draughty telephone box until the urge to weep had passed. He fished in his pocket for the shopping list and saw that he would have to go to the greengrocer's. He wondered what Linda's reaction would be if he bought her flowers.

Chapter Twenty-One

June 1940, Northern France

'Do you really think we're going to get home, Rupert, old chap?' Charlie Meredith asked his old friend.

'Of course we are, Charlie. We're in a proper queue now, aren't we?'

Charlie Meredith, his dirty, stubbled face etched with weariness, looked at the line of men stretching from where they stood to the sea where vessels of all shapes and sizes were waiting. He laughed. 'And how long do you think it will take to get this lot on board?'

'They're doing their best,' Rupert told him.

'Of course they are,' Denis Vincent, who was standing behind them, spoke up.

Charlie glanced at him briefly, then turned to point out to sea. 'But look at them,' he said. 'Look at that one – it's a ruddy paddle steamer. What's it doing crossing the English Channel?'

'It's here to take us home,' Denis said. 'And you should be grateful instead of whingeing all the time.'

Charlie looked at him in surprise. 'Whingeing? Me? You've hurt my feelings, old chap. And as for the paddle steamer: Roll up! Roll up! Any more for the *Skylark?*'

Charlie and Rupert laughed.

Denis looked at them, envying their camaraderie. He had known them at school, where he had been a year below them, and then met up with them again at Oxford. They had good-naturedly allowed him to join their group of privileged young men but they had never been real friends. Their backgrounds were too different.

A scholarship had taken Denis to Oxford, where he had shone. His father, a teacher in a minor public school, was inordinately proud of him, and his mother had been overjoyed when Denis had been taken on as a private secretary to a government minister. His parents had thought it only natural that Denis had been commissioned straight away. Rupert and Charlie were still waiting, so Denis as a second lieutenant was their superior in rank, although Charlie did not seem to grasp this.

The bulk of the British army had been driven to the coast and was trapped here at Dunkirk. The men thought that nothing but a miracle could save them from the German onslaught. Then the

369

miracle came in the form of a vast fleet of little boats. Some of them would make their way back across the English Channel; some of them acted as ferries taking the men to the larger vessels waiting offshore because the waters were too shallow. These vessels had become the main target for the Luftwaffe.

At the moment the skies were clear and the shelling from the German front line had paused. Hundreds of men had taken advantage of the hiatus to form more or less orderly lines. All of them were praying that they would be taken aboard before they came under attack again. Grubby, unshaven, hungry and thirsty, the men were desperate to get away, but most of them were resilient and some even managed to find humour in the situation; including men like Charlie Meredith and Rupert Hylton. And then, while the lines of men shuffled forward, Denis heard the distant drone of approaching aircraft. All around him he saw men looking up at the sky.

'Oh, Christ,' Rupert Hylton said, 'the bastards are coming back.' All around them the lines began to break as the men ran for the shelter of the dunes. 'Come on, Charlie,' Rupert said. 'Time to take cover.'

'You go, if you like. I'm staying here. If we leave we'll lose our place in the queue.'

'If you stay you'll lose more than that.'

Charlie's answer was to lie down on the sand. Rupert stared at him helplessly as the first of the Stukas appeared overhead. Soon the sky was full of enemy planes and the dreadful screaming of their engines as they dived. They sought their target among the ships but some of the pilots chose to bomb the beach.

Rupert bent over and grasped Charlie's legs and tried to drag him backwards. He saw Denis standing there indecisively and yelled, 'For God's sake, help me!'

'Meredith!' Denis said. 'As your officer I order you to pull back.'

He would never forget Rupert Hylton's expression of amazed derision. 'Thanks a bundle,' Rupert said and then Denis turned and fled.

He had no sooner reached the dunes than there was a deafening explosion and the air filled with sand, stinging his face and filling his eyes. The blast threw him bodily into the marram grass.

Later that day, when the attack subsided, Denis found a place on the paddle steamer. 'Any more for the *Skylark*,' he muttered as weary, uncomplaining men took whatever place was available. Tears streamed down Denis's face as he remembered Charlie Meredith's brave humour. He knew he would never understand why Rupert Hylton had not tried to save himself.

15th July 1940

Dear Linda,
You would have to have a heart of stone not to weep for Mrs Hylton now. Not only has she lost her son, but when he heard the news from France Mr Hylton had a stroke – a severe one – and it's doubtful if he will recover. Or even if he wants to. Cordelia has come home, but in her own sorrow

she's not much help to her mother. Mrs Hylton was asked if she would take in some evacuees, children from the cities. In other circumstances I'm sure she would have done, but now her days are devoted to looking after her husband.

This is not the house that you first came to, Linda. You would be sad if you could see it now. More than half the rooms are shut up with the furniture draped with dustcovers. Mrs Hylton, God bless her, suggested that they should stop using the dining room and that they would eat in the kitchen with Brenda and me, but Cordelia wouldn't hear of it. So there the two of them sit at mealtimes in that cold, draughty dining room with no coal for the fire while Ivy and Albert and I keep warm in the kitchen. At least Cordelia doesn't expect us to take her meals to her room on a tray. Mr Hylton never leaves his room and we save what coal we can to keep it warm for him.

We had a visitor staying with us for a few days, a Mr Denis Vincent. He said he had been on the beach at Dunkirk with Rupert and Cordelia's husband, Charlie, when they died. He wanted to tell Mrs Hylton how brave Rupert had been. Apparently he died trying to save Charlie, and Mr Vincent said that it would haunt him until his dying day that he had not been able to do more. He said he'd tried to help but the blast of the explosion that killed them blew him yards away. A consequence of this is that he is now deaf in one ear and has had to leave the army. He was working in the Houses of Parliament before the war started and now he's hoping that they'll take him back.

Cordelia and he seemed to come close – perhaps

sharing grief. Nothing happened, of course. After all, she's in mourning for her husband, but I think they will keep in touch.

You'll see by this that one aspect of Fernwood Hall hasn't changed at all. The servants find out everything that goes on!

Linda, I wish you and Florian were here with us. They say that it can't be much longer before the Germans start bombing London, and I know you're supposed to be all prepared with air raid shelters and sandbags and the like, but it would be much safer to be here in the country.

Can't you persuade your husband to come home? I know his mother has written to him – I posted the letter myself last week – and she hasn't had an answer yet. I suppose he has every right to be angry with her for the way he was treated, but in times like this he should swallow his pride for the sake of you and his daughter, if not for his own.

War or not, nothing much changes in the village, although everyone is grumbling about the food rationing. Luckily a lot of folk round here keep hens, so there are always fresh eggs, and there's no one left here to see if a few rabbits are being snared in the woods.

Write soon, Linda, won't you? I worry about you.

Love,
Vera

'A letter from your friend at home?'

Rosa was slicing vegetables on the kitchen table and she paused and asked her question when

Linda put the pages back in the envelope.

Linda was sitting at the table where she had been trying to make sense of the ration books when the post had arrived. 'Yes, it's from Vera.'

'You look worried. Is it bad news?'

'Not bad news, just sad news.'

'They are grieving over the loss of Mr Hylton's brother?'

'And his brother-in-law. Yes. His mother wants him to go home.'

'And you, too?'

'I suppose so, although I haven't read her letter and Florian doesn't want to talk about it.'

'I think he is too proud, no?'

'That could be so.' Linda sighed and rose from the table. 'It's time Imogen woke from her nap. I think I'll take her for a walk.'

Florian was in his study. He had started work on a new play. It was set in a country house, beginning as the First World War came to an end and ending as the next war began. The family who lived there saw the old order vanishing and eventually realized that if they were going to survive they would have to change. Linda thought it a brilliant concept and had been pleased whenever he discussed his progress with her. In the early stages he had been careful to explain that there was no part in this play for Nadine. She would be fully occupied as it looked as though *The Shadow Wife* was going to run for years.

Linda could have pointed out that often the cast of a play would change as the actors moved on, either to another play or to take part in a film. However, she did not want to do anything to halt the progress they were making as they strove to be happy again; so she kept quiet.

Once Imogen was ready to go, Linda paused at the study door, wondering whether to go in. She listened to the clatter of his typewriter and realized that he was in full flow so she decided not to disturb him. Rosa gave her a paper bag full of stale crusts and Linda and Imogen set off to feed the ducks.

Florian heard Rosa call goodbye to Imogen and his daughter's excited reply. Then he heard the front door of the apartment close. He waited for a moment and went into the kitchen where Rosa seemed to putting everything she could find into a large pan to make one of her mother's soups.

He smiled and asked her where Linda was. Rosa told him that his wife and daughter had gone for a walk by the river. He told Rosa that he was sorry that Linda had not asked him to go with them and then said it was just as well, because he'd reached a sticky bit in his writing and should get back to work as soon as Rosa had made him some coffee.

'Sticky bit?' Rosa said and she frowned.

'Difficult,' Florian explained. 'So after you've brought my coffee I would be glad if you didn't disturb me.'

Rosa assured him that she wouldn't, and a few minutes later she brought his coffee into the study and closed the door behind her.

Florian wasted no time before he reached for the phone and dialled a number. When Nadine answered she sounded cross.

'What is it, Florian? You should know by now

that I don't like to be disturbed when I'm getting ready to go to the theatre.'

'You have ages, yet.'

'I like to relax and get myself in the mood. Besides, you took a chance. Gerald comes home early these days for a meal before he goes off on his fire-watching duties.'

'Nadine, I'm sorry if I've disturbed you, but we haven't got much time and I want to talk.'

He heard her sigh but her voice softened when she said, 'Darling, we agreed it was all over between us.'

'For the moment.'

'All right, for the moment, but we can't meet and you're only prolonging the agony when you phone like this.' There was a long silence and she sounded exasperated when she said, 'Don't sulk, Florian, it doesn't become you.'

'Nadine, do you still love me?'

'Oh, my Lord, what brought this on?'

'Do you?'

'Yes, I do, even when you behave like a spoilt child and phone me for no reason whatsoever.'

'I have a reason. My mother has written and asked me to come home.'

'Are you asking me whether you should go?'

'I suppose I am.'

'Do you want to?'

'No.'

'Then don't.'

'It's not as easy as that. My elder brother was killed in action, along with my sister's husband, and my father has had a stroke.'

'Good God, that's appalling.'

'And that's not all. The best men at the pottery are in the forces, and my mother is struggling to run the business as well as nursing my father and trying to keep the ship afloat.'

'The ship?'

'Fernwood Hall. It takes a great deal of looking after.'

'Your family home? You've never talked about it.'

'Because I thought I had done with it.'

'It sounds rather grand.'

'Grand enough. And as my mother points out that I will inherit it one day, along with the wretched pottery, she thinks I ought to go home and take up my responsibilities.'

'Florian, you've got to go home.'

'Why?'

'Because it's the right thing to do.'

'I was hoping you would beg me to stay in London.'

'Listen, my love. Take your wife and daughter home; find someone you can trust to run the business for you so you can get on with your writing. You can always come up to town now and then on business.'

'Business?'

'To talk about the next play, of course. Incidentally, how is it going?'

'Very well.'

'No squalling babes to interrupt you?'

'Imogen doesn't squall any more and Linda makes sure I'm not disturbed.'

'The good little wife.'

'Don't talk like that. She doesn't deserve sarcasm.'

377

'Feeling guilty? Well, I'm sorry, but I do find her too good to be true sometimes, and you know what, Florian, darling? Your home in Northumberland will be just the right place for her.'

The bagful of crusts was soon emptied and the faithless ducks deserted them to swim downstream in search of other delights. Usually this would have brought a howl of frustration from Imogen, but the day was warm and she was tired. She settled back against the pillow and Linda adjusted the pram parasol to shade her eyes from the bright sun. It wasn't long before she was asleep.

As Linda straightened up she heard a burst of laughter from further along the river bank. A lively group of young men and women in khaki were feeding the ducks. But they weren't making it easy for them. They were hurling the tasty morsels as far away as they could then laughing as the ducks raced en masse towards them.

Linda, guessing that they were on leave, was moved by their high spirits. As she walked towards them she hoped that this would be a day for them to remember in the dangerous and difficult days ahead. Eventually they quietened down and turned towards each other, some of them with heads bent as they lit cigarettes. Linda guessed they were discussing what to do next. Then it seemed they came to an agreement and they set off in the direction of Linda's favourite café. All but one of them.

One of the men stayed behind and, hands in his pockets, forage cap angled jauntily forward, he stared down into the river where a few ducks paddled hopefully back and forth. Linda had already closed most of the gap between them before the shock of recognition hit her. She stopped and stared, trying to deny the way her heart had leaped so joyfully and knowing that she must turn around and walk away. She gripped the handle of the pram and stared down at her sleeping daughter as if seeking guidance from her beautiful innocent face.

Suddenly, without turning to look at her, the soldier spoke. 'My father used to listen to John Snagge commentating on the boat race on the wireless.'

The boat race? What did he mean? Of course. The boat race used to start just along there at Putney Bridge. He still hadn't turned to look at her and the moment felt surreal. Linda remained silent.

The soldier continued, 'Dad supported Oxford, the dark blues. I told you once how keen he was on history, and you see Oxford remained loyal to King Charles during the Civil War. I supported Cambridge, just to tease him, and he would joke and call me a Roundhead.

'It's strange how a working man could have been so taken up with the idea of two boatloads of privileged youth fighting it out on the river, isn't it? Tradition, he used to say. He thought tradition important. I thought I'd honour his memory today by coming along to see where it all took place. I don't suppose there'll be another boat race for a while. At least not until this war is over. John Snagge has more serious matters to report on now.'

Still she hadn't spoken and he said, 'I know you're there, Linda. I saw you a while ago. I wasn't sure what I should do. I wanted to leave the others and walk towards you but I knew how unwise that would be.'

'Why?' Linda whispered. It was the first time she had spoken.

'Because I wanted to see you too much for my own good. But at the same time I couldn't walk away. So I played a game with myself. I thought, I'll leave it to fate. So I decided to stay here and look at the river – not to turn round – just wait to see if you came in this direction. I wasn't even going to speak to you if you walked straight past me. But you stopped. I knew you had recognized me. I couldn't help myself. Blame it on the war.'

'What do you mean?'

Graham Forsyth laughed softly and at last he turned to face her. 'All this heightened emotion,' he said. 'Men and women torn away from their everyday lives, not knowing if they will return. And not knowing whether they will see the people they love again.'

Linda was unable to meet his eyes. He came towards her and his shadow fell across the pram. 'I've embarrassed you. I'm sorry. Do you want me to go away?'

She looked up at him. 'No, I don't. But please don't...'

'Don't what?'

'Don't play any more games.'

He looked at her searchingly for a moment and then he smiled. 'I promise I won't. What shall we do? Find somewhere for a cup of tea?'

'No. It's a lovely day. Let's just walk by the river.'

Florian stared pensively at the neat pile of manuscript pages lying next to his typewriter. His work was going well and he'd already had interest from a production company. Would he be able to work at home in Fernwood? Nadine, bless her, was right about one thing. Someone else would have to run the business if he was to get on with his writing.

Later that night he talked to Linda about it, not of course telling her that it had been Nadine's suggestion, and he was pleased to find that Linda agreed with him.

'I'll help as much as I can,' Linda said. 'I'll make sure that you're left alone.'

'You don't mind?'

'Not at all. I'd like to help you.'

'What I meant was, do you mind going back to Fernwood? After all, my mother and sister haven't exactly been friendly since we got married.'

'They haven't been friendly to you either. We'll deal with them together.'

'I don't deserve you, Linda.'

'You probably don't.' Linda tried to keep it light, although for some reason she felt like crying. 'Florian, if we go back to Fernwood what will we do about the apartment?'

'Keep it, of course.'

'And Rosa? Would we have to let her go?'

'I'm afraid so. Does that upset you?'

'It does. She has become a good friend.'

'She's young and intelligent. She'll get another job easily but I could always ask her to keep an eye on this place. Pop in now and then to keep it clean and aired. Send on any correspondence that might arrive. That sort of thing. I'd pay her something, of course.'

'Thank you, Florian. That would be wonderful.'

'Let's not talk about it any more tonight, Linda. As Scarlett O'Hara would say, let's think about it tomorrow.'

The next day brought a telegram that left them no time to think: 'Your father died in his sleep. Would appreciate it if you came home for the funeral. Emerald Hylton.'

Florian took the sleeper from King's Cross that night. Linda and Imogen would follow as soon as they could. They reckoned it would take at the very least a week to pack up and send anything they needed from the apartment.

Linda and Rosa both wept when it was time for them to say goodbye. Rosa wanted to go with them to the station, but Linda told her she'd rather remember her in the kitchen of the apartment than standing forlornly on the station platform as the train pulled away.

Rosa had to stay in the apartment until the carrier arrived to take the heavy luggage. 'I will keep this place nice for you,' she told Linda. 'And whenever you come up to London, no matter what other job I'm doing, I shall come and cook for you.'

Even the first-class carriages were full, and not only with men and women in uniform. Linda wondered where all these people could be going and why they were making such journeys in wartime. At first Imogen was fractious, but the repetitive rhythm of the train seemed to hypnotize her, and for much of the six-hour journey she slept. As the train rattled northwards Linda wondered if she would ever return to the apartment and if she would ever see Rosa again.

'Has she changed much?' Muriel Sinclair asked her husband when he arrived home.

He laughed. 'Give me a chance to take my coat off. But no, not at all. She's as bonny as ever. Although obviously she looks a little strained at the moment.' He followed his wife into the kitchen where she had the table set for a supper of soup and sandwiches.

'And the baby?' Muriel asked as she lit the gas and began to stir the soup.

'She's got her father's blond hair and her mother's dark brown eyes.'

'They say that's supposed to be a sign of great beauty.'

'In this case I think the old wives' tale is going to be proved true.'

Muriel filled two soup plates and sat at the table with him. 'Linda must have been surprised to see you.'

'She was, but I explained to her that as Aslett is wary of handling the big cars the Hyltons are without a chauffeur and rely heavily on taxis. She knows Florian doesn't drive and she was touched that he had asked me to meet her at the Central Station.'

'And use up your precious petrol coupons to boot!'

'I didn't mention that.'

383

'Of course not. You're a good man, John.'

'And you're a good cook.'

The Sinclairs smiled at each other and went on chatting as they ate their supper.

'Did you go in with her?' Muriel asked.

'Into the Hall?'

'Mmm.'

'Yes. I helped her in with her luggage. Florian was pleased to see them.'

'I should hope so.'

'But he seemed distracted.'

'And Mrs Hylton?'

'Didn't make an appearance. Neither did Cordelia. Florian explained that they had both gone to bed.'

'Poor Linda.'

'Why do you say that?'

'You would have thought one of them at least would have stayed up to welcome her.'

'Yes, you would. But there's no need to worry. Linda will cope. And she has Vera Saunders.'

'Ah yes. Vera was a friend of Linda's mother, wasn't she? I'm glad the girl will have an ally.'

Later, in bed, John Sinclair pondered over his wife's choice of words. An ally was more than a friend or a supporter. You needed allies when you had enemies. He hoped that Linda was not going to have troubled times ahead.

Chapter Twenty-Two

August 1940

Rain smeared the soot-stained windows of the dreary little room in the house in Station Road. For three generations now Armstrong & Sons had dealt with small town concerns such as the sale and purchase of property, minor court cases and wills. His father was long gone and Harold, the only surviving son, had rarely had to deal with anything as intriguing as this.

'Would you like a cup of tea?' he asked the coldly beautiful woman sitting at the other side of his desk.

'No, thank you.'

Her tone, like her eyes, was hollow and Harold Armstrong felt a surge of pity. She was not the first war widow to climb the lino-covered stairs to his first-floor office and he feared she would not be the last. *Widow* ... he mused. Strictly speaking, she was no such thing. But the man she had taken up with had cared enough for her to provide for her and his child.

'That will be all,' Harold told his secretary, who was hovering by the door.

'Very well, dear, but if the lady changes her mind I can make a fresh pot and I've got some nice Garibaldis.' She went out and closed the door.

Harold, flushing, smiled at his client and said,

'Er ... my mother. She came in to help when Miss Jackson left to join the land army.'

If he had expected a smile he was disappointed. Mrs Wade, or Miss Delafontaine as she really was, was in no mood for gentle humour. And why should she be? The man she must have loved had died in action at Dunkirk and she was now an unmarried mother with an uncertain future. Rupert Hylton had made sure that she would not starve; there might even be enough to send the boy to a good school, but there were strings attached.

The Hylton family's firm of solicitors in Newcastle had got in touch with him and asked him to take care of Rupert Hylton's mistress. He was to take her 'under his wing', advise her of her position and instruct her that she must never get in touch with the Hylton family. If she did the money would stop. Harold wasn't too sure of the legality of this, but he hoped that he would never have to go to battle with such an old and eminent firm.

Poor girl, he thought. She's had a rough ride. First finding out that her father is an utter scoundrel, and now this. And saddled with an illegitimate child as she was, he doubted whether she would find it easy to meet a man who would marry her.

'Mr Armstrong?'

With a start, Harold realized that he had not spoken for some time. 'Miss, ah – Mrs Wade. First of all, may I say how sorry I am for the loss of your – er – for your loss. And now, if you like, I shall explain the terms of the will.'

'Poor dear,' his mother said as she stood by the

window a little later and watched Harold's new client emerge from the door and cross the street. 'Is she going to be all right?'

'You know I can't tell you, Mother.'

'I'm not asking for details. I just want to know that she will not suffer hardship.'

'No, no hardship.'

'Then why do you look so sad?'

'It's the war, Mother. It's the war.'

His mother turned from the window and smiled ruefully at him. 'I never thought I should say this but I thank God for your weak chest.' She patted his arm. 'And now I shall go and make that pot of tea.'

Harold remained by the window, and as he watched Pamela Delafontaine hurrying through the rain he felt a surge of anger and contempt for the late Rupert Hylton who, despite dying in defence of his country, had nevertheless behaved totally dishonourably.

'How has he been?'

'As good as gold,' Polly said. She had been looking after David while Pamela had been out. 'Let me have your coat,' she said. 'It's soaking. We can't have you catching cold.'

'Stop that, will you? I'm not a child.'

'I'm sorry. Do you want a cup of tea?' The young maid looked abashed.

'No. I want a large gin and tonic. Can you manage that?'

'I can, and you shouldn't talk to me like this.'

Pamela's eyes widened. 'What do you mean?'

'Every time I try to help you, you snap at me.'

'I don't need your help. I just need you to do as you're told. Where's David?'

'He's having a nap, and while he's sleeping I think you and I should have a talk.'

Pamela was astonished. Polly, her maidservant, was talking to her as if they were equals.

'I don't want to talk to you,' she said.

'Well, don't talk. Just listen. Go and sit by the fire and I'll bring you your gin and tonic. You might find that you need it.'

To Pamela's further astonishment, when Polly brought her drink she actually sat down. 'This won't take long,' she said.

Pamela gave an exaggerated sigh. 'Go on then.'

'I was thinking about leaving, but the news came through about Mr Wade and I thought that would be a really rotten thing to do. My mam said I should stay and see you through the bad times.'

'What business is it of your mother's?'

'None, I suppose. She's just a kindly soul who thought you might need help or comforting.'

'So you took it upon yourself to comfort me?'

'I tried, but obviously I've failed.'

'Look, Polly, I'll try to explain. You're not my friend or anything. You're just a maidservant.'

'Not much longer.'

'What do you mean?'

'I had my nineteenth birthday last month.'

'Oh, dear, did I miss it?'

'There's no need to be sarcastic. I've only told you because now I can join up.'

'Join up? What are you talking about?'

'The army – well, the ATS.'

Pamela laughed. 'For goodness sake, Polly, don't

388

be taken in by those posters and those uniforms that look so attractive. I bet in real life that ghastly, scratchy khaki is far from glamorous.'

'I'm not joining up to look glamorous.'

'Well, why exactly are you joining up?'

'Because there's a war on and I want to help win it.'

'Oh, very noble. You've been seeing too many films. You have no idea what you'll be getting into.'

'I'm not stupid. I know very well that I'll probably end up peeling potatoes or cleaning floors, but with any luck I could work on the anti-aircraft guns.'

Pamela was astonished. 'You would be happy doing that?'

'I want to do my bit to—'

'To win this war. This bloody war.'

Suddenly, without warning, Pamela burst into tears and began to sob uncontrollably.

Polly rose from her seat. 'Mrs Wade, I...'

'Don't come near me. Or rather, fill up this glass and then go and cook the bloody dinner.'

'Very well, Mrs Wade. I'll cook the dinner since that's what you're paying me for, but you can fill up your own glass.'

'Polly!'

'What?'

'You really are leaving, aren't you? Otherwise you wouldn't speak to me like this.'

'That's right. I'm leaving. I would probably have been called up anyway. Working as a maid for a woman young enough to do her own housework isn't exactly a reserved occupation, is it?'

'But what shall I do?'

'Find someone who's too old to join up. And if no one else will put up with you, you'll have to do your own cooking and cleaning. As far as I can see, there's no reason why you shouldn't.'

Polly went to the kitchen to start preparing the meal. Pamela stared across the empty room and then she began to shake with a mixture of fear and rage. Fear because now that Rupert was dead she did not know what was going to happen to her, and rage because he had left her in this position. She was all the more angry because it was her own fault. She had deliberately set out to seduce Rupert Hylton, thinking that he would do the honourable thing and marry her. How wrong she had been. For all their grand airs and graces, the Hyltons were self-interested and shallow.

Her father was an out-and-out criminal who had ruined people's lives. He had deserved to go to prison. Her mother, in her misery, had not cared enough for the daughter she had left alone in the world. But no matter how wretched she felt, at least she had David. She knew now that it was up to her and her alone to make sure that her son grew up to be decent and honourable. And in doing that she would make her own happiness.

'I had no idea that William had made another will,' Emerald Hylton said.

James Grayson, the head of the firm of the Hyltons' solicitors, had come to Fernwood Hall himself to explain to the family the terms of William Hylton's last will and testament. They sat in the library where Vera Saunders had managed to get a small fire going, for although it was the height of summer the days had been cold and rainy.

Linda had worried over how she should arrange the chairs. She had not wanted to seat Mr Grayson at William Hylton's desk, but Florian had assured her that would be all right. So now Emerald and Cordelia, and Florian and Linda herself sat and faced Mr Grayson like students while he read out the lesson notes.

The solicitor explained that when Rupert had joined the army his father had thought it best to assume he might not survive, in which case the pottery was to be left to Florian and Cordelia jointly and the Hall to Emerald as long as she lived. When she died or if she remarried it was to pass to Florian or his descendants, as Cordelia already had Green Leas.

Apart from that, the arrangements for various trusts and all bequests were to remain unchanged.

'So Florian and I must take charge of the pottery?' Cordelia said.

'Yes. You will be equal partners.'

Cordelia frowned and Florian stared at Mr Grayson glumly. 'But I know nothing about the damn pottery and neither does my sister.'

'Your father was not unaware of that, and his suggestion was that you should find a good man to manage the place for you.'

'All the good men are away at the war,' Florian said. 'For instance, what will we do without Graham Forsyth? He's our top designer, isn't he?'

In the blink of an eye Linda saw Graham spreading the designs for Cordelia's dinner service across the desk. She remembered how they had smiled at each other when Cordelia finally made a decision.

She forced herself to return to the present.

'Don't worry,' Mr Grayson said. 'I understand he has trained his team well. And as for finding a manager, I'll start making enquiries, shall I?'

'Please do that.'

'Wait a moment,' Cordelia intercepted. 'I haven't agreed that would be the best thing to do, and if we are to be equal partners it should be my decision, too.'

Florian turned on her angrily. 'Are you saying you want to run the bloody place? If so, you're welcome to it.'

'No, I'm not saying that. I'm just saying you should have consulted me.'

'Oh, for Christ's sake,' Florian said. 'You can see what this is going to be like. A bloody shambles.'

'Florian!' his mother said. 'Please. This is difficult enough without your forgetting your manners.'

Florian raised his eyebrows in disbelief. 'My manners?'

'Yes, your manners. Mr Grayson did not come here to listen to your bad-tempered squabbling.'

'It's all right, Mrs Hylton,' the solicitor said. 'I am used to the way people react in unhappy circumstances. But let me assure you, Florian – and Cordelia – I will find a man to manage the place as soon as I can. In fact, in anticipation of your reaction I already have someone in mind. He is recently retired–'

'Retired!' Florian said. 'Some decrepit old man.'

'He is in his sixties but far from decrepit. In fact, he is the same age as I am.' At this point Mr Grayson looked disapprovingly over his reading glasses. 'Mr Redman has been working at a pottery in the Midlands for all his working life. By the time he retired he was assistant managing director. He is a widower and he has come north to live with his married daughter. I can arrange for you to interview him, if you like.'

'I don't think there's any need for that,' Florian said. 'Not if you think he's suitable. Forgive my burst of temper a moment ago. I'm very grateful to you for finding someone.'

'You've done it again, Florian! You've made a decision without asking me, and I say we should interview him,' Cordelia said.

'Really? And what exactly would you ask him?'

Cordelia threw him a scornful glance. 'I'm not entirely stupid. My suggestion is that you and I and Mr Grayson should interview Mr Redman. Mr Grayson will ask the questions and if we're satisfied we will make a decision together.'

'Really, Cordelia—'

Florian began to lose his temper again but Mr Grayson interrupted him. 'If you don't mind my saying so, I think that is an excellent suggestion. This is a family firm and Mr Redman ought to know who he is working for.'

Cordelia's smile was smug and Florian looked as if he would burst with the deadliness of it all. 'Very well,' Florian said. 'We'll leave the next step to Mr Grayson.' And then, remembering something, he added, 'Is that all right with you, Mother?'

While Florian and Cordelia had been squabbling Emerald had been staring into the mid-distance. Linda had no idea what it was she saw. At Florian's words she blinked and then stared at him uncomprehendingly. 'What did you say?'

'I asked if you agreed that we should leave Mr Grayson to arrange an interview with Mr Redman.'

'I haven't the remotest idea what you're talking about. If it's about the business I want nothing to do with it. Your father left it to you and Cordelia, so please get on with it.'

'Come for a walk?' Florian asked Linda.

'I'd love to.'

'What about Imogen?'

'I've just put her down for a nap.'

'Then grab a coat – there's a nasty little breeze – and let's go.'

Linda told Vera she was going for a walk and asked her to listen out for Imogen. By the time she was ready to go Florian was waiting in the hallway. He had put on an overcoat and was holding a walking stick. Linda couldn't remember the exact moment when the stick had become necessary and they had never talked about it. Florian preferred it that way.

'Where are we going?' she asked him.

'To the woods. Is there anywhere else to go?'

Linda shook her head and they smiled at each other as they set off across the open ground that lay in front of the house.

'That was pretty grim, wasn't it?' Florian said.

'The meeting with Mr Grayson or the lunch that followed it?'

Florian laughed. 'Both. I feel ashamed about the way I behaved at the meeting.'

'And so you should.'

'But the blame lies entirely at my mother's door for that miserable luncheon.'

'I thought the corned beef rissoles were very tasty. And the rice pudding was a treat.'

'I don't mean the food – especially as I know you helped prepare it. I mean the way my mother sat in total silence and made no attempt whatsoever to respond to the poor chap's polite conversation.'

'Don't be too hard on her. She's finding life very difficult. I'm sure Mr Grayson will understand.'

'Of course she is, and of course he will. And now you've made me feel twice as guilty.' Suddenly Florian stopped walking and turned, and grinned at Linda. 'But I don't feel at all guilty about wanting to strangle my sister. Honestly, Linda, I never wanted to be involved with the family business and now that I am, I'll have Cordelia to put up with, too.'

'Perhaps once you have someone to manage the pottery–'

'Mr Redman.'

'Yes, Mr Redman. Well, perhaps then Cordelia will get bored with it and be content to leave the decisions to you.'

'And that's supposed to comfort me?'

The wind caught at their coats and tried to push them forwards. Florian steadied himself with his walking stick and set off towards the woods again.

'Florian, wait–' The wind caught her words and threw them away. She hurried to catch up with him. 'Florian.' This time he heard her but he kept on walking and stared straight ahead. She caught at his arm. 'Darling, I know how wretched you must feel.'

He stopped and turned towards her. 'Do you?'

'Of course I do. You never wanted anything to do with the business; you wanted to concentrate on your writing. And now, when you are becoming a successful playwright, you find yourself responsible for it.'

'Linda, what am I going to do?'

'What do you *want* to do?'

'I've thought of giving it away.'

'Giving it away?'

Florian's smile was strained. 'Not literally. I mean I could sign the whole thing over to Cordelia, but that would be the end of Hylton's, wouldn't it?'

'Not necessarily. If you appoint a good manager.'

'No matter how good he was, Cordelia would drive him crazy. She's so contrary. You know that as well as I do.'

Linda sighed and linked her arm through his. They began to walk towards the woods again. 'Yes, I suppose I do.'

'And you must see that I can't let my mother down like this. What would people think of me? I'm stuck with it, aren't I?'

'In name you are.'

'What do you mean?'

'You could leave a lot of it to me. I mean, you could tell me what you want to do and then trust me to deal with Cordelia.'

'Do you think she would listen to you?'

'She has in the past.'

'She can be difficult when she gets a bee in her bonnet.'

'Leave me to take care of that so that you can

get on with your writing. And, do you know, it might just be the case that Cordelia would get bored with the business eventually and leave all the decisions to you.'

They had reached the pathway into the woods and Florian stopped and smiled at her. 'You could be right. Linda, will you really do this for me?'

Linda looked at her husband. His handsome face was marred by ill-concealed petulance. Why, she wondered, should she be willing to help this man who had betrayed her so hurtfully? She knew that if she did help it wouldn't be so much for Florian as for her daughter who would inherit the pottery one day. But it was more than that. She would also be doing it for herself. Once more she remembered the day that Graham had arrived with his designs and how interesting she had found them. Perhaps if she got involved she could do something good with the business, and even help the war effort.

'Linda?' Florian was looking at her anxiously.

'Don't worry, Florian,' she said. 'I will.'

Suddenly the wind grew stronger and a swirl of early autumn leaves surrounded them. Florian released her arm and stood back and looked at her.

'There's a leaf in your hair,' he said.

Linda reached up and took the leaf. She was about to throw it down when he caught her hand. 'Know'st thou not at the fall of a leaf, How the heart feels a languid grief...' he said softly.

'"Autumn Song", Rossetti,' Linda said.

'Do you remember?'

'I do.'

'I took a leaf from your hair that day and put it

in my pocket. I kept it, you know. I pressed it in one of my books. I can't remember which one. It could still be there.'

He smiled as he remembered and let the leaf fall.

Linda closed her eyes, remembering how Florian had taken her in his arms that day and how he had kissed her.

'Goodbye, Linda,' he had said. *'We'll meet again when I'm home for Christmas, won't we?'*

It had been years before they had seen each other again.

'What are you thinking?' Florian asked.

'Mmm?'

'You were miles away.'

'Not miles. Years.'

She might have said more, but he had already started to walk away from her. 'Let's go back,' he said and half turned to look over his shoulder. He was smiling broadly. 'I'll tell Saunders to find a good bottle of wine to go with tonight's meal, even if it's another rabbit stew.'

'I like rabbit stew!' Linda said and she began to follow him.

She looked ahead and caught her breath. The afternoon sun catching the windows made the house look as if all the lights were on. As if the Hall was lit up for a ball, Linda thought, remembering her childhood fantasies. This had been a magic place; a house of enchantment where attractive, vibrant people dwelled. Had she broken the spell by coming here? She, an ordinary mortal. She knew it was fanciful, but she couldn't help wondering if it was her intrusion that had caused the magic to fade and the shadows to gather.

Linda hurried back to Fernwood Hall, knowing she must do her best to help these people. For, magic or not, the gift she had received from them was her daughter, Imogen.

Florian had been right. It was rabbit stew for dinner. The stew was followed by semolina with a dollop of jam each. Despite rationing they had plenty of jam made by Ivy Aslett over the years with fruit from the Hall's own gardens and stored in the pantry. Now most of the gardens had been given over to a local farmer for the duration of the war. Those that were left were producing an abundant harvest of weeds.

Florian had gone down into the wine cellar himself and come up with a bottle of vintage champagne. Cordelia looked at it and said, 'Don't you think we should save that until we have something to celebrate?'

'There's plenty more down there. And, anyway what do you mean, "something to celebrate"?'

'Victory?'

'Are you sure we're going to win?'

'Well, the end of the war, then, whether we win or not.'

'If we lose the war I'll smash the bottles and pour every drop of champagne away myself rather than let the Germans have it.'

After the meal they sat for a while over their coffee but the conversation was half-hearted. Emerald hardly spoke and Cordelia wondered aloud whether she would ever be called up for war work.

'If I am I want to drive an ambulance,' she said.

'But you can't drive,' Florian told her.

'Actually I can,' she said. 'Paul taught me.'

'Have you taken the test?'

'No.'

'Then how can you drive ambulances?'

'They've suspended the tests for the duration of the war.'

'Then remind me to walk ahead of you with a red flag,' Florian said, and that was the evening's only attempt at humour.

Soon Florian excused himself and went to his old bedroom where he already had a desk, so he could use the room as a study.

Emerald went to bed early and Cordelia decided to listen to the wireless in her room. Linda went upstairs to check on Imogen and then she went down to the kitchen to help Vera with the washing-up. Although Vera had objected, Linda helped with a lot of the housework. Fernwood Hall was too big for Vera and the Asletts to manage on their own, although they did have occasional help from women in the village. Needless to say, neither Cordelia nor Emerald Hylton lifted a finger.

'Will Mr Hylton want a bite of supper?' Vera asked. 'I can manage some spam sandwiches.'

'Yes, I'm sure he'd appreciate that.'

'I'll take them up before we go to bed. Unless you want to?'

'No, you take them. I think I'll go up and read for a while.'

Leaving the nursery door open, Linda settled in bed with a copy of *Dumb Witness* by Agatha Christie. She tried to get involved in the plot but very soon guessed what was going to happen and found it too unsettling. So instead of reading she lay there hoping that sleep would not evade her for too long.

She wondered if Florian would come to join her, but when midnight struck she decided that he would not. He very rarely did these days. His old room still had a comfortable bed, and if he worked late on his writing it was easier just to stay there. He had told her that he often woke up early with ideas that must be got down on paper straight away, and it would only disturb her if they slept together. He had been working so hard that Linda could only hope that his writing was going well. He had not allowed her to read any of it for some time now.

Florian thanked Vera for the sandwiches and poured himself a generous glass of whisky to wash them down. As he ate them he glanced moodily through the typewritten pages he had placed on the desk. He sighed. He wasn't satisfied with any of it. It was frustrating, because he knew what he wanted the characters to say but he could not find the right words. It had been like this ever since they had come back to Fernwood, but sheer pride had made him keep up the pretence to Linda and his family that all was going well. He poured himself another glass of whisky.

When the house was quiet he went downstairs. He didn't put any lights on and as he clung onto the banister rail his eyes filled with tears as he remembered his grandmother's accident. Poor old Clara, he thought. But perhaps it was just as well. She had been growing more and more dotty. He could only hope that the end, when it came, had not been too painful. He felt the tears streaming down his face and realized he was drunk.

The curtains in the library had not been closed. No one had been in there that night. The moonlight showed him the way to the desk. He sat down and dialled a long-distance number. When he heard it ring at the other end he replaced the receiver immediately and waited. It wasn't long before the phone rang and he picked it up quickly, hoping that no one upstairs could have heard it.

'Are you alone?' he asked.

'Of course or I wouldn't be phoning you,' Nadine said.

'Gerald is out fire-watching?'

'He's out there with his bucket of water and bucket of sand.'

'And don't forget the stirrup pump!'

They laughed softly then Florian said, 'We shouldn't make mock of him. He's doing his bit, whereas I...'

'Don't start that, darling. You couldn't be a soldier and no one blames you for that.'

'I know. But I feel I ought to do something.'

'Well, you may be able to.'

'What do you mean?'

'Max Hulbert has been asked to form a small film unit. They'll make films to encourage the population.'

'Propaganda.'

'Yes, propaganda. I happen to know that he has put your name forward as a scriptwriter. There's only one problem. You would have to come back to London.'

'You call that a problem?'

'Well, what about your family? Your mother and your sister and the blessed pottery? Who would take care of all that?'

'There's no problem at all. When you see Max, tell him I'm ready and able. As for the family and the business, I can leave it all to Linda.'

Part Four

Chapter Twenty-Three

September 1943, Italy

He would always feel guilty about taking the over-coat. The clothes in the battered suitcase were clean but old and patched, whereas the coat was obviously new and likely to be Alfredo's prize possession.

Graham and his young guard were in the station's waiting room where a cheerful fire blazed. Who would have thought Italy could be so cold? Alfredo had entered, smiled hesitantly at the grey-uniformed soldier and, taking his offhand shrug as permission, had sat down. He put his suitcase on the floor at his feet and began to unwrap a large paper parcel. It contained sausages, cheese, bread, olives and a bottle of wine.

The young soldier looked at the food longingly and Graham thought he might have demanded a share had not the door opened and another soldier, Graham guessed an officer, ordered him to come with him. Graham had picked up enough German to understand that his guard was to stand outside on the platform.

'*Jawohl!*' the soldier said and a moment later Graham heard footsteps marching away.

The Italian was looking at him. '*Inglese?*' he asked.

Graham thought the question unnecessary.

407

Surely his British army battledress was enough of a giveaway.

'I am Alfredo,' the newcomer said. 'And you?'

Graham remained silent but the man took no offence. He went on to tell Graham that he had been taken prisoner in the First World War, then he took a knife from his pocket and carved off a lump of sausage and passed it to Graham with a smile.

'You are alone?' he asked.

Graham did not respond. Although his new friend might have been totally innocent and certainly seemed sympathetic, he thought it best not to explain exactly how he had escaped the first time, who had helped them, or where the others were headed. The young German who was guarding him spoke no English and it was just possible that Alfredo had been set up to befriend Graham and get information from him.

'You are wounded?' Alfredo asked.

'How do you know that?' Graham asked sharply.

'I see your bandage.'

Graham glanced down and saw that the bandage on his leg, filthy now and unravelling, was hanging down over his boot.

Alfredo offered him the bottle of wine and Graham took a swig.

'Good?'

'*Molto buono,*' Graham said and Alfredo smiled.

'The train is late,' he told him. 'It is getting dark. We may have to wait until morning. Then where will they take you?'

'I don't know.'

'Probably to a camp in the North. But there is

much troop movement. Your journey will be difficult.'

Graham had already worked this out so he went on eating his sausage.

'Here, have some bread and cheese. Do you like olives? Have another drink of wine. As much as you like.'

Graham was tempted, but the combination of good food and wine had already made him relax his guard. Perhaps too much. He took one small sip and returned the bottle to Alfredo.

When they had finished eating Alfredo wrapped the remains of the feast in the paper and tied it with string. He shoved the cork back in the bottle of wine and placed it on the floor at his feet. He closed his eyes and seemed to have no difficulty in going to sleep. Soon he was snoring. The window was a darkened square; there was no light except the fire and that was dying. Graham took the last two logs from the basket and arranged them carefully in the smouldering ash. He wondered if there was a station master and decided if there was he had probably decided discretion was the better part of valour and surrendered his station to the Germans, who so recently had been his allies but were now his enemy.

Eventually he wondered why his guard had not even opened the door to check on him for an hour or more. Could the young soldier have fallen asleep? Graham crept quietly across the tiled floor and began to open the door. It was no more than half open when some force pushed it inwards, knocking him onto the floor. Thinking his last moments had come, he stared up at the fearsome figure looking down at him. It was not the German guard. This was no clean-shaven Wehrmacht soldier in battledress; the outline showed a stocky, bearded man in rough clothes and carrying a rifle. A partisan.

'*Inglese?*' the man asked.

Graham nodded.

'Get up.'

Alfredo had woken up with a start and he began a heated conversation with the intruder in Italian. Graham heard the word *Tedeschi* and guessed he was asking about the German soldier who was supposed to be on guard.

The newcomer laughed and made the age-old and unmistakeable gesture of drawing his finger across his throat. Then, to Graham's surprise, he strode across to where Alfredo was sitting and snatched the suitcase. He threw it in Graham's direction.

'Open it,' he said.

Graham did so to find it full of clothes.

'Put them on.'

Graham realized that the partisan wanted him to get dressed in Alfredo's clothes. Wary of the rifle still pointing in his direction, he did so as quickly as he could.

'Put your battledress in the case,' he was commanded. The man looked like a peasant. He had probably been living rough but his command of English was good. Graham guessed him to be an educated man.

'Take the coat. It is very cold in the mountains.'

He swung the rifle round to point it at Alfredo, who responded with a burst of furious indig-

410

nation, but when his fierce fellow countryman took a step nearer he shed the coat quickly.

'Put it on.'

'My uniform?'

'This *fascisto* will get rid of it.'

Alfredo responded furiously. 'I am no fascist!' he said in English. 'I have risked my life to shelter other *Inglesi*. And to this one I give what is left of the food. Here, take it.'

Graham buttoned up the overcoat and stuffed the parcel inside. Alfredo put the bottle of wine into one of the silk-lined pockets.

'*Grazie, Alfredo,*' he said, knowing his words were totally inadequate.

The partisan gestured towards the open door with the rifle and Graham stepped out into the moonlight. The air was sharp. He could smell wood smoke and hear a dog barking in the little town. He took a step forward and nearly stumbled over a dark form lying on the ground at his feet.

'Careful,' his companion said and took hold of Graham's arm to steady him.

He turned towards the partisan. '*Mille grazie.*'

'Keep to the shadows,' his saviour said unnecessarily. He lowered his voice. 'Go south towards the allied lines. There are those who will help you but you must make your own judgement about who to trust.' He laughed. 'Don't let anyone see your feet.'

Graham glanced down at his British army boots and groaned. They would surely give him away.

'Mud. Dirt. Make them filthy. That's all you can do. Now go. That way.'

Graham set off on a journey that was to last until Christmas.

December 1943, Redesburn

There had been only a light fall of snow but it was enough to support the runners of the old sledge. Vera had told her to look at the back of the garage which had once been the stables.

'There it is,' Vera said when they found it propped up against a wall. 'And it's in pretty good condition.'

'Good, because I want to use it today,' Linda told her.

'Are you going to take the bairn out to play in the snow?' Vera asked her.

'We're going to the village to buy a Christmas tree. Imogen can ride all the way there but I'll put the tree on the sledge and we'll pull it back together.'

'It's a long walk for a little lass.'

'Not for Imogen.'

'No, you're right. She's a tough one. Good little walking legs. Takes after you.'

'Yes, well, we'd better be off if we're going to get back in time for lunch.' Linda changed the subject quickly. She was pretty sure that Vera had not been referring to Florian's disability but the words had been too close for comfort.

Imogen was in the kitchen, the warmest room in the house. She was sitting in the old armchair by the range looking at her book of nursery rhymes. She loved books and she had more than most little girls. Linda had found a treasure trove of children's books in the old nursery, some of them very old, and she and Imogen had spent many happy hours together looking at the quaint illustrations. Linda loved the time just before Imogen went to bed when they would curl up in this very chair and Linda would read to her daughter. One day she realized that Imogen had mastered some of the words. She would be well on the way to being able to read by the time she started at the village school in January.

Vera dressed Imogen warmly in her coat and knitted pixie hood and mittens. She managed to put on two pairs of socks before she eased her feet into her wellington boots. Although it was difficult to get new shoes, there was no shortage of boots of all sorts in the boot room. The Hyltons had never been good at throwing things away. It was the same with clothes. In fact, the coat Imogen was wearing today had once belonged to her aunt, Cordelia.

Emerald and Cordelia complained that there was nothing new but they still had wardrobes full of good clothes. Cordelia found someone in the village who did alterations, so she and her mother were able to follow the latest fashions.

The previous winter had been appalling and Cordelia, in one of her generous moments, had told Linda to make free with Clara's furs. 'My grandmother would love you to have them,' she'd said.

Linda thought this might be true so she chose a black beaver that almost fitted her. It had a couple of braided buttons, one at the neckline and one at the waist. She put it on for her trip to the village and added an old leather belt to prevent it from flapping open. Then she pulled on a black woollen turban hat. To complete the picture, she added a long woollen scarf, wellington boots and a pair of sheepskin mittens.

'What do I look like?' she asked Vera.

'Height of fashion, darling,' Ivy said in a fair imitation of the way Cordelia talked.

They laughed.

'As long as you're warm,' Vera said. 'Can't have you catching cold. This place would go under without you.'

'Not so long as you were here,' Linda replied.

'Well, maybe Ivy and Albert and I could see to the house but we couldn't run the business for them. If you left us that would be the end of Hylton's.'

'And on that cheerful note my daughter and I will go and buy a Christmas tree.'

Linda tried to be light-hearted but Vera's words had depressed her. Since Florian had gone back to London she had tried her best to carry out his wishes concerning the pottery, even though she didn't always agree with them. As she had predicted, Cordelia soon tired of business matters, although every now and then she would take up some detail, become obsessed with it and make Linda's task very difficult.

Emerald hardly ever interfered. She was a shadow of the warm, vivacious woman who had greeted Linda on her first day at Fernwood Hall. She had very little interest in the world around her, never expressed gratitude for anything that was done for her, and what hurt Linda most was the fact that she ignored Imogen.

'Her own granddaughter!' Vera had said. 'And Cordelia's not much better. You would think she would want to make a fuss of her little niece but most of the time she barely notices her.'

'She does let her dress up in her old clothes and shoes and play with her make-up,' Linda said.

'Only when she's bored,' Vera replied. 'But I shouldn't talk like this, should I?'

'No, you shouldn't,' Linda said. But she was smiling.

The air was crisply cold and Imogen's cheeks were soon rosy. Halfway to the village Linda stopped so that her daughter could run about and get warm. Fir trees of various sizes were propped up outside the village shop. Linda chose the smallest – it was the only one that would fit onto the sledge.

Getting it back to Fernwood wasn't as simple as she had thought it would be. The tree kept falling off the sledge. It was Imogen who solved the problem.

'I think you should tie it on with your scarf, Mummy,' she said.

Linda looked at her daughter and smiled. 'You're absolutely right!'

The scarf was just long enough and the tree wobbled precariously. By the time they got home they were weak with effort and laughter. And Imogen was very excited.

'Will Daddy be coming home for Christmas?' she asked.

'I'm not sure. He said he would do his best.'

Imogen looked grave. 'What does that mean?'

'It means he will come if he can,' Linda said,

and seeing Imogen's frown she added, 'He has to work hard, you know.'

Imogen looked pensive but the mood didn't last, and she settled down quite happily when Linda began to read the story of the Gigantic Turnip, one of Imogen's favourites.

Later, when Imogen was in bed and Linda was dressing the tree, she couldn't help remembering that first Christmas at Fernwood and the night she had found Florian sitting in the window seat behind the Christmas tree.

The overhead light and the lamps had been switched off and the only illumination had come from the dying fire and the tree lights; the colours reflecting on the tinsel streamers and the glass baubles.

'Come and sit behind the tree with me,' he'd said. 'Let us both escape from this cruel world for a moment or two.'

Linda remembered the fresh smell of pine and the way the little silver bells had tinkled on the trembling branches. She remembered shivering in the cold draught from the window and how Florian had put his arm around her.

Here in this enchanted world of fairy lights and sparkling tinsel he had kissed her and they had imagined themselves in love.

'Linda, how good of you to do a Christmas tree! It isn't as big as we used to have but it does look cheerful, and we could all do with some good cheer.'

Linda turned in surprise to see Emerald Hylton had entered the room. In defiance of the cold she was dressed in a black satin evening gown which had once hugged her figure but which now hung loosely. The square neckline was low enough to reveal the two deep hollows above her collar bones. Her blonde hair, swept up and secured with diamond spray hairpins, had lost its lustre and her cheekbones were far too prominent.

Linda was overcome with guilt. Is my mother-in-law ill and have I not noticed it? she thought. Emerald Hylton did not listen to anything Linda had to say these days, so all she could do was resolve to have a word with Cordelia. But she thought she ought at least to ask why Emerald had dressed the way she had. And then she had a horrifying presentiment. Was she becoming eccentric? Dangerously so? For a confused moment Linda wondered whether Emerald had inherited Clara's illness and then she remembered that they were not related.

'Why are you looking at me like that?' Emerald asked her. 'Is my make-up smudged? Is my hair coming down?'

'No. You look lovely. I was just wondering why you have dressed so elegantly.'

'Really, Linda. Are you losing your memory? We have a guest for dinner tonight. If the train arrived in Newcastle on time, he should be here any minute.'

'Florian?' Linda asked. 'Is Florian coming home?'

Emerald frowned. 'Not as far as I know. You are his wife. You shouldn't have to ask me.'

'Then who are we expecting?'

Emerald suddenly looked less sure of herself.

'Do you know, I've forgotten his name.' She smiled self-consciously. 'Vincent, is it? Yes, Vincent something.'

'You mean Denis Vincent.'

'That's it.'

'He's coming for dinner? All the way from London?'

'Not just for dinner, silly. Vincent is coming to stay over Christmas. Cordelia invited him. Didn't you know?'

'No, I didn't.'

'I can't imagine why. It's no secret. Cordelia has been writing to him, you know.'

'Yes, I did know that. I've posted some of her letters for her. But I certainly didn't know that he was coming here for Christmas.'

'Perhaps Cordelia felt a little embarrassed about it. I mean, it is all right, isn't it?'

'Cordelia has been a widow for more than three years now. I don't think anyone could object to her seeing someone else.'

'Oh, I didn't mean that. I meant ... well ... he's not exactly from the sort of family we're used to. But he has a very important job in Whitehall, doesn't he?'

'Don't worry. Times are changing.'

'That's what Cordelia said. How clever you are.'

'Where is Cordelia? Linda asked.

Emerald glanced at her wristwatch. She frowned. 'Still getting ready. She'd better hurry. Saunders will be calling us for dinner soon.'

'Oh no!'

'What is it?'

'Has anyone told Mrs Aslett that we are having

a guest for dinner tonight and that he will be staying over Christmas?'

Emerald looked surprised. 'I really don't know. Does it matter?'

'Of course it does.'

'Then you had better go and sort things out. Would you do that, Linda? I think I'll go up and help Cordelia. I have a feeling tonight will be important.' Emerald Hylton smiled vaguely and turned to go. Then she looked back. 'Oh, did I thank you for arranging to have a Christmas tree?'

'You did.'

'We always had a tree, you know, when the children were small. And even when they grew up we carried on the tradition. Did you know that?'

'Yes, I did.'

Her mother-in-law gazed at the tree speechlessly for a moment and then said, 'Of course, in those days we had a much bigger tree than that.'

Emerald left the room. Linda packed away the baubles she had not used and shoved the box behind the tree. She paused long enough to switch on the lights and smiled. Imogen would be pleased and excited, no matter that the tree was small by Hylton standards. Amused rather than offended by her mother-in-law's attitude, she hurried through to the kitchen to break the news that there would be an extra guest at dinner tonight.

Denis Vincent did not arrive until nine o'clock and then he had to go to his room to dress for dinner. By the time he appeared at the table the meat loaf was in danger of drying out but Vera solved that problem by bringing in another jug of gravy. This

419

was followed by bread pudding – except the butter had been replaced by margarine.

At least the wine was good. Cordelia had chosen it before Denis arrived. Linda knew very little about wine but when Emerald raised her eyebrows and said, 'Are you sure, darling?' she guessed that whatever it was it must be expensive.

Cordelia looked sensational. She had swept her hair up into an explosion of curls. Her strapless gown of ice-blue crêpe had a matching bolero with tiny-puffed sleeves. There was no decoration other than her grandmother's diamonds. Or rather, her own diamonds, as they had been left to her in Clara's will.

The twenty hundredweight of coal that each household was allowed was far from adequate for a house such as Fernwood, and Linda, mindful of the fact that there would be no fire in the draughty dining room, wore a black velvet evening skirt and a dark red high-necked long-sleeved sweater. She livened the outfit up with a shiny lacy jet necklace and matching drop earrings but nevertheless was treated with a look of cool disbelief by Cordelia.

'You don't believe in making an effort for our guest, do you?' she asked.

Linda tried to keep her vexation from showing. 'I'm sure our guest will have eyes for no one but you.'

'Well, perhaps not,' Cordelia responded with a flash of her old good humour. Then her smile faded and was replaced by an expression of anxiety. 'I think he's going to pop the question tonight.'

'And what will your answer be?'

420

'Oh, I shall accept, of course. I have no intention of remaining a widow like so many women did after the last war.'

'They had no choice.'

'Exactly. If I don't marry Denis now I might not have another chance.'

When Denis, resplendent in evening clothes, joined them for dinner Cordelia was polite and charming. She flattered him by asking about his work – 'Oh, but I shouldn't ask, should I? I'm sure it's all highly secret.'

Emerald smiled at him encouragingly and all went well until the coffee was served, when she began to sob silently. Everyone turned to look at her.

'Mother, darling,' Cordelia said. 'What is it?'

'Rupert,' she said and she began to weep in earnest. She scrubbed at her face with her napkin and looked round at the shocked faces. Her mascara and lipstick were smudged, her nose and cheeks mottled.

'I understand, of course,' Cordelia said. 'It's nearly Christmas and you wish he were here.'

'It's not that. I feel he already is here.'

Cordelia rose from her seat and dropped her napkin on the table. One end of it dipped in her coffee. Emerald glanced up at her face and produced a wavering smile.

'No, it's all right,' she said. 'It's a good feeling I have, and I have Denis to thank for it.'

Denis Vincent started visibly. Linda thought she could see the colour draining from his cheeks.

'What do you mean?' Cordelia asked.

421

'You see, Denis was with Rupert when he died.'

'He was with Charlie, too,' Cordelia muttered.

'Yes, I know. He was the last person to speak to them and he tried his best to save them, didn't you, Denis?'

Denis, obviously aghast, nodded dumbly.

'I shall be eternally grateful to you. And just having you here makes me feel close to Rupert,' Emerald said. 'God bless you.'

Emerald rose to her feet and wavered uncertainly. 'I think I'll go up now. Would you help me up the stairs, Linda?'

'Of course.'

Linda put an arm round Emerald's waist to support her. At the door she turned and told Cordelia not to worry. She saw that Cordelia was shivering. 'There's a fire in the drawing room,' she said. 'Ask Vera to bring you a fresh pot of coffee and I happen to know she found a tin of chocolate biscuits on the top shelf of the pantry.'

As Linda helped Emerald up the stairs Cordelia and Denis walked through to the drawing room. She heard Denis say, 'Oh, a Christmas tree. How splendid.' He sounded rather strained.

Cordelia laughed and said, 'Yes, it's important to try and live life as normally as possible, isn't it? I told Mother that.'

She has deliberately given him the impression that she is responsible for the tree, Linda thought. She was amused rather than angry.

Emerald was exhausted. Linda helped her undress and sat with her until she went to sleep. When she left the room she met Vera on the stairs.

'Didn't you hear the telephone?' she asked.

'I did but it stopped ringing quite soon. I thought someone must have answered it.'

'Cordelia answered it,' Vera said. 'She talked for ages and then rang for me to come for you. It's Florian.'

'Oh, thank you.'

Linda knew what Florian was going to say. She sat in the large chair at the desk in the library and stared at the telephone.

'Linda? Are you there?' she heard a tinny voice say. 'Someone's there – I can hear you.'

She picked up the receiver. 'Yes, Florian, I'm here.'

'What took you so long?'

'I was upstairs with your mother. She was rather upset.'

'Yes, Cordelia told me. She also told me the good news.'

'Well, that didn't take long.'

'What do you mean?'

'Denis must have proposed to her the minute I went upstairs with your mother.'

'Apparently. They haven't set a date yet, but now Mother will have something cheerful to look forward to.'

'Florian, why did you phone tonight?'

There was a pause and he sounded cautious when he said, 'Why shouldn't I phone my wife?'

'You're not coming home for Christmas, are you? If you were you would have said so straight away.'

The pause was even longer, then he said, 'No, I'm not coming home.'

'Why?'

'I'm just too busy. We're making a film about the Fire Service. I haven't started the script yet. I'm going to different fire stations and spending days and nights there. Those guys are heroes and we want to get this right. And their work doesn't stop just because it's Christmas.'

Linda felt rebuked. 'Of course not.'

'So you understand?'

'I do. But perhaps you could phone on Christmas morning and speak to Imogen. She ... she misses you.'

Even as she said this Linda wondered if it was true. Imogen had seen so little of her father since he had returned to London that sometimes Linda wondered if she actually realized that the glamorous stranger who made fleeting visits was of her own flesh and blood.

'Of course I will. I planned to.'

'Florian, where will you spend Christmas Day?'

'Most likely in some fire station, but if you're asking if I'm going to have some sort of Christmas Dinner, Nadine and Gerald have invited me round on Boxing Day. It's Sunday so the theatre will be closed.'

'Well, enjoy yourself.'

Linda made no attempt to disguise her anger and there was a pause before Florian replied. When he did he chose to ignore the sarcasm.

'I shall. By the way, Linda, I meant to tell you. Rosa doesn't come to the apartment any more. She's working in a canteen for servicemen on leave. She'll be writing to you.'

'Have you taken on anyone else?'

'I've got a woman to come in and clean twice a

week, but otherwise I look after it myself. Not that I spend much time at home.'

'No, I don't suppose you do.'

'What do you mean by that?'

'Oh, just that you'll be out and about with the film unit most of the time.'

'That's right. Linda, what's the matter?'

'Nothing. Nothing at all. Perhaps I'm tired.'

He paused again and then said cautiously, 'Yes, you must be.' When Linda didn't respond he added, 'I know how hard you work and I'm very grateful.'

'Are you, Florian? Well, that's nice, but I think I need to go to bed now. Goodnight.'

'Linda – wait–'

Linda replaced the receiver. She was sorry their conversation had ended in this unsatisfactory way but she was finding it more and more difficult not to believe that Florian and Nadine had renewed their affair. Even if they had not, she was certain that they spent too much time together.

The next day was Christmas Eve. Linda and Imogen got dressed early and hurried downstairs to have breakfast in the kitchen. To Linda's surprise, instead of the usual cheerful banter, Vera, Ivy and Albert were sitting at the kitchen table staring glumly at their cups of tea.

'What is it?' Linda asked.

Ivy looked up, saw Imogen and made the effort to smile. 'Sit the bairn down,' she said. 'I've made some porridge and it's just what's needed on a cold winter's morning.'

While Ivy had been speaking Vera had already

ladled some porridge into two bowls. She added a spoonful of black treacle to each one.

When Imogen was occupied with her breakfast, Vera reached into the pocket of her pinafore and took out a telegram. She handed it to Linda and, glancing in Imogen's direction, she shook her head slightly.

Linda took the telegram from its envelope and opened it out. She stared at the strips of paper bearing the printed message. She read it twice just to make sure then looked up and said, 'This says he's missing. It doesn't say anything more definite than that. It says they'll let you know if they have any more information.'

Vera spooned tea leaves into the large brown teapot then filled it up with boiling water. Albert smiled sadly. 'Bobby was always good at going missing, wasn't he? Especially if I had a job for him to do. I shouldn't think he did this deliberately. He'd never be a deserter. When I think about what could have happened, I only wish he was.'

'He could have been taken prisoner.'

'Aye, there is that. We'll just have to wait and see. And say a few prayers.'

'How is it that you have been informed?' Linda asked.

'Bobby didn't have any family. He put me down as next of kin,' Vera said.

'Oh, no!'

'What is it?'

'Remember we all thought he was seeing that lass? The one he got pally with at Mrs Hylton's funeral?'

'Yes, I remember.'

'Well, I wonder if anyone's told her.'

'Don't worry. She's a cousin of the Hyltons; I can ask Florian how to find her.'

'Well, leave it for now,' Vera said. 'With any luck we'll get another telegram saying that he's turned up safe and sound.'

Knowing Bobby and how resourceful he was, Linda allowed herself to hope that this was so.

Chapter Twenty-Four

April 1944

'Do you mean to tell me that you can't come up with anything other than this ghastly institutional ware?'

Cecil Redman remained calm in the face of Cordelia's scorn. 'I can come up with whatever style you want, Mrs Meredith, so long as it's–'

'White!'

'Correct.'

Linda, Cordelia and Mr Redman were in the library at Fernwood looking at designs for a dinner service. Although Linda thought it quite unnecessary, Cordelia was demanding new tableware for her marriage to Denis Vincent. Even her mother had been against the idea.

'You have the beautiful Hylton Dragon ware, darling,' she had said. 'Why do you need another dinner service?'

'Mother, you can't expect Denis to like using

things that were designed for Charlie.'

'For *you* and Charlie.'

'Exactly. For my marriage to another man. Surely you can see that's rather second-hand and shabby?'

'What will you do with the Dragon ware?' Emerald asked.

'Oh, I don't know. Maybe I'll sell it.'

Emerald had retired shocked and defeated, and the next day Cordelia had summoned Mr Redman to Fernwood.

It was the first time Mr Redman had been to the Hall but he seemed quite at ease. He had not seen Cordelia or Florian since his initial interview; all his dealings had been with Linda, who went to Newcastle regularly to discuss business and relay instructions. They had worked well together. Until now he had had no idea how difficult Cordelia had made life for Linda.

Florian had very soon been content to leave it to Linda to make decisions for him, and most of the time Cordelia was too. Until she remembered she was a partner in the firm. Or when the matter was personal, as it was now.

Cecil Redman leaned back in his chair and smiled at Cordelia. 'Mrs Meredith,' he said. 'You know very well that wartime restrictions mean we can manufacture no coloured ware, but that does not mean that what we do produce has to be absolutely plain.'

Linda observed the man with respect. He had refused to be offended by Cordelia's high-handed manner and he was exercising great patience. Neither Cordelia nor Florian realized it, but the

Hyltons had been very lucky to find Cecil Redman.

'Explain,' Cordelia said imperiously.

'You could have a raised pattern round the
edge.'

'Such as?'

'Scrolls, ivy leaves, even a dragon.'

'White dragons?'

'Why not? It would certainly be original.'

'Yes, it would, wouldn't it?' Cordelia looked
thoughtful. 'But Mr Forsyth is in the army. Who
would be good enough to do the design?'

'There's a young woman coming along nicely,
Caitlin; I could set her to work.'

'Could you show me some drawings? Mr
Forsyth brought lots of drawings along with him.'
She smiled suddenly. 'Do you remember, Linda?
We had fun that day, didn't we?'

'Yes, I remember, although I'm not sure that
Mr Forsyth thought it amusing.'

'Oh, dear, I was difficult, wasn't I?'

'You were.'

'And now I'm being difficult again.' She sighed.
'Mr Redman, please go ahead and develop the
idea of the dragons. And now I'll leave you in
Linda's capable hands. Linda, could you organize some sort of lunch for Mr Redman? Some
sandwiches or something?'

Cordelia swept out of the library and Cecil Redman shook his head. 'I don't envy you,' he said.
'I'm glad I don't have to deal with her. Tell me,
does she have any idea of how difficult it has been
with most of the old workforce called up and the
number of apprentices we can take on limited?'

Linda did not want to be seen to criticize Cordelia, so she compromised. 'I have had to explain things very carefully to her. Luckily my husband told her that he trusted me to act for him and that she should take my advice. Now, I've already arranged for some sandwiches for you, and if you don't mind I'll bring mine in and keep you company. We can talk business while we eat.'

When Linda returned she was carrying a tray bearing a pot of tea and a plate of sandwiches. 'Let's sit by the fire – such as it is. Would you bring that little table over?' she said.

She poured the tea and Cecil Redman looked at the sandwiches curiously. 'What are they?' he asked.

'Grated raw carrot and shredded cabbage bound with chutney. One of Vera's specials. They're delicious, I promise you.'

When they were settled she discovered that Mr Redman was still brooding about Cordelia's behaviour. 'Doesn't Mrs Meredith realize that the "ghastly institutional ware" as she called it has saved Hylton's from going under?'

'I don't suppose she does,' Linda said. 'After all, some of Hyltons' more exotic designs were world famous. I'll never forget Mrs Meredith's expression when I showed her the photographs of our first hospital order. "Bedpans and chamber pots!" she said. "How utterly disgusting!"'

Cecil Redman laughed. 'Disgusting or not, that was the first of many, and as a matter of fact I've heard back from the army medical department. It was a good idea of yours to ask me to approach them. They want feeding cups, inhalers and the like. Would you like me to go ahead?'

'Certainly.'

'Will you have to OK it with Mrs Meredith?'

'No, she's far too taken up with her wedding plans, thank goodness.'

'And Mr Hylton?'

'He'll be happy to leave the decision to me.'

'They are very lucky to have you.'

'And I am lucky to have you.'

They smiled at each other.

'Seriously, Mrs Hylton, I don't think I could deal with any of the family. If you were not here I would probably retire.'

While they had been talking it had begun to rain. Linda looked at the clock anxiously.

'Is something the matter?' Cecil Redman asked her.

'No. It's just that it's time to go and meet my daughter from school.'

'You're going to get wet.'

'I'll take a couple of umbrellas.'

'Allow me to give you a lift to the village. No, don't object. I'm going that way anyway.'

On the way to the village Mr Redman began singing 'April Showers'. At first Linda was embarrassed but he was so unaffectedly cheerful that to her surprise she found herself singing along.

When they pulled up near the school Mr Redman turned to her and said, 'I quite fancied myself as a crooner when I was younger. My wife thought I was as good as Al Bowlly, but that way of life didn't appeal to us. Show business, you know. All in all, I made the right decision. I'm just sorry that we didn't have more years to-

431

gether. But I must be embarrassing you with all this personal talk.'

'No, not at all. I feel that while we have been working together we have become friends.'

'Well in that case, forgive me for saying this, but you don't seem to be having much of a life up at that gloomy house. It seems to me that none of them realize how much they expect of you. They don't seem to have any idea of the effort you've put in to make sure the pottery survives these difficult times.' He paused and smiled at her sympathetically. 'And with your husband in London most of the time you must get lonely.'

'At least I see him sometimes. Think of all the women whose men are away in the forces. And some of them won't be coming back.'

'You're right, of course. But your husband is not in the army, is he?'

'No, but his work is very important. Mr Redman, you really shouldn't talk like this.'

'You're right. I shouldn't. It's just that I like you a lot and I don't like to see you unhappy.'

'What makes you think I'm unhappy?'

'Lonely, then.'

'Oh, but I'm not lonely. I have my daughter and Vera.'

'Vera?'

'She works at the Hall. Vera and I have been friends from the first day I went there. There's no need to feel sorry for me, honestly there isn't.'

Mr Redman looked abashed. 'You're annoyed with me and you have every right to be.'

'No, it's all right, really. But look, the children are coming out of school.' Linda was glad of the chance to change the subject. 'Thank you so much for the lift. It was very kind of you.'

'I can take you back if you like.'

'No, the rain's easing off. It will be fun for Imogen to walk back with the umbrella.'

Linda opened the door of the car but then she turned and smiled at Mr Redman. 'You haven't upset me. I know you meant well, but there's no need to worry about me, really there isn't.'

She got out of the car, unfurled the larger of the two umbrellas and hurried towards the school gate. She heard the car start up and turned to wave. Mr Redman was a kind man and Linda hoped that he would not be embarrassed next time they met. Any further musings were swept aside when Imogen hurtled towards her.

'Have you got an umbrella for me?' her daughter asked. 'The red one with white spots?'

'Of course I have.'

On the way home they bumped into Jane Millard, Linda's tenant. She was putting the brakes on her pram outside the village shop. The pram's hood was up and the rain-cover meant that Linda could not see the baby. Mrs Millard looked pleased to see her. John Sinclair had told her more than once that the Millards wanted to buy the house in the village. Ralph Millard, because of his long experience working in the Middle East, was working in intelligence, but when the war was over he would be coming back to his archaeological work, and now that they had a child the Millards wanted to settle down.

Linda stopped long enough to enquire after the baby.

'He's fine,' Jane Millard told her. She looked as though she wanted to stay and talk.

'Must hurry. This rain,' Linda said and, feeling guilty, she waved cheerily and hurried on.

When she passed her old home she noticed that the Millards had made a good job of the small front garden. They had also put up new curtains with a cheerful red geometric pattern on a cream background. Nina Bernard would approve! Despite the drizzle the house looked cheerful; much more cheerful than it looked when I was growing up there, Linda thought. I don't know why I'm hanging onto it. Perhaps I ought to let it go.

Ever since she had got into Cecil Redman's car something had been hovering at the back of her mind. Now, as she and her daughter walked back to the Hall, she remembered that other rainy day when Graham Forsyth had given her a lift to the village and how he had come into the house with her and made himself at home.

He had been unashamedly curious about her life at the Hall and whether she was happy or not. At the time she had thought herself foolish to imagine that his interest was anything more than friendly.

Cordelia had thought he had 'taken a shine to her'. Linda remembered a snatch of their conversation.

'... *you were rather stricken, too.*'

'*You're mistaken. I definitely wasn't stricken. What a silly word.*'

'*If you say so.*'

It had been obvious that Cordelia had not believed her.

When Cordelia had asked her to phone

434

Graham's house she admitted now that she had been looking forward to speaking to him. And then how hard she had gripped the receiver when she discovered that the woman who answered the phone was his wife.

Later that night Florian had returned from Scotland and he had made his feelings for her quite clear. For the first time Linda acknowledged that this had eased her hurt, and she wondered whether she'd have been so responsive to Florian if Graham Forsyth had not been a married man.

Where was Graham now, Linda wondered. When he had taken leave of her that day by the river nearly four years ago he had told her he was going back to camp, but that was all. She had no idea where the camp was or where he would be going next. Perhaps he was not allowed to say.

In fact he hadn't said very much at all after they had started walking along the path by the river, Linda pushing Imogen's pram. Sunlight dappled the water, dazzling their eyes. When they sought the shade under the trees, the shadows of the leaves made patterns on the path ahead of them. They had been content to walk in silence; perhaps because neither of them dared find the words for what they wanted to say.

More than one person they passed smiled sympathetically at them. An old man stopped them and said, 'Good luck, son. May God bring you safely home to them.' He had walked on, leaving them speechless.

He thinks we are married and this is our child, Linda thought. She looked up at Graham and saw the lines of his face taut as if he were battling

435

with some strong emotion. He saw her looking at him and quickly looked away. She wanted to speak, to make a joke of it, but found her throat constricted. She closed her eyes.

'Your daughter is awake,' she heard him say and opened her eyes to find him smiling down into the pram.

Imogen stared up at him, puzzled at the sight of a stranger, and Linda was prepared for a howl of surprise and fright. But instead her daughter had gurgled with pleasure and had returned his smile.

Linda wondered what had happened to Graham since then. Had he survived the war so far and would he come safely home, one day? Home to his wife. Trying to dismiss all thoughts of that homecoming, Linda took her daughter's hand and they hurried home through the rain.

September 1944

'And where are you off to, madam?' Dora Forsyth eyed her daughter-in-law suspiciously. She had arrived at her son's house to find Sonya 'dressed up to the nines', as she put it.

Sonya was standing in front of the mirror above the mantelpiece. Before answering Graham's mother, she spat on her block of mascara and rubbed the little brush on it before carefully applying it to her eyelashes.

'Dancing,' she said without looking round.

'Who with?'

'Margery, of course. Us girls have to keep our spirits up, haven't we?'

436

'I don't see why.'

'The war effort.'

'Don't be daft. How can you going dancing do anything to help win the war when your poor husbands are somewhere over there risking their lives for us?'

Sonya put her mascara back in her make-up bag and raised her eyebrows humorously. 'Over there, eh? Just like the song.' She began to sing.

'Stop that!' Dora said. 'That's a Yankee song.'

'So?'

'That's where you're going, isn't it, to the dance at the American air base?'

'Canadian, actually. And why shouldn't we go along and cheer them up?'

'Cheer them up! That's one way of putting it.'

Sonya turned to face the older woman. 'Why Dora,' she said. 'What on earth are you suggesting?'

'You know damn well what I mean.'

Sonya stared at her for a moment and then shrugged and turned to the mirror and began to apply her lipstick. When she was satisfied with the result, she sprayed herself with perfume.

'That's right,' Dora said. 'Smell nice for him.'

Sonya dropped her make-up bag and scent spray into her handbag and reached for her coat which was lying on a chair. She looked coolly at her mother-in-law. 'Why did you come here tonight?'

'Graham said he hasn't had a letter for a while. He wanted me to see if you were all right.'

'He wanted you to keep an eye on me, you mean. Well, I can hardly stop you from staying here but don't expect to see me until tomorrow morning. I'll be staying at Margery's house.'

'You and who else?'

Sonya laughed. 'Nobody else, of course. Just us girls together. Margery is my friend but you wouldn't understand that, would you? I don't believe you have any friends.' She slipped on her coat and then opened her handbag and took out some coins. 'Here you are, five shillings, that should be more than enough.'

'What for?'

'As they say in the nursery rhyme, the cupboard is bare. Can't have you writing to Graham and telling him that I didn't even feed you. Go and get yourself some fish and chips and a bottle of pale ale.'

'You know I don't drink.'

'Well, a bottle of pop then. I haven't time to stand here arguing.'

'I don't want your money.'

'Oh, for goodness sake!'

Sonya dropped the coins on the table and tried to control her rage. Dora turning up like this had spoiled her plans. Margery was always funny about taking the guys back to her house, but to-night she would have to be talked into it. She sighed. It was foolish of her to have stopped writing to Graham. She supposed she'd better start again. Surely it wouldn't be for much longer.

Dora stared at the table and battled with herself over whether she should take the money. The battle didn't last long. After all, Sonya had managed to avoid taking any kind of job by saying that she had a weak constitution. Huh! Dora would bet

438

anything that she had completely bamboozled the doctor. So this wasn't Sonya's money. It had come from Graham. Her son wouldn't want her to go to bed without supper. She slipped the coins into her handbag and set off for the fish and chip shop.

December 1944, London

Gerald Grey poured himself a glass of whisky and looked at the note Nadine had left for him. It was New Year's Eve the next day and, as it was Sunday, the theatre would be closed. Nadine was going to give a party. Most of the guests would be from the world of entertainment. The party was not just to celebrate the New Year. It was also to mark the success of *The Shadow Wife,* which had been running for five years now with Nadine as the star.

If it had not been for the war she might have already moved on. However, Florian had been too busy working for the film unit to concentrate on his new play and Nadine, although much in demand, would not consider anything else.

Gerald smiled as he folded the note and put it in his pocket. His wife must think he could perform miracles. Cigarettes and alcohol were not officially rationed but were in short supply, and many shopkeepers kept their limited stocks for their favourite customers. Luckily Gerald had made friends with quite a few shopkeepers while performing his duties as a firewatcher, and he was hoping that the main problem would be how to get his booty home.

That night he called in on one of his friendly

439

shopkeepers and struck lucky. It was midnight and his shift was over. The streets were dark and silent. Gerald was used to that. He kept his torch pointed downwards as he picked his way over the rubble. A gas explosion, the official line had been, but Gerald knew better. The flying bombs, or buzz bombs, had at least given some warning. You could hear them coming. Even so, there was very little you could do once the engine noise stopped and the device began its descent. Now the V-2 rockets approached silently and dropped on unsuspecting targets, giving no chance of escape whatever. Thousands had died without knowing what had hit them.

The haversack Gerald had thought to bring with him was bulging with bottles and cartons of cigarettes. That's surely enough, he thought. In any case, well-trained guests will bring their own contribution. Gerald was on his way to the underground station when he heard a loud explosion. A powerful rush of air lifted him from his feet and threw him into the road. Before he had time to register what had happened, he was buried under a mountain of falling masonry. Gerald's war was over.

31st December 1944, Fernwood Hall

Denis had come to stay for Christmas and New Year again. Emerald fawned on him and encouraged Cordelia to treat him like a war hero. Vera wasn't impressed.

'Now that he's married to Cordelia he's started

to throw his weight around,' Vera told Linda one day. 'Acting like the master of the house. Actually asked me if Mr Aslett would clean his shoes. I told him those days are long gone. As politely as possible, of course.' Vera grinned.

'What did he say?'

'Just pulled a sour face, but I could tell he was angry.'

'It's as well he doesn't come here too often,' Linda had replied.

'Just wait until the war's over. Apparently they've decided he should resign from his post in London and come north to run the business with Cordelia.'

'How do you know that?'

Vera smiled. 'I've told you many times; servants know just about everything that goes on in a house.'

'Well, he's always very polite to me,' Linda said.

'Prudent of him. He knows this place couldn't function without you. He wouldn't want to upset you until he's ready to take over.'

'My goodness, Vera, you make him sound like a politician.'

'That's what he is, isn't he? At least, he works for the government. I wouldn't trust any of them.'

'You're too cynical, Vera.'

'Maybe. But sometimes it's hard not to be. And another thing,' Vera added. 'I'm beginning to wonder if they have any intention of opening up Green Leas and going to live there. It's much cheaper for them to stay here.'

'Mrs Hylton likes having them here,' Linda said.

'Yes, she does, and that's the only good thing

about it. She's got very little to be happy about these days.'

'Well, that's her own fault!'

Linda had spoken uncharacteristically sharply and Vera looked surprised. After a moment her eyes widened and she said, 'You mean Imogen?'

'Of course I do. I know I'm biased, but my daughter is a lively, lovely child. She could bring so much pleasure to her grandmother if the woman allowed her to.'

'The more fool her,' Vera said. 'Perhaps some women are just not cut out to be grandmothers.'

'You may be right.'

But Linda sensed this not to be true in this case. Emerald Hylton had never forgiven her son for marrying Linda in the first place. No matter that Linda had been made welcome at the Hall and almost treated like one of the family; to them she would always be a girl from the village who should have known her place.

Vera had just implied that times were changing. Maybe they were. But Emerald Hylton would forever mourn the life she had had before the war, and maybe she would never be truly happy again.

That evening Emerald, Cordelia and Denis sat at the table in the draughty dining room dressed in evening clothes while they ate mock goose followed by an eggless sponge pudding, accompanied by champagne. Cordelia had sent Denis to the wine cellar to choose it. He came back with two bottles of Veuve Clicquot and a bottle of Moscato, a sweet dessert wine which was slightly fizzy.

'Do you think you could get Saunders to find

the ice buckets?' he asked Linda. 'If we're going to have champagne we may as well serve it at the right temperature.'

Linda felt like laughing at his self-important manner. She also felt like telling him to stop being so bloody pompous and to go and tell Vera himself, but she restrained herself, because she knew how infuriated Vera would be. Especially as the bottle of Moscato was a 'treat for the staff', suitable because of its 'low alcohol content'. When he told her this, Linda decided she would eat in the kitchen. She also decided to nip down to the wine cellar herself and exchange the Moscato for a couple of the best bottles of champagne she could find.

Florian phoned that night after dinner and Linda took the call in the library. For a while she listened to him in silence. He stumbled over his words but she gave him no encouragement.

When it finally seemed he had no more to say she said, 'So you're not coming home. I think that's pretty poor of you.'

'Be fair, Linda, I never said I would.'

'That's not true. You promised you'd try. Just for a few days to spend time with Imogen.'

Florian's sigh expressed his exasperation. 'I don't think I promised, and please don't let's quarrel about this. And I must say, I'm surprised at your reaction when I've just told you that Gerald has been killed in an air raid.'

'I liked Gerald and I'm very sorry that he has died, but I can't help feeling that Nadine is not as bereft as you claim she is.'

443

'How cynical you sound.'

'How cynical you've made me.'

'Linda, this is pointless. Nadine is alone.'

'What about her children?'

'You know very well they are in Canada.'

'Oh, yes. How convenient.'

'She sent them there for their own safety.'

Suddenly Linda was weary of the conversation. 'Of course she did. And you're right. We shouldn't quarrel. It's pointless.'

'Linda?'

'What?'

'I ... I'm sorry.'

'So am I.'

'I'll be in touch. Why are you laughing?'

'The clock, Florian. Can't you hear it? It's striking midnight. Listen.' Linda held the receiver out in the direction of the clock on the mantelpiece. 'Six, seven, eight, nine, ten, eleven, twelve,' she said. When the clock had stopped chiming she replaced the receiver and closed the line, but not before she had whispered, 'Happy New Year.'

Chapter Twenty-Five

May 1945

'Florian Hylton needs his brains examined,' Muriel Sinclair said.

After a cold, snowy start to the year a succession of warm days promised an early summer and they

444

sat with the French windows open so they could enjoy a view of the burgeoning garden while they had their evening meal.

'Why so?' her husband asked her.

'Oh, come along, John. I know it has to be confidential, but everybody knows that there is going to be a divorce. You can admit that much at least.'

'I suppose so.'

'And as I said, he needs his brains examined. Fancy walking away from a wife like Linda. And all for the sake of some actress.'

'How on earth do you know that?'

'From the newspapers. Quote: "Leading lady, Nadine Temple, has been seen out on the arm of successful playwright, Florian Hylton."'

'The gossip columns.'

'Of course. You know I enjoy them.'

'So what else did you learn?'

'That Florian Hylton wrote *The Shadow Wife* especially for Nadine Temple and that he is working on another play in which she will play the lead.'

'It doesn't say that he left his wife.'

'No, not in so many words. It says that Nadine's husband Gerald Grey died in a bombing raid while he was doing his fire-watch duties and that the heartbroken actress had sought consolation in the company of the couple's old friend Florian Hylton. Poor Linda.'

'Don't say that.'

'Don't say what?'

'"Poor Linda". She would be mortified if she thought people felt sorry for her. She has too much pride. And she is coping with the situation

445

with great fortitude.'

'All the same, I do feel sorry for her. She doesn't deserve to be treated this way.'

'No, she doesn't.'

'You will do your best for her, won't you, John?'

'You shouldn't need to ask that.'

'I know. You're a good man. But...'

'But what?'

'I wish you had agreed to take Linda in that day when her mother died.'

John Sinclair sighed. 'So do I, Muriel. So do I.'

Earlier that day the solicitor had been to Fernwood Hall to discuss the divorce with Linda. As he told his wife later, Linda, in what must surely be a distressing situation, was bearing up bravely. She'd answered the door herself and led him to the garden room.

'Let's make the most of the sunshine,' she said. 'No matter what time of day it is, the sun never seems to penetrate the gloom of the library.'

Vera Saunders brought them tea and biscuits and told Linda not to worry because she would send Bobby to meet Imogen from school.

'Bobby?' John Sinclair said. 'You mean the lad who used to work here?'

Linda smiled and nodded.

'But I thought he was killed in action.'

'No. He was missing. Unaccounted for. In fact he was taken prisoner and has spent the years since trying to dodge the prison guards and probably causing them all sorts of trouble, which may be why he was recommended for one of the prisoner exchange schemes.'

446

'Is he all right?'

'He lost an eye.'

'Oh, I'm so sorry.'

Linda smiled. 'He's not the sort to let it get him down. He'll be fitted up with a glass eye, but meanwhile he wears an eyepatch which makes him look very roguish. Imogen thinks he looks like a pirate in a storybook. She loves him.'

'And the Hyltons have given him his job back.'

'Yes. I did.'

With those three words John Sinclair was reminded that Linda had been virtually running Fernwood Hall, and therefore it was no surprise that Florian, even though he wanted a divorce, did not want her to leave the place.

Even though she appeared to be perfectly composed, Linda seemed to want to delay getting down to business. She asked John about his own grown-up children. His son and sons-in-law had all survived so far, and with victory in Europe expected to be declared any day now John had every reason to hope that it would not be too long before they would be safely home.

When John told Linda that the Hyltons' solicitors, acting for Florian, had been in touch with him, her first question was, 'How long is this going to take?'

'Before I answer that, I have to ask you if you are willing to go ahead with this divorce.'

'I am. What would be the point of trying to delay things? Florian is not going to change his mind.'

'I'm sorry, Linda.'

'Don't be. Just help me make the best of the situation.'

447

'In answer to your question about how long it will take to end this marriage, the quicker option is to opt for adultery.'

'You mean I should have an affair?'

'No, I don't mean that at all, I mean – oh, you're joking.'

Linda smiled. 'Sorry, I know this is no laughing matter, but there's no need to be miserable, is there?'

'I suppose not.'

'But it's no to adultery. Florian is most anxious that Nadine's name should not be sullied.'

'And you're willing to comply?'

'There's no point in being vindictive, is there?'

'That's very good of you.'

'No, I'm not being good. Florian is Imogen's father, and even though he has been a somewhat absent parent I don't want to do anything that would spoil any future relationship between them.'

'So we'll go for desertion?'

'Yes.'

'Then once Florian has been away from you for more than three years–'

'Nearly a year of that time has already passed since he last visited Fernwood.'

'And he did not have your consent to be away?'

'No. For Imogen's sake, I asked him to come home more often.'

'And he intends to stop living with you?'

'That's why you are here today, isn't it?'

'Also to make sure that proper provision is made for you and your daughter. Obviously he will pay maintenance and wants you to stay here at Fernwood. He feels very keenly that this should be

Imogen's home – and yours for as long as you need it to be. He says that he knows how much this house means to you.'

Linda remained silent.

'Are you all right?'

'Yes, thank you. Am I to go on running the business for him?'

'He hopes that you will. For Imogen's sake.'

'There may be problems there.'

'What kind of problems?'

'Once the war is over Cordelia intends that her husband, Denis, will take over.'

'Then that is something that Florian must sort out with his sister. Don't worry. I'll see to that.'

Before John left, Linda brought up the subject of her house in the village. 'I know that the Millards want to buy it,' she said, 'and I know how happy it would make them, but I still can't bring myself to part with it. Perhaps it's because I think of the house as truly my own.'

'There's no hurry. So long as you wouldn't turn them out.'

'Of course, I wouldn't!' Linda smiled. 'Now you're joking.'

'Then think about it very carefully. Whatever you decide, I will do my best for you.'

As John Sinclair was leaving, Imogen arrived home from school with Bobby – the useful lad, as he used to be called. The little girl had her mother's dark eyes and her father's angel-fair hair and was radiantly pretty – and full of exuberant good nature. What a fool Florian Hylton was, he thought, to leave such a child. But how fortunate Imogen was to have such a mother as Linda.

449

Whatever the future brought them, John knew with certainty that mother and daughter would survive.

Just a few days later Victory in Europe was celebrated throughout the British Isles. In Redesburn red, white and blue streamers, garlands and paper chains had appeared like magic to decorate the village hall. The trestle tables groaned with plates of sandwiches, cakes and bowls of jelly and custard. Every child had a flag to wave and a paper hat to wear – if their fancy dress costume allowed it.

Muriel Sinclair greeted the party from Fernwood at the door. 'There are seats at the table for the children and the old folk,' she said. 'The rest of us will be helping out, if you don't mind.'

'What about wounded heroes?' Bobby asked.

After a moment when nobody was sure if he was joking or not Muriel smiled. 'Of course you must have a seat but, if you don't mind, you must make yourself useful.'

'How can I do that?'

'Keep order at your table; like a school prefect. You'll find they're all very excited.'

'Leave it to me,' Bobby said.

Imogen elected to sit with Bobby and Linda, Albert went to help Ted Crawford find extra chairs and Ivy started to pour drinks of orange squash. Vera chose to go and help Etta Crawford, who was in charge of the kitchen.

She greeted her with raised eyebrows. 'What about the ladies of the house?' she asked. 'Are they not coming?'

'Mrs Vincent – Cordelia – has gone to London

450

to some grand celebration at her husband's office – apparently Mr Churchill will be there – and Emerald Hylton is rather tired.'

That was only partly true. Emerald Hylton was simply not interested in going to the Victory Party.

'We can't leave you here on your own while we are all celebrating,' Linda had told her.

'It's quite all right. I shall relax and listen to the wireless. Please, the rest of you, just go.'

'Pity,' Etta Crawford said. 'But then she was never as enthusiastic about this sort of thing as her mother-in-law, was she? Nothing would have stopped that old girl from coming along.'

That was true, Linda thought, catching this remark as she came into the kitchen. During the ensuing happy chaos she thought back to the time when she came to the Autumn Fayre with Clara, and later to the Christmas party. What a scare Clara had given them when she wandered off to find the carol singers and how anxious Florian, Paul Stevens and Linda herself had been until they found her. It was hard to believe that was more than seven years ago and that that had been the last village party that Clara had enjoyed.

When all the food on the tables had gone, Etta's husband Ted ordered everyone outside for games on the green, starting with the fancy dress parade. Jane Millard had been appointed judge. It was thought that as her own child was too young to enter the competition and also because she was a relative newcomer to the village, she would not be tempted to give the prize, a box of chocolates, to a friend or favourite.

Imogen, influenced by Bobby's eyepatch, had

insisted on coming as a pirate and she looked marvellous. Or at least Linda thought she did. But not even the fondest of parents was surprised when the child who won the competition was the little girl swathed in a Union Jack who had come as Little Miss Victory.

Linda wondered whether it was altogether wise to have organized running about games and races after the children had eaten so much food, but everything went well. After the games the children trooped back into the hall for a sing-song but Vera told Linda that she would go back to Fernwood and give Emerald Hylton her tea.

'Do you have to?' Linda asked. 'Surely she's capable of getting something to eat for herself.'

Vera shook her head. 'She won't change now, and I don't mind really. Haven't you noticed she's been a little washed out lately?'

Linda thought about it. 'More washed out than usual, you mean?'

'Look, Linda, I don't blame you for getting impatient with her, but I try to remember what she was like in the early days, when she first came to the Hall as a bride and then when she started her family, and what a happy house it was then.'

Linda felt chastened. 'Am I turning into a cantankerous old tartar?' she asked.

'Not you. I know how much you have to put up with, and I know you get little thanks. So don't you worry about Mrs Hylton. You can leave her to me.'

Ivy and Albert decided to walk back with Vera, but Bobby stayed and helped to lead the sing-song. Only the children and the old folks were there by now. The younger folk had gone home for a rest before coming back for the dance.

On the way home Linda asked Bobby if he was going to the dance.

'I certainly am. Hope you're coming with me.'

'*Me?*'

'Don't sound so astonished. You're not one of the old crocks yet.'

Linda laughed. 'Thanks very much. But Imogen–'

'Vera will look after her. You've no excuse. Get yourself dolled up and come out and enjoy yourself. It's not every day we win a war.'

Linda could have reminded Bobby that although there had been victory in Europe the war in the Far East still had to be won, but this was not the day to do it. 'All right,' she said. 'I'll come.'

The band consisted of a pianist and a drummer. Both were local lads who, thankfully, knew all the latest dance numbers. Bobby proved to be an excellent dancer, although he kept telling the girls that as he only had one eye he would have to hold them tight so they could steer him round the dance floor without mishap. Most of them seemed happy to go along with this.

Linda lost track of the men she danced with. Everybody seemed determined to dance with everybody else. This reminded Linda of the letter she had had that morning from Rosa. There had been an impromptu victory party at the servicemen's canteen where she worked. 'I danced all night,' she told Linda, 'and I had three proposals of marriage from very handsome men. I cannot now remember who they were.'

The letter had gone on to say that Rosa was hoping to go to college and perhaps be a teacher like her father was. Linda hoped that her old friend's dreams would come true.

When the dance was over, everyone sang the national anthem with added fervour. Then they spilled out into the quiet village streets, still singing and dancing. On the way home to Fernwood Bobby didn't say very much. The moon silvered the road ahead of them and the further they got from the village the quieter the world became.

'Flora didn't wait for me, you know,' he said suddenly.

There was no need to ask who he was talking about.

'I met her at Mrs Hylton's funeral.'

'I know that.'

'At first she thought I was one of the family, but even when I told her I was just a servant she didn't seem to mind. We met as often as we could and when I went into the army we wrote to each other. Then, not long after I was taken prisoner, the letters stopped. My letters to her were returned unopened. Then I got a letter from her mother saying that Flora had got engaged to an officer in the Royal Navy. An officer – she made that clear. So that was that.'

'I'm sorry,' Linda said.

'Don't be. It's all part of life's rich tapestry, isn't it? Is that a cliché or an idiom? Or both?'

Linda turned her head to look up at him and saw that he was smiling. 'I'm too tired to work that one out,' she said. Then she asked, 'Are you going to be all right, Bobby?'

'You mean tonight or for the rest of my life?'

'From now on, I suppose.'

'I'll get by. And you?'

No, she wanted to howl. I'm not all right at all. In fact I've never felt so lonely and so apprehensive in all my life. But when she thought of what Bobby and others like him had to cope with, she smiled up at him and said, 'Oh, yes. I'll get by.'

Chapter Twenty-Six

September 1945

The corporal storekeeper looked Graham up and down and said, 'Forty, long. That rail over there.'

'That's it?' Graham said. 'Aren't you going to get the tape measure out?'

'Where do you think you are? Bloody Savile Row? Now move along, sir, and go and choose your suit. Officers and other ranks all the same, and you keep your uniform in case we have to call you back.' The storekeeper's attention was immediately focused on the man who had been standing behind Graham in the queue. 'Right, sergeant, another forty long, I think.'

The two men made their way across the crowded hall of the demob centre in York to the rail with the notice 'Forty, Long' hanging above it.

'Doesn't look like there's much choice,' the sergeant said. 'In fact, none at all.' He shuffled the hangers along the rail and back. 'Every one of these is a grey three-piece pinstripe.'

'And I don't suppose for one moment that we can try them on?' Graham said with a smile.

'What would be the point? They all look the same to me and the storekeeper said you're forty, long, so forty, long you are.'

They both laughed and then the sergeant, who had taken one of the suits from the rail, paused, and said, 'Hey, wait a minute, don't I know you?'

The two men looked at each other and it was Graham who made the connection first. 'Were you the Hyltons' chauffeur?'

'That's right. Paul Stevens. And you worked at the pottery, didn't you?'

'Yes. Graham Forsyth.'

Sergeant Stevens glanced at Graham's uniform. 'Second Lieutenant Graham Forsyth.'

'I was a sergeant like you, but one very bad day at Monte Cassino our officer bought it and I had to take command. A commission was confirmed later.'

'Battlefield commission?'

'Yes.'

'Well, I'd congratulate you, except it must have been a hell of a day.'

Graham didn't answer him so Paul grinned and said, 'Come on, let's collect all the other odds and sods and go and change into our demob suits.'

The other odds and sods were contained in a box given to each man and consisted of two shirts with detachable collars, collar studs, cufflinks, two pairs of socks, shoes – luckily they were allowed to try the shoes on – a raincoat and a trilby hat.

When they had changed, the two men surveyed each other. 'What do you think we look like?' Paul asked.

'A couple of actors in a B movie,' Graham said.

'You don't have to keep the outfit, you know.'

'What do you mean?'

'You can put it all back in the box, suit included, and sell it to one of the shady characters with slicked-back hair and wide-lapelled suits who you'll find hanging about outside the demob centre.'

'A spiv, you mean?'

'That's what they call them.'

'How much would I get for my demob box?'

'I've heard as much as a fiver.'

'And then the bastard who stayed at home and made a fortune while other men died would sell it on the black market?'

Paul nodded.

'I'll pass on that one,' Graham said.

'Well, I must admit I could do with the money, but I'll give it a miss, too.'

They were issued with travel warrants, and with everything they now owned packed into their kitbags, Graham and Paul made their way to the station. The platforms were seething with men, who had obviously passed through the same demob centre.

Paul looked around and laughed. 'These guys are all extras in the same movie as we are,' he said.

'Look, this is hell on earth,' Paul said. 'Why don't we go back into town and find somewhere for a damn good meal then come back later?'

Graham found himself agreeing and at last

admitted to himself that he had mixed feelings about going home. Sonya had stopped writing to him for a while, but after he had asked his mother to go and see if she was all right, she had started writing again. She had made no excuse nor given any reason for her silence. Her letters were lively and interesting. She had the gift of observation and her descriptions of wartime everyday life were vivid.

But there was never anything personal in her letters. And even though the letters ended with love and kisses, she never said that she missed him or was worried about his welfare. The letters had stopped again when Graham had told her he was coming home. Perhaps she didn't think them necessary now that he was back in England. Or perhaps she just didn't care.

He surveyed the plates of fish and chips, the pot of tea and the plate of bread and butter that Paul had ordered and found himself laughing.

'What's the joke?' Paul asked.

'No joke. It's just that if I had managed to get home in time for supper I think this is exactly what my wife would have provided.'

'Well, get that down you and then we'll go and find a cosy saloon bar. We'll stay there until closing time.'

The two men spent the night in a crowded waiting room in the station. Those who had got there first were stretched out along the benches or even on the floor, using kitbags as pillows. At first light they made a dash for the tea bar, and after a bacon sandwich and a cup of tea strong enough to stand your spoon up in, they went to look at the information board.

'You won't have to wait too long,' Paul said. 'The overnight from King's Cross will be pulling in shortly. You'll be back in Newcastle by lunchtime.'

'What do you mean, *I* won't have to wait too long? What about you?'

'I'm not going back to Newcastle.'

'So where are you going?'

'I'll get the first train to London, and then make my way back to Germany and Magda.'

'Your girlfriend?'

'Who will be my wife as soon as we can work our way through all the red tape.'

'Are you going to bring her home?'

'By home you mean England?'

'Yes.'

'No, there's nothing here for me. I'm staying in Germany. I'm a qualified mechanic and there's going to be plenty of work. They've got a country to reconstruct. What are you going to do?'

'Go back to Hylton's, I suppose. They said they'd keep my job open for me.'

'Is that what you want to do?'

'Why do you ask?'

'I don't know. You just don't seem very enthusiastic.'

'It'll take a bit of getting used to, won't it? Settling back into the old routines.'

'Well, good luck to you.'

'And to you.'

They looked at each other awkwardly for a moment, both knowing that it was unlikely that they would ever see each other again.

'That's my train coming in,' Paul said.

The men shook hands and then Paul hurried through the barrier to where a train was pulling in and slowing down with a hiss of steam. Others followed him and soon Graham lost sight of him in the melee of passengers trying to get aboard in time to secure a seat. When the train pulled out he thought he saw someone standing by the window of a compartment and waving to him. He waved back, although he knew it could have been any one of the hundreds of soldiers going home to try and reconstruct their lives.

Newcastle was grey and cloudy. Graham joined a tired-looking crowd at the tram stop and tried to work out why he wasn't moved to be home again. Although it was nearly noon, many of the houses he passed after he left the tram had lights on; but not his own. The gate creaked and weeds grew tall in the front garden. Graham was not an ardent gardener but his sense of order and colour had impelled him to keep the small plot harmonious throughout the changing seasons of the year. The place looked so dismal that he wondered if it had been abandoned; whether there would be anyone there to answer the door.

However, as soon as he rang the bell he heard footsteps hurrying along the passage and the door swung open to reveal his mother.

'Graham, I'm so sorry,' were her first words. Not, Graham, my son, I'm pleased to see you. Or, I'm so grateful that you've arrived home safely. No, her first words were, 'Graham, I'm so sorry.'

'Sorry to see me, Mother?' he asked.

'No, of course not. But don't just stand there,

460

come in.'

She invited him into his own house and in truth he did feel like a stranger. He wondered whether he should hug his mother or kiss her, but while he thought about it she told him to shut the front door and she scuttled along the passage to the breakfast room.

'Come along, lad,' she called over her shoulder. 'I've got a fire going in here. Are you hungry?'

Graham dumped his kitbag in the hall and hung his coat and hat on the coat stand. By the time he entered the breakfast room his mother had donned a pinafore and gone into the kitchen, where he could see her opening cupboards and shaking her head in mock despair.

'There's not much here for you,' she told him. 'Not unless you fancy dried egg.'

'I'll settle for a cup of tea.'

Dora sniffed. 'She might have done some shopping before she ran off.'

So that was it. Graham wondered why he wasn't surprised. 'Sonya has left home?'

'Yes, she has. Disgraceful, isn't it? Graham, I'm so sorry.'

'You've already said that.' Graham sat down at the table. 'You'd better tell me about it.'

'Well, at least I can make us a cup of tea.'

She remained silent while she filled the kettle and put it on the gas stove. Graham saw her reach for the tea caddy and then spoon tea into the teapot. She brought the tray through and resumed her tale.

'She left as soon as she got notice that you were coming home.'

461

'How do you know that?'

'Because at least she had the decency to write and tell me. And she sent me her keys.'

'Did she say why she was leaving?'

'She didn't have to.' His mother pursed her lips and shook her head slowly. 'It's bad, I'm afraid. Very bad. While you've been away Sonya has been carrying on with other men.'

'Do you know that for a fact? Other *men?*'

'Yes, at first, anyway. Her and that pal of hers, Margery, started going dancing, and I'm pretty sure they weren't dancing with each other.'

Suddenly the coal settled and shifted in the grate, sending out a burst of sparks. His mother made to get up but Graham motioned for her to stay where she was. 'I'll see to it,' he said.

As Graham saw to the fire he tried to control his anger, which was not directed at the absent Sonya – not yet – but at his mother, who was so obviously relishing the telling of this sorry tale.

'Dancing isn't exactly carrying on, Mother,' he said when he went back to the table.

'Well, I know. But you were away fighting for King and country and there she was, out galli-vanting. It wasn't right.'

Graham sighed. 'No, I don't suppose it was. But you're going to tell me it gets worse, aren't you?'

'I'm really sorry, Graham.'

'You keep saying that.'

'Well, I suspected that she was more than pals with one of them. I can't prove it, but I think she brought him here.'

'She brought a man here?'

Graham's mother couldn't meet his eyes. 'As I

say, I can't prove it, but a couple of times when I called to see her it looked as though there'd been some kind of party. Empty beer bottles, over-flowing ashtrays. Well, anyway, I put a stop to that.'

'How?'

'I called one night and told her I knew what she was up to. I don't think she dared bring anyone home after that. I suspect they went to Margery's house instead.'

'So what did she say in her letter?'

'Not very much. Just that she wouldn't be here when you got back and to tell you that she'd be in touch to get things sorted. No apologies. Not even a proper goodbye.'

What was a proper goodbye? Graham wondered. His mother was looking at him with genuine sympathy but there was also a hint of satisfaction. She had never liked Sonya. She had warned him that no good would come of it and she had been proved right. To his surprise, her hands began to shake when she attempted to pour herself another cup of tea. And then she began to cry.

'Don't cry. Please don't cry, Mother,' he said.

'I can't help it. I know I didn't like Sonya, but you love her, and I would have given anything for this not to happen. For her to be waiting for you when you came home. And I can't even find any-thing to make a meal for you,' she added incon-gruously.

Moved by her genuine sympathy, Graham reached across the table and took her hands. 'Don't worry about that. We can do some shop-ping in the morning. But now you're going to go and lie down and rest while I unpack and make myself at home, and then I'm going to take you out for a meal.'

Dora Forsyth reached into the pocket of her pinafore for her handkerchief. She blew her nose and then smiled tearfully. 'Upstairs at the chippy on Shields Road?' she asked.

'Definitely not. This is an occasion, isn't it? My coming home? I've got six weeks' pay in my pocket. I'm taking you into town to the County Hotel.'

Pamela could hardly bear to look at the photographs in the local paper; photographs showing happy reunions as servicemen and women came home. She tortured herself by wondering whether Rupert, if he had survived, would have gone to his parents first or whether he would have come to her and his son. When she thought about it she knew the answer. Like a dutiful son of the house, he would have gone to Fernwood, and who knew how long it would have taken him to remember her and David.

Pamela had spent the last few years distributing food parcels and clothes to the people who had been bombed out. She had made friends with other volunteers this way and she had been delighted when they seemed to accept her unquestioningly. One woman in particular, Jeanette Harvey, the mother of Peter, David's best friend at school, had taken to dropping in at teatime – always bringing a contribution for the table – and the two women would gossip while the boys played with David's train set.

However, Jeanette never called in the evenings. Once David was in bed, Pamela would settle down to read or listen to the wireless. Sometimes she would treat herself to a glass of sherry, but more often than not her night-time drink would be cocoa. One dismal day when the sun had never seemed to break free of the heavy grey clouds, Pamela decided to go to bed early and listen to the play on her portable radio.

She looked in on David. He had fallen asleep while reading, and his book, *Treasure Island,* had slipped down onto the floor. Pamela picked it up and put it on his bedside table. She made sure he was covered up properly then went downstairs to make her cocoa. She had only got as far as pouring milk into the pan when the doorbell rang. Puzzled, but thinking it might be someone with a message about the next lot of food parcels from America, she went to open the door. Then stood there motionless with shock.

Her visitor was a man who had once been handsome but whose face was now drawn and grey-tinged. His hair, which he had once had expensively styled, was cut brutally short and his Savile Row suit looked as though it had been tailored for a more substantial man. He was carrying a small suitcase and, rather pathetically, Pamela thought, a bunch of flowers. Chrysanthemums. Pamela shivered. She always thought of chrysanthemums as funeral flowers.

Once so confident, he now looked hesitant and unsure of his welcome. 'Pamela?' he said.

She sighed. 'You'd better come in, Father.'

For the next few days Dora Forsyth acted as if there had been a death in the house. She crept around as quietly as she could and had a permanently solicitous expression. She did the best she could with their two ration books and cooked for Graham as if he were an invalid. Eventually he sat her down and told her that he was very grateful but he thought she ought to be getting off home.

'Aunt Edna will be missing you,' he said.

'I don't like leaving you alone, son. You really didn't deserve this, you know. Her running off like that just when you were coming home.'

'No, Mother, if Sonya was going to leave me it was the best time to go. It's saved any unpleasant scenes. And, as for my not deserving it, maybe I did.'

'How can you say that? You've been a very good husband.'

'Have I?'

'You've worked hard, you provided for her. You could even say you kept her in luxury. She didn't have to lift a finger. She even had that cleaning woman before the war started, though I know Mrs Slater went off to earn more money in the munitions factory.'

'Maybe that's all true, Mother, although I think "luxury" might be a bit of an exaggeration, but when it comes down to it, none of that makes up for the fact that I neglected her.'

His mother was shocked. 'Neglected her? How can you say that?'

'I wasn't the kind of husband she wanted. Sonya wanted to go out, have a good time.'

'The hussy!'

'No, she wasn't a hussy. She wanted to go dancing, go to the pictures, dine out.'

'Dine out indeed. She never learned to cook, that's for sure.'

'Listen, Mother, I knew all this when I married her. I must have been crazy to think that marriage would change her. When I sensed we were in trouble, instead of trying to sort things out, I just threw myself into my work. I've known for a long time that it would end like this. I actually feel sorry for her.'

'Sorry for her!' Dora Forsyth shook her head. 'And now I suppose there will be a divorce?'

'Almost certainly.'

Graham's mother looked at him shrewdly and then she said, 'Well, at least you don't seem heartbroken.'

'I can't deny that I'm sad and that I will always regret what happened. But I'm not heartbroken.'

'Then, good riddance to her.'

'So you see, it's quite all right for you to go home now.'

'But what are you going to do? Can you manage on your own?'

'The housework and cooking, you mean? There's no need to worry about that, Mother. The army has taught me how to keep things spick and span, and I'm sure I can manage to put a meal or two together.'

'Will you be going back to Hylton's now?'

'Not straight away. I've got six weeks' paid demobilization leave. I'm going to use the time to develop a few ideas to show them. It's a new world and I believe it's time for a change.'

Pamela was thankful that David had been in bed the night her father arrived. Her first question had been, 'How did you find me?'

'I have friends.'

'That sounds sinister.'

Jack Delafontaine put his suitcase down and rested the bunch of flowers on top of it. 'Look, can I sit down somewhere? And a drink would be nice. Presuming you keep anything decent in the house.'

'Wait here,' Pamela said and she opened the door into the sitting room and drew the curtains before she put the lights on.

'It's all right, I'm not on the run,' her father told her. 'I'm a free man.'

'So answer my question.'

'As soon as you bring me that drink I'll tell you all you need to know.'

Pamela didn't miss the significance of the word 'need' but she brought him his drink. 'Sherry,' she said. 'I know that's not your favourite tipple, but that's all I've got.'

'It'll do.'

They sat and faced each other at opposite sides of the hearth. Jack gazed thoughtfully into his glass for a moment, took a sip, then smiled at her. 'You didn't think I'd abandoned you, did you?'

Pamela was outraged. 'You don't call going to prison abandoning me, then?'

'I told you. I've got friends. I've known where you were all along, and even if that scoundrel hadn't written to me I would have come to you the moment I was released.'

'What are you talking about? Who wrote to you?'

'Rupert Hylton.'

'Rupert wrote to you? When?' Pamela was shocked and confused.

'When he joined the army. He thought it only right that should he not return I should know where you were and that he had provided for you and your son. At first I thought that was decent of him until I realized that he had said *your* son, not his.

'And then he went on to say that if he did survive the war his family would expect him to get married and then it would prove difficult to continue with your relationship. He said that in his heart he knew that, no matter what I had done, father and daughter should not be separated.

'Devious hypocrite! I was tempted to put the word out to a friend of mine to pay him a visit, but it was too late. The bastard was already overseas, about to meet a hero's death at Dunkirk. So here I am,' Jack said. 'I'll look after you and the boy.'

Pamela was aware of the tears streaming down her face as she stared at her father, but she kept her voice steady when she said, 'I can look after myself – and David. We don't need you.'

For the first time since he had arrived, her father's confident manner faltered. 'You mean that, don't you? That's not just pride speaking?'

'I mean it.'

Jack drained his glass and held it out towards Pamela. 'Any chance of a fill-up?'

'The bottle's empty.'

'Pamela...?'

'What is it?'

'I was hoping you'd come away with me.'

'You've only just arrived. Where are you going?'

'South Africa. It's been planned for a long time.'

'Why South Africa?'

'It's complicated.'

Pamela stared at him. 'You have some money there?'

'Yes. Enough to keep you and me and the boy in luxury for the rest of our days.'

'Money that doesn't really belong to you.'

'Don't worry. No one will ever be able to prove that it isn't mine.'

She stared at him in silence.

'Just think, Pamela, no more dreary making do. You'll have a lovely home. There'll be sunshine, servants, anything you want.'

'What I want right now is that you should leave.'

Jack looked astounded. 'Leave?'

'Yes. Tonight. Find a hotel. I don't want you in this house when David wakes up in the morning. I don't want him to meet you.'

'But he's my grandson!'

'I know. But if he meets you he might grow to love you – as I still do – but I don't want the kind of life you offer either for me or my son. I'm sorry, Father, but my mind is made up. You'll have to go.'

After her father had gone Pamela found the bunch of flowers lying on the floor and took them through to the kitchen. When she took the paper off, a shower of petals fell onto the bench. They won't last long, she thought, but nevertheless she found a vase for them and put them on the table in the entrance hall.

Lying in bed that night, she mused that the

whole episode had been surreal. After all those years, had she really seen her father again? She might have thought it all a dream, save for the fact that when she went downstairs the next morning she was met by the bitter-sweet odour of chrysanthemums.

Chapter Twenty-Seven

October 1945

Graham found he was strangely reluctant to leave the house. Familiar streets seemed alien to him. He did some basic shopping, applied for his petrol coupons and then waited until they arrived. For the duration of the war his car had been left with Ted Coulson, an old friend of his father's who owned a garage. When Graham went to collect his car he found it jacked up on bricks.

A young lad who looked about fourteen years old told him that had been a precaution. 'Had to keep the tyres off the ground to keep them in good condition,' the lad said. 'Leaving the car stationary for all this time they might have been damaged.' The lad looked as though he was going to launch into a lecture, so Graham held up his hand.

'I'll take your word for it,' he said. 'How long will it take to get the car back on the road?'

'About ten minutes to get it down,' the lad replied. 'And then I'll check it over for you.'

Graham drank tea in the untidy office with his

father's friend, who unfortunately wanted to talk about the war and Graham's part in it.

'An officer?' the old man said. 'Your dad would have been proud of you.'

Graham wondered if that were true and decided it probably was. Then, after all that had happened to him over the last six years, he found that this was the moment that he welled up with emotion. How wonderful it would have been to come home to find his father waiting and to have been able to share some part of his experiences with him, instead of returning to find his wife gone and his mother fractious.

Mr Coulson refused any kind of payment and would have kept Graham talking for a lot longer but Graham said he had work to do. And that was true in a way. He had phoned but not called in in person at Hylton's yet. When he did go, he wanted to show them his new ideas, and he wanted to prepare what he was going to say.

That evening he was just about to make himself some sandwiches when the doorbell rang. When he opened the door it took him a few moments to recognize the young woman standing there.

'Caitlin?' he said.

She grinned. 'That's right. I've grown up, haven't I?'

When Graham had last seen her at the pottery, Caitlin had been a reasonably pretty, fresh-faced girl. Now she was an attractive woman. More than attractive; she was beautiful. And she knew it.

'Well, go on then, invite me in.'

'Sorry. Of course.'

Graham stood back, and as she entered there

was a waft of a rather heavy perfume. It wasn't unpleasant but Graham thought it too old for such a young woman. He smiled. I'm only thirty-one, he reminded himself, and I'm thinking like a middle-aged man. It's the war that has aged me.

Without being asked, Caitlin went along the passage and entered the breakfast room. She turned to face him. 'Aren't you pleased to see me?'

Graham marvelled at her confidence. 'Of course I am. But to what do I owe this pleasure?'

'Ooh, hark at him,' she said. Then she laughed and sat at the table without waiting to be asked.

'We knew you were home,' she said, 'and we wondered why you hadn't come to work yet.'

'How did you know I was home?'

'You phoned Mr Redman, didn't you?'

'The new manager? I did. But I didn't expect him to make an announcement.'

'Oh, don't be so stuffy. He didn't do anything wrong. He just told us that he was very pleased you had come home safely and that he was looking forward to meeting you.'

Graham was curious. 'What's he like?'

'He's a good man. Some say that Hylton's would have gone under if it hadn't been for him – and Linda, of course. She worked like the very devil to make sure Hylton's kept afloat. Not that the rest of the stuck-up beggars seemed to notice.'

'Linda? Florian Hylton's wife?'

'That's the girl – although she won't be that two-faced rat's wife for much longer.'

Graham paused to let that bit of information sink in. 'Caitlin, I think you'd better tell me what's been going on.'

Caitlin opened her coat and slipped it off her shoulders. 'You've got it nice and warm in here. Now put the kettle on and make a pot of tea. And is that a tin of spam I spy? Shall I make some sandwiches?'

His unexpected guest didn't wait for an answer but busied herself in the kitchen. Annoyingly, the girl refused to talk until they were sitting at the table with their cups of tea and a plate of roughly cut sandwiches. To his dismay she lit a cigarette and proceeded to smoke while she was eating. He considered asking her not to smoke but decided against it. He just wanted her to get on with it.

She took a large bite of her sandwich, sipped her tea, then took a long drag on her cigarette. When she exhaled she screwed up her eyes and gazed at him through the smoke. 'Well, I suppose you know Mr Hylton had a stroke and died?' she began.

'Mr Redman told me when I phoned. He said he was of the opinion that it was the death of his son Rupert at Dunkirk that caused the stroke. We didn't talk for long, but I assumed Florian would take over.'

'Not a chance! But for goodness sake, eat your sandwich. And your tea's getting cold.'

With a certain sense of relish, Caitlin told him everything she thought he ought to know. Florian had gone to London, written a play and fallen in love with an actress. Old Mr Hylton had expected that Florian and Cordelia would manage the pottery between them but Florian left everything to Linda, who worked hard at it, whereas Cordelia caused nothing but trouble. Especially now that she wanted her husband to take over.

Graham was surprised. 'Charlie Meredith?'

'No. He died alongside his pal Rupert at Dunkirk, and then this bloke, Denis Vincent, turned up at the Hall and told them he'd been with them when they bought it. Tried to save them by all accounts. Anyway, Cordelia married him and a right pain he is, too. I sometimes think if it wasn't for Linda, Mr Redman would walk out. And then we'd be done for. Shall I make another pot of tea?'

Graham nodded. He considered everything Caitlin had told him and tried not to think too deeply about the fact that Linda's marriage had failed.

'What are you thinking?' his guest asked.

Graham frowned. 'What do you mean?'

'You were miles away.'

'Was I?'

She nodded.

'I was just thinking about everything you've told me.'

Graham noticed Caitlin was no longer smiling. She lit another cigarette and didn't look him in the face when she said, 'I take it you are coming back to Hylton's?'

'Why shouldn't I?'

'Well, things have changed. You know what I mean.'

'No, I don't know,' Graham said, but then the penny dropped. 'That's why you came here. You've been doing well while I've been away and you're worried that when I come back you might be demoted in some way.'

Caitlin looked uncomfortable. 'I've got used to being the team leader. It's natural for me to want to hang onto that, isn't it?'

'Yes, it is natural, Caitlin, but being my top assistant wouldn't actually mean you'd been demoted, would it?'

She sighed. 'I think it would. But there's nothing I can do about it, is there?' She wasn't expecting an answer and she stood up and put her coat on.

'Wait a minute, Caitlin. What made you think that I might not come back to Hylton's?'

'Lots of men coming back from the war aren't satisfied with their old life. I thought you might think it time to move on.'

'Where would I move on to?'

She grinned. 'It pains me to say this, but you're a bloody brilliant designer. You could get a top job anywhere. Don't say you haven't thought of that?'

Graham shook his head.

'No?' She sighed. 'Well, I'll be off then.'

After she had gone, he thought about what she had said. He hadn't been entirely honest with her. He had not thought about getting a job with another pottery. What he would really like to do would be to found his own firm. But even though his plans were modest, he would have to work out how he was going to raise the money. For the moment he would have to be content with going back to Hylton's.

Cordelia and Denis sat in the living room at Fernwood with Emerald and Linda. Their train had been delayed and they had missed the evening meal, so Vera had made them coffee and sandwiches.

Despite their tiring journey, Cordelia seemed energized. 'I wish you had come with us, Mother. Florian's play was brilliant.'

They had been to London to visit Florian. Linda had a good idea what the real motive had been, but Cordelia pretended that she thought it time to heal the rift with her brother.

'And you would love his apartment. So fashionable. He had Nina Bernard do it up, you know.'

She's talking as though I had nothing to do with it, Linda thought. She's completely forgetting that it was my home, too.

'Next time we go you really must come, too.'

Emerald sighed deeply. 'But your father—'

'I know, Mother. Father wanted Florian to forget about writing and be a businessman. But if poor old Dad could have known how successful Florian would be, I think he would have been proud of him.'

'But the business...'

'Denis and I can run the business, Mother. You know we can.'

Am I invisible? Linda thought. Is everything I've done to be discounted?

'Does Florian agree to that?' Emerald asked.

Cordelia smiled. 'Oh, Florian and Denis got along like a house on fire, there's no worry there.'

That's not an answer, Linda thought, but Cordelia hurried on.

'And you would just love Nadine,' she said. 'She's so beautiful and so talented, and she absolutely adores Florian. It's no wonder that he—' She stopped and stared at Linda as if she had just remembered she was there. 'Oh, dear,' she said.

'Linda, I...'

'Don't worry,' Linda said. 'We all know how beautiful Nadine is. And how devious. I wonder if Florian has ever wondered if she will adore him quite so much if his next play is not a success. Or whether she will find another promising young playwright to further her career.'

No one spoke. Linda rose and hurried towards the door. When she got there she heard Cordelia say, 'Poor Linda. She's a sweet girl but not one of us. Florian should never have married her.'

Linda knew that Cordelia had meant her to hear that. She wants to drive me away so that she and Denis can run the business without me, she thought. If only she knew that her words can't hurt me. I stopped loving Florian long ago. But I loved him once and we have a daughter. I promised Florian that Imogen would grow up here at Fernwood. No matter that her grandmother ignores her, she has Vera and Bobby and the Asletts who all adore her. She is happy here. The countryside, the woods, this house. This is her rightful home.

The telephone rang early next morning. Linda and Imogen were having breakfast in the kitchen.

'Go on, answer it,' Vera said. 'I'll see that the bairn eats up her porridge.'

Linda hurried through the draughty hall to the library. There was still only one phone in the house, although Cordelia was talking about having extensions fitted in her bedroom and in her mother's little sitting room. Cordelia and Denis had taken over Emerald's cosy little room. Once the fire got going it was easier to keep warm. Emerald wandered about the house like a displaced person. She always carried her handbag with her, just as Clara once did, and when she settled temporarily she would take out her cigarettes and light up.

Once Linda followed the trail of smoke to the garden room and found Emerald sitting on the window seat, staring out at the rain-drenched grounds. She sensed Linda's presence and she spoke without turning round. 'I used to play out there with the children,' she said. 'It doesn't seem so long ago, does it? The sun was shining then, of course.'

Linda closed her eyes and remembered the beautiful woman and the handsome children, their laughter echoing across the lawns to the woodland where another child stood and watched them, longing to be part of the happy scene. Overwhelmed by a sense of loss, she turned and left the room.

Linda picked up the receiver and gave the number. There was a slight pause and then a voice she thought she recognized said, 'Is that you, Linda?'

'Yes. Who is this?'

'Graham. Graham Forsyth. Remember me?'

She closed her eyes.

Sunlight dappling the water ... the cool hush of the shade under the sheltering trees ... the silent companionship of two people who sought a moment's contentment in a world gripped by turmoil...

'Of course I do.'

The line went silent and Linda wondered if he

479

was still there. And then he said, 'Will you meet me? This morning. There are things I want to talk about.'

'Things?'

'Business.'

'Oh.' Linda couldn't imagine why she was disappointed. 'I'm not sure if I can come into town this morning.'

'You won't have to. I'm here.'

'Where?'

'In Redesburn. I'm phoning from the call box in the village. I intended to come straight to the Hall but I lost my nerve.'

'Am I so formidable?'

'No. It's not that.'

He paused and the silence stretched uncomfortably. Linda heard the clock ticking and the rustle of leaves against the windowpane. Some instinct told her that she shouldn't ask what he meant.

'So will you come?' he said at last. 'I'll wait outside your house.'

'All right,' Linda said. 'I'll meet you as soon as I've taken Imogen to school.'

Graham sat in his car and watched children hurrying to school. When he heard the school bell ringing he knew it wouldn't be long. Then there she was, a slim, dark-haired young woman in a red belted coat hurrying along the grey morning street towards the car. His heart leaped. Or it would have done if he had been one of the film stars in the romantic movies that Sonya so loved.

He wasn't a film star, he was an ordinary guy who had come through the war and had come home to find that his wife hadn't waited for him, and the marvellous thing was that he didn't care. Should I care about Sonya's betrayal of me? he wondered. No. He knew she would be happier without him. And in going the way she had, she had set him free. Free to hope. To hope for what? As the young woman in the red coat drew nearer Graham found himself suffering an agony of uncertainty. But he hadn't time to ponder further. He got out of the car to greet her.

Linda looked up into his face and saw what the years at war had done. He was still a handsome man but his dark hair was laced with grey and his features were leaner than they used to be.

They looked at each other awkwardly, and then his first words were laughably mundane. 'I was hoping for a cup of tea,' he said, 'but I see you've sold your house.'

'What makes you think that?'

'The young woman and the little chap who came out and went across to the shop.'

'No, I haven't sold it. The Millards are my tenants, although they want to buy it.'

'Then why don't you sell it to them?'

'Because it's mine. Because it's all I own.' The words came out more vehemently than she had intended and she was embarrassed. She was grateful when Graham changed the subject.

'Then we'll have to make do with biscuits and pop,' he said.

'What are you talking about?'

'A picnic. I popped into the village shop and bought half a pound of mixed biscuits and a bottle of Dandelion and Burdock. Oh, goodness, do you like it? It's my favourite but I know it's not everyone's choice.'

'I love it.'

'That's a good start.'

They looked at each other and smiled, then Linda said, 'We can't just stand here. We're attracting attention. See the curtains twitching?'

Graham looked nervously at the row of terraced houses. 'I do. Let's go.'

'For a picnic? You're serious?'

'That's what I said.'

'At this time of the year?'

'It's a fine day. Not too cold, and the skies are clear. While I was waiting for you I remembered somewhere I used to go with my father. It's not far away and it's the perfect place for what I want to say.'

Not long after they had left the village Graham took the old road that wound up into the hills and Linda knew where they were going.

'The Roman fort?' she asked.

'You've been here before?'

'Of course. My guardian, Miss Taylor, used to bring me when I was a child.'

'It's a long walk from the village for a woman and a child.'

'You never met Miss Taylor! Of course, when she became ill the visits had to stop.'

'Do you miss her?'

Linda gazed out at the grey-green countryside and ancient drystone walls. A lonely farmstead nestled against a wooded outcrop, the smoke from its chimney curling up into the wide Northumbrian sky.

'Miss Taylor had spent most of her life teaching in a poor part of Newcastle. It was her dream to retire to the country. She loved it here. And yes, I miss her. Taking in an orphaned child could not have been part of her plan. But tell me, did you come here often?'

'Only two or three times.'

'With your parents?'

'My father. My mother didn't care for old ruins.' He smiled wryly. 'She had that in common with Sonya. I could never have brought her here.'

'Sonya?'

'My wife. She's left me, you know.'

'I ... I'm sorry.'

'Don't be.' Graham's expression was unreadable. After a moment he shrugged and said, 'Poor old Dad. He used to say that when he retired he and I would follow the Roman wall from coast to coast.'

'You never did?'

'The minute he retired he died.'

'I'm sorry.'

They travelled in silence for a while and then Graham said, 'I think this is where I'll have to park the car.'

He pulled in and reached for a kitbag that was resting on the back seat. 'Are you any good at stiles?'

They set off up the hill. As they climbed higher the air became fresher and then turned into a worrying little wind. Linda turned up her coat collar.

'Are you cold?' Graham asked as he surveyed

the tumble of ancient stones.

'A little.'

'Don't worry. That wall is tall enough to provide shelter.'

Graham put the kitbag down. He took out a travelling rug and spread it on the ground beneath the wall. 'Come and sit down,' he said. No sooner had she done so than he wandered away and she watched, puzzled, as he stooped now and then, picking things up and putting them in his pockets. When he returned he offered no explanation.

'Has the walk made you hungry?' he asked.

'A little.'

'Good. We'll eat before we get down to business.'

He delved into the kitbag again and brought out a paper bag of biscuits and the bottle of Dandelion and Burdock. He frowned.

'What is it?' Linda asked.

'I haven't got a cup. We'll have to drink from the bottle. Do you mind?'

Linda shook her head. 'I don't suppose it will kill me.'

While they ate their biscuits and drank the pop they talked about the people who had built this outpost and who had lived here centuries ago.

'I wonder what they were like,' Linda said.

'Not very different from us, I imagine. Their daily lives might have been less complicated, but they still had to sleep and eat and give birth, overcome illness and misfortune and eventually die.'

While he was speaking he began to take things out of his pockets and lay them on the rug. Linda looked closely and saw that they were bits of

484

broken pottery. All quite small, but you could still tell whether they had come from a dish or a plate or a jug.

Graham looked up and saw her watching him. 'This is how it started for me,' he said. 'My father was interested in kings and battles and victories. I was fascinated by the evidence of people's daily lives. These pieces here are all everyday stuff, but each has its own history. Who ate from this plate? Who drank from this cup? What did the woman of the house keep in this bowl? Did she cry when it was broken? As I said, all bits and pieces from everyday life. And then there's this.' He reached into the kitbag and brought out something else. 'Hold out your hand.'

Linda did so and then stared at the blue and gold object he had placed there. 'It's an owl,' she said, 'a pottery owl.'

'Look carefully.'

Linda turned it over with her other hand. 'A candlestick,' she said. 'An owl candlestick. It's lovely! Where did you get it?'

'In Italy,' he said. 'I was on the run from the Germans and this was a gift from a family of potters that sheltered me for a while. Linda, I wish you could have seen their ware. Bottles, bowls, urns, vases, candlesticks, mugs, plates, tea sets and coffee sets. All made from Mediterranean clay and decorated in the colours of the earth, the sea and the sky.'

'And very different from what we produce at Hylton's?'

'Yes.'

'So what are you telling me? That you want to

produce ware like this?'

'No. Not exactly like this. It wouldn't be right for our Northern clime. But what I saw in Italy has inspired me to try something different. People are starting to live all over again. Young couples want something new, something different both in design and in colour.'

'And you want Hylton's to recognize this?'

'I do.' Delving into his kitbag yet again, Graham brought out a sketchbook. 'Look.'

Linda put the owl down and took the sketchbook. She didn't say anything while she turned the pages, then she looked up and said, 'So that's why you wanted to talk to me today? Because you think I have some influence at Hylton's?'

'Yes. I admit it.'

'I see. Well, they're brilliant, of course.'

She gave him back the sketchbook and got up. She walked away from him to the brow of the hill and looked down at the fields and the winding road below. Sunlight glinted on the roof of his car. Away from the shelter of the old wall, the wind caught at her hair and blew it across her face. She pushed it roughly aside.

What had she been expecting? Had that meeting by the river meant nothing to him? Had her memories of that day been no more than a hollow dream?

'Linda.'

She turned to see him hurrying towards her. 'Yes.'

'That wasn't the only reason.'

'No?'

He reached out for her. 'I wanted to see you

486

because I love you,' he said. After a moment's hesitation, when they looked at each other searchingly, he took her in his arms.

Chapter Twenty-Eight

November 1945

Graham was still in his dressing gown when he opened the door. 'Linda! Have I overslept?'

'Don't worry. Bobby's taking Imogen to school so that I could catch the early train. May I come in?'

'Sorry. Of course. Would you like some breakfast? I'm very good at burning toast.'

She smiled. 'A cup of tea will do. I came because we need to talk. We must present a united front when we have the meeting with Cordelia today.'

'Cordelia and Denis.'

'Oh, yes, Denis. He pulls the strings these days.'

'Have they told you what they think of my new designs?'

'Not a word.'

'And is that really why you came?'

'What do you mean?'

'This nonsense about a united front. Tell the truth; you came because you can't keep away from me.'

'There is that.'

Graham glanced at the clock on the mantelshelf. They looked at each other and smiled then he pulled her into his arms.

Cordelia sat behind the desk in the chair her father used to occupy, with Denis and Mr Redman flanking her. Linda realized she had arranged this on purpose so that Graham and Linda herself seemed like supplicants; or schoolchildren summoned to the headmaster's study. She even kept them waiting a good minute before she asked them to sit down. Then she patted Graham's sketchbook which lay on the desk in front of her.

'Denis and I have studied your designs, Mr Forsyth, and I'm afraid they won't do,' she said. 'Now that the restrictions are being lifted, Denis and I want Hylton's to be the firm it used to be, to produce the lovely traditional ware that we are famous for and that our customers expect.'

Linda would have spoken, but Graham, hearing her intake of breath, leaned forward and spoke first. 'Have you considered that you may have a different kind of customer now? Young couples starting out who have aspirations for a better life. They want tableware that's fashionable and modern.'

'I disagree,' Denis said. 'I believe people don't want any of that New World stuff. They want the comfort of the familiar. They want the world to be as it used to be.'

'I'm not saying we should discard the old designs,' Graham said. 'But if we don't cater for the new market I believe Hylton's may very well go under.'

'Nonsense,' Cordelia said. 'Hylton's is an old established firm. And whatever you may believe,

488

Mr Forsyth, our customers will always be faithful to us.'

'May I ask Mr Redman's opinion?' Graham said.

The older man shook his head. 'It's no use asking me, son. Now that Mr Vincent is going to take over I've decided to retire.'

This was news to Linda. 'No,' she said, 'you can't!' She knew very well that if Cecil Redman retired she would have no influence whatsoever on the running of the pottery.

'I'm afraid that's true, Linda,' Cordelia said. 'We have already accepted Mr Redman's resignation. However, I'm quite willing to hear his opinion.'

Cecil Redman looked embarrassed. He cleared his throat. 'I'm sorry, Graham,' he said, 'but I think your designs are too avant-garde. It would be an interesting experiment but I do believe there'd be a risk involved. And I don't believe we are in a position to take risks.'

'Well, I think that settles it,' Denis said.

'No, it doesn't,' Linda spoke up. 'We haven't asked Florian's opinion.'

'We phoned Florian last night,' Cordelia said. 'Didn't you know? He said he would be happy to go along with whatever Denis advised. You know, now that Denis and I are working together we don't really need you, Linda. After all, once the divorce is final, you won't even be one of the family.'

Graham stood up quickly, his chair scraping back across the polished floor. He picked up his sketchbook and turned for the door. 'Coming, Linda?' he asked. 'It seems neither of us is needed here.'

'Mr Forsyth – wait–' Denis Vincent began. 'We didn't say that we didn't want you to go on working for us. We simply want you to work our way.'

'I'm sorry, I can't,' Graham said. 'Well, that's not quite true. The fact is I don't want to.'

Linda followed him out of the office. 'I'm sorry it's come to this,' she said.

He grinned. 'Thanks for trying, but this could be the best thing that's ever happened to me.'

'What do you mean?'

'Do you have to go back to Redesburn now?'

'I can't stay too long. I must be back to meet Imogen from school.'

'If I take you back we have time for lunch somewhere. Fancy a run down to the coast?'

They left the car in the deserted and boarded-up pleasure park and walked along the promenade. The sea and the sky were uniformly grey, battleship grey, Linda thought, and the beach, still with its barbed wire barriers, was dismally uninviting.

The café was warm. Steam from the coffee machine fogged up the windows. Graham and Linda were the only customers.

'My mother and Aunt Edna used to bring me here when I was a child,' Graham told her. 'Real bucket and spade and sand in your sandwiches outings. I loved the place. I've fancied living by the sea ever since.'

They paused while the waitress brought bowls of hot soup to the table and then Linda said, 'What are you trying to tell me?'

'I'm leaving, Linda. I'm going to start up my

own business.'

'Where?'

'I haven't decided exactly, but it will be somewhere on the south coast. I want a completely new start.'

'How... I mean, can you afford to do this?'

'I have some savings. There's nothing to stop me going right away. Tomorrow even, to have a look around. I'll sell my house and by the time I find somewhere suitable – somewhere where there is a tradition of pottery and ceramics – I should have enough money to start up in a small way. Just.'

'Oh.'

'Don't look at me like that. I want you to come with me. I want you to be my partner in every sense of the word.'

'Graham, I can't.'

'Why not?'

'Imogen.'

Graham grinned. 'For goodness sake, I didn't mean that you should abandon her. I want Imogen to come, too.'

Linda shook her head. 'It's no good. Imogen is a Hylton. She belongs at Fernwood. It will be hers one day.'

'Not if Cordelia has her way. I think she wants the business, the house, the lot.'

'It doesn't matter. Whatever she might want, Florian wouldn't betray his own daughter.'

'He already has. He did that when he went off with Nadine.'

Linda shook her head. 'This is different. He told me he wanted Imogen to grow up at Fernwood. He asked me to stay.'

The waitress took their soup plates away and brought the next course, shepherd's pie, but Linda had lost all interest in food and pushed the mashed potato and mince around her plate until it became a soggy mess. To her chagrin, Graham gave every sign of enjoying his.

They hardly spoke on the way back to Redesburn. When they drew up outside the Hall Linda said, 'Graham, if I phone Florian this evening, and if I can persuade him to go along with your plans, would you stay at Hylton's?'

He sighed. 'If that's what you want.'

'And if he doesn't agree?'

Graham stared bleakly ahead but all he said was, 'I don't want to lose you, Linda.' Then without another glance he drove away.

Linda phoned the apartment first on the off chance that Florian was there. Now that Nadine had come out of *The Shadow Wife* and was in rehearsal for the new play, Linda never knew where Florian would be. She let the phone ring half a dozen times before deciding he wasn't there.

She tried Nadine's house and was met with hostility. 'Really, Linda, I can't have you phoning here every five minutes. You should wait until Florian phones you.'

Linda got the impression that Nadine was about to replace the receiver so she said quickly, 'I need to speak to him *now*.'

There was an offended silence and then Nadine said, 'Oh, very well.'

At least five full minutes went by, during which Linda could hear raised voices. When Florian came to the phone he sounded flustered. 'What is it?'

'I need to speak to you about Graham Forsyth's new designs. I told you about them last time we spoke.'

'Oh, yes. Cordelia phoned last night. She says Denis gave them the thumbs down.'

Linda was stunned. 'And you're happy to go along with that?'

'I don't understand, Linda. Why shouldn't I?'

'I thought you wanted me to represent your interests.'

Florian laughed. 'Represent my interests? That makes it sound so formal. I asked you to keep an eye on what Cordelia does. But that was before Denis came along. He's a good bloke.'

Linda gave it one more try. 'I think the designs are just what Hylton's needs.'

'Look, Linda, I haven't time for this. Nadine and I are going out to dinner. So is there anything else? No? Goodnight, then.'

Linda replaced the receiver and sat down at the desk. She stayed there until Vera came looking for her.

'Everything all right?' her old friend asked.

'No, it isn't but there's nothing I can do about it.'

'Then take my advice and let it go.'

Linda stood in the shadow of the bare-branched trees. Ahead of her the grass stretched like a frozen lake, each blade crisp with frost. The night pressed down on the darkened house and a pale moon shining intermittently through the scudding clouds did little to

493

disperse the shadows.

Once upon a time the windows had blazed with light and the family who lived there,William Hylton, Clara, Emerald, Cordelia, Rupert and Florian had enchanted her with their gaiety. She had longed to be part of that family, to be taken in and accepted, and for a while she thought her dreams had come true. But the dreams had not withstood the harsh light of reality.

Clara,William and Rupert had gone. Florian had betrayed her and Cordelia and Emerald had forsaken her. There was no more magic in the house which once had seemed to be enchanted. Now Cordelia and her husband acted like usurpers and Emerald, poor Emerald, once so vibrant, had become a wraith wandering through the empty rooms seeking the shades of times past.

Linda pulled up the collar of her coat and stepped out of the shelter of the trees, meeting the wind head-on. The cold knifed through her and the force of the wind was so strong that she could have believed that it was trying to push her away. But tonight she had to go back to the house she had once loved. Her daughter was there. The daughter whose father had not even mentioned her when Linda had phoned him hours earlier.

This would be the last time Linda walked across these lawns, looked through these windows, grieved for what might have been. She had made her decision. She would sell her village house to the Millards and she would leave Fernwood. The spell was broken.

Linda and her daughter would make a new and different life for themselves. With Graham. The man she loved.

The publishers hope that this book has given you enjoyable reading. Large Print Books are especially designed to be as easy to see and hold as possible. If you wish a complete list of our books please ask at your local library or write directly to:

Magna Large Print Books
Magna House, Long Preston,
Skipton, North Yorkshire.
BD23 4ND

This Large Print Book for the partially sighted, who cannot read normal print, is published under the auspices of

THE ULVERSCROFT FOUNDATION